The
Seed
Woman

The Seed Woman

THE SEED TRADERS' SAGA
PETRA DURST-BENNING
TRANSLATED BY EDWIN MILES

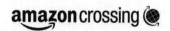

Previously published as *Die Samenhändlerin* (*Die Samenhändlerin-Saga, Band 1*) by Ullstein Buchverlage GmbH in Germany in 2005. Translated from German by Edwin Miles. First published in English by AmazonCrossing in 2017.

Published by AmazonCrossing, Seattle

www.apub.com

ISBN-13: 9781542047814
ISBN-10: 1542047811

Cover design by Shasti O'Leary Soudant

Printed in the United States of America

And the earth brought forth grass and herb yielding seed, each after its kind, and the tree yielding fruit, whose seed was in itself, each after its kind. And God saw that it was good.

—Genesis 1:12

Chapter One

The man felt the sweat trickle down his chest and back and gather at the waistband of his trousers. He was finding it difficult to breathe, so he loosened his belt a notch. When he raised his mug to his lips, a little beer dribbled down his chin to the collar of his shirt. Instead of wiping it away, he merely grinned. When he stood up from the table, he would be able to afford to have a new shirt made. Not just one but two or three or four!

He'd never had a hand as good as this in his life. And today! Today of all days . . .

He slapped his cards hard onto the table.

"Oh, God damn it!"

"Die, you miserable—"

"That . . . is that really . . . ?"

The men around the table gaped incredulously at him.

"Gentlemen"—he tried to sound blasé, but his pulse was pounding at his temples—"looks like Lady Luck is on my side today." With trembling hands, he scraped together the bills and coins spread across the table and scooped the pile into his money bag. Get it out of sight fast. Best to separate these men from their money as quickly and painlessly as possible.

The proprietor was the first to find his voice again. "Why the hurry? Can't a man as newly rich as you at least buy a round?"

The question was met with approving murmurs from the others, though Friedhelm Schwarz thought he heard mutterings of "swindle" and "cheat" among them.

The tavern was old and tumbledown, its walls blackened by years of smoke. The smell of poor-man's food mixed with the fetor of desperation, aggression, and apathy.

Friedhelm looked around, repulsed. Hadn't he sworn never to set foot in a place like this again? But if he had not, his money bag wouldn't now be so fat and heavy that it hung almost to his knee. Ha! Ilse would be in for a surprise.

Suppressing a smile, he swung his damp cloak over his shoulders. "Time I was back on the road."

As he tied his cloak at his throat, he glanced out through the tiny windows. It was still light outside—if one could use that expression at all in that godforsaken valley in the mountains of Switzerland. The surrounding mountains swallowed each ray of sunshine before it reached the meadows and fields lower down. Farming the land in that shadowy existence meant a backbreaking and meager life.

But it was not *his* meager life, Friedhelm told himself. Not today!

He'd been in that dingy corner of Switzerland for weeks, trying to come to terms with the farmers, but he had managed to get rid of only half of his vegetable seeds. And even so, some of the farmers had promised to pay him only after the next year's harvest, when they would have enough money to cover their debts. Friedhelm had not managed to sell even a single pack of his flower seeds. He did not think any worse of the people of the region for that, however. Violets and anemones don't fill your belly. And when your stomach is growling, you have little time for a flower bed, however pretty it might be.

Oh, he had had it up to here with these high valleys and the taciturn, poor, embittered people who survived there. Why wasn't his life like that of other seed dealers, who pursued their trade in better regions? And why couldn't he count any wealthy farmers among his customers? Or any nurseries or rich gardeners? Why had his father left him no more than this miserable territory in Switzerland in which to peddle his seeds?

He grasped his money bag, the weight of which helped him keep a lid on that last question before envy and anger and hate could overwhelm him. All the others could go to hell! Today, he was king. He'd done his business well today, yes sir.

He wanted to go home. To Gönningen, his hometown, a village at the foot of the Swabian Mountains, hundreds of miles from this dismal spot on a map. He was hurrying now, shouldering the seed sack that contained his flower seeds and bulbs. Bulbs! Why had he even bothered hauling them all this way? He raised his hat, taking his leave.

"Where do you think you'll get to on foot today? You'll never make it down to the bottom of the valley," said one of the card players, who looked at him with a sour expression.

In his mind, Friedhelm traced the roads he would have to cover. The man was right. It was a good twenty miles to the next valley, with only two or three villages in between. But what other choice did he have? The last thing he wanted to do was spend the night in that wretched place. He could practically guarantee that he'd end up with his head bashed in, or drugged and robbed, or—

"I'm in a hurry. I want to be home for Christmas."

"You weren't in no hurry earlier," grumbled one of the men.

"That's right. You had plenty of time to win the shirts off our backs," snarled another.

"Easy!" the proprietor said to the men. "If you want to play, you have to be able to lose, right?" He nodded to Friedhelm, who returned the gesture.

Friedhelm knew the muffled growl in the belly only too well, the feeling that comes only when you realize that you have risked everything in the game. The euphoria of the moment abates, the concentration lapses, and the bewilderment at one's own stupidity sets in. *Lady Luck is a whore. She'll sleep with whomever she pleases,* Friedhelm thought. He also knew that such well-intentioned aphorisms were no consolation to a losing man. He kept his mouth shut.

The proprietor accompanied him to the door. He cast a glance back into the room, and then he beckoned Friedhelm closer. A contorted grin crossed the proprietor's face.

"I know how you can get much farther today. You can drive with old Öschen-Bürli. He'll get you down into the valley tonight. If you like, I'll have a word. I'm sure he'll take you along." There was something sly in the man's eyes.

Friedhelm hesitated. From previous gambling nights, he knew Öschen-Bürli as a singular drunkard and cantankerous to boot. Friedhelm had been glad the man was not there that evening, and he was not thrilled at the idea of riding with him, especially as he remembered the man's worn-out old nag and the wheels of his wagon, with half of their spokes broken. But a long way on bad wheels was better than nowhere on foot.

"Good. I'll wait for Öschen-Bürli," Friedhelm said.

He was about to turn back into the tavern when the proprietor grabbed him roughly by the arm.

"Don't," he whispered. "You know what those fellows are like. They'd begrudge a man the butter on his bread, let alone the pile you've won today. Better they don't set eyes on you again."

Friedhelm glanced over the man's shoulder into the barroom. The card players were talking among themselves, leaning close. Though he felt no desire to rejoin them, he wasn't eager to trudge up the steep hill to Öschen-Bürli's farm, either. But what choice did he have?

"Then I'll be on my way," he said with a sigh, and turned his chin toward where he knew the man's hut to be.

The proprietor shook his head. "You don't need to slog up there. I've got a better idea."

An hour later, Friedhelm reached the meeting point the proprietor had told him about. He looked around, checking the landscape to make sure he was in the right place. On his left were the three fir trees the proprietor had described. "They lean toward each other as if they're round-dancing," he'd said. Friedhelm had smiled inwardly at that—he had not expected such a poetic description from the boorish proprietor. On his right was a canebrake, and beyond that, the path forked. A narrow, deeply rutted track curved away to the right across a field—probably the way to a remote farmstead. Another track, no less rutted, led to the left. Would Öschen-Bürli be coming down one of those paths? He was angry at himself for not asking the proprietor about that. And why couldn't he just have met the man at the edge of the village?

It was completely dark now, and only the thin layer of snow offered a little light. Friedhelm felt goose bumps spread across his back. He narrowed his eyes. No wagon, no Öschen-Bürli—not from the left track or the right, although he could not see very far.

He was already thinking about continuing on foot and forgetting all about old Öschen-Bürli and his broken-down wagon when he heard something crack in the bushes on his right. He spun around in fright. Nothing. He had been holding his breath, and now he exhaled a dim cloud that hovered in front of him. *Easy now,* he told himself. But his hand moved instinctively to the bag containing his money.

It was not the first time that he had been out traveling alone at night. He knew that doing so was risky. Foolhardy, even. Few seed dealers ventured out alone. The dangers were too great. Two traveling together were better off in the face of a possible robbery. Four eyes and four ears simply saw and heard more. But who was there to go with him to that godforsaken corner of the world?

And yet, this trip had been a complete success! His wife, Ilse, would be proud of him, and Seraphine would marvel at the weight of his money bag. Seraphine, his beautiful daughter. The real treasure of his life. In Bregenz, he would buy her the finest lace and a fat roll of silk cloth to go with it. He would place the money on the counter like a rich gentleman ought and not even bat an eye.

He did not hear the rustling among the reeds or the footsteps approaching. His body did not alert him in any way to the danger he was in. He was too distracted by visions of his triumphant return to Gönningen.

Like a king. He would go home a king . . .

Chapter Two

Gönningen, Germany, December 1849

"Lord, where have I landed?" Hannah muttered to herself. She narrowed her eyes and peered along the street. *The back end of nowhere . . .*

"Ten minutes on foot," the farmer who had driven her from Reutlingen to that junction had assured her. That's all it would take. A ten-minute walk to Gönningen. When she peered ahead, she could, in fact, make out the buildings through the swathes of fog drifting down from the surrounding mountains. But the only thing that Hannah could see clearly were bare fruit trees. Hundreds of fruit trees, left and right, in front of her, behind her—in spring, when the trees flowered, it would be a pretty sight.

Hannah let her traveling bag drop to the snowy road and pressed her hands to her back, which was as stiff as a wooden puppet's. She looked around, but there wasn't a hedge in sight. If she didn't find a place to urinate soon, she was sure her bladder would burst. She momentarily considered simply squatting beside a tree or right there in the road . . . but she rejected the idea when a coach suddenly appeared from around a corner behind her. The driver nodded to her, but he did not stop to offer a ride.

Well, then don't! Hannah bent to pick up her traveling bag. In the few moments it had been out of her hand, the mix of mushy snow and horse dung that covered the road had soaked through the bottom and sides. Hannah's skirt, too, was sodden up to her ankles. In anger, she kicked at a particularly disgusting pile of the slush, but the sudden movement only increased the pressure on her bladder. She stalked off down the road. Soon, something she could hide behind would appear. Then she could lift her skirt, untie her underwear and . . . *stop thinking about it.*

The chill was so clammy and piercing that Hannah felt as if she were completely naked, but in reality she was wearing almost every piece of clothing she had with her. She pulled her shawl closer around her head and shoulders. The damp material made her cheeks itch, but Hannah stopped herself from scratching. Once she started with that, she would never stop. Seven days and seven nights in the same clothes, with little more than a lick and a spit to keep herself clean. She shuddered at the thought.

She would give anything for a hot bath! Since climbing up beside that stinking farmer on the driver's seat at midday, all she could think of was sinking into a tub of warm water. Her aching bones would become weightless; every pore of her skin would open. She would wash her hair, twice even—she didn't care if it took half a block of soap. A blissful sigh was smothered in the dank fabric of her shawl, and she tried not to think of the rim of black she would surely leave around the bath. She had never been this filthy in her life.

The day had never really brightened, and now the fog was eating away at the last strands of daylight. Hannah could not say whether it was three, four, or maybe even five in the afternoon. She trudged on.

At least the village could boast a church, she thought a few minutes later, when the outlines of a bell tower grew clearer. There had to be rooms to rent somewhere, with or without a bath. If need be, she would make do with a bowl of hot water.

Hannah was so focused on hurrying ahead to find a bed for the night that she heard the wagon only when it was almost on top of her. It sped past without slowing down, and Hannah jumped clear just in time. Mushy snow splattered against her skirt.

"Lout!" she shouted after the driver.

"Be careful there, girl," the farmer who had taken her as far as the junction had warned. He came from one of the neighboring towns, he said, and when she had alighted from the wagon, he explained, "The Gönningers are good-for-nothings. They'll drink away all they own in a night, the miserable beggars."

Hannah frowned and kept walking, jumping over a particularly deep puddle a moment later.

Of course, the farmer had wanted to know what had led her there, to the edge of the Swabian Mountains.

"A family matter," she had answered curtly, and he had looked at her askance.

A family matter was also the reason she gave the office in Nuremberg when she applied for traveling papers. That had been less than three weeks before, but to Hannah it felt like an eternity.

She never would have guessed that the journey from Nuremberg would drag on for a week. No doubt her mother thought she had reached Gönningen long ago; she probably knocked the mailman off his feet every morning, hoping for a letter or card from her daughter.

Seven days. And every single day, Hannah had had trouble getting from A to B. There were many trains that started from Nuremberg. She could easily have traveled to Augsburg, Munich, or Leipzig, or even as far as Hamburg or Danzig, but there was no direct train, or even an affordable connection, to Stuttgart. At first, the man at the ticket office could not even find Gönningen, about thirty miles south of Stuttgart. But of all the places she might want to visit, it was to that remote southern corner of Württemberg that she had to go. Mail coaches, goods wagons, farmers' carts—she had changed from one to the other countless times, sharing narrow wooden benches with people whose dialect grew stranger and stranger the farther south she went, until Hannah didn't think she understood any more than half of what she heard. At the start, she had made sure she always had a roof over her head at night, but from Stuttgart on, she could no longer afford that luxury, and she had to count herself lucky when she was picked up at all.

And now she had arrived at the foot of the Swabian Mountains.

Ten minutes later, Hannah's need to relieve herself was all but forgotten, replaced by a sense of amazement that she thought might never pass.

Since reaching the first buildings of Gönningen, she had passed three shoemakers, four butcher's shops, a hairdresser, and at least five food stores. There was an inn named The Swans, but there were no lights on inside, so Hannah assumed it was closed. But with so many shops in the village, there certainly would be another inn. What an unusual little place. Most of the businesses were located in rather stately houses, quite a few of which were built from a cream-colored stone that Hannah did not recognize. And there were small gardens in front of or on the sides of many of the houses; the gates to these gardens were made of wrought iron and were as richly decorated as the entrances to magnificent mansions. The roads were well lit and exceptionally clean. Although carts and coaches were passing by all the time, she saw no horse dung anywhere. Did someone sweep it up, perhaps? And, like the Nuremberg quarter where Hannah's parents ran their inn, here, too, there was a great deal of general busyness. Women bustled past quickly on their way to church—well-dressed women, she realized at a glance, which made her feel all the more shabby in her dirty clothes. And men were on the streets, too, arms slung around each other's shoulders, most likely on their way to the nearest tavern. "*They'll drink away all they own in a night*"—Hannah was reminded of the farmer's words. Despite the bad weather, she saw children everywhere: toddlers playing together, older children arguing, adolescents giggling. When Hannah glanced down a side alley, a horde of young ruffians jumped out in front of her, demanding a toll to let her pass, tittering and jostling each other.

"Shoo, all of you!" Swinging her traveling bag, she tried to chase the little gang away, but they just laughed and danced around her. Hannah kept on, and she soon came to a market area. She stopped in the center of the cobblestoned square. "Oh my . . ."

The Lamb, The Crown, The Fox, The Sun. An inn on every corner!

Now the real problem became the question of where she should spend the night—a different kind of problem than Hannah had anticipated.

"One inn is as good as another," she murmured to herself, knowing perfectly well that that was not true. Why did so many travelers in Nuremberg seek out her parents' Golden Anchor even though it was not particularly central? Because one inn was *not* as good as another. Because the travelers knew that the food, the service, and the beds at The Golden Anchor were solid and affordable.

Hannah blinked. Back home, the first guests for the night would already have arrived, and her mother would have her hands full in the kitchen and restaurant. Homesickness leaped onto Hannah like a tick. Before it could suck out the last of her strength, she steered for one of the smaller places, its sign adorned with a pretty image of the sun.

"You're in luck, we have one room free," the proprietress said. "How long will you be staying?"

"I don't know yet," Hannah said quietly. To one side was a door that opened into the restaurant, which was full of men who clearly had something to celebrate; the room was loud. Was The Sun the right choice? In the small reception area where she and the proprietress stood, rows of sacks were piled against the wall, and getting past them meant pulling in her stomach and turning sideways. Why was the place so busy?

The woman followed Hannah's gaze and said, "The gardeners from Ulm arrived today. They come every year; that hodgepodge of sacks belongs to them. It's their last chance to earn a bit of money before the year is out." She laughed.

"The gardeners from Ulm—aha!" Hannah nodded knowingly, as if the woman's explanation clarified everything. Hannah leaned across the counter and whispered, "Excuse me, but can you tell me where the . . . lavatory is?"

"The lavatory? Oh, you mean the outhouse!" The woman smiled understandingly. "Go out this door to the back. You can't miss it. You can leave your bag here, and I'll have my daughter take it to your room." She nodded in the direction of a young woman just then coming out of the restaurant with a stack of dirty plates—she dragged her right foot a little as she walked, making a strange scraping sound.

"There's something else . . ." Hannah took a deep breath. If she did not ask now, she felt she would explode with uncertainty. "Where can I find Helmut Kerner? The seed dealer?"

"Helmut?" The proprietress's brow furrowed. "As far as I know, he got back just yesterday. He and his brother. They will certainly drop by this evening. Normally, they would be among the ones who only come home at Easter, but this year"—she winked confidentially—"now that wedding bells will be ringing . . ."

"Wedding be—" That was all Hannah could get out. She was suddenly so dizzy that she had to hold on to the edge of the counter.

The proprietress screwed up her nose. "I know, I know! It took a lot of us by surprise to see them finally decide to take things seriously. But then, it's hardly a miracle. Helmut is twenty-five now, after all."

Without another word, Hannah dashed out through the back door.

Chapter Three

Seraphine squinted. She had already tried three times, in vain, to coax the thread through the needle's tiny eye, and now she glared angrily at the oil lamp that cast its dingy, flickering light across the table. The miserable cottage didn't even have enough light! Ignoring the trembling in her fingers, Seraphine tried again. Finally! With a sigh, she began to rummage through the reams of fabric in front of her.

"You're not starting your sewing again now, are you?" her mother asked. "The soup will be warm in a few minutes, then we'll eat. And if you have to do it, I'll thank you to make room at the table. You heard what the miller's wife said. She wants all those things finished in two days."

Seraphine looked first at her mother and then at the pile of clothes that needed to be repaired. They had just been handed to her that afternoon.

"The miller's wife shouldn't go making such a fuss. I've set aside this evening to sew lace along the hem of the skirt."

She spread the mountain of cloth out on the table and was about to get to work when she caught the penetrating smell of the cabbage stewing on the stove. She screwed up her face and hastily threw a table-cloth over her sewing. Aside from the miller's wife's clothes, Seraphine couldn't have her own beautiful dress reeking of cabbage! But a moment later, Seraphine's face relaxed again, as it always did when she held the dress in her hands.

Her wedding dress.

So many hours of work. The bodice was covered with tiny, silvery, shimmering beads that her father had brought back with him from his last trip. The sleeves were adorned with four layers of the finest lace, and two rings of lace of different widths encircled the neckline. Seraphine had sewn dozens of folds into the skirt, exceptionally fine folds, each precisely as wide as the next, each carefully ironed flat. She had spent most of summer and fall working only on the skirt.

A warm shiver ran through her just looking at it. She would look like a queen when she wore it. Or a princess. The princess of the moon. Furtively, she pulled her long braid over her shoulder and held it against the black taffeta traditionally used for wedding dresses. The silky black fabric made her hair look even lighter. She would not paint on any red-apple cheeks. She would wear her fair skin like a noble lady. Painted cheeks were for country bumpkins. And she was no bumpkin.

She was Seraphine. The most beautiful girl in the village. Everybody said so. But even without the admiration of the men or the envy of the women, Seraphine knew that she was uncommonly beautiful. No one had hair as smooth and silvery blond as hers. No one had eyes the color of polished granite. Seraphine's lips radiated a sensuality that stopped men in their tracks. And her stature reminded them of a fine horse—slender, with long legs and perfect proportions.

Some of the villagers called her vain behind her back. But vanity was a sin, as the priest told them. Seraphine knew that her beauty was the only thing she possessed in this world. Did realizing that make her conceited?

Dreamily, Seraphine traced the contours of her lips with her right index finger. Her skin immediately began to tingle at the touch. Soon she would be woken with a kiss, like a sleeping princess. Woken by her prince. By Helmut, whose family was one of the richest in Gönningen. And whom she had loved for as long as she could remember.

Seraphine put down her needle and thread. A deep sigh escaped her, filling the room. If only that day were already here . . .

She had been waiting for years, sometimes more patiently, sometimes less, but always in the knowledge that one day *the* day would come. The day on which the error that had caused her to be born in that wretched cottage would be corrected. It was clear to Seraphine that an error must have been made. Even her father had said so.

"They say that when the fairies leave a changeling in a human cradle, the changeling is an ugly creature, always. But the fairy that came to us must have made a mistake. She took away the ugly duckling and left you in our cradle instead," her father had said, and then had laughed so loudly that anyone would have thought that *he* had personally managed to trick fate.

Seraphine had come to believe that the fairy's mistake was a fateful one indeed. Perhaps the star fairy had been blinded by a particularly bright star when she was distributing the newborn babies, and for that reason could not see inside the woebegone walls in which she had laid her special daughter. That's how it must have been. Seraphine's looks, her unusual name, which her father had brought back with him from his travels—was any more proof necessary that she was destined for something better? So far, that certainty had helped her endure.

But now that *the* day was less than three weeks away, her patience was at an end. She could not wait any longer to lie in Helmut's arms. Her prince, her savior. The man who would carry her out of poverty, who would lavish her with care and attention. Helmut and her, united as man and wife.

Passion welled up inside her. Warm and untouched. Seraphine thought about going to the Kerners' house, but she remembered that Helmut had mentioned a meeting that evening among the Gönningen seed merchants and the gardeners from Ulm. No doubt he and Valentin and the old man were already at The Sun.

It was strange. The entire year, the people of Gönningen made a big secret of where they obtained their seeds. Everybody wanted to keep the most reliable seed growers and market gardeners for themselves. But when the gardeners from Ulm came to them, everyone sat peaceably at one large table. She had to ask Helmut why that was.

The next moment, the dress caught her eye again. She had too much to do to see Helmut that evening.

More determined than ever, she picked up the packet of lace, unfolded it, and was shocked to discover how little was left. That would never be enough for three rows around the hem of the skirt!

"I hope Papa remembers the lace he said he'd bring home," she said.

"He has to *get* home before he can give you anything," her mother grumbled. "Almost all the men are back, all except Friedhelm. Yet again, I might add. I don't want to think what's held him up this year." Ilse squinted out the window as if she expected to see her husband coming around the corner just then.

An uneasy feeling sprouted inside Seraphine.

"Do you think he . . ." She could not finish the sentence. But Father knew her wedding was coming up. He knew it!

"I don't know, child," her mother replied flatly.

Seraphine bit down on her lip.

What if Father had broken his promise? *"I'll drop down dead before I let some oaf talk me into anything again."* His words still rang clearly in her mind. No more dice, no more cards, no more betting on anything. He was done with that, and he had sworn as much to her mother before he left.

What if he came home with empty pockets again? As he had one time in late summer, returning from the Jakobi trade . . .

Seraphine shuddered. It had been humiliating—terribly humiliating, really—to have to go to Helmut and tell him about her father's unfortunate situation. Helmut declared that Friedhelm Schwarz would not be the first to buy his seeds from the Kerner family on credit. That same evening he had talked to his father, and the next day Gottlieb Kerner came by with a selection of vegetable and flower seeds. Seraphine wanted the earth to swallow her up when her father signed the bond for the seeds, although doing so did not seem to bother him very much. Something like that could happen to anyone, he had said with a lopsided grin. A thoughtless moment, certainly: he'd been happy about how good business had been, had felt that pleasant sense that comes when coins are clinking in one's money bag, and then a couple of beers to quench the thirst, and the boisterous mood in some of the taverns, Gottlieb knew how it was . . .

Seraphine had seen the look on her future father-in-law's face. She knew what he was thinking.

The orchards that extended for miles around Gönningen brought in a rich harvest for the villagers every year, and the Schwarz family owned several fields of their own. They dried the apples and pears that grew in the lee of the Swabian Mountains, and then sold the dried fruit during the Jakobi trade—a good source of income, especially for those Gönningen residents who lacked the funds to invest in flower and vegetable seeds. People like Friedhelm Schwarz. Though instead of realizing how tenuous his situation was, her father had gambled away his profits and now went cap in hand, like a beggar.

Oh, star fairy, how could you do this to me? Seraphine pressed a hand to her mouth to smother a cry. Then another terrible thought came to her: It might well be true that the Kerners sold their goods to many people in the village on credit, but what would happen if her father was the only one who did not pay them back?

She would never forgive him for that. Never! Not in this life, not in the next one.

When Seraphine saw the stony look on her mother's face as she stared out the window, the unconscious desperation she had sensed so often returned.

Why couldn't her mother be more confident? And why didn't she go with her father on his travels, like other women? As she had when she was younger? Her left leg had given up on her, but Seraphine was not certain that her mother wasn't exaggerating her suffering, wasn't hiding away behind all the clothes she mended for the women in the village, the same women who had no time to do it themselves because they were away traveling with their husbands. It never occurred to Seraphine that she might go with her father in her mother's place.

As if she could read her daughter's mind, Ilse Schwarz turned away from the window and fixed her eyes on Seraphine.

"Even if I'd gone with him, I don't know that I could have stopped him. You've never seen your father when he gets that glassy look in his eye. All he has to do is get wind of a dice game or card game and you won't get a sensible word out of him. Oh, I used to plead with him to get away from the table before it was too late. But the other men laughed and asked him who wore the trousers in our house. When he heard that, your father threw more coins on the table. As if he had to prove something. That's how it was."

Seraphine gulped. "But now that we owe money, he wouldn't . . ."

Ilse laughed scornfully. "*Maybe* he wouldn't. I have no more illusions about your father. Don't trouble yourself. Everything will work out for the best. And if worse comes to worse, we still have the money I've put aside from my sewing."

Her mother—a woman who had to take in sewing. *Oh, star fairy, how could you . . .*

Seraphine moved her dress to make room for the plates her mother brought to the table. She would go back to work after they ate. Her wedding dress, her key to happiness.

Chapter Four

Hannah slipped down inside the tub until her chin reached the water. When her knees, which were then protruding into the air, grew cold, she changed position. But no matter which part of her body was underwater, she felt chilled through. And not just because her room was unpleasantly cold.

"Bath day here is Saturday," Emma Steiner had said when Hannah told her what she wanted. A moment later, however, she patted Hannah's hand and said, "But I know how it is when you're traveling. I can't count how many times I would have loved to be able to have a good wash." She added that there was nothing to stop Hannah from taking a bath as long as she put on the water to heat in the kitchen by herself. She could help Hannah carry the tub into her room, but she had no time for anything else.

Hannah had spontaneously embraced the woman. On her entire journey, no one had shown her so much kindness.

Hannah dunked the washcloth in the water and wiped it over her arms and the back of her neck again, as she already had several times. She waited expectantly for the warm feeling she wanted so much, but it simply would not come.

Not long now and she would see Helmut. Helmut, getting married in three weeks . . . damn it! Hannah slapped her hand onto the water so hard that it sprayed in all directions. That was it; she had lost all interest in the bath. She climbed out of the tub and began to dry herself.

What could she do? Helmut was promised to another. Only three weeks from now, he would be a married man! The proprietress's revelation, mentioned so casually as she helped Hannah carry the tub, dug into Hannah like a splinter driven deep under the skin. What was to become of her now?

She had set off on this journey with no illusions. Or at least, *almost* no illusions, she silently corrected herself. Helmut was a dashing young man, and she liked him very much indeed. He was cheerful and told stories well; he also knew not to hold forth forever, unlike other men. And the way he had looked after his sick brother! Helmut was just . . . nice. The sadness that Hannah had felt when he left had been a new experience for her. She could have given him her heart forever. But that's how it was with the guests at The Golden Anchor. Here today, gone tomorrow. She had come to terms with that.

Except that, in the vaguest of terms, Helmut had suggested that his travels might lead him back to Nuremberg the following year. No declaration of love, no word about eternal fidelity. Hannah wouldn't have paid any notice if there had been; she knew men well enough to know how much such words were worth.

Who would ever have thought that she would see Helmut again so soon?

The farther south she went, the more she realized how much she was looking forward to seeing him again. At the same time, of course, she knew he was no prince astride a white horse who could rescue her from her unfortunate situation.

Unfortunate situation! How could she have been so stupid? So careless? So . . . bad? Why couldn't she simply have listened to her mother?

"Do you always have to go batting your eyelids at the nearest young man? People already talk about you. Woe betide you if your father ever gets wind of it! No good will come of it, mark my words. Sooner or later, one of them will leave you with a big belly. And what are you going to do then?"

Hannah had asked herself the same question four weeks after Helmut's visit to Nuremberg, when her monthly bleeding didn't come. That had been at the start of November, and at first she had not wanted to believe what had happened.

Drat and blast it! Of all the businesses they could have started, why had her parents chosen to open an inn? And why was she so foolish? Her intentions had always been good: a bit of merrymaking, maybe a little peck, and then she would go to her room and the guest to his. Anything else, she knew well enough, was not proper. And most of the time, that was how it went. Once in a while, though, she threw all her good intentions into the river and gave in to the moment. Her bad conscience only returned the next morning. How many times had she silently sworn, never again? But then why did the hands of men feel so good?

She ran her fingertips gently over her belly, then across her breasts. No tingling, no thrill . . . no more than goose bumps.

With the towel wrapped tightly around her body, Hannah tiptoed across the icy floor. She lifted the Hungarian blouse carefully from her bag. The red straps against the white fabric contrasted nicely with Hannah's almost black hair, and the high collar made her wide face with its striking cheekbones look narrower. At home, she had thought it was a good choice, but now that she had seen the Gönningen women in their finery, Hannah doubted herself. Would the outfit—there in that well-to-do village—come across as too showy? Or, God forbid, provincial?

Well, there was nothing she could do about it now. Resolutely, Hannah buttoned the blouse. She was wasting precious time. Helmut was probably already sitting in the restaurant.

Throughout her journey to Gönningen, she had been preoccupied with finding her next ride or a reasonably safe place to spend the night or any one of a dozen other uncertainties. She had neither the time nor the peace of mind to think about what would happen when she reached her destination. And what would have been the point? What mattered most was finding Helmut; then everything would fall into place. What choice did he have but to marry her? Hannah could not contemplate any other outcome.

Of course, she knew that in Nuremberg, in certain houses, there were doctors or so-called angel-makers who helped women out of such "unfortunate situations." But she had never even considered seeking one of them out. She may have been depraved and wicked, but certainly not that depraved and wicked! A sin like that was not something she would burden herself with. And because she would not, with the courage of desperation, she had set out on this journey. "Please, dear God, let me find Helmut. If you do that, I will atone for every sin I have ever committed. I will be the best wife he could wish for, the very best!" She had prayed every night. And God had listened. She had found Helmut.

The fact that he had long been promised to another woman—Seraphine—and that they had even set a date for the wedding . . . Hannah had not reckoned with that. If she had, she would have formulated her prayers differently!

Seraphine. What kind of woman had a name like that?

Hannah grasped her skirt and with the flat of her hand began to beat it vigorously, as if to drive out not only the dust but every fearful thought along with it.

"And if you don't find him because he left you a false address, or if he doesn't have an honorable bone in his body, or if anything else comes to grief, then come home again. It will work out that way, too. You would not be the first girl to fall into disgrace," her mother had whispered when Hannah was about to leave. And she had kept looking back toward the kitchen, making sure that her father didn't catch wind of any of it. Her mother was brave. Hannah and her mother convinced her father that his daughter wanted to visit her cousin Elfriede in Baden. He resisted for days and offered many objections: A young girl, traveling alone? And so close to Christmas? Wouldn't a visit now be an inconvenience to their relatives? Mother and daughter had talked as if their lives depended on it, and her father had finally relented.

Hannah lowered her skirt again, its hem still filthy with the grime from the road. She did not want to put her parents through the embarrassment of her return to Nuremberg as an unwed mother. What kind of future would she have there? The people would point their fingers at her for years to come, and the likelihood of finding a husband who would accept her and a bastard child was slim at best. Hannah had no illusions about that. She had one chance only, and that was here, in Gönningen.

She finished dressing quickly, combed her still-wet hair in front of the tiny mirror on the wall, and wove her hair into a braid that she pinned around her head like a wreath. When she stepped back and looked at her reflection, she was satisfied with what she saw: Her hair did not look commonplace, and might even be considered a little daring, but wasn't that exactly what the men liked about her?

Let's hope Helmut remembers that, she thought grimly as she made her way downstairs.

What had she gotten herself into?

Chapter Five

The fist came down on the table with a crash. "For all the Ulmer Giants I'm buying, I expect a better price. I'll tell you that here and now so that ev . . . everyone can hear it!" The man began to slur his words, and he raised his tankard of beer to his lips and drank.

Beside him another man laid one arm around his shoulders to placate him and said, "We can all hear you very well, Schorsch, but the quantity you need to run your business, honestly, you could sweep that up beneath my table at home. If *anyone* here deserves to get a good price, it's *me*. And not only for the Ulmer Giants."

The man laughed uproariously, as if he had said something very funny indeed, and the others around the table joined in. Schorsch, however, pulled free of the placating arm, offended.

"Tight bastard," he muttered. He tried to stand up from the table, but the man sitting opposite pushed him back down.

"Now hold your horses. Every customer of mine has walked away with a good and fair price!" The man smiled jovially at the others gathered around the table.

"I'd like to see that," Schorsch said, his eyes glinting combatively.

Hannah held her breath. All it took now, she knew, was one spark to trigger an explosion. She looked around for the proprietress, but she was nowhere to be seen. Her own father would have been at the table long before to make sure no one came to blows. Hannah sighed. Well, others' fights were not her concern that evening. She glanced toward the door again. How many times had she looked now? From her seat behind a wooden pillar, she had a good view of the entrance, but she would not immediately be seen by anyone coming in.

Helmut was not yet there, but the innkeeper had assured her that was not unusual. Unlike the other men, the Kerners usually ate at home and came to the inn later to transact their business.

Hannah lifted her bowl and spooned the last bit of soup into her mouth. She took a deep breath, exhaled, and looked around.

The clash of beer mugs raised in a toast, the smell of food, Käthe Steiner—Emma's daughter—her cheeks red from her effort . . . all of it reminded Hannah so very much of The Golden Anchor. Only with an effort did she withstand the urge to run behind the counter, grab some tankards of beer, and deliver them to the waiting tables. At the same time, The Sun and its guests had nothing in common with the usual bustle of an inn.

"More soup?"

Hannah jumped in surprise. She had been so absorbed that she had not heard Käthe approach. She shook her head, then beckoned the proprietress's daughter to come closer.

"May I ask you something?" she whispered.

"Asking's free," replied the young woman with a shrug. At the same time, she looked toward the counter uneasily, where more beer mugs were already waiting to be served.

Hannah nodded toward the middle of the large room, where the men who were arguing sat with a dozen or more other men at several tables that had been pushed together in a long row. Spread out across the entire length of the table were many small bowls and jars containing grain-like substances. Now and then, one of the men would pick up one of the jars and shake the stuff inside it; others would sprinkle or spoon a little of the contents into their palm. They sniffed at it, weighed it, looked at it from all sides, packed small quantities into little paper bags. Strange names flew across the table like a swarm of flies: Pride of Söflingen, Viennese Yellow, and German Peerless.

Hannah shook her head. "What is that all about?"

"What it's all . . . about?" Käthe Steiner seemed not to understand the question.

"I mean, what are those men doing? What's in the jars?"

Käthe brightened. "Oh, you don't know? Those are vegetable seeds of all kinds! And the Ulmers will have brought some flower seeds, too; you can count on it. Before the Gönningers buy anything, they want to at least see what they're getting. Of course, you can't tell if a seed will germinate just by looking at it. But you can certainly tell if it smells good, or if maybe it smells a bit moldy. And then there's the usual haggling." Käthe raised her eyebrows and smiled conspiratorially.

"Yes, but then those men are . . . are they also seed dealers? I thought only Helmut and his brother . . ."

Käthe looked as if she understood even less than before, but a moment later she hooted with laughter, and a few heads immediately turned toward them.

"Did you really think the Kerners were the only ones?" Through her laughter she said, "All of us here, we're *all* seed dealers!"

All of us? What did she mean by that? Hannah frowned.

Käthe Steiner tilted her head thoughtfully and looked at Hannah. At the same time, she waved to placate her mother, who was gesticulating wildly behind the counter. Then she sighed and sat down opposite Hannah.

"I really don't have the time, but I think someone has to explain a few things to you about Gönningen."

Before you make an idiot of yourself again. Hannah thought she heard the unspoken words.

26

"Helmut, wait a moment!"

Helmut had not even closed the inn door behind him when Emma Steiner grabbed him by the sleeve and pulled him off to one side.

Impatiently, he watched his father and Valentin make their way toward the center of the room. He had a thirst for a good mug of beer, for the camaraderie of the other men and their tall tales, for a crude joke or two.

After almost four months on the road, he and his brother had arrived home only the day before. And as much as he had been looking forward to being in Gönningen again, he was finding it difficult to adjust from the traveling life to that of the village. Every year and every journey he made, the adjustment became more difficult. When he awoke that morning, it took him some moments even to remember where he was. An inn? But which one? And where? When it finally dawned on him that he was lying in his own bed, he was strangely disappointed.

"What is it, Emma?"

"There's a young woman back there. A Miss Brettschneider. She was asking about you."

Helmut followed Emma's gaze, but he could only see Käthe's back and not who was behind the pillar. Of course Käthe had to go sticking her nose in! None of the men in the village had any interest in her, and that only seemed to make her more interested in other people's business. Helmut grimaced.

"Brettschneider . . . the name doesn't mean anything to me. What does she want?"

Emma twisted up her mouth. "Why would she tell me? Anyway, I just thought you ought to be warned." She shrugged and went back behind the bar.

"Hold on, she must have told you something."

Emma crossed her arms. "I don't know if I should tell you. She's a guest in my house, after all."

"Emma," Helmut growled.

The proprietress frowned. "She's from Nuremberg. And she's staying for an 'indefinite period,'" she added, with a meaningful arch of her eyebrows.

Nuremberg. There was something . . . Helmut rummaged through his memories of his most recent travels, trying to call up the right one. A strange feeling twanged in his belly. Nuremberg. From there, they had gone on to Bohemia. In Nuremberg, Valentin had been sick, and he—

"Helmut, are you coming, or have you put down roots over there?" he heard his father call.

At the same moment, a head popped out from behind the pillar. "Helmut!"

Chair legs scraped across the floor, red bands practically glowed against white fabric, and a wide, angular face appeared.

Helmut blinked. That was . . . could . . . could it be?

Käthe jumped up from her chair and hurried past him, unvarnished curiosity and something else, too, in her eyes.

Looks of surprise, curiosity, and even envy followed Helmut as he walked toward the table. Who was this pretty stranger? And what did she want with the elder Kerner brother?

"Hannah?" Helmut's word was a question mark. At least he remembered her name. "What are you doing here?"

He had a lump in his throat like a fist and had to choke out every word. He held out his hand tentatively. Unable to stop himself, he found his eyes drawn to the neckline of her blouse. The memory of his time in Nuremberg abruptly returned. His face grew hot.

He had feared this day like the devil feared holy water. The day that one of his liaisons caught up with him. Blast it, why had he let himself get mixed up with an innkeeper's daughter, someone who only had to look in the guest book to find his address?

"I was looking for you," Hannah answered, her lips trembling. Her cheeks were red, and her left eyelid twitched slightly. She seemed very excited as she grasped Helmut's proffered hand. "Oh, I am so happy to see you again!" Hannah was smiling radiantly and really seemed to mean it.

Helmut was having trouble sharing her joy at their reunion. His body stiffened and he clamped his lips together. With their hands clasped, her skin was against his for so long in front of so many people that it made him uncomfortable. He was standing there with a woman no one had ever seen before, and holding her hand—that would make some tongues wag! No doubt Seraphine would hear about it by sunrise. And she already suspected him of making eyes at any woman who so much as said hello to him.

He waited without hope for her to make some trivial remark, like "I was just passing through." But a girl like Hannah was never just passing through, and if she were passing through anywhere, then her route certainly would not include the foothills of the Swabian Mountains.

"What are you doing here?" he asked softly, for the second time. He managed to extract his hand from hers. He took a step back and crossed his arms over his chest.

The radiant smile on Hannah's face vanished, and her expression took on a new determination. "We have to talk."

Chapter Six

"Say, don't I know you from somewhere?" Valentin murmured to his brother when Helmut, his face a stone, finally sat down next to him.

His father had dug an elbow into Valentin's ribs more than once, trying to send him to check on Helmut. "What do they have to talk about so long?" Gottlieb Kerner had hissed at him. "It's not proper. Tell your brother that!"

Valentin had acted as if he had not heard, though in fact, he had kept one eye on Helmut and the woman the entire time. Whatever they were talking about, their conversation was animated, even agitated.

"Where's she gone?"

"Later," Helmut said and nodded placatingly to his father, ignoring the barbs from around the table. If anyone had been expecting an exciting tale, they were disappointed. Helmut did not say a word over his encounter with the good-looking mystery woman. Instead, he lifted his mug of beer and drained it in a draft. The other men grinned. Talking with a woman could really give a man a thirst.

By the time Helmut joined them at the table, the talks with the Ulmer market gardeners were almost complete. And, as usual, Gottlieb Kerner had placed the biggest orders. Valentin made detailed notes about the dozens of types of seeds that the men of Ulm would deliver to them for the next year. Also as usual, Gottlieb and Valentin had bickered about the selection and quantities. Gottlieb had insisted on the traditional sorts, but Valentin was in favor of adding a few new varieties to their range. Their customers wanted a wider choice, he argued, while his father held that they would be safer with the better-known seeds. The gardeners went to pains to point out the quality of the new varieties, everything from the Unikum cucumber to the Guérande carrot. But because Helmut had been talking with Hannah, there was only Valentin there to argue things with his father, so the matter had quickly been settled.

Whether for old varieties or new, the haggling had been a hardfought affair. The Ulmers complained that Gottlieb was bleeding them dry, but in the end they conceded to practically every demand he made.

The other seed merchants at the table also seemed satisfied with their purchases and now turned to the most important part of the evening: a decent drink to seal the business. Käthe Steiner couldn't refill the beer mugs fast enough, though she hobbled between the bar and the tables as quickly as she was able.

When spirits were at their highest, Helmut abruptly stood and signaled to his brother to follow him outside.

The cold air hit Valentin like a fist.

"God damn it, I've drunk too much," he groaned and had to hold himself against a railing. But one look at his brother's face was enough to make him at least partway sober again. Valentin hooked his elbow into his brother's and hoped Helmut would see the gesture as comradely. His brother had always mocked him for his inability to hold his alcohol.

Both brothers hobbled along—due not only to the drink but also to the half-frozen toes they had brought home with them from their most recent travels. Valentin's little toe, especially, was cause for concern. Just that afternoon, the doctor had told him that it would perhaps be better to remove it, but Valentin did not want to hear a word about that. A few days of warmth and different shoes and it would be back to its old self.

"So what was that all about just now?" Valentin, in the meantime, had recalled where he recognized the woman from: she was the inn-keeper's daughter from The Golden Anchor in Nuremberg.

"I'm . . . going to . . . be a father," Helmut said in a monotone.

"Whaaaaat?"

"That's what she said." Helmut sounded rather amazed. "'You're going to be a father.' Not, for example, 'I'm pregnant' or 'I'm having your child.'" He laughed helplessly. "Being a father takes some doing, doesn't it?"

Valentin nodded, dazed and unable to say a word.

The brothers walked on in silence. It was approaching midnight, but lights burned in most of the houses.

"What now?" Valentin finally asked, feeling stupid the moment the question was out. He cursed the alcohol fogging his brain. He had a thousand questions on his lips and did not know which one to ask first. Seraphine . . . his heart began to beat wildly. What if Seraphine found out about the stranger? The wedding was set for January 6.

Helmut sighed. "I have no idea." Every word hung in the air as a little cloud in the icy winter air.

"Yes, but you must have said something to her. Is it possible? I mean . . . oh, damn it!"

Of course it was possible. Valentin knew his brother well enough to know that. Then something else occurred to him.

"Hold on . . . It was in Nuremberg that I nearly died from that horrible diarrhea. The doctor spent the whole night with me."

He had been too weak to crawl out of bed and use the pan. The doctor had had to help him. The memory of what had been the worst night of his life still made him shudder. Instantly, he was sober.

"I was lying there, at death's door, and you couldn't think of anything better than to jump in the hay with a girl?"

"What do you think I should have done?" Helmut cried. "I was beside myself, worrying about you, but the doctor told me there was not a thing in the world that I could do. Hannah said the doctor was good, that he really knew what he was doing, and so I should try not to worry anymore. Then we had something to drink. I had to spend the time somehow, didn't I? And then"—he raised his hands helplessly—"one thing led to another. It didn't take much persuading on my part, believe me."

Valentin sniffed. "Then another question: How do you know you were the only one who didn't need to persuade Miss Hannah very much?"

Helmut's expression brightened for a moment. "I asked her that, of course. She almost snapped my head off! 'Do you think I would have traveled all this way if it weren't you?' she said. Then she asked me what kind of person I thought she was . . . What was I supposed to say to that?" After a long silence, Helmut groaned loudly.

"Everyone saw Hannah and me! Tomorrow, the whole village will know that I sat and talked for a long time, alone, with a strange woman. That will get the gossips going. How in the world am I supposed to explain it to Seraphine?"

Valentin almost asked his brother why he had to go and cheat on his bride-to-be as often as he did. But he choked back the question like a tough chunk of meat.

But how could he cheat on *Seraphine*, of all people? She was so virtuous and pure. "*I'm not married yet*" was all Helmut said whenever Valentin mentioned his licentious behavior. Or "*Better to sow my wild oats now than later, right? As long as you keep your mouth shut, Seraphine won't find out a thing.*" And how miserable, how endlessly miserable, Valentin had felt, covering up Helmut's affairs, but his brother did not care in the slightest about Valentin's feelings.

Valentin forced himself to speak casually. "You have to feel something for Hannah, don't you? I mean, she's a beautiful woman, no question, and you are the father of her child."

Helmut groaned again. "She's very nice, of course. And cheerful. Back then, that night, I was really worried about you, you know? She was there, she took my mind off you and onto . . . other things, literally! Somehow, she's . . . not gloomy."

Valentin nodded. Anyone else would have wondered at Helmut's choice of words, but he knew what his brother was talking about. Seraphine was different from other young women her age. More serious and somehow more dreamy. *Enigmatic,* Valentin thought. Helmut had often complained about her seriousness, about how little she laughed. So she dreamed herself off to some faraway place? Was it any wonder? Friedhelm and Ilse Schwarz fought all the time, and there were the money problems, the dismal cottage they lived in with its damp walls. If Helmut weren't so insensitive, he would have realized that long ago instead of complaining all the time about "gloomy" Seraphine.

"Hannah can laugh like . . . like I don't know what, and I admire that. She's an open book, and if there's something to be done, she's in there with her sleeves rolled up. You should have seen how fast she grabbed her coat and went off to find your doctor! You don't have to tell her anything more than once—" He caught himself raving and changed his tone. "Oh, to hell with it. I thought you'd help me, but all you do is ask stupid questions."

"Well, you're in a tricky situation, certainly." Valentin realized that he found some cruel pleasure in Helmut's predicament, but the feeling made him ashamed. "Does Hannah know that you *actually*"—the stress he put on the word made it sound purely rhetorical—"are set to marry someone else in three weeks?"

Helmut nodded despondently. "I told her I had to think everything through. That a solution could certainly be found, but that I would need some time," he replied flatly. He kicked at a pile of snow. "The whole thing, it's like being ambushed! I mean, who would have thought that something like this would happen? I feel like packing a bag and just taking off and leaving everything behind." He stopped and grasped Valentin by the shoulder. "I don't really want to get married at all, you know? Not to one, not to the other! If Mother hadn't been going on about Seraphine all the time . . . you can understand that, can't you? I mean, we've both seen a lot."

Valentin knew very well what his brother meant, but he wasn't going to do him the favor of admitting it. Let him stew in his own juices a little longer!

Yes, on their travels, they saw too much. In particular, when their road took them into remote regions, they often came face-to-face with the misery of life in all its brutality. In the lonely mountain villages and narrow valleys, where the only way to earn one's bread was to till the land. The hard days, the eternal gnawing in the belly, the constant exhaustion of the women—was it any surprise to find discord and quarreling in those houses? The careworn faces of the women, the never-ending nagging, the sour stench of rubbish and unwashed bodies—Valentin and Helmut were always glad when they were able to leave. But the husbands of the wives, the fathers of the children . . . they had to stay. Often, what little money they earned went to drink. And then there was nothing left with which to buy seeds for the following spring. Sometimes the hardship was so bad that the brothers were tempted to leave the necessary seeds on credit. And sometimes they did, knowing well that they were unlikely to ever see their money again.

Valentin sighed. Once you had seen enough families like that, you could lose all interest in marriage. For better or worse. Who needed it?

And one did not have to look far. Even in Gönningen, misery was a permanent guest in some houses. Here, too, there were people who bought their seeds on credit, with no certainty that they would ever be able to repay their debts.

At the same time, their grandfathers and great-grandfathers had all started with the same basic prerequisite: a few extra seeds to sell. In earlier times, there had been no great differences between the families in the village; at least, that was how the old men told the story. Anyone who was poor in Gönningen now usually had only himself to blame for his misfortune, because he had not invested his profits from the seed trade back into the business, and had squandered them instead. And sometimes, of course, sickness or death or some other stroke of fate was behind the unlucky card that some of the village's residents had drawn.

Helmut and he, God knew, were not among those poor bastards. They were the scions of the most successful and wealthiest traders in the entire village. If anyone could afford to start a family and put food on the table, it was them, and Helmut's remarks were no more than evasions. He had no idea how lucky he could count himself with Seraphine.

But now things had taken a very unexpected turn. And Valentin's heart began to beat a little harder. If Helmut and Hannah . . . Then it would mean that Seraphine was free again.

"Is Seraphine's father back yet?" he suddenly asked.

Helmut shook his head. "At least, he wasn't back this afternoon, but maybe he got in late. When I think that I . . ." He groaned. "My God, Valentin, what am I going to do?"

Chapter Seven

It was Christmas Eve. Hannah sat on the bed and counted her money, which had dwindled away to not very much at all. If something did not happen soon, she would have to write to her mother and ask for money.

She had now spent four nights at The Sun, and lodging there was not especially cheap. Perhaps she should have gone in search of somewhere else to stay after her first night, but Emma was a friendly proprietress and did not ask many questions. The latter was reason enough for Hannah to feel she was in good hands. Curious questions and spiteful remarks about the reason for her visit, perhaps even open hostility, were not what she needed.

She looked out the window. A ground-hugging fog had wrapped the village like a damp, downy blanket for days. Only the church tower and the highest rooftops loomed spookily above the whiteness. Snow lay on the surrounding mountains, but in the village the last mushy snow had melted and now flowed in muddy runnels through the streets and alleys. Hannah pulled the shawl around her shoulders a little closer.

How much longer?

How much longer would she have to sit there and wait?

Since the departure of the Ulmer gardeners, she was the only overnight guest at The Sun. Hannah felt as if she were the only person visiting Gönningen at all. And while Emma certainly made her feel welcome, Hannah suspected that the proprietress would rather be alone with her daughter. It was not as if Hannah caused them any great difficulties. She ate breakfast with the two women in the kitchen, then helped Emma with whatever needed to be done. Hannah was not suffering the way she had seen other pregnant women suffer, and she found doing nothing more trying than washing sheets, polishing floors, or mending tablecloths. At the start, Emma had tried to fend her off, saying it wasn't right for a guest to do that and that she didn't want word to get around that she was making her guests work. But she finally relented and let Hannah do what she wanted, insisting only that she eat for free. That was certainly good for Hannah—a few more pennies saved. At midday, there was always a pot of tea and buttered bread, and Emma served an early dinner late in the afternoon, before the bar and restaurant grew busy.

There were a dozen men who were regular visitors to The Sun: the mayor, the village schoolteacher, the local minister, a few businessmen—the so-called better citizens, Emma had explained to her. Helmut's father, too, was a frequent guest. Anyone wanting only to drink went to one of the other inns. The Sun was a place to do business and to discuss what was good for Gönningen.

Gönningen.

Hannah let her little purse drop onto the bed, stood up, and crossed to the window.

What was this strange village she had wandered into?

For more than a hundred years, most of Gönningen's citizens earned their living from the trade in flower and vegetable seeds. Käthe had explained that to her on her first memorable night at the inn. *We're all seed dealers!*—and Käthe had not been exaggerating. According to the most recent census, of the 2,500 residents, 1,200 were involved in the seed trade. The shoemaker, the butcher, Emma and Käthe.

"Women too?" Hannah had asked in disbelief.

"Women too!" Käthe had confirmed with a smile, then explained that there were families in which both the husband and wife went out on the road—in different directions, of course. And they traded not only in seeds but also in honey, cheese, dried fruit; some of them were practically wandering markets.

"If a woman knows something about the business, she can sell as well as any man," she had added, not without pride.

The trade was closely tied to the seasons, Hannah had learned. There were times of year when the village was all but abandoned, with half its residents away. In autumn, especially, when the work in the surrounding fields was finished, the seed traders went on the road.

"But then winter is already on the way," Hannah had objected, thinking of her own strenuous journey to get there.

"Of course the traveling is hard, but what can you do?" Käthe had shrugged. "In the cold months, it is much easier to catch people at home. In summer, most of them are out in the fields or at the market or somewhere else. You have to go back to the same house several times if you want to speak to the owner, and that costs you time. And time is money, as they say." Because of that, she and her mother only went out in the winter, unlike many Gönningers, who were kept busy with the Jakobi trade in summer, too, Käthe had added.

Jakobi trade? Hannah had no idea what that was, but Käthe had continued on before she could ask.

The ones who made journeys out to foreign countries stayed away until Easter. Others, whose *Samenstrich* was closer, interrupted their travels to spend Christmas at home.

Samenstrich—what a strange word that was! A combination of "seed" and "line." In her mind's eye, Hannah saw children drawing a line with chalk across cobblestones. And along that line, she saw the Gönningen seed dealers balancing their seed sacks, filled with all kinds of seeds, across their shoulders. She had laughed at her mental picture, and Käthe gave her a scathing look. The *Samenstrich*, she had explained, and as Hannah had already understood, was a seed dealer's sales territory, where his or her customers lived. Most of them had known their customers for years, some for decades. For the people who lived in a dealer's territory, it went without saying that they would buy their seeds every year from that dealer. As a rule, the dealers respected each other's territory, although there certainly had been some ugly exceptions.

Some sales territories lay as far afield as Russia or even America, Käthe had explained, and when she talked about those well-traveled dealers, there was admiration in her voice. Helmut and Valentin were among the long-distance merchants—their territory saw them traveling through Bohemia—while their father traveled around Alsace and their mother did not go out at all anymore.

Hannah had soaked up all Käthe's information like a sponge. What an exciting life! But what about the children when their mothers were away from home for weeks at a time? Who kept the house in order? And how was it possible for so many to know so much about growing vegetables and flowers? She would have asked many more questions, but then Helmut arrived, and suddenly none of the seed dealers in the world—with the exception of one—meant anything.

Hannah sighed loudly and deeply. Her sigh was the only sound in the inn. There was no banging of doors, no rattling pots to be heard down below—Emma and Käthe were probably getting ready to go to church. They had invited her to go with them, but Hannah had declined. Putting up with all the curious looks on her walks around Gönningen had been more than enough. Emma had encouraged her to get out and look at the village. Gönningen had a lot that was worth seeing. The stately houses built of tuff—Hannah learned that that was the name for the odd yellowish stone she had noticed when she arrived— the pretty creek, and all the shops, of course. But shopping was the last thing she could think about given her meager funds. And she was not really in a mood for sightseeing, although she had gone to look at the house that belonged to Helmut's parents, inspecting it from the front and back. Three floors! It was one of the biggest in the village. On the right side of the house was a garden, though it was not as large as one might expect for a seed dealer. A step led to the front door, which was flanked by columns also made of tuff. Hannah thought the columns looked silly, but the large house and garden fascinated her. This is where she would live if Helmut proved himself to be a man of honor and took her as his wife. Behind which window would their bedroom be? How would it feel to live in a house like that?

Despite the fascination it held for her, the Kerner estate was also to blame for her regular panic. Was she really expecting the elder son of the richest seed merchant in the village to marry her? A nobody like *her*? When she thought about it like that, she wished that he lived in one of the poor huts out on the edge of the village.

She had not been invited anywhere other than church, but Hannah had still put on her pretty Hungarian outfit. It was good to dress well for Christmas Eve, even if you were only going to spend it alone sitting on a bed in a tiny, cold room.

Hannah laid one hand on her belly. She and her child, forgotten by the world. Was that loneliness now going to be her constant companion? Oh, if only Helmut would at least come by today!

He had visited the previous three days, and each time he had found a different excuse for why he could only stay for a short while.

"No male visitors in the rooms!" Emma had told her sternly when he visited the first time. Then she turned to Helmut and asked, "Does Seraphine know that you're here with a guest?" When Helmut answered no, she shook her head disapprovingly, but a little later she brought a plate with some dry *Hefekranz* to their table in the restaurant, then disappeared back into the kitchen without another word. It was early in the afternoon and there were no other guests. The silence between them hung over the table like the pall of tobacco smoke that would hang there later. *He's a stranger. I have nothing to say to him.* That realization had all but pulled the floor out from beneath Hannah's feet. Together, they ate the *Hefekranz*, Hannah picking at it and choking it down crumb by crumb. Helmut asked her questions about her journey, and her replies were taciturn, fool that she was. She soon saw they were not getting anywhere like that.

"Come back tonight," she had whispered to him as he left. "When the inn is full, I can let you into my room without anyone seeing." Helmut had nodded.

And he came. So late that Hannah had given up on him. He could not come any sooner, he explained, because his father wanted to go through an important account with him.

Hannah had embraced him and said that it didn't matter, that nothing mattered now that they were together. The hours of waiting, the worry, not knowing what would become of her—she had been so desperate. Tears ran down her cheeks. Then she had felt Helmut's arm around her, so warm, so protecting. Looking back, Hannah could no longer recall how she had gotten out of her dress or Helmut out of his trousers. With her kisses, she smothered his mumblings about how it wouldn't be right. Suddenly, they were lying in bed. The familiarity between them was back, and along with it, the floor under Hannah's feet. He was not as strange and foreign to her as he had seemed that afternoon, not at all, and she felt no surprise that she had fallen for him back then, in Nuremberg. Her smile had returned, and also her sense that everything would work out.

When the lust of the moment had been satisfied, Helmut began to tell her about Seraphine—openly and honestly. About how it had been a given for years that they would one day get married. His mother had been after him about the wedding for so long, but his father allowed him more leeway.

Listening to him speak about Seraphine hurt Hannah. She did not dare question him, much as she wanted to: *Do you love her? I'm carrying your child. How can you lie there and tell me about someone else?*

Of course he liked Seraphine Schwarz. They had known each other since they were children, and everyone's time came sooner or later. But his betrothal to Seraphine was really a kind of arranged marriage, a marriage of convenience, Helmut had told Hannah.

Which, to Hannah's ears, sounded nothing like a love story.

Now, of course, the situation had changed dramatically. He had to talk with his father. And with his mother, too. But that meant finding a suitable moment; she could understand that, couldn't she?

Of course. Hannah understood.

He also had to talk to Seraphine, which would be the hardest of all. Seraphine was already sewing her wedding dress. She had been for months. He needed to find the right words for her and had yet to prepare them.

Of course. Hannah understood everything, and she covered Helmut's face in tiny kisses.

If only Seraphine's father were back from his roving. They had been waiting for him to return for days, but he didn't come and didn't come. He would have to talk to him, and to Seraphine's mother, Ilse Schwarz, too. He did not yet know how he was supposed to explain everything to everyone, but he was sure he would come up with something.

On his next visit, Helmut had consoled her again, murmuring something about finding the right moment.

But when would that moment be? When would he find the words?

Poor Seraphine was just a few buildings away, sewing her wedding dress, not knowing another woman sat here expecting a child from her husband-to-be. For a moment Hannah could sympathize with her, but her sympathy quickly evaporated, swept away like smoke in a good chimney.

And Christmas Eve had come! The wedding was planned for the sixth of January. Hannah had seen the marriage announcement pinned to the glass-fronted board outside the church. When was Helmut going to tell his fiancée that she would have to live without his "I do"? Perhaps when he was walking her down the aisle?

An engagement could not be dissolved just like that, could it? The humiliation—Hannah did not like to imagine how it must feel to be a spurned bride.

With her index finger, she cleared a peephole on the fogged glass. It was a hazy night, but almost all the windows of the houses were lit. No doubt the women inside them were busy making the last preparations for dinner after their visit to the church. And children were running around excitedly. For them, going to church was a chore, no more, while at home there would be plenty to eat and maybe even a small gift waiting for them.

She wondered what Helmut was doing right then. Was he perhaps with his Seraphine? While she sat there, lonely and sad and . . .

Like a lamb to the slaughter.

Hannah didn't like the thought, which had come from nowhere. No, she didn't like it one little bit. She might well have been a fool back then, in Nuremberg, when she let Helmut . . . with her, but she was no lamb to the slaughter. If she felt that way, she might as well have stayed home.

She had hidden away in her room for too long. Away from the curious eyes of the Gönningers. Away from the questions about why she was there. Away from Helmut's family. Away from meeting Seraphine.

Enough! Her patience was at an end.

She picked up her coat and ran down the steps. She hoped that Emma and Käthe were still there. And if they were not, then she would find her way to the church by herself, though her knees trembled at the thought.

Chapter Eight

Every bench in the church was packed. She had entered with Emma and Käthe, but while they pushed through to the middle of a pew where someone had kept two places for them, Hannah remained almost out of sight behind a column next to the last row. She nodded to a few women who turned around to look at her. Was one of them Seraphine?

The church smelled of soap, fermented apples, and camphor—a strange mixture that was unfamiliar to Hannah and yet belonged there. She had never in her life felt as lonely as she did then. If at least her mother had been there with her . . . Tears were burning behind her eyelids, and she blinked quickly; the last thing she wanted was to burst into tears in front of everybody. She should have stayed in her room, but there, too, the loneliness would have settled like frost on her skin.

"Chin up, especially if you're drowning," she suddenly heard her father's words. She sniffed loudly, and a few churchgoers looked askance at her. She swallowed. Her father was right. Crying never made anything better. She looked ahead to the altar.

It was an evangelical church, which surprised Hannah but also pleased her. She was evangelical herself, which was nothing unusual in Nuremberg, but on her travels through Württemberg she had passed through many Catholic regions. Gönningen was not the only evangelical village in the region, Emma had explained just before they entered the church. Since the Reformation, there were many evangelical towns and parishes.

Normally, Hannah quickly absorbed the solemn atmosphere of a church service and listened to the Christmas story every year as if she were hearing it for the first time. Today she was far too preoccupied to concentrate on the minister's words. She looked surreptitiously along the rows until she finally discovered Helmut's tousled shock of hair. Beside him sat Valentin, and beside Valentin an older man who must have been their father.

The service only lasted about an hour, though it felt like an eternity to Hannah. But as it drew to an end, she grew apprehensive and wished that the priest would start singing another hymn.

Hannah was the first out the door and waited to the right of the steps. She forced herself to smile pleasantly at everyone who walked by, and did her best to ignore the whispering and the curious looks behind her once they had passed. Let them get a good look at Helmut Kerner's future wife. Rocking back and forth on tiptoe, she craned her neck to look inside. It could not be much longer.

There! The older Mr. Kerner. And behind him . . .

"Why are you standing around in the cold, girl?" asked Emma, who was suddenly beside her. "Why haven't you gone home? I gave you a key."

Then Käthe plucked at her sleeve and said, "Come on, we've got something special for dinner!"

Hannah shook Käthe off like a bothersome fly, but she kept her forced smile in place. "I'll be along soon!" She was very close to physically pushing both of them on their way. She had just spotted Helmut, and he would reach her any second.

One more deep breath, and then she stepped out into the middle of the path.

"Helmut! How lovely to see you." Her voice only trembled a little. She smiled first at Helmut, then at his brother, then at their parents, who nodded back in confusion. Behind them was a blond girl of such ethereal beauty that Hannah's breath was momentarily taken away. Seraphine.

Helmut looked around as if the devil incarnate were behind him. All he managed to get out of his mouth was a croak. He jabbed Valentin with his elbow, but his brother could only stare at Hannah in bewilderment.

Hannah's smile froze. He still hadn't spoken with his family, let alone his fiancée.

"Helmut, aren't you going to introduce me to your family?"

"I think that would be an excellent idea," the older Mr. Kerner remarked, furrowing his brow. He shifted his weight impatiently. He was well aware that a crowd was watching. Apparently, it was no longer so important to get home and pull the Christmas roast out of the oven. Whatever was playing out between the Kerners and the beautiful stranger, who'd already been in the village for several days, was far more interesting.

"Yes, uh, this is Hannah, uh, Brettschneider. She—" Helmut turned to Valentin, looking for help.

"She's from Nuremberg, just visiting Gönningen," Valentin said, finishing his brother's sentence. Then he took Helmut and his father by the arm and urged them forward. "And now we should all see that we get home, or my half-frozen toe will fall off right here."

Perplexed, Hannah could only stand there and watch them hurry off into the darkness.

"Who was that woman and what did she want? I'm asking you for the last time!" Gottlieb Kerner pointed his fork at Helmut. Gravy dripped onto the tablecloth, which drew an annoyed "tsk-tsk" from his wife, Wilhelmine.

Helmut looked around. His parents, Valentin, and his sister, Marianne, who had come from Reutlingen for Christmas with her son and husband—all of them were staring at him. He was in a corner, and he could not get out of it. Damn it, why did Hannah have to make her big entrance tonight, of all nights? The only consolation was that Seraphine and her mother were not with them at the table. They wanted to be home in case Friedhelm returned. On the other hand, if she were here, he could put the hardest part of all behind him.

"Helmut! If you don't open your mouth now—" his mother threatened. She glanced angrily at the Christmas goose that nobody at the table, just then, really seemed to appreciate.

"Don't be so modest," said Valentin. "You weren't so modest back there in Nuremberg."

Helmut turned sharply to his brother. *Oh, thank you! Yet again, you're a great help!* Then he looked up at the ceiling beseechingly. Silent night, holy night . . . well, that was about to end.

"It's all a bit complicated . . ."

Hannah picked at a chunk of carp. She had no appetite at all, and she had never liked carp. Back home, Christmas Eve always meant a big bowl of sausages and a mountain of mashed potatoes. Then again, even the best Nuremberg bratwurst would probably stick in her throat today. She looked around at the deserted tables. Emma had set the regulars' table to mark the occasion, but for Hannah, the voices of the three women practically echoed in the large, empty room. Why couldn't they have eaten in the kitchen where it was warm and cozy? A little, just a little, like home.

Oh, Mother, I miss you so.

To distract herself, Hannah asked the first question that popped into her head: "Why are there so many inns in Gönningen? Is that also because of the seed trading?"

Emma and Käthe looked at her.

"Yes and no," said Emma, her mouth full. Her cheeks were flushed from the glass of wine that she had treated herself to. "The men like a drink, and they like the atmosphere in the inns, especially in spring, when the money flows."

"The women too!" Käthe added with a laugh.

Emma nodded. "But it isn't just the Gönningers who come here. There are a lot of visitors who come for the Swabian Mountains. Gönningen is one of the last villages in the valley before the road goes up."

Hannah tried to look interested. But her eyes kept drifting away into space.

Helmut had looked so fearful. Was it a mistake to talk to him like that, in front of everyone?

"Gönningen once had four mills, too, which meant that a lot of farmers came to us from all around. After they dropped off their grain at a mill, a mug of beer was always welcome. But that was a long time ago."

And then there was that beautiful girl. Seraphine . . . she was probably eating dinner with Helmut's family right now.

"The market people still come through," Käthe said.

Emma flicked her hand dismissively. "They don't count. They come twice a year, and that doesn't help."

Käthe shrugged. "Other villages would be happy if they had market rights."

Next to that Seraphine, I'm just fat and ugly! She looked at her own white arms, disgusted at the way the flesh seemed to bulge out of the gathered sleeves.

"Other villages would be happy if they had *anything* that Gönningen has," said Emma proudly. "Which is why the Gönningers tend to keep to themselves."

Käthe held the plate of carp out for Hannah. "More fish?"

Hannah shook her head. Anything but more of the spongy fish. She drank a sip of wine to ease the nausea she felt rising. Should she tell them about how the farmers from one of the neighboring villages called the Gönningers a bunch of drunkards? Better not . . .

"What do you mean, they keep to themselves? I thought they were always out traveling?" Hannah frowned.

If Helmut and I were man and wife—would he go off traveling alone? Or would I have to go along?

"That's true, but when it comes to marrying, a Gönningen man would rather find a wife from his own village. And the women are the same . . ." Emma glanced at her daughter, who began scraping her plate.

Hannah's heart sank even lower. She had tried to choose the most harmless subject in the world to divert herself from her own misery, and this was what she got: the Gönningen men look for their wives locally.

"I guess Gönningen is a very special village," she murmured, and was surprised at the tone of longing in her voice. She had only meant the remark to sound polite, something to please her hostess. Instead, she realized that the village was starting to fascinate her.

"You're right about that. Gönningen sits under a lucky star," Emma mused. "The fruit trees in our fields alone are a treasure. It's really no surprise that other villages look at us with envy. When I think about how miserably things have gone for most people in this country in the last few years, I'm glad that we Gönningers can still stand up and smile."

Fruit trees? What did fruit trees have to do with wealth? Hannah was about to ask when someone knocked loudly and without stopping on the front door.

Chapter Nine

"I wanted to see for myself the woman who claims my son dishonored her." Gottlieb Kerner's face was a stony mask. With his right hand, he gestured to Emma to leave the room. She had retreated behind the bar almost as soon as the older Kerner and Helmut had stepped inside. Only when Emma had disappeared through the kitchen door did he turn back to the stranger.

Hannah slowly stood up from the table, took a few steps toward the center of the room, and turned a full circle. "Like this?"

Was she trying to get his back up? Gottlieb looked at Helmut, who was trying to stifle a smile. His son would change his tune soon enough, even if he had to clip him on the ear!

"Emma, bring us something to drink. And clear away the leftovers," he called toward the kitchen door. The two women were probably just on the other side with their ears pressed to the wood, not wanting to miss a word of it.

He was not in the habit of bursting in on other people on Christmas Eve. But extraordinary situations demanded extraordinary measures, a rule he had seen confirmed many times in his life. And Gottlieb Kerner knew without a doubt that he was facing an extraordinary situation.

This affair had to be closed and put behind them, the sooner the better. He had no tolerance for loose talk in the village.

As far as Emma and her daughter were concerned, he would have to think of something. He snorted when he realized just how difficult a position Helmut had put him in: for one thing, he owed the innkeeper something for barging in on her like this, and for another, he had to make sure she kept her mouth shut. No doubt half the village would know the story by tomorrow evening, after church.

He nodded toward a table. "Sit." He noted that Helmut and the woman chose two seats side by side. Aha, the two malefactors together! Not that either of them looked particularly remorseful. Quite the opposite, in fact: Helmut, who had squirmed like an eel at home, seemed far more comfortable here. Time to get down to business.

"What do you want, young lady?"

She could name her price. If it was within the realm of reason, he would pay it. He glared furiously at Helmut again. Spreading his seed across the entire country, the rogue.

"I am having your son's child. The child of a seed merchant. And I want my child to be a seed merchant, too! I would like my child to carry his father's name. It is an honorable name, isn't it?"

Gottlieb Kerner could not believe what he was hearing. This was . . . insolence!

But it was Helmut who replied. "Of course our family is honorable! You can ask anyone. And we are among the most successful seed merchants in the entire village. Isn't that right, Father?"

Under the table, Gottlieb kicked as hard as he could, but he contacted a table leg instead of Helmut's shin. Was the boy crazy? He'd start counting out the Kerner assets next.

"This is not about money," Hannah said, as if reading the old man's mind.

Again, Gottlieb Kerner felt he'd been made a fool of. By a woman, at that!

"Money is not unimportant," Hannah went on. "No one wants to starve, after all. But I have learned that money does not come for free. It takes hard work, honesty, and respectability, as my parents taught me from when I was a little girl. That is what matters to me."

Gottlieb took a mouthful of beer. This conversation was not going at all as he had foreseen it. The sack of money he had brought with him hung heavy and useless inside the leg of his trousers. The strings had been snatched from his fingers within just a few minutes, and it was Hannah who was pulling them.

To win time, he took his pipe out of his pocket and made a show of packing it. So she didn't want money. Hmm. That made things easier. He would have to think of a new strategy, then, one that would fit with this stranger's approach to things. As inconspicuously as possible, he looked across at her.

She was not the most beautiful woman around, and no comparison to Seraphine, but he certainly could not call her ugly. A little . . . coarse, perhaps.

On the other hand, there was something about the woman. She was not one of those string beans who'd get knocked down by the first decent breeze. And the spark in her eye! She had guts, he'd give her that. Not a word to excuse the fact that she had gotten herself mixed up with Helmut. There was nothing about her that said "fallen woman," nothing at all. Her expression was open and without the slightest trace of shame.

"I can work. I can work hard. I'm used to it. And I was born with a good constitution!" Hannah laughed. "I can't remember the last time I was sick."

Gottlieb Kerner waved it off. "You don't have to sell yourself like a cow at market," he said with unnecessary harshness.

Hannah flinched at his words. "I just thought it would be important for you to know what kind of daughter-in-law you are getting."

Daughter-in-law?

Before he could say anything, she went on. "I will be a good wife to your son." She took Helmut's hand in hers and he, though taken aback, let her. "In good times as in bad, isn't that what they say? Back then, when your brother was so ill"—looking now at Helmut—"and you were beside yourself with worry for him, I was there for you. I will always be there for you. And I will learn everything I need to be a good seed merchant's wife."

Now utterly speechless, Gottlieb looked from one to the other. Was that his son sitting there, smiling like an idiot? Where were all of Helmut's fine words? His son, the big mouth! He sniffed. It was obvious to him who'd wear the breeches in this marriage. But he was terrified when he realized how far-reaching the consequences of that thought would be. Blast it all, he already had a future daughter-in-law. What would he do with two?

For a moment, he considered going home and discussing the situation with Wilhelmine. But she had been no great help earlier: wide-eyed and disbelieving, she had listened to Helmut's confession, then jumped up and come back with the prayer book that she had put on the sideboard on their return from church, leafing through it frantically as if she might find the solution on a certain page.

Gottlieb Kerner drew on his pipe as if he could inhale wisdom with the tobacco smoke. There were moments in life when neither the Lord above nor a man's own wife were much use.

Silence settled over the table. Helmut shifted on his chair uneasily while Hannah remained calm and collected, at least on the outside, drank a sip of wine, and smiled at Helmut as if this were an everyday encounter among old, good friends.

Nothing seemed to unsettle the woman, a circumstance that Gottlieb Kerner could only marvel at. And he marveled that it surprised him just as much.

He was fifty-two years old. He had been going out on the road for thirty-six years, and there was nothing he hadn't seen, as he liked to say.

His customers prized his advice—and not only when it came to rotating their carrots, kohlrabi, and beans. "We are so glad to see you," he heard regularly. "We have a problem, but we thought we'd wait until our seed man came." His mere presence meant whatever problem they had was already half solved. A drunken husband, a dispute with neighbors or relatives—a man as well traveled and worldly as he would surely have an answer for the everyday questions that plagued his customers. And he usually did.

Now here he sat, completely at a loss. He sighed. Then he turned to Helmut. "And would you be willing to marry this woman?"

How that sounded! As if he were the parish priest in person. He popped his pipe in his mouth and sucked on it.

"I would, but . . ." Helmut lifted his hands in a hopeless gesture.

"But there's still this other matter," said Gottlieb for his son.

This other matter—instead of being ashamed at his choice of words, he took new courage from it. Better to tackle the matter now than to put it off. This woman was carrying his son's baby. A mishap, certainly, and one that fundamentally changed the entire situation. Helmut *could not* marry Seraphine Schwarz now. And in truth, he had never been particularly enthusiastic about his son's choice. Seraphine was a vision, to be sure, but when he thought of her father . . . and she had never been much good in the trade, or she would have gone out on the road herself long ago instead of leaving it all to her good-for-nothing father. It was Wilhelmine whose heart had gone out to Seraphine. "Seraphine is the most beautiful girl in the village. She's so delicate and gracious—she will make you a good wife." She had never tired of telling Helmut that, and to Gottlieb she had said many times that "she would be like a second daughter to me."

With Seraphine as her second daughter or not, Wilhelmine would soon be a grandmother again. He would again be a grandfather. The realization made him choke on his pipe smoke, and he began to cough and splutter. Hannah instantly jumped to her feet and thumped him on the back, and he thanked her with a not unfriendly look.

From that perspective, Helmut had no other choice. This Hannah was not the kind of woman who would be paid off—that much was clear. The engagement with Seraphine would have to be called off. But how did one proceed in such a case? He could not recall anything similar, ever, in the village. God, this would set some tongues wagging. He would have to come up with something for that. And of course Seraphine would have to get something to compensate for the ignominy, as would her parents. He would make an appointment with a lawyer in Reutlingen. It couldn't hurt to get some legal support in such a precarious matter; he didn't want anyone casting aspersions on his family later for behaving like villains. No, no, everything would have to go forward officially, legally, and correctly. He already sensed that the affair would prove expensive, but he would have to pay. What else could he do? The boy had made a mistake, and now he had to face it like a man. *He* had raised his son that way, after all.

Satisfied with himself and his wisdom, Gottlieb felt a smile spread across his face as he looked at Hannah and Helmut.

Half an hour later, he embraced his future daughter-in-law, Helmut kissed his future wife, and together with Emma and Käthe, who both shed some tears, they toasted the happy moment.

Chapter Ten

"And that happened on Christmas Eve?"

Emma nodded.

"My heavens, what a drama!" Elsbeth Wagner, the wife of the pharmacist, shook her head. "And I thought *we* were having a big night when Grandpa lost a tooth on Christmas Eve and it fell into the soup pot."

The two women giggled.

Her arms folded across her breasts, her lips pursed accusingly, Almuth Maurer looked from one to the other. With all due respect for their little chat, did the women actually think she was standing there in the icy cold of her shop just for the joy of it? The first day after the holiday was always a good day. Every house ran out of something that had to be replaced urgently. Today, however, nothing seemed more important to the women than the news that Emma and Käthe Steiner were crowing about.

"Where is this Hannah now?" Elsbeth asked Emma.

"In her room," Käthe said, speaking first. "The poor thing seems to sleep all day. She probably didn't get a wink of sleep before"—she raised her eyebrows meaningfully—"the *revelation*."

Gertrude, one of Emma's neighbors, took such a deep breath that her chest heaved considerably. "Well, when I think about a Miss Hannah coming from who-knows-where and claiming that my boy Eugen knocked her up!" She rolled her eyes dramatically. "I always say what I don't know can't upset me, but . . ."

The others nodded. None of them really wanted to imagine what their husbands got up to in the long months of traveling.

"There are sluts like her in every town and every village! Making eyes at our men! You can hardly blame the men for a moment of weakness, can you?" Elsbeth looked around at the women for agreement.

Emma snorted with laughter. "And what about the women? There's more than one of us that's come back with a pea in the pod, right?" She turned a meaningful glance on Gertrude, who looked away. Everyone in the village knew that at least one of Gertrude's five brats was not her husband's. It wasn't hard to add up.

Annchen, the youngest of the women present, blushed. "What? Do you think—"

"Well, this is something completely different," Elsbeth interrupted the young woman. "Are you on this little slut's side?" She glared angrily at Emma.

"Who are you calling a slut? She's a decent young woman, take it from me!" Emma said protectively, like a mother hen. Hannah, in a manner of speaking, was in her care, living under her roof after all. She could hardly stand by and listen to the other women attacking and denigrating her like that.

"Poor Seraphine," said Annchen. "I wonder how she took it?"

All eyes turned back to Emma, who wondered if she should say anything at all about that.

Elsbeth spoke up before she could make up her mind. "Not well, I'm sure. She and Helmut have been engaged since, well, forever, and now he's marrying someone else in just a few days?"

Elsbeth's words were met with a collective sigh that even Emma had to join in.

"Hannah says that Gottlieb and Helmut went to see the minister yesterday to sort out everything for the wedding. They want to keep the date and time they already had," Käthe added almost breathlessly. "Well, I for one think it's not proper. Is it even legal? Why does one even bother to register a marriage at all—that's what I'd like to know. Couldn't they at least have picked another Sunday? And I can't believe the minister is just letting this happen."

"I'll bet it's costing Kerner senior a pretty penny."

"It's indecent, *all* of it, if you ask me!" Annchen said indignantly. "Because . . ." She fell silent, her face red when she felt Emma's stern eyes glaring.

"Hannah is a solid, respectable young woman, and I'll be glad to say it again. And as for what happened in Nuremberg . . ." The innkeeper shrugged. "I know Helmut. And I can well imagine him making eyes at her. She did not know he was already promised to another; she told me that herself. Of course it isn't as it should be, but . . ." She lifted her hands, palms up, and shrugged, as if to say, *That's the way life is.*

"But what's to become of Seraphine?" said Annchen.

Looking away absently, Gertrude picked up a handful of sugar from an open sack beside her and let it trickle through her fingers.

Almuth Maurer frowned. That was going too far. Everyone knew that Gertrude was not the most particular when it came to hygiene and cleanliness. And she had the gall to stand there and run her fingers through the fine sugar! She reached across and covered the sugar sack with an upturned tin plate.

"Seraphine is young and beautiful. She will find someone else soon enough, you can be sure of that. Our young Mr. Kerner is not the only bachelor in the region, after all. Well, can I help any of you?" She nodded meaningfully toward her stacked shelves.

"Beautiful!" Gertrude blurted disdainfully. "We see once again how far one gets in life on beauty alone. Ha! The way she paraded through the village, with her nose high in the air and her gaze off somewhere as if the rest of us weren't even worth noticing. But pride goeth before a fall, right? Well, our pretty Seraphine won't be holding her nose quite so high anymore. And besides—"

The doorbell rang just then, causing Gertrude to fall silent, and the next moment she let out a small, muffled squeal.

"Holy Mary-and-Joseph, speak of the devil and he comes at a run," murmured Almuth.

"And another pound of butter for me!"

"I need semolina. The mice got into mine. And our old tomcat just lay there and watched 'em."

"And a bottle of sugar syrup. For the grandson—"

"Good morning, Seraphine," said Almuth, with feigned indifference. "What can I get you?"

Seraphine, who had stopped in the doorway, looked up. "But it's not my turn. All these others are ahead of me," she said and laughed.

"No, no, it's quite all right." With an eager smile, Annchen pulled Seraphine to the front.

"If there's any way we can help you . . . ," said the pharmacist's wife, taking a step to the side.

Gertrude nodded vigorously. "There's only so much one can do, of course. But with a thing like this, I mean, it goes without saying that we all . . . ow!" She looked around, annoyed, and saw Annchen, who had jabbed her hard in the ribs.

"I've got some peppermint sweets in and unpacked them just this minute. Here!" As if she were dealing with a child, Almuth Maurer pressed a sweet into Seraphine's hand. "I know you love them."

Seraphine looked in confusion at the piece of candy in her hand. "Thank you."

"Idiots all," murmured Emma. She took a step toward Seraphine. "Just ignore these silly clucks." She put one arm across Seraphine's shoulder and squeezed her gently. "We're sure it isn't easy for you, and—"

Seraphine twisted free of Emma's awkward embrace. A small vertical crease appeared between her eyes.

"What has gotten into all of you?" She laughed helplessly. "It isn't the first time that Father has come home later than expected. I mean, it would have been nice to have him home for Christmas, but that's just like him, isn't it? Helmut also says we shouldn't go getting ourselves all worried for nothing. I'm sure he'll be back in time for the wedding."

Her last words vanished into the bewildered silence of the other women.

Seraphine shook her head. "Now I've completely forgotten what Mother sent me here to get." She chewed her bottom lip, but the memory would not come. "Doesn't matter. I'll come back a little later." She gave the women a cursory nod, and left.

The women looked from one to the other, their faces showing a mix of surprise and horror.

Almuth finally broke the silence. "She doesn't know."

Chapter Eleven

"Helmut. You're very early, you know. The food isn't finished yet."

Seraphine jumped at the sound of her mother's voice. Helmut was already here? And she was still standing in the tiny pantry, a broom in her hands, dreaming away! She frantically tried to sweep the little dust balls and grit into one corner. After that, she only had to get out to the courtyard unobserved to wash her hands and tidy her hair. Helmut could not see her in such a slovenly state.

"Friedhelm still hasn't come back?" she heard Helmut ask.

"People are already starting to talk. Seraphine said that when she was in Almuth's shop earlier, a few women there were acting as if he were already dead. I had no idea that everyone worried about us so." Ilse Schwarz's words bore more than a trace of irony.

Seraphine stood behind the curtain that separated the pantry from the kitchen, the broom in her hand as she eavesdropped.

Ilse sighed. "I'm slowly beginning to fear that something has happened. It's been more than three weeks with not a word. And now it's only a few days until the wedding! If Seraphine's own father isn't there . . ."

"The wedding . . ." Helmut cleared his throat, which degenerated into a coughing fit.

"Oooh, that doesn't sound good," Seraphine heard her mother say, followed by a loud pounding sound. "Pushed things a little too far on the first day of the holidays, did you?" She laughed. "And now that I see you close up, you look like you haven't slept a wink for days."

Seraphine twisted up her mouth. Helmut's drinking habits were not her mother's business. It was customary in Gönningen that fathers and their sons went from inn to inn on the first day of the Christmas holidays.

"It wasn't so bad at all this year," Helmut replied, his voice scratchy.

"If I'm supposed to believe that, I guess I'll believe anything." Ilse laughed.

Seraphine licked the fingertips on her right hand, then ran them over her forehead and hair. That would have to do. She had to rescue Helmut from her mother. She pulled back the curtain and stepped into the kitchen.

"Seraphine."

"Helmut."

She swept angelically toward him. She held his hands, which were raw and hard from hauling the heavy seed sack. A ripple of love ran through her. "I dreamed about you last night. A lovely dream. Should I tell you about it?" she whispered, hoping fervently that her mother would have the decency to leave them alone. What beautiful eyes Helmut had . . . eyes only for her. She felt slightly dizzy, suddenly, and the ripple spread to her skin, making it tingle.

"We can sit and talk about it in the front room," Helmut said.

What? What had he said? Whenever she took Helmut's hands in hers or they embraced or even kissed, it became hard for her to think clearly.

"What's going on in here? You didn't even get the floor clean. That's what daydreaming gets you!" she heard her mother say. She had pushed past her daughter and drawn the curtain aside. "Before you two turtle-doves make yourselves at home in the front room, my precious daughter here is going to finish her work. Lord knows, it can't be too much to ask for a little sweeping and dusting, can it?"

Helmut gently freed his hands from Seraphine's and stamped his right foot dramatically. "My God, none of that matters now," he practically screamed. "I have to talk to Seraphine, now, and everything else can wait!"

Perplexed, Ilse stood and watched her future son-in-law pull her daughter into the next room.

"But . . ."

The door slammed.

"Did you hear me? Seraphine!" Helmut shook her arm.

Seraphine sat dazed and numb in the front room, which had just enough space for an old sofa, an armchair, and a wobbly table. The room was rarely used. More than once, Seraphine had asked to be allowed to use it as her bedroom, just to escape the chilly hole she currently had in the back part of the house. But Ilse insisted it had to be kept as it was: a front room was part of a proper and decent house.

The fingernails of her right hand dug into the frayed upholstery. Seraphine picked at the loose threads, dug down, pulled up new threads, picked deeper.

Of course she had heard him. She was not deaf.

She looked up, finally, with an absent smile. When she saw his face contorted into a grimace, his eyes wide and desperate, his lips trembling, the warm ripple washed through her again. There was a buzzing sound in her ears, and her heart beat rapidly. Her Helmut! He was putting himself through so much pain. There he was, stammering like a schoolboy in distress, groaning, starting sentences only to leave them hanging, unfinished. So much hard work, and all that came out of his mouth was rubbish. His journey to Nuremberg, a girl named Hannah, Valentin getting sick—what did all that have to do with her?

What did it have to do with either of them? She felt like throwing her arms around him, pressing her body to his, rubbing against him like a cat. Instead, she raised her right hand and stroked his cheek gently. The black stubble of his beard was as rough as the old, worn fabric of the sofa. Oh, Helmut.

"Seraphine, say something!" He jerked away from her, his breathing heavy, nostrils flared, and her hand was left in emptiness. The silence began to feel intimidating.

Nuremberg. Hannah. Nuremberg.

The room rocked, the sofa rocked, contours blurred, and dizziness threatened to lift her high and away, like a leaf in a storm. Seraphine had to hold on to the sofa with both hands. But when she looked at Helmut, he was sitting calmly, not moving. Could it be that this quaking was only in her? Reluctantly, she took a deep breath, shuddered, exhaled. Out, out with all those words that had nothing to do with her.

"I wanted to tell you about my dream. We were traveling, but it was not a normal journey, not on foot, but in a coach made of silver. The two horses were also silver."

Seraphine closed her eyes. The glow! As if the star fairy had sprinkled everything with silver dust.

"We were sitting very close to one another. There was no coachman on the seat; the coach drove itself. Isn't that odd?"

Helmut jumped up and paced like a caged lion between the door, window, and sofa. "My God, Seraphine, wake up!"

The coach dissolved. Her dream transformed into a shrill scream. Seraphine held on to the sofa tightly, fearing the quaking would return. But . . . nothing.

"How can you babble about dreams now? This—*this*—is the bitter reality. Don't make it so hard for me. Scream at me. Berate me for the bastard I am. Hit me, if you want!" A furious sob escaped him.

"Why would I do that"—Seraphine looked up at him in astonishment—"if I love you?"

"But I am not worthy of your love, damn it." Helmut sat down again. He looked at her strangely, not like he normally did. Almost brutally. Seraphine felt an uneasiness rise inside her. "Seraphine, we can't get married, do you understand that? The wedding is canceled. I have to marry another woman. I *have to*, you understand? My father is going to Reutlingen this week, to a lawyer, to find out what compensation you are entitled to. We . . . I will do everything to make up for this, please believe me."

Compensate, make up for . . . Seraphine smiled and closed her ears. Smiling was painful and her cheekbones hurt from it. But then the silence passed and the buzzing grew louder, spreading through her head like a swarm of bees. Thoughts formed and dissolved, feelings galloped away so fast that no one could have rounded them up in time. The star fairy, perhaps. Yes. But she was not there. Not in that cottage. Not then. Seraphine sighed.

"Of course I understand." Her eyes sought out Helmut's face again, his beautiful eyes, and locked onto him. "But we love each other! The two of us, we belong together—nothing has changed about that, has it?"

"Yes . . . no!" He shook his head despairingly. "Of course I love you, but . . ."

Of course. He loved her. The world was good. Seraphine took a deep breath, exhaled. The other words didn't matter.

"But I can't follow the call of my heart, you see? The heart has to take a back seat. We both have to be strong."

"Yes," she sighed and nodded, trusting him. "We belong together, forever and ever, and nothing else is important." She smiled. Brave. Strong. Away with the unimportant words. Everything was all right. He loved her.

"My God, I'm glad you see it like that." He glanced covertly toward the door, then pulled Seraphine into an embrace and pressed a kiss to her cheek. "You would not believe how ill I felt, coming here." Helmut jumped to his feet, suddenly in a hurry. "Tell your mother that I can't stay to eat. But I will come back and talk to her and your father, when he returns. My father will come, too. He will arrange everything. You should not suffer any hardship, after all. I . . . blast it, Seraphine, I'm sorry. Forgive me."

Helmut ran from the room, almost colliding with Ilse Schwarz.

Seraphine watched as he left. She wanted to call after him, but every word was engulfed by the buzzing of the bee swarm. Why was he asking her to forgive him? That's what you did if you stepped on someone's foot. Or if you accidentally elbowed someone in the ribs. But not if . . . The whole world came crashing down. Away, away with the words that did not belong there!

"Child! Sera! I . . ." Her mother's voice, choked, more a gurgling noise, then arms around her, the odor of sweat and sauerkraut, and pressure, so hard, so hard against the inside of her chest that it made breathing almost impossible.

"How can he . . ." Then the gurgling again, full of snot, full of spit. "Break your heart . . ." Tears, wet and hot, drenching her dress. "Your lost honor . . . the people in the village . . . the talk . . . Who will have you now?"

"Mother! Stop it!" Whimpering, Seraphine freed herself from her mother's arms. She wiped her damp hands on her skirt, but small fibers from the upholstered sofa still stuck to her fingers. "There is no reason to cry." Was that her voice? So metallic? So empty?

"But child, he just . . ." Her mother, helpless as ever. She looked confused, anxious, no shine in her eyes at all. Almost sickened, Seraphine turned away and placed a cushion over the hole she had picked in the upholstery. She stood up. She was hungry suddenly. Wasn't that strange?

"Helmut talks some rubbish, doesn't he? Men do that sometimes. You must know that better than me. Helmut and I, we belong together, and nothing will change that, absolutely nothing. We are like the sun and the moon—our lives are inseparably interwoven. There's no need to worry. Everything will work out, you'll see."

She would burn with love, and if she had to, she would die for love. What difference did a few silly comments make? To burn with love . . . passionately, and not with a snotty nose or cried-out eyes. The star fairy had promised her, but her mother knew nothing about that, of course.

Chapter Twelve

Hannah whirled amid the turbulent events of the next few days.

Gottlieb Kerner invited her to his house so Wilhelmine could get to know her future daughter-in-law. Helmut's sister, Marianne, had returned to Reutlingen with her husband ahead of the looming scandal, which left only Helmut's Aunt Finchen, Wilhelmine's sister, at the house on the day Hannah visited, along with Helmut, Valentin, and their parents. The mood was oppressive, and no one seemed to know what to say. Luckily, there were many details that had to be discussed and clarified: Hannah did not even know where the reception was to take place, let alone who had been invited. It struck her as rather strange that the guest list remained unchanged, but that was certainly not the only strange thing, considering the situation.

Of course, she wrote to her parents and invited them, and in a separate letter she asked her mother to explain everything to her father. She held no great hope that they would appear. It was unlikely her parents would be able to close The Golden Anchor for a few days on such short notice, and for this reason she also asked her mother if she would send her things to Gönningen. Hannah did not have much she called her own: a few dresses, a small trousseau, a few bits and pieces that were special to her. An extra room would be emptied out for her and Helmut,

Wilhelmine explained to her in an icy voice. Hannah planned to make it as cozy as possible.

Many other visits followed that first formal visit to the Kerner house. Helmut literally took her from door to door. In each house, Hannah was scrutinized as if she'd just come from the moon. Sometimes she was greeted heartily, and other times with more reserve, but Hannah was satisfied, all in all. Who could blame the people of Gönningen for not welcoming her with open arms, considering the suffering she had brought to their own Seraphine?

Helmut and Hannah stayed away from one small house: the Schwarzes'. But as they were visiting one of the neighbors, they saw Valentin saying goodbye to Seraphine. Both of them looked over toward Hannah and Helmut with undisguised hostility. What was her future brother-in-law doing at Seraphine's house? Was Valentin stirring up trouble behind their backs? Or had he gone to see the spurned bride out of the sheer goodness of his heart? Hannah tended toward the latter. Valentin was an amiable young man, and she could not believe he would do anything to harm them.

And, of course, they had to visit the parish priest. Several times, in fact. He, too, was less than happy with the way the entire affair had developed. Hannah thought she could sense exactly what the man thought of her: for him, she was no more than some no-good trollop. And the way he stared at her belly! As if he could actually see the bastard child inside through her clothes and skin! She had gritted her teeth and let Helmut do all the talking. She had no idea and did not want to know what arguments he or his father had used to explain Helmut's change of heart, or if they had simply told the priest the truth.

Then they had to talk through the various courses for the meal at the inn after the ceremony. Hannah had insisted on at least one Franconian dish, a specialty of her home district: roast pork with potato dumplings. Neither the proprietor—who had never made potato dumplings in his life—nor Wilhelmine, who had fixed the menu weeks before with

Seraphine, was especially taken with the change. But Hannah held her ground. She wanted to have a little influence on the celebration. It was *her* wedding, wasn't it? So the next day, she found herself in the inn-keeper's kitchen, showing him how the dumplings were made. While she was there, Helmut and his father drove to Reutlingen to find out where they stood legally with the dissolved engagement. Both returned in a peevish mood, and it took several glasses of wine at The Sun for Helmut to win back his usual cheerfulness, but he did, and Hannah sighed with relief to see it.

On the morning of the wedding, there was a knock on Hannah's door while she was still in bed. "Whatever it is, it can wait," she growled unenthusiastically at the door, and buried her face back in her pillow. She was finding it harder to get out of bed with every passing day, and she had become a late sleeper, though back home she had been up by five every morning.

"What I want to do *can't* wait!" Helmut strode into the room, bringing a blast of wintry air with him. With a swift jerk, he pulled the bedspread off, and it fell to the floor. Hannah screamed. What was he doing here? Intent on not leaving her legs exposed any longer than necessary, she reached out, angling after the quilt with her fingers.

"Who knows when the weather will be this good again? We have to make the most of it while we can. Come on, pull something on. I'll wait for you downstairs with Emma. Boots, coat, a scarf for your head—better put on everything you've got! Where I'm taking you, it can get distinctly cold."

The way he laughed, so bright, so freely! Like a young man in love, and not one about to be dragged forcefully to the altar. *He can't really have loved Seraphine that much,* Hannah thought, not for the first time. "She took it quite calmly" was all he had said about his conversation with Seraphine. Calmly, hmm. It was inexplicable to her that Seraphine could be so understanding. To find out a few days before your wedding that the bridegroom had been unfaithful and . . . the very thought almost drove Hannah wild. The truth must be that Seraphine had not felt much love for Helmut, either. All the better. A jealous adversary could only make her life in Gönningen harder.

Hannah sat up halfway. "Helmut, we're getting married today. Can you imagine that a woman might like to prepare herself for an occasion like that?" She watched while Helmut paced around her room, putting her clothes into a pile. She did not know what *he* was planning to do, but *her* plans were clear: Emma had promised her a bath, and she and Käthe would carry it together up to the room. After that, Käthe was going to experiment on Hannah's hair—Hannah pictured something high and complicated and held in place artfully with hairpins, but she did not know if Käthe's skills went that far. Emma was going to use that time to go to work on Hannah's Hungarian outfit. She was going to remove the red straps—"Red is not proper for a bride," she had said with a sniff—and sew on black silk straps instead. And now Helmut was there making a lot of noise about some kind of outing?

A good hour later, Hannah was standing on top of Rossberg, the highest peak she had ever climbed. She clenched the wooden rail of the survey tower, ignoring the crust of ice biting into her fingers. The entire construction seemed too flimsy to her, and she hardly dared move. Unlike Helmut, who marched around on the platform like a general as he pointed out Stuttgart, Tübingen, the Swiss Alps. His cheeks were glowing, and his eyes were at least as bright as the winter's day around them. The air was as pure as crystal.

"It's beautiful," Hannah said, dazed at all the distant sights. Their viewing platform was higher than anything else around. Higher than any building, higher than the trees around them, higher than most of the other summits of the Swabian Mountains. She had to resist the urge to reach up with her hand and snatch at the sky—it seemed close enough to touch.

"It makes me feel solemn. Awed."

Helmut nodded, and she could see he knew how she felt. He wrapped one arm around her shoulders. "I used to love coming up here even when I was a little boy. Whenever the village got too crowded for me, I climbed Rossberg. Then I imagined what it would be like when I went traveling through all those faraway, wonderful lands. I couldn't wait to grow up, get a seed sack on my back, and take off. To see the Alps up close, to march through the Black Forest on my own two feet. Back then, I couldn't imagine going any farther." He laughed. "And these days, as a rule, Valentin and I cover a thousand miles or more each year."

A thousand miles. The number alone frightened Hannah. "And this year? Will you go that far again?"

Helmut nodded. "Even farther. Valentin and I have big plans."

Hannah waited for Helmut to add something to his tantalizing remark, but instead he took her hands in his. He looked into her eyes, and his smile disappeared.

"You're marrying a migratory bird, Hannah. You have to realize that. The life of a seed merchant's wife is not always easy."

She nodded. The main thing was just to get married, she almost said. But instead she replied, "This rambling around, not knowing in the morning what the day will bring or where you're going to sleep that night—that's not for me! For me, just going from Nuremberg to here was enough. And dangerous, too. On the very first day, our coach broke an axle, and we nearly crashed into a ditch." The thought that she, too, might one day have to travel from house to house with a sack of seeds and bulbs over her shoulder drenched her like an unexpected thundershower. She, who was lucky to tell the difference between a tulip and a rose! She, who still looked back on her journey from Nuremberg with such unease. She held her breath and waited for Helmut's reaction.

Helmut laughed. "You could just as easily break an axle in the middle of the village. I'm not saying those kinds of things aren't annoying, but all the beautiful moments that you get to experience when you travel make up for trifles like that a dozen times over. Being free to think what you like—it's worth facing any danger."

His gaze wandered off into the distance. When he continued, there was an unexpected vigor in his voice.

"Sometimes, when I'm home, I feel as if my brain is freezing solid, and I can't even think properly anymore. It actually feels hard to breathe, as if something is robbing me of the breath I need to live." He shook his head, suddenly surprised. "You should know by now that the people down there in the village are a very special kind. They don't laugh as much as people in other places, and they grumble a lot more. But at the same time, they have far less to grumble about than in those other places. Oh, we have poor people living among us, it's true, but you find poor people in other places, too, more than here, and in those other towns and villages you still find a certain . . . cheerfulness. Ha, I only have to think about Baden and how the Catholics there celebrate Shrovetide—something like that would be unthinkable in Gönningen. They dress in costumes and run around like lunatics—how blasphemous that would be here! Don't be surprised if the dance floor isn't full tonight; there are a lot of folk in Gönningen who've never even learned a waltz."

"What do you mean?" Hannah asked uncertainly. Everyone could dance! Back home in Nuremberg, a guest only had to take out a harmonica, and tables and chairs would be pushed aside and people would be swinging each other around for all they were worth.

"Well, we younger ones like a dance, but the older folk . . . you won't get them up easily. My God, that would be an open display of high spirits! Many of them don't want to believe that now and then they might find an opportunity to make this life a bit more enjoyable. They keep their eyes trained on heaven instead, where all their sacrifices in life will be made good."

"But these sacrifices—don't they really impose them on themselves? I mean, the seed trade seems to bring in quite a lot." The skepticism in Hannah's voice was unmistakable. What Helmut was telling her simply did not fit with the picture she had formed of the village with its beautiful buildings and its well-dressed inhabitants.

"The trade brings in enough, of course, but instead of using the money they make to do something nice for themselves, they invest the profits back into the business. I'm not saying that isn't pragmatic. But what about those who don't want to wait for heaven? Those who want to have a better life here and now? Who want to ride a beautiful horse instead of going everywhere on foot? Or wear a coat for five years instead of ten?"

"You're looking at it pessimistically, aren't you? It's nice here," said Hannah.

He laughed. "What have you seen of the world to compare it with? Just wait, in a year or two you might get bitten by the same bug as me, and then you'll understand what I mean."

Hannah looked thoughtfully at her future husband. His enthusiasm, the poetry in his words when he talked about traveling . . . it had nothing in common with what Emma had told her about the hard journeys and months of deprivation of the seed merchants. About the life-threatening diseases that could strike you down in foreign climes, about men who returned to Gönningen more dead than alive, failed, broken. Admittedly, Emma's eyes had sparkled brightly when she talked about her own travels, but she had generally been more reserved than Helmut.

How little I know about you, Hannah suddenly thought. *How little I know about what is going on inside you.* The feeling frightened her. She was tempted to break the solemnity of the moment with a carefree, silly remark like *Well, starting today, no more freedom at all!* But at the same time, she sensed that this moment could be the foundation for everything that shaped their lives in the future. She felt uneasy, as if the floor of the platform under her feet really were swaying. Afraid to upset the balance and weight of the moment, she said simply, "Tell me more."

Helmut flinched briefly, as if he'd almost forgotten that she was there. After a moment of silence, he went on. "Out there, out in the big, wide world, in countries like Hungary, Russia, and America, people think differently. They lead lives that we can't imagine, lives we can't even begin to guess at. They don't just dream of better times, they make them for themselves."

His words seemed to have warmed him, and a flush appeared on his cheeks. He told her about the opportunities that one could take advantage of if one approached life with open eyes and courage in one's heart.

Hungary, Russia, America. Hannah could not get the countries out of her head as they made their way back to the village a little later. Until now, those places had always been just patches on a map.

Why had he told her all that? What did it mean for her and for their future life together? The freedom, all the opportunities he talked about, would they exist for her as well? All she wanted was for her child not to have to grow up with the disgrace of being fatherless. She wanted to be provided for and to be a good wife, but she had not thought beyond that when she set off from Nuremberg.

Freedom, exploiting opportunities, not waiting for a better life but creating it for yourself—with every step toward Gönningen, a feeling of unreality grew stronger inside Hannah. Helmut's words were like a stone that fell into the water, forming ripples that spread in circles, washing along new, strange, threatening ideas, but also ideas that she sensed were full of promise.

Until now, Hannah had simply lived her life. She had done what her parents told her to do. It had never crossed her mind to question any of it. As a kind of balance, she had enjoyed her nights with one traveling man or another, never thinking of the consequences until her period did not come a few weeks after Helmut's visit. That another life might be possible, a life beyond that of a maid at her parents' inn . . . she had never allowed herself even to dream of such a thing.

But hadn't she taken the first step toward a better life just by going off in search of Helmut? Maybe they weren't so different after all. Was there perhaps a seed of Gönningen industriousness hidden inside her, too?

She hooked her arm into the crook of Helmut's, enjoying the feeling of comradeship with her husband-to-be. One thing was plain to see: her new life would not be dull.

Chapter Thirteen

The wedding was a merry, boozy occasion. In the evening, the guests—more than a hundred all together—met at The Eagle, the largest inn in Gönningen. By the time they all found their seats at the long tables, waiters were already bringing out bowls of steaming potato dumplings, yolk-yellow spätzle, roast pork in a heavy dark-brown gravy, and many other dishes. Beer mugs were emptied so quickly that the innkeeper and his helpers were hard-pressed to keep up.

Whether it was because Emma had not missed an opportunity to speak up for Hannah or because Hannah's straightforward nature and radiant face had won the hearts of the Gönningers, everyone seemed to have come to terms with Helmut's choice of bride, despite the scandal surrounding Seraphine and the fact that Hannah was an outsider. Complete strangers raised toasts to the bride, who had to shed a tear or two because her parents had been unable to travel to her wedding. Commercial obligations? An inn they could not just close at the drop of a hat? Yes, the Gönningers knew that kind of problem.

"She may not be as beautiful as Seraphine, but she can work hard, if Emma's to be believed," Gottlieb had told the pharmacist after the service. Thanks to the pharmacist's wife, Elsbeth, who had been standing beside her husband with her ears pricked, that particular piece of information circulated very quickly indeed. Hard work—that was something the Gönningers could understand. Beauty? Not so much.

After the meal, chairs were rearranged so that people could talk privately at other tables, and among the younger, a few courageous souls began to dance, while their parents smoked their pipes and sipped their drinks and watched.

The men congratulated Helmut on his choice and clapped him on the shoulder admiringly, as if the bridegroom had come home with Hannah after years of searching for a wife. None mentioned that the wedding was effectively forced on him. The women were less euphoric, Wilhelmine especially, but they also made an effort to welcome Hannah into their circle. It would be unwise to lose favor with the wealthiest family in the village. Besides, maybe Hannah would put in a good word for one or the other of them one day . . .

It was, in a way, as if the Gönningers were celebrating themselves that evening, satisfied with who they were and with their worldly ways that allowed them to master even unusual situations. Soon everyone was caught up in the party, dancing and singing and eating and drinking everything the inn's kitchen and cellar had to offer. If anyone gave a thought to the unhappy girl sitting in her cottage at the other end of the village, then they did so only fleetingly.

The evening was already well advanced when Gottlieb Kerner instructed the musicians to play a fanfare. Swaying slightly, he rose from his seat, but had to hold on to the arm of his wife's chair, which drew a frown of disapproval from her. It took a few moments of waving his hand about for it to have the desired effect and for the guests to fall silent. Listening to the groom's father make a speech was a trying obligation, no more. Of *course* he had to welcome Hannah to the family. Of *course* he wished the newlyweds every conceivable happiness, and of *course* he compared them to himself and Wilhelmine twenty-five years earlier. Everyone had heard it before, the words spoken at every wedding, sometimes with more fire in the voice, sometimes with less.

"The time has come for a fundamental change."

Now he had their attention.

"Now that you, my dearest Helmut, have laid the cornerstone for a family of your own, I would like to add something to the foundation myself. After all, the dwelling place of marriage should be built on solid ground!" He gazed around the assembled faces, seeking approval for his eloquence, and only after a few appreciative murmurs and nods did he continue.

"You all know that among the Kerner men the seed trade is in our blood from the moment of birth. My own grandfather . . ." And the interest of the audience faded again. This story, too, was familiar, and every family could claim something similar. Guests covertly wiped their foreheads, sipped at their beer, puffed on their pipes.

"It is time for me to say farewell to the trade. I cannot say that this decision has been an easy one for me, but . . ."

What? What was that? Had they heard right? Was the old man sick or something? Gottlieb's next few sentences were lost in the rumble that spread through the room.

He cleared his throat and moved on.

"You, my dear Helmut, as the eldest son, are to inherit my *Samenstrich* in Alsace. I am certain that my honored customers will find an honest counterpart in you, and I am happy to know that it is you who will succeed me."

He looked next at Valentin, who was leaning casually against a post.

"And you, Valentin, will also benefit from this. That is to say, I would appreciate it very much if my two sons were to continue to travel together. A good partnership is not something to be cast aside lightly. Am I right?"

Helmut set his beer mug down decisively. "But, Father, if you don't go out traveling, what in the world are you going to do? I mean . . ." He fell silent and looked across at Valentin, who only shrugged.

"What your son is trying to say is that you're still too young for the scrap heap!" called someone from the back, and the crowd laughed raucously.

Gottlieb took the joke in stride. "And he's right!" He grinned at his audience. "There's more juice left in these bones than many a younger man can muster! Which is why, when a higher power calls, I won't say no." He paused to let that sink in. "This year, after Easter, I intend to register my candidacy for the parish council. Here in Gönningen we live in singular circumstances, although that fact does not yet seem to have reached the right ears in Tübingen. Representing Gönningen better and more effectively at the regional level requires a great deal of personal effort and commitment. Our esteemed mayor"—here he nodded in the direction of that gentleman, Mr. Schultheiss—"can count on my unmitigated support. For the well-being of Gönningen, I will not shy away from any task or errand for which I am called upon."

Gottlieb Kerner's announcement was the main topic for the rest of the evening. The almost unanimous opinion was that his chances were excellent. Schultheiss was always keen to have the best men for his council, after all.

Valentin sighed when he saw his brother coming his way. He had steered clear of Helmut the entire day, although he could not have said why exactly. As Helmut's wedding day had approached, the thought of Helmut and Seraphine together filled Valentin with dread. But now that everything had turned out differently, the relief he expected to feel had not come, and Valentin felt somehow out of place. Superfluous. *What am I even doing here?* he asked himself.

But before he could come up with an answer, Helmut had grabbed him and dragged him into a side room.

"Did you know about Father's plans?" Helmut asked, the moment they were alone.

Valentin shook his head. He had not known, but it had come as no surprise that their father had exploited the wedding like that—he had always been good for a surprise, and he was given to grand gestures. "Alsace! Not bad. Congratulations are in order," he said drily.

"Oh, shut up!" Helmut hissed. "You know as well as I do that I don't give a damn about Alsace. What I want to know is what we're going to do about our plans for Russia."

Valentin had been asking himself the same question. On their most recent travels through Bohemia, they had talked about nothing else for weeks but how exciting it would be to make the long journey to Russia, finally! Before them, only a handful of Gönningers had ever dared go there, and they had returned with the most unbelievable stories. The brothers knew very well that there was enough money for them to make the journey; the question was whether their father would finance such an adventure. They already had one contact in the country: Leonard, a distant cousin of their father's, who had immigrated to Russia during the famine more than thirty years earlier, and who asked in every letter he sent when someone from the family would finally come to visit him. He was a wealthy man, apparently, head of a large trading company, and his wife, Eleonore, had excellent contacts inside the czar's court. The brothers agreed: there was money to be made there. Everybody knew how much the Russian czars cared about their expansive gardens and parks. And because of that, they would take only flower seeds with them to Russia, the most extraordinary varieties. And the best bulbs, by the sackful, of course. Russia would be so completely different from visiting the same farmers year in, year out in Bohemia or Alsace, peddling a few kohlrabi seeds here, a few carrot seeds there.

If it were up to Valentin, he would have chosen America over Russia. The stories he heard about America were even *more* colorful, *more* adventurous. But Helmut had no interest in going overseas. Why?

Spending weeks aboard a ship, out of sight of land? That was a touch too exciting for him. And he rejected Valentin's argument that he would have to go by ship to get to Russia, too. A harmless boat trip down the Danube did not compare to sailing across an ocean.

"If Father starts preparing for his election now, he'll already be expecting us to take over his customers in spring. Which means we can forget any plans for Russia, at least for now," Valentin said, and shrugged. He was surprised at how little that notion moved him. Russia—what did he care about Russia if he knew that Seraphine was sitting home alone, probably crying her eyes out?

"Alsace is for old people and women." Helmut curled his lip in disdain. "No, no, I'm not going to give up so fast. I'll talk to Father tomorrow. If he won't budge, we'll have to find another way. There are other people with money."

"Would you really borrow money from a stranger?" Valentin frowned.

"If there's no other way, yes. You'll have to pick Father's jaw up off the floor if I threaten to, I'll tell you that."

Valentin nodded. Gottlieb Kerner was one of the biggest money-lenders in the village, and other traders would go to him to finance a trip. If his own son went somewhere else, maybe even to one of those Tübingen cutthroats . . .

"And what about your wife? You'll have a baby soon," Valentin said, although one look at Helmut's expression made it clear he was serious about his plans.

"What does that have to do with Russia?" Helmut answered. "The child will come into the world whether I'm there or not."

Valentin felt the faintest trace of relief. Wedding or not, married or not, as far as their business relationship was concerned, nothing seemed to have changed, at least from Helmut's side.

The next moment, Helmut slung his arm across Valentin's shoulder. "Let's get back in there. We're here for the party, aren't we? And you've been standing around by yourself the entire evening, looking as grouchy as if you'd been left out in the rain all night. Don't think I didn't notice. Is it possible that you haven't danced with a single girl all night? You've got some catching up to do! Now I'm going to go and stumble across the dance floor with Käthe, our own little wallflower." Helmut sighed theatrically. "My Hannah has told me I must, so I'd best put it behind me as soon as possible." He jumped up and was gone.

My Hannah . . . Valentin watched his brother go, hardly recognizing him. Was this the same man who had all but broken down in tears at the miserable hand he'd been dealt? The same man who had not found the courage to tell Seraphine, the love of his young life, the truth, and who had put off clearing the air between them for days? And now he was out there dancing so wildly that other couples fled the dance floor to escape his flying elbows and heels.

And Valentin realized then that Helmut was happy to be free of Seraphine. He recalled a remark that Helmut had made during their most recent travels, the evening before they reached Gönningen.

"You know, it isn't easy with Seraphine. Sometimes, when I'm around her, I feel so . . . simple. As if she expects something of me, something I should already know, but which I really don't have the faintest clue about, you know?"

Helmut seldom talked like that. There were rarely any problems in his life, and if one did rear its head, he did his best to ignore it.

Valentin had nodded silently. But every word was like a knife to his heart, and he hated his brother as he did every time he talked about Seraphine. *She is too fine and too good for you, that's all!* he wanted to shout in Helmut's face. At the same time, he hated himself for his jealousy and resentment.

But those times were now past. There was no reason to hate his brother anymore.

Valentin took a deep breath. His heart fluttered. Seraphine was free. It was time to do what he had to do.

Chapter Fourteen

She was not in the kitchen, nor was she in her tiny room in the back of the house.

"I don't know where she is. She . . . took the dress . . . ," Ilse Schwarz sobbed.

Valentin asked repeatedly where Seraphine was, but he got nothing more out of the woman. Ilse's grief filled the small cottage completely. He placed one hand on her shoulder, squeezed gently, reassuringly, then went outside again.

It was a moonlit night, and the stars seemed to hang so low that it looked as if one of them could fall and be extinguished on the layer of ice that lay over the landscape.

Where was he supposed to look? Where could Seraphine have run off to? Had she run away forever? Had she done something to herself? The frost settled on Valentin's skin, freezing his mind, and for a few moments he was incapable of forming a single clear thought. He cursed himself and his lethargy, which had kept him at the wedding reception until now. If Seraphine had . . . He would never forgive himself.

In a panic now, he ran behind the house, tramped through the small vegetable garden, giving no thought to the fallow beds, Brussels sprouts, or berry bushes. Nothing. Valentin tried to organize his thoughts. He had been feeling horribly dizzy since leaving The Eagle. Why had he drunk so much?

The Eagle . . . she may have gone there and stared in through a window while her heart was breaking with loneliness. That would have been just like Seraphine. Valentin could well imagine how much she was suffering, although Helmut had blathered about having a sensible conversation with her.

He ran back along the streets of Gönningen, slipping several times on the icy cobblestones. There was no sign of Seraphine at The Eagle.

Go in, get help, start a search party. His mind raced; his heart pounded. But who was he supposed to ask for help? Everyone inside was merry, drunk, dancing. And what if Seraphine had simply gone to visit a friend? Hysterical as he was, he would only make a laughingstock of both of them. But then, Seraphine had no friends. She had . . . no one.

Valentin made up his mind to return to Seraphine's house and if necessary shake Ilse until she was able to give him answers to his questions. *How is it possible for a mother not to stand by her daughter on such a dark day?* he wondered, in a fury. *And where were* you *all day?* whispered another, poisonous, voice.

The next moment, he stopped abruptly. Was that something glittering over there, beside the waters of the Wiesaz? Valentin squinted to see better. The stream went around a bend there, and two weeping willows grew on the opposite bank. Between them stood a bench, its seat weathered silver over the years. On warm summer evenings, the young people of the village met there, mostly when their parents were away traveling and life for the children was more carefree. Valentin did not know if it had also been a meeting place for Helmut and Seraphine. If Seraphine, feeling sentimental . . . But it was bitterly cold! It was not possible that she would hide away there, was it? His eyes traced the outlines of the bench, but saw no more than an indefinite black shadow. He moved a little farther along the street, his eyes never leaving the bench and the opposite bank of the stream. There! A movement, almost imperceptible.

The next moment, he heard a woman's voice humming. Soft, gentle, and unmistakable. Seraphine! He began to run.

She was sitting on the bench. The dress she wore, adorned with layer upon layer of lace, beads, and silk trim, billowed out beside her, spread carefully across the seat. In the moonlight, the black fabric gleamed, soft and silvery. Seraphine's hair glittered. The entire tableau was so ethereally beautiful that Valentin stopped and recoiled a little. What a fool he was! How could he imagine for a moment that a woman like her could ever be interested in him? He was no expert in women's clothes, God knew, but he had some idea of the hours Seraphine must have put into her wedding dress. Hours in which she had done nothing but think of Helmut and dream of a different, better life. And now there she sat, lonely, robbed of all her dreams, and the symbol of her eternal happiness had reverted to scraps of cloth.

When she looked up and saw him standing on the other side of the stream, there was no fear in her eyes, not even surprise.

"Today is my wedding day. Did you know that?" she asked in a voice he did not recognize. Then she began to hum again, a melody that Valentin did not know.

"Seraphine, what are you doing here? You'll die out here in the cold." He leaped across the stream, and then he was beside her, pushing aside the folds of the dress, taking her in his arms. "You're as cold as ice! Sera, come with me, let's go." He tried to pull her to her feet, but she fended him off and stayed seated. Her eyes were on the waters of the Wiesaz, the moon's reflection forming a milky oval on its sluggish surface. She smiled.

"Look. How lovely . . . do you know that feeling? When something is especially lovely, it hurts in your heart."

Which is just how I feel when I look at you, Valentin was tempted to say, but he held his tongue. What was he supposed to do? How was he supposed to act? Seraphine was so strange. Not that he would ever reproach her for that, God forbid, but . . .

"*Sometimes, when I'm around her, I feel so simple*"—his brother's words came back to him. While he sat there trying to think what to do, he began to understand what Helmut had been trying to say.

"The moon, the stars—so much beauty tonight of all nights. Isn't that a gift?" She looked at Valentin.

"*You* are the beauty," he blurted. "Not that moon. It isn't even full anymore."

She turned slowly, looking up toward the sky. She seemed to tense, withdrawing from him, turning back inside herself completely, but the next moment her face relaxed again.

"The sun and the moon—that is Helmut and me. We belong together."

Valentin had no choice but to nod.

"Like the sun can't exist without the moon, or like the way there could be no night without the day, that is how we belong together. Forever and ever. Nothing will change that." She nodded, her head moving up and down like an old lady's. The little beads that she had woven into her hair bobbed in rhythm. *But blast it, Helmut doesn't want you. He's dancing around drunk and blissful with Hannah—she is his sun, not you!* everything inside Valentin screamed. But he pressed his lips together hard.

"You will shine like the sun even without Helmut," he finally said.

"I am not the sun!" Seraphine replied, horrified. "*Helmut* is the sun. He makes me laugh, and when he is close I can finally come to life. Alone, I am only the moon. Always in the shadows, surrounded by darkness."

Valentin swallowed. Had Seraphine lost her mind?

"Every person on earth has a dark side," he said vehemently. "There is nothing special about that. We can't feel like laughing all the time." Helmut, the sun . . . ha! More like a shooting star, fleeting and fickle.

Valentin knew he could not help Seraphine when she was like this. She barely reacted to his words. He tried a new tack: "If the moon freezes to death, it won't please the sun, will it? And you are already half-frozen. Let's go somewhere warmer."

This time she let him help her up. She stumbled beside him stiffly, taking small steps, his arm around her shoulder, his free hand supporting her at her hip. Seraphine hummed as she walked, as if no care in the world could burden her.

But now where to?

Not back to the Schwarz home, that much was certain. Valentin shuddered to think of Ilse and her tearstained face. As strangely as Seraphine was acting, he did not want to leave her alone, but he could hardly take her home with him—what if someone from the wedding came home early and found them in the kitchen?

Just before the bridge that would lead them to the center of the village, he had a flash of inspiration: the old hut! It was some distance away, certainly, between two of his family's fields, and it would not be very warm there, but it would be better than being out in the bitter chill. And no one would look for them there, he knew.

Seraphine seemed not to notice that the path they were following was leading them back out into the fields. When they arrived at the hut, Valentin rattled at the bolt on the door without releasing Seraphine, afraid that she would run away from him. Finally, with a loud creak, the door swung open. He sniffed the escaping air; it smelled of earth and potatoes and apples.

"I've been here before. With Helmut," Seraphine cried as she followed Valentin inside.

With Helmut, of course, he thought as he struggled with the damp matches to light the old oil lamp hanging from the ceiling. He pushed aside all the gardening tools and rummaged wildly through the decrepit cupboard beside the door. Somewhere, he knew, there were a few old blankets that were used in summer to spread on the ground when the workers had lunch in the field. He found them in the bottom drawer, spread them out on the floor quickly, sat down, and patted the space beside him. Seraphine's knees cracked as she lowered herself onto the blanket.

"The cold has gone all the way to your bones," he said. "Come, I'll warm you up a little." He spread his arms out wide, and was overcome with terror when she willingly nestled against him. A second fright overcame him when he felt the sharpness of her shoulder blade press into his side. She was no more than skin and bone! Was money so tight in the Schwarz household? Or had her misery destroyed her appetite completely?

They sat like that in silence for a while. The moon had wandered on and now cast its light in pale beams across the room.

Here we are, and I have her in my arms, Valentin thought. How many times had he dreamed of this moment? How many times had he imagined how Seraphine would feel? Soft, warm, feminine, and mysterious. She trembled like a starved chick fallen too early from its nest. Valentin's heart overflowed with love.

The next moment, Seraphine tore herself free and jumped to her feet. "What a fool I am!" She banged her fist against the wooden wall of the hut so hard that it shook.

Valentin flinched, not prepared for such an outburst of emotion. Before he could say anything, she swung one hand over her head in frustration and impatience.

"All around me, I see women throwing themselves at the seed dealers, whispering sweet words, and lifting their skirts. And me?" She laughed hysterically. "'A stain on the white cloth of chastity is like red wine on a tablecloth,' my father always told me. 'Neither one will ever come out.'" Her face was suddenly transformed into a twisted, whitewashed grimace. "And what do I have to show for my unsullied chastity?" She glared provocatively at Valentin.

"Seraphine . . ." He reached for her arm, wanting to pull her down beside him again on the blanket, but she recoiled from his touch.

"I was stupid. Stupid, stupid, stupid! There I was, protecting my virginity like a treasure, and what is it worth now? Not a cent!" She spat the last words out like venom.

Valentin held his breath. He was not sure which state he preferred her in: as melancholic and confused as she had been beside the Wiesaz, or as furious as she was now. But she could be as furious as she wanted at Helmut! Finally, she realized what a scoundrel he really was.

Seraphine looked down at Valentin. "You're one of these revelers in the night, too. How many times have I heard you and the others stomping through the village. I know perfectly well that there are always girls with you, though they might act like butter wouldn't melt in their mouths the next day. There's always one who can't help but brag about her conquests." Seraphine narrowed her eyes and looked critically at Valentin. "Did you ever see me in one of those drunken packs?"

He shook his head. He had wished many times that she were there when, on warm summer nights, they would light a fire in the fields outside the village and sing and dance. Helmut had complained at times that she never joined them, but he used her absence as a chance to flirt with the other girls. Valentin sniffed contemptuously. So Seraphine was not as ignorant as Helmut thought.

"See?" she went on. "How can I think badly of Helmut if he falls into the clutches of some harlot? By holding back like I did, I practically drove him into her arms! I'm to blame for him marrying a woman he doesn't even like." Her anger went out like the air from a bellows, and she sank beside him on the blanket. "But how can I live with this guilt? What have I done to him?"

Valentin did not think he had heard her correctly. *She* was to blame? "What rubbish is that?" he cried. He was close to grabbing her by the shoulders and shaking some sense into her, but one glance at her unhappy face held him back. "Oh, Seraphine," he said sadly.

She threw her arms around him, suddenly effusive, as trusting as a child who has woken from a nightmare. "Hold me! Hold me as tightly as you can," she sobbed. "This is my wedding night. I should really be . . . but . . . I'm here . . ." Whatever words followed were swallowed by her despair.

Valentin rocked her softly in his arms, his eyes closed. Hope kindled inside him. Her cheek at his chest, her trembling heart so near, the scent that rose from her hair to his nose. One day, one day she would realize that he loved her, truly and decently. But he would be patient; he already had been, so long . . .

A moment later, he felt her bony elbows in his ribs. Hasty movements, the rustling of fabric, restless legs, her body so close to his, closer, closer, his hand on . . . on her breast?

He opened his eyes and blinked hard, as if waking from a bewildering dream. He pulled his hand back from her naked skin as if he had burned himself.

With a final, impatient movement, Seraphine freed herself from the bottom of her dress. She screwed it carelessly into a ball, as if it were no more than an old apron, and dropped it beside her.

And then she lay there, naked and shivering before him, her legs slightly spread.

"Love me!" Not a question, not a breathless request.

Her eyes were on him, determined, demanding.

Valentin stared at her in shock. He reached for her dress, wanting to cover her with it, but she threw it away again.

"Sera . . ." He swallowed. His throat was suddenly tight. He felt his own arousal, hard and insistent, pressed against the buttons of his trousers. Ashamed of himself, he slid out of the ray of moonlight and into the shadow.

What had happened? Where had the tenderness gone? His eyes flew around the room but came back to Seraphine the next moment. He did not know what to do with his hands; every touch had taken on a language of its own, a language that was alien to everything he associated with Seraphine. As she herself was alien to him. The hunger in her eyes as she lay there, offering herself to him—alien.

He had, of course, imagined many times what it would be like with her. But not today, not here and now! Not while Seraphine was in such an emotional state. Only a swine would exploit the situation she was in. Her savior—that is what he wanted to be. He tried in vain to find words that could express what he felt.

I am not a swine, not a swine, not a swine—unable to turn his eyes from her nakedness, he repeated the words to himself silently, but with every repetition they lost more and more of their meaning.

"What is it? Don't you find me desirable? Am I not *woman* enough for you?" she screamed at him.

He shook his head mechanically. Her small breasts, the pink-brown areolas, so perfect, as if a sculptor or painter had gone to particular pains with them. Her long legs, that silver triangle of the finest little curls, ruffling so curiously with every movement she made.

He sensed his breathing accelerating, opened his mouth, took a deep breath. With the index finger of his right hand, he reached down to the silver, cautiously, as if he were handling a figure molded of the finest porcelain.

What am I doing? What am I . . . What . . .

With a hoarse laugh, Seraphine grasped his hand, pushing his fingers deeper. Her juices, sweet as those of a ripe fruit, on his fingers . . .

And then she was fumbling at his waistband.

"I have been ready for this night for so long . . ." Words, swaying, trembling like the legs she wrapped around him.

Her hand on him now, drawing him out, so certain, so sure.

She is a virgin, a girl, still a child. What is she doing?

Groaning, he pushed her aside, unbuttoned his trousers himself.

This is all too fast, too fast.

Awkwardly, his mouth sought hers. She turned her head aside, and his lips caught her hair. Then she pulled him on top of her. He pressed his elbows against the rough wooden floor, afraid he might crush Seraphine with his weight.

She screamed, unsatisfied, impatient. Her right hand positioned him between her legs.

He looked at her a final time. Her eyes open very wide, filled with desire, no bashful glance from half-closed eyes.

She wants me. My God, she wants me!

Her body pushed up against his. He could not, did not want to keep her waiting any longer; he pushed back, pushed inside her.

Cries united them. And through the window, a tired moon looked on.

Chapter Fifteen

The next morning, Ilse and Seraphine sat at the table having breakfast in near silence. Ilse had asked her several times where she had been and why she had come back in the middle of the night. Seraphine said nothing, and she stopped stirring her porridge only when someone knocked at their door.

"Who can that be? Friedhelm?" Ilse frowned, looking across at her daughter. "Why would he knock?" She jumped to her feet and opened the door.

In front of her stood Adolf Rausch, the village constable. His expression was even more dour than usual. "May I come in?"

"We have to go to Switzerland. Make some inquiries ourselves." Ilse looked up from her bowl, her eyes wet with tears. The porridge had gone cold, and a dry crust had formed over it. "Maybe . . . maybe it's all a mistake."

Seraphine took a deep breath. "*That* is no mistake," she said and pointed to her father's seed sack, which the constable had brought with him. A handful of seed packets, a few bulbs, and her father's sample book, which Seraphine had painted for him some years before—that was all the seed sack contained. No traveling papers, no money, nothing else that would point to Friedhelm Schwarz's identity. Without Seraphine's sample book, in which she had painted her father's name in large letters on the first page, the sack could have belonged to anyone. "Those are Father's belongings, there is no doubt about that." As she spoke, she felt her brimming tears about to overflow.

Her father was dead. Or missing, at least.

"From their investigations, my colleagues in Switzerland believe that Friedhelm fell victim to a crime. He has not been seen anywhere. All trace of him has simply disappeared," Adolf had said in a solemn voice. "In the region around"—he had taken out a note and read off the name of a village that meant nothing to Seraphine or her mother—"it seems that robberies are commonplace. The Swiss gendarmerie writes that it is not advisable to travel there alone. The proprietor of the inn where Friedhelm had been shortly before his disappearance stated that he warned Friedhelm expressly not to travel unaccompanied."

At that point, the constable had fixed a presumptuous glare on Ilse and Seraphine.

Seraphine had wanted to scream at the arrogant man: *My father was poor, and he was traveling in one of the most poverty-stricken territories there is. Who was supposed to accompany him?* But instead, in a tremulous voice, she asked, "His . . . body has not been found?"

Adolf had shaken his head vigorously. "As I said, it is rough, inhospitable territory. Friedhelm could be anywhere. And there is still the possibility that he fell, and died that way. But if that were the case, his body would not have disappeared without a trace. His seed sack was found lying right beside the road, and the gendarmes searched all around the area." Another self-important shake of his head followed—murder and manslaughter were rarities in Gönningen, after all. "Friedhelm certainly would have had money on him from what he had sold. No sign of that, either. Everything points to a crime. It's a disgrace!"

"How could he? How could he?" Ilse beat the palm of her hand on the table. The spoons in the porridge bowls clattered against the stoneware. "He'd been betting again, you can count on it!" With shaking hands, she cleared the table and moved the bowls to the sink. "Instead of coming home, he holed up in an inn somewhere and played cards."

"And what if he did? What difference does that make now? Father is dead! And you stand there and accuse him!" Seraphine screamed.

Father . . . I will never see him again? There was something unreal about the thought. Seraphine banished it as quickly as she could.

"Don't you understand?" Ilse yelled back. "It was probably one of the crooks he'd been sitting at the table with! Dice, cards—this is money, and those men take it seriously. Oh, you don't know how many times I had to sit and watch it." Her bottom lip began to shake. "And now all the . . . the goddamned betting . . . has killed him."

Seraphine looked at her mother, who was crying, shoulders quaking, leaning with both hands on the sink to stop her from falling down. She should have gone to her and put her arms around her. In her mind was a buzz, a hum: It is not true. None of it is true. First Helmut, then her father . . . where was the star fairy? No doubt she would come soon and set Seraphine free from this nightmare.

Ilse turned around and took a step toward her. She poked one finger against Seraphine's chest. "Your vanity will perish soon enough. Sitting there as if none of this has anything to do with you. How are we supposed to pay the rent? Now that Helmut is married to another, his father won't have any scruples about tossing us out on our ears. And then there's the debt that Friedhelm went into with the Kerners. How can we pay them back? We'll end up in the poorhouse. We—" But her next words were lost in a sob.

Money, money, money. Her mother thought of nothing else. Money and her own misfortune. *She hasn't asked me how I feel even once,* Seraphine thought. Then another knock sounded at the door.

Both heads turned.

Cautiously, Valentin stepped into the room. His eyes bulged from his corpse-pale face.

"I came as fast as I could. Adolf . . . he was just at our place. My father wants you to know that you can count on our support. You don't need to worry, he says. I . . . what I want to say, Seraphine, is that I am so, so sorry." He slipped in beside Seraphine on the bench and put one arm around her shoulders, which she did not resist.

Ilse looked at him. "That's very nice, Valentin," she said slowly. Since he'd come in, a little color had returned to her cheeks, and her eyes cleared a little behind the shine of tears. "Tell your father that we appreciate his help very much. In our hour of . . . loss, one is thankful for every friendly gesture."

Valentin cleared his throat. "Perhaps it is not the right moment, or maybe it is exactly right, I don't know, but . . . I would like to talk to Seraphine."

Ilse nodded encouragingly.

"I mean, alone," Valentin added, and he pulled Seraphine into the front room.

Ilse, a little taken aback, was left in the kitchen. Hadn't she just been through this recently? When Helmut disappeared with Seraphine into the front room and . . .

On tiptoe, she crept across the room and positioned herself behind the door to listen to what the younger Kerner boy had to say to her daughter.

"And you sit there and jabber something about time to think! Why didn't you just say yes?" Ilse set down a cup of tea in front of Seraphine so roughly that the hot liquid lapped over the sides.

"You were eavesdropping."

"Of course I was eavesdropping. This is about our survival! And your future. Now that Friedhelm isn't . . . Then it is up to me to make sure you have a future."

"My *future*." Seraphine practically spat the words out. The smell of peppermint rising from her cup made her feel nauseous.

"Yes, your future. Now that not only Helmut but also your father has left you in the lurch—"

"Father did not leave me in the lurch," Seraphine shouted. "He loved me. And Helmut loves me, too," she added softly.

"Love!" Ilse Schwarz laughed contemptuously. "Some men only love themselves."

Seraphine turned away.

"I love you more than life," Valentin had told her. "I've loved you as long as I can remember. But . . . I couldn't. Because of Helmut. But now, after last night . . ." He had fallen silent then and pressed an awkward kiss to her cheek.

How could she respond to that? How could she tell him that the previous night had meant something completely different to her than it did to him? That she had been trying to bury her love for Helmut? Like a mother wolf scraping a hole in the forest floor to bury her afterbirth.

Forever and ever.

The muscles in Seraphine's face tightened. If only what she had tried to do had worked. Instead, she only felt more keenly than ever how deep, how all-engulfing her love for Helmut was. Nothing, nobody would ever be able to take his place.

"He loves you. He is a fine young man from a good family. What more do you want?" Ilse asked, not comprehending. "Valentin's proposal is like manna from heaven. On this terrible day, of all days!"

"He is not Helmut," Seraphine said, her voice toneless. "Helmut and I . . ." She trailed off. It made no sense.

Valentin loved her? Had always loved her? Strange . . .

"Helmut, Helmut—you always play the same tune. Where is your fine Helmut now? Probably lying in bed with his bride and doesn't yet know a blessed thing about our sorrows. But Valentin . . ."

He had been resolute, certainly. Almost a little like Helmut. It was certainly odd. All these years, Seraphine had barely exchanged five sentences with Valentin, had never really been aware of him at all, and now he talked to her as if they were the closest of friends.

"I know that I can only ever be your second choice. But as my wife, you would lack nothing. And while you don't love me, not yet, can you imagine loving me one day? Like . . . last night?" The look in his eyes terrified her. *What are you trying to do?* she felt like screaming at him. *You have no right to look at me like that.*

No, she should have answered. *No, I can't imagine that.* But instead, she asked Valentin for a little time to think. He had been full of understanding. The news about her father's death, now his proposal. It was a lot all at once, of course. He had taken his leave, saying that he would return again tomorrow.

Seraphine snorted. As if anything would change in a day!

"What's there to sniff at?" Ilse flared. "Valentin would lavish every care and attention on you. He said it! I heard him say it! Child, don't you understand what that would mean? You would be provided for for the rest of your life. You would never have to worry about anything. And there would be a place for me somewhere, too."

Lavished with every care and attention—how she had longed to hear those words. But from the wrong man's mouth they rang hollow.

"You expect me to marry for what I get out of it. For my own interests. To be provided for. Is that all I have earned in your eyes?" Seraphine stared at her mother in bewilderment and disbelief.

"For your own interests—oh God, child! Am I asking you to marry a monster? Valentin is a good, charming young man, and you would have taken his brother with pleasure. But no, you keep up your pigheadedness. You keep on dreaming. Ha, I married for love, and look where it got me!" Ilse's voice had grown shrill. Shocked at her own vehemence, she stopped and took a sip of her tea. When she had calmed a little, she went on quietly. "My parents warned me. Again and again, they warned me to stay away from Friedhelm. He was a good-for-nothing, they said. Someone who could not handle money, and that it was a curse on everyone in the Schwarz family. But I didn't want to hear it." She took Seraphine's hand in hers. "Believe me, I know what I am talking about. Can you blame me for wanting something better for my only child? Valentin's proposal is a gift from above." When Seraphine said nothing, she continued. "Have I spoken a single word of reproach about last night? I heard enough to know what happened. Do you think every mother would be as understanding? That must show you that I only mean well by you."

Seraphine laughed. Her mother, the eavesdropper! Abruptly, she pushed back the bench and stood up.

"And the answer is still no. I can't marry a man I don't love. I would rather die."

The rest of the day, the door of the Schwarz house hardly closed. Gönningen's residents, one by one, came to give their condolences and sate their curiosity, then go home again with the feeling that fate favored them more than it did Ilse and Seraphine. Between mother and daughter hung a reproachful silence. If the visitors noticed the strange atmosphere in the tiny cottage, they put it down to the sad circumstances of the day.

When Seraphine went to bed that evening, she was more exhausted than ever in her life. She had the feeling that an earthquake had shaken their house to pieces, and she lay helpless and hidden under the rubble. Alone, too weak to move, unable to call for help, powerless to free herself from all the thoughts that had buried her. Helmut and Hannah, her father, Valentin, her mother, who followed her every step so disapprovingly . . . it was all too much.

Helmut. He was the only one who had not come. His wife had probably forbidden him. Hannah was most likely one of those women who would eat him up alive like a spider, its prey entangled in its web.

She threw herself restlessly onto her other side and pulled the blanket up so that it half covered her face, as if, like that, she did not have to look the truth in the eye.

She had driven Helmut to marry another. With her overplayed morality, she had destroyed not only her own life but his as well. Little Miss Touch-Me-Not, he had always called her, teasing, when she fended off his ardent embraces. But at the same time, there was nothing she wanted more than to hold him close. She would have guided his hands into her lap, would have arched her breasts toward him. How many times had she imagined what it would be like when he made a woman of her? She had dreamed endlessly of her wedding night. At home, in her narrow bed, she had explored her body with her hands and fantasized that they were his, had pressed her lips to her forearm and fingers and imagined those lips were his. Many a cold night had she warmed like that, and the star fairy had always whispered, *Soon, soon it will come.*

Hannah had not let herself be satisfied with dreams, and had gotten pregnant. By Helmut.

"Helmut was not forced into anything," Valentin had told her at midday that day. "He and Hannah both had their fun. He could just as easily have said no, couldn't he?"

Could have, should have, would have . . . what did Valentin know? He was probably just jealous that Helmut was so desirable to women. No, no, the woman had *tried,* had been *determined,* to lure Helmut, that was clear. And Hannah had succeeded while she, Seraphine, had exercised noble-minded restraint.

And then along came Valentin, wanting to marry her. Ha! Then things had gone for her just as they had for Helmut. She snorted so powerfully that her pillow puffed up.

But wasn't that a kind of justice?

Seraphine sat up with a jolt and stared outside.

Why should things work out any better for her than they had for Helmut? He had to stand up for the mistake he made, and she had to take responsibility for the faults of her father, whose presumed death had left them in dire straits. The poorhouse was looming, her mother had said. Wasn't that at least as good a reason to marry? Wasn't her hour of need at least as serious as what Helmut had had to face?

She and Valentin—the words tasted as bitter as overbrewed tea.

On the other hand, he was Helmut's brother. In many ways, they were not unalike. Last night, in his arms, she had been able to imagine, at times, that he was Helmut. If she married Valentin, it would mean that she would never be far from Helmut. And she would be able to keep an eye on that terrible Hannah, would be able to make sure that she didn't make his life any harder than it already was. Helmut would be able to come to her with whatever was bothering him. She did not want to abandon him ever again as she had in the past.

And then something completely new occurred to Seraphine. Wilhelmine Kerner would become her mother-in-law as she had always wanted to, despite Helmut marrying another woman. Wilhelmine, who stroked her hair and called her a fine young woman, and who no doubt liked her more than any Hannah-come-lately.

A smile crossed Seraphine's face. Valentin, a gift from heaven? Yes. For her and for Helmut. And she was almost too stupid to see it for what it was.

Thank you, star fairy.

A week later, Seraphine Schwarz and Valentin Kerner announced their engagement.

The wedding was set for the second Sunday following the Easter holiday. On the first Sunday after Easter, the election for the new local council was to take place.

There was no more talk about the brothers leaving for a journey through Russia. Nobody had the time to dedicate to such exacting and intricate plans.

Chapter Sixteen

Gönningen, January 18, 1850

Dearest Mother and Father,

Forgive me that I only now manage to sit and write a long letter to you, but until today I have had hardly a minute to myself.

I want to start by telling you about the wedding. It was such a wonderful occasion, and my heart is still broken that you could not be there. Everybody asked after you and sends you their very best regards. Oh, Mother, if you could only have seen the beautiful gifts Helmut and I received. There was even a samovar, all the way from Russia, can you believe it? I had no idea at first what it was for until Helmut explained that you can brew fresh tea with it. And we were given some lovely crockery, too, although I'm really not sure what I'm supposed to do with all of it. We all cook and eat together, so I can hardly go setting out special porcelain for Helmut and me.

Nibbling at the end of her quill, Hannah paused. She would not tell her mother about the horsehair paintbrushes or sewing supplies she had been given. Her with a needle? She could not even sew on a button! Unlike Seraphine, about whose artistic talents and sewing skills Wilhelmine had gone on at great length.

Those special gifts had no doubt been sought out by the wedding guests for the *other* bride and had now ended up in her possession more by accident. No, she would not tell her mother a word of that, or she would have to go into the whole story of Helmut's dissolved engagement.

With a flourish, she dipped her quill in the inkpot again and began a new sentence.

The people of Gönningen really outdid themselves, and for an outsider like me! I was met with open arms, and I am sure I will find a friendship or two among the young women here. Then there is Emma, who runs the inn where I stayed when I first arrived, and Käthe, her daughter. I owe them a lot. They are such good-hearted people, and it hurts me even more to know that none of the young men here have any interest in Käthe. She is lame in one leg, but do the men have to reject her so completely for that? Of course, she shed some tears at the wedding, and I think they were tears of emotion not only because of me but also from regret for her own circumstance.

Helmut's parents are also very nice, especially his father. He wants to run for the local council, imagine that!

She stopped again, leaving a small spot of ink on the paper. Should she write that Helmut's mother was extremely aloof and formal with her, or would that just make her mother worry? On the other hand, maybe she had some advice about how Hannah could handle Wilhelmine? No, she would have to come to grips with that herself. *All I have to do is pick up the Bible more often and pretend I'm reading it,* she thought mockingly. Then Wilhelmine might find an occasional word of praise for her.

The way people here live is also so different from home. All they ever think about is business! From sunup to sundown, the whole family is in the packing room, and we sometimes even eat lunch in there, which—as I'm sure you can imagine—is not particularly lavish because they have so little time. Usually there's just bread and soup, and they eat it all down as fast as they can so they don't lose any time.

Someone gives me a spoon and points at a sack of seeds, and I measure off the right amount of whatever seeds are in the sack into little paper bags. They might be carrot seeds or kohlrabi or flowers, I really don't know. There's never time for explanations—Helmut and Valentin are leaving the morning after next to visit their customers, and the seeds have to be packed; that's just how it is. But I am determined to find out more about all these strange seeds in the next few months so that I—

"Hannah? Are you coming? The others are already in the packing room." Helmut looked in.

With a sigh, Hannah put the quill aside. She had finally managed to sit down and put pen to paper, and she wasn't finished. Hadn't Wilhelmine told her she would only have to help with the packing after lunch?

She looked up and saw that Helmut was dressed for going out. Frowning, she pointed at his green-dyed fur cap. That and the long cape he wore were meant to be his traveling clothes. "So what is the lord of the manor up to while the rest of us are breaking our backs?"

Helmut grinned. "The lord of the manor is preparing himself for his journey. I have to pick up my new boots today. Actually, I should have been breaking them in for a week or two already, and I'll have to pay for not doing that with bloody blisters . . . After that, I'm stopping by the Heinzes. He and his brother are leaving the same day as Valentin and I. We may be able to ride a good part of the way on their cart."

Hannah swallowed. Until now, she had successfully managed to push aside the idea that Helmut would be leaving so soon. She stood up and went to him.

"Do you really have to go? I mean, couldn't Valentin, this once . . ." But even as she spoke, she was angry at herself for broaching the subject. She was a seed merchant's wife now, and the sooner she began to behave like one, the better.

A shadow drifted across Helmut's face. "You know perfectly well that he can't. Traveling alone is far too dangerous. Just think of Seraphine's father."

Seraphine . . . now it was Hannah's face that darkened. In a few months, she would be living in the Kerner house, too, and Hannah did not yet know what to think of her. She had met her for the first time at the small engagement party a few days earlier, and she had not really come across as a calculating female—although Hannah had ascribed precisely that trait to her when Seraphine so suddenly shifted her favors from one brother to the other. She said little and laughed even less—far from the picture of a happy bride. But if Helmut made a joke or asked her a question, she came to life. She had not exchanged a word with Hannah, though, which came as no surprise. For Seraphine, she was the evil woman who had stolen her promised husband . . . and that was something Hannah could understand.

She sighed. She and Seraphine would never be friends.

Helmut screwed up his face. "My dear Hannah, don't look so sad. It doesn't make things any easier for me." He sat on the bed and patted the mattress beside him. "Come and sit with me."

Reluctantly, she joined him. Just now she could do without platitudes like "Don't be like that. You have to get used to being alone." So she was all the more surprised when Helmut put his arm around her and drew her close.

"You know, it has never been this difficult to pack for a journey as it has been this time." Now it was he who sighed deeply. "I'm looking forward to traveling again, naturally, and I'd be lying if I said anything else. But . . . I will miss you terribly."

"Hmm," she murmured, doing her best to sound unimpressed. But she instinctively held her breath, not wanting to miss a word he said.

"I never would have thought that we'd understand each other as well as we do. I mean, I liked you when I first saw you, back then, in Nuremberg. Or I never would have . . . you know . . ."

"Hmm," she murmured again, smiling inside. Let him struggle a little to find the right words. That was the least she deserved. She nestled closer against him and stroked the back of his neck the way she knew he liked.

Helmut took a deep breath. "In any case, what I wanted to say is that I'm happy the way everything has worked out. I would never have believed that marriage is . . . such a fine thing." He laughed softly. "As a young man, you think all kinds of dumb things, and one of them is that once you're married, the good life is over. But that's not true, I know that now. It's the opposite, in fact. You have made my life so much better. Your smile gives every gray day a little color, and even my father said to me just yesterday that he finds your happy nature to be very refreshing. And something like that, from him . . ." Helmut sounded genuinely amazed.

Hannah smirked and kissed him on the cheek. "If you don't complain, it counts as praise, right? People don't say that about you Swabians for nothing." She snuggled against his shoulder again, enjoying his lovely—and rare—words, when Helmut turned her face to his. His lips were warm and tasted of apples, and with a low moan she gave herself over to his caress. The next moment, they lay side by side, arms and legs wrapped around each other. Helmut's fur cap fell to the floor. Hannah felt her nipples stiffen, felt goose bumps prickle all over her body and her skin tingle with lust. Everyone else was down in the packing room, but there, upstairs, they were alone . . .

Hannah hastily began to unbutton her blouse.

Helmut muttered a soft curse, then began to pry himself free of her embrace. Hannah groaned, not wanting him to go.

"Oh, Hannah, don't make me lose my head! Not that I would mind. I'd like nothing more than to lie here with you right now," he said, honest regret in his voice. "But there isn't the time. I'm sorry."

He swung his legs abruptly over the side of the bed, grabbed his cap, and put it back on his head.

"I have to go, really." He lifted Hannah's chin lovingly and kissed her passionately. "I'll bring you back a surprise. Now hurry. The others must be wondering where we are."

Hannah stayed behind, disappointed, after he left. A surprise from the shoemaker? Or from his upcoming travels? She lay there for a little while longer, squirming into the warm hollow left by Helmut's body. Her husband.

He had never spoken to her like that before. So . . . intimately. Oh, how she would miss him. How cold the nights would be without his warmth. How empty this room would feel.

She looked around their bedroom thoughtfully.

Before the wedding, Helmut's Aunt Finchen had lived there. Now she lived in a smaller room on the floor below, which she apparently found very convenient. "Finally, no more climbing all those stairs," she had said.

A large bed, a wardrobe, a small table and two chairs by the window. That was all the furniture they had. Everything about the room was marked by austerity: no pictures, no colorful patchwork rug or pretty lightweight curtains to let the light in. The room radiated a coldness that made Hannah shiver. All the other rooms in the house were similarly sober. Only the front room and Gottlieb's office—that is, the rooms where the family received visitors—were more elaborately decorated. Both contained wall clocks, porcelain figurines, and heavy brocade curtains to impress guests. But the Kerners seemed to need little to satisfy themselves. Not that they didn't have enough money!

While Helmut is away, I'll make our room a little prettier, she resolved. She would ask Wilhelmine at the first opportunity how she might obtain some colorful fabric. The thought cheered her, and she rolled over and sat up, in a good mood again.

As she left the room, she glanced at the unfinished letter, the open pot of ink, the dried quill. With a pang of conscience, she stopped and cleared it all away. No more time today for something like that, but as soon as Helmut was gone, she would write to her mother every single week!

Helmut had not returned by dinnertime. Hannah suspected that he and Valentin had continued their "provisioning" in one of the inns. *He might have taken me along,* she thought, silently annoyed. It was one of their last nights together, after all. Spontaneously, she reached for her coat.

"I'm just going to drop over and see Emma and Käthe," she called toward the kitchen, where Wilhelmine was slicing bread. She was out the door before her mother-in-law could raise any objections. At least she would get to say goodbye to the innkeeper and her daughter, who were leaving the next day.

"Underwear down at the bottom! How many times do I have to say it? If you open your bag on the road, you don't want to be showing your underwear to everyone, do you?" Shaking her head, Emma turned back to her own packing.

Käthe glowered but did as she was told.

Hannah smiled at her. "That's all you're taking for six whole weeks?" She nodded toward the two travel bags that stood on the table. A few pairs of underwear, a couple of bodices, a nightdress, soap, and a comb—the two Steiner women had so far packed no more.

Emma let out a laugh. "I'd have nothing against a dress or two to change into." She pointed to the two seed sacks, stuffed with seed packets, that leaned against the wall. "But we already have enough to carry, so vanity has to stay here."

"When you go on the road, you have to do without a few things," Käthe added, her cheeks flushed with anticipation. "I can hardly wait to be going!"

"Where will the road take you this time?" Hannah asked enthusiastically. Käthe's eagerness was infectious. The seed trade must have something special about it—first it was Helmut talking about new worlds, new opportunities, and now here were Emma and Käthe, practically glowing with the urge to be under way. *And I have to stay here,* thought Hannah, suddenly gloomy. And at the same time, just a few days earlier, she had been proclaiming to Helmut about how happy she was to have her own traveling experience behind her.

"Hohenlohe," Käthe replied proudly. "It's a good territory. My father, God rest his soul, did business there himself in the past. Schwäbisch Hall is a wealthy town. The salt—they also call it white gold—has made the people there rich. And we profit from that. We sell hundreds of packets of our seeds there. I'm looking forward to visiting the salt baroness the most," she said with a sigh.

Emma nodded. "Dorothea von Graauw is a wonderful woman. Unlike the other rich people we visit, she's not above talking through everything with us personally. Her family got rich on salt. The Graauws mine the salt using a method that Dorothea apparently introduced as a young woman, which I'm sure wasn't easy for her. The men in Schwäbisch Hall run things there just as in other places. But the salt baroness never had much time for convention and always followed her own road, however stony it was," she told Hannah. "And if you've once seen her garden . . . oh, 'garden' isn't the word, it's a *park* is what it is!"

Hannah wriggled on her chair. On the one hand, she was fascinated by Emma and Käthe's stories. On the other hand, it hurt, somehow, to hear about such things, never to see them herself.

"But what does a rich woman like the salt baroness need your vegetable seeds for?" Surely she has enough money to have her vegetables carted in from a farmer.

"Vegetable seeds? Heavens, no!" Emma and Käthe shook their heads vehemently, and Emma said, "We don't have anything to do with that side of the business. We sell flower seeds. Pansies with their pretty faces, bright-yellow sunflowers, lobelia shrubs with hundreds of blooms—that's our line. But there's nothing common about our range at all, let me tell you!"

"And we don't only sell. We also give advice," Käthe added proudly. "When it comes to a rose garden, you have to be especially picky. Let's say you have a gorgeous red rose, and then you plant marigolds around it—it would look horrible!"

Hannah nodded, although she could not actually see what was so terrible about combining red and yellow like that.

"Some roses only bloom for a few weeks of the year, and others will keep producing flowers all summer. If we're talking about the first kind, we tell our customers to plant annuals like sweet peas or maybe sunflowers beside them, so that they can enjoy the sight of flowers all summer."

"I can see you know your craft." Hannah sighed, though with the slightest touch of mockery. My Lord, they made it sound almost like a science. "It seems to me that Gönningen women are cut from the same cloth as that salt baroness," she added, though more to herself. When she saw the inquiring looks of her two friends, she had to elaborate. "I mean, it's certainly unusual to have women going off traveling alone—except here in Gönningen. Here, you go your own way, and I mean literally."

Käthe smirked. "Thank you for the compliment, but we haven't actually earned it, you know. Do you know the saying, 'Better a sore foot than a broken back'?"

Hannah shook her head.

"Well, it means that—for us, at least—the seed trade is an easier way to earn money than spending the whole year mucking out stables or slaving in the fields, like the women in the other villages. And besides, as a seed trader, you simply get to see and hear a lot more than if you spend all day milking cows and making cheese."

"And there's something else, too," Emma added. "A woman who earns her own money can choose who she marries. She doesn't have to accept the next Tom, Dick, or Harry who comes along just to be provided for."

Hannah wanted to know what was wrong with being provided for, but instead she asked, "So why is it that some women—a woman like Seraphine, for instance—don't go on the road?"

"Well, one does need to have what it takes," said Emma, with a trace of arrogance. "There's no room for daydreams, God knows!"

Hannah nodded. Seraphine, the daydreamer. In their few encounters, that was the impression she had made on Hannah.

"I have to be going!" She picked up her scarf from the chair and began to wrap it around her head. Then she embraced first Käthe, then Emma, wishing both of them a safe journey. Halfway out the door, she paused. "One last question: Why are you leaving only now? I mean, you were here all through autumn. But Helmut and Valentin spent autumn visiting their customers and taking orders, and now they are going out to deliver them."

"We do things differently, but we are the only two in Gönningen who do," said Emma after a brief pause. "We don't go as far afield as most. We write to our customers in autumn, ask them what they would like, and request a written order. And that's what we are delivering now. Keeping up the personal contact is important to us, you see. And we always carry more than we have on our order cards. The people are sometimes a little . . . thrifty with their orders."

"Taking your orders by post—that's an excellent idea," Hannah said. "You save yourselves a long, tiring journey. I wonder why the Kerners don't do it that way?"

"The Kerners? They'll be the last to give up the old way of doing things. You'll find that out for yourself soon enough." Emma came over to her and patted her cheek one last time. "'We've always done it that way,'" she said in a mimicking voice. "You'll hear that a lot in the future!"

Chapter Seventeen

A few days later, Gönningen was deserted. *A ghost town,* Hannah thought to herself as she strolled back to the Kerner house after picking up a few things at Almuth's store. Snow hung in the air like smoke. She wondered how Helmut and Valentin were doing and hoped they had a solid roof over their heads every night.

Of a good dozen shops in Gönningen, only two remained open, and Almuth's store was one of them. Some had even barricaded their windows, afraid the night watchman might overlook a burglar. Most of the empty houses, too, had their shutters closed day and night. No more hustle and bustle on the streets, just older people and schoolchildren, who, while their parents were away, had all the time in the world to get to school. And it was much nicer to throw snowballs or go plashing through the slushy snow or beg sweets in Almuth's store. Hannah was present when Almuth took pity on the little rascals, giving each of them a piece of candy.

"I feel a little sorry for them," she had said afterward, in an almost apologetic voice, to Hannah and Wilhelmine. "It isn't easy to see your parents go away all the time, never knowing if they'll come back again."

"Nonsense!" Wilhelmine shot back. "Unruly little brats, that's all they are. And you reward them for it."

Hannah, who did not think Almuth should be scolded for her generosity, said, "But it's no wonder they're like that. There's no one here to look after them."

Even two- and three-year-olds tottered through the streets on their little legs, watched over indifferently by older siblings, or sometimes by no one at all. Infants, some no more than six months old, were left in the care of relatives when their mothers went on the road. Käthe had told Hannah that it was the usual practice to stop breastfeeding the children before the regular departures in January or October so that they could be handed over to others. Hannah swore to herself that she would never be part of that practice.

Hannah's retort led to the first open conflict with her mother-in-law. And because it happened in Almuth's store, everyone in the village would know about it within a few hours. Wilhelmine sneered at Hannah, saying that of *course* they looked after the children. Was Hannah suggesting they didn't know how to do that?

Hannah bit her lip, stifling an answer.

Children in Gönningen simply went along with the state of things, and not much fuss was made about them, Hannah quickly realized. On the other hand, Helmut had told her that in the schools in Gönningen they taught French and English, and that the teachers in general attached great importance to a good education—how could these attitudes be reconciled?

Helmut's warnings made little difference: Hannah could never have imagined how Gönningen would transform from a busy village into a deserted town. Even the Kerner household had grown quiet, with only Wilhelmine, Aunt Finchen, and Hannah still resident. Despite his announcement at Helmut's wedding, Gottlieb Kerner had departed for Alsace to deliver the ordered seeds. "Who am I supposed to court to support me for the council?" he had said. "All the men are traveling. And the organizational side has long been taken care of."

It was the middle of February, and Hannah found herself missing Helmut all the time. She missed his teasing when others were around, his tenderness when they were alone, his warm body in bed—and she was amazed by how much she ached for him. She pressed her face into his pillow, but the scent of him grew weaker by the day. Every week or so, a letter came, but he usually only wrote about business matters, with names of customers that meant nothing to her, or from places she did not even know existed.

If at least Emma or Käthe were here! Or Annchen, the young woman she had met and chatted with at her wedding. An afternoon visit would have made Hannah's days easier. But Annchen had gone off with her husband for the first time and had been even more excited than Emma and Käthe put together. So there were only Wilhelmine and Aunt Finchen for company. And her unborn child.

To save herself from dying of boredom, Hannah did what she had done all her life: she worked. She took over the laundry duties, so once a week, she carried the soiled clothes and linens to one of the washhouses in the village and rolled up her sleeves. She met few like-minded young women, however, because most of them were away, and the heavy work of washing was left mostly to crook-backed old women. Hannah found it hard to talk to them, the Swabian dialect still barely comprehensible to her. Still, she looked forward to washday, when the hours seemed to pass more quickly.

Hannah also tackled the packing room. She boiled soapy water and scrubbed from top to bottom. Wilhelmine, who found her daughter-in-law's zeal for work a little odd, offered a few words of praise but no help. When it came to housework, the Kerners did what was necessary, but having enough seeds in stock and well organized mattered much more than polished floors and dusted surfaces. This was quite different from Hannah's mother, who scrubbed the restaurant at their inn every morning front to back.

Hannah started with the enormous storage cupboard that took up the entire length of the room. Its bottom section consisted of small brass-handled drawers, each of which was filled with different seeds. The little paper packets for the seeds were kept in one extra-large compartment. The upper part of the cupboard was taken up by open shelves, where they kept index cards, the names and addresses of customers, and the orders and invoices from seed suppliers. Neatly arranged on a wooden batten were various spoons of different sizes that they used for filling the packets. A large number of stamps dangled from a second long batten. These were used to stamp "Green onions, sow July–August" or "Kohlrabi" or other information on the individual paper packets, a job that Hannah particularly enjoyed.

In a special locked drawer, they kept what Helmut called their "Holy Grail": a small book containing the names and addresses of highly regarded seed suppliers. He had told her that it was crucial to them to have good seed producers as their partners. The fastest way to lose customers was to anger them with low-quality seeds. A housewife who had a field to plant behind her home did not know how to check the quality of the seeds she was offered. She could only decide if the seed merchant selling them to her was trustworthy. And the Kerners prided themselves on being trustworthy. In fact, they tested almost all their seeds to ensure they would germinate. A certain number of seeds were placed in a damp glass bowl, and one could see how many of them actually began to grow; because of those controls, they rarely had to deal with a complaint, Helmut had told her with pride. Apart from the Ulm gardeners, the precious little book held the names and addresses of seed suppliers from France, Central Germany, and Italy. Dutch suppliers were also listed, and it was from them that they obtained their bulbs.

Holland, bulbs . . . how strange and exciting it all was! Hannah breathed in so deeply that she had to sneeze. The smell of the vegetable seeds—earthy, slightly bitter, a little like wild herbs—tickled her nose.

When the cupboard and the floor were practically gleaming, Hannah allowed herself a break. She picked up the seed catalog that lay beside the stamps and made herself comfortable at the long packing table. She leafed through the pages for a few minutes, flicking back and forth, amazed at the variety. She had spent years in her parents' kitchen cleaning and dicing carrots, not knowing how many different kinds there were. "Carrots, long, red," she read. "Carrots, semi-long, light red," "Carrots, red, short, no heart"—no *heart*? How could their customers even tell the different kinds of carrots apart? And how did Helmut and Valentin do it?

After the carrots came parsley, celery, beetroot, and countless varieties of lettuce. Then kohlrabi, peas, and other vegetables for the pot. But she searched in vain for the pansies with their *"pretty faces,"* as Emma had described them. Was the Kerners' range more of the common or garden sort that Emma had spoken of so disparagingly?

Hannah set herself the task, before Helmut's return, of learning by heart at least some of the different kinds of seeds on offer. But how was she supposed to distinguish between all the different carrots? The catalog didn't even have pictures! If they at least had decent names, names she could actually remember—but "Carrot, long" and "Carrot, semi-long"?

Dispirited, Hannah closed the catalog and picked up her cloth and bucket again.

I have so much to learn, she thought as she scrubbed hard at the surface of the packing table. *But there is time enough for it.*

Chapter Eighteen

The weeks that followed passed in monotonous harmony. After breakfast, Wilhelmine sat at the kitchen window with either her Bible or a piece of knitting, and spent the time until lunch watching the street and passing judgment on anyone who walked by. Because cleaning and washing did not nearly fill her time, and because the kitchen was the warmest room in the house, Hannah took over the cooking: simple, hearty food, the same food her mother served in their bar. And sometimes, stirring away, busy with two or three pots at once, she could, for a blessed moment, imagine that she was once again in Nuremberg with her mother, who always had a song on her lips. She missed her mother at least as much as she missed Helmut. *Here I am, a wife, and no husband in sight,* she wrote in one of her numerous letters.

In the afternoons, Wilhelmine went off to join one of the local Bible groups. Out of sheer boredom, Hannah went with her once—for the first and last time, she promised herself afterward. Sometimes, too, Wilhelmine visited old people who were confined to bed or too weak to get out of the house.

Some afternoons, Aunt Finchen also went out, although she invariably waited until Wilhelmine had left. And unlike Wilhelmine, she never asked Hannah if she wanted to join her. If she had, Hannah would have thanked her and declined. But she soon realized Finchen came home in the evenings in a cheerful mood, with red cheeks and a slight scent of alcohol. Wilhelmine always stared sullenly at her sister when she returned from one of those outings.

"Do you know what, Aunt Finchen, I think I'll come along today!" Hannah said one day, hooking her arm into the old lady's before she could raise any objections. In a few minutes, she found herself in The Stork, one of the two inns still open. Inside, Hannah met a very illustrious crowd indeed. The pharmacist's wife was there, with the wife of the mayor and a handful of other women, sitting with glasses of liqueur and spirits at the table their husbands occupied at other times of the year. The innkeeper's wife served them—the innkeeper was off traveling. There was gossip and giggling, and Hannah quickly grew to like the group, although the other women were all considerably older than she. Women drinking at an inn—nothing like that ever went on in Nuremberg!

"Wilhelmine thinks I'm visiting the sick," Finchen confessed, giggling. Hannah promised not to say a word, although she was fairly certain that her mother-in-law had seen through Finchen's "visits" long ago.

Seraphine only rarely showed her face. Hannah assumed that after her engagement to Valentin, she would be a regular visitor to the Kerner household—another wedding had to be planned, after all—but her visits were sporadic. When she came, Wilhelmine instantly dropped whatever she was doing, served coffee and sometimes even cake, and vanished into the front room with her future daughter-in-law to work out wedding details . . . again.

Hannah was not expressly invited to these little coffee circles, but she joined them nevertheless. Although she still felt a little uneasy in Seraphine's presence, it would be wrong to avoid her future sister-in-law. The sooner they both forgot the start of their acquaintanceship, the better.

These meetings were never easy. Seraphine hardly said a word and showed little interest in Wilhelmine's preparations for the wedding. Whenever Hannah ventured an idea or even to comment on one of Wilhelmine's, all she earned from Seraphine was a hostile glare.

"I don't know what's going on with that girl," Wilhelmine said to Hannah one day. "Here I am, trying to get everything arranged as nicely as possible, and she sits there looking like it's been raining for a month! I find it a little ungrateful, really."

Did Seraphine's lack of interest have to do with her groom? Was she still in love with Helmut? Hannah pushed the thought aside as quickly as she could—it was much easier to think of Seraphine as no more than a shy young woman who was finding it difficult to come to terms with the hand she'd been dealt. Hannah felt an urge to help Seraphine with the situation—she felt guilty about what had happened, after all. But she sensed that Seraphine would turn down any help she might offer, and she refrained from making any more attempts. While she yearned for a close friend, someone she could really talk to, Hannah doubted that Seraphine would ever fill that role.

Hannah looked forward more and more to the birth of her baby. When the boy—she was convinced it would be a boy—was finally there, she knew all the tedious days would be over.

Winter withdrew, bit by bit. For Hannah, who in her closed-in corner of Nuremberg had never had much sense of the passing seasons, it was a time of never-ending wonder. In mid-February, the countryside still lay beneath a thick layer of snow, the unaltering contrast between black and white tiring to the eye. But by the middle of March, after several warm days, the landscape looked like a blanket full of holes. Here and there, grass began to show, and the patches of snow shrank and shrank. Although the sun had to struggle into the sky each day, the air actually did begin to warm a little, and the warmth brought with it a little bit of spring promise. As if touched by a magical hand, the fields in which the fruit trees grew were suddenly covered in tiny blue flowers. The apple and pear trees themselves were not yet budding, but looking closely one could sense the fresh juices flowing through their veins. The first crocuses, too, began to show, and a few premature daffodils and tulips appeared from beneath the old, matted grass. For Hannah, every flower that spring was like a little miracle. How was it possible for the shriveled bulbs she had seen in the Kerners' packing room to transform into such beauties?

In the mornings, Hannah was woken by the music of thrushes, titmice, and finches. And spring itself finally arrived in all its glory: the forsythias bloomed, turning entire gardens into yellow fire, and the air smelled sweet, of new grass and wildflowers. Hannah grew more and more restless. Finally, finally . . . Easter was drawing near, and Helmut would come back home.

On Good Friday, someone knocked at the Kerners' door.

Hannah, counting the hours until Helmut's return, jumped up so fast from the kitchen bench that she made herself dizzy.

Adolf Rausch was at the door. Hannah let out a sharp cry. "What . . . ?"

The village constable stared at her belly for a moment, then, abashed, removed his official cap.

"Is Valentin not yet back?"

Hannah shook her head. She was so afraid that she felt as if all her breath had been knocked out of her. She struggled to think clearly.

"Has . . . has something . . . happened?"

"Yes. I mean, no. I mean—"

Hannah instinctively grasped the man's arm. "What is it, sir? Speak!"

Adolf pried her hand free in annoyance. "Another hysterical woman is the last thing I need," he muttered, pinching an invisible foreign thread from his uniform before continuing, "I have yet to visit the Schwarzes. Friedhelm's . . . body has been found. And the last time, Ilse . . . well, with all her wailing and thrashing, she only made the whole affair worse. So I thought it might perhaps be better to have Valentin along this time. As Seraphine's fiancé and as masculine comfort, so to speak. But if he is not here, then so be it." He turned away, but Hannah managed to grab hold of his sleeve.

"Seraphine's father has been found? Where? By whom?"

The constable shook his head. "A mad story, it is!" He turned back and stepped closer as if to be certain his news did not reach the wrong ears. But he was practically bursting with the need to tell somebody.

"He was found just a few miles from the village where he had last been seen, buried in a shallow grave, like a dead dog!"

Hannah grimaced. She hoped the man would choose other words when he broke the news to the dead man's widow and daughter.

"He was not even a stone's throw off the road. And at that place—I can still hardly believe it—for the first time, daffodils sprouted." Adolf glanced at Hannah as if waiting for her approval.

"Daffodils," she repeated, her brow furrowing. What was he talking about?

"Yes, daffodils. That was what made my Swiss colleagues suspicious. They just happened to be passing by, and they had to ask themselves, 'Where did the daffodils come from?'"

"And where did they come from?" Hannah said, gritting her teeth. With all his theatrical talent, the man should have been on stage.

Adolf Rausch waved Hannah closer. Then he whispered, "Friedhelm had the daffodil bulbs in the pocket of his trousers. God alone knows why."

"In his . . ." That meant that the flowers were . . . on the body . . . Hannah's hand flew to her mouth. "Oh, that's horrible!"

Rausch nodded benevolently—finally, this thickheaded woman seemed to have grasped the tragedy of the situation.

Both were silent for a moment, their minds in Switzerland, where a handful of bulbs had contributed to solving a crime. Then Hannah breathed in sharply.

"I'm coming with you!" She took her scarf from its hook and wrapped it around her. "Seraphine will need someone to stand by her."

Surreptitiously, Hannah counted the chimes of the church bell. So late already! She should really have been home long before to help Wilhelmine and Aunt Finchen get supper on the table. *What am I doing here at all?* she wondered silently. *I should just stand up and leave.*

Seraphine had not spoken a word since their arrival. She listened to Rausch's announcement without the slightest sound or movement . . . in contrast to her mother, who collapsed instantly in tears. Hannah made Ilse a cup of tea and put her to bed. Now, as they sat with Seraphine, an occasional sob reached them from the other room, but the sound seemed not to disturb Seraphine at all.

Finally, Seraphine said, "My father loved me."

Two silver tears glittered in the corners of her eyes. She threw her head back, and the tears left wet trails down her cheeks. Her hair, only loosely braided, swirled around her finely hewn face.

How beautiful she is, Hannah thought. Her eyes involuntarily looked down at her own rough hands, her swollen belly, her plain apron. Next to Seraphine, she felt like a hideous, clumsy peasant.

Why did I even come here? How did I imagine I could help Seraphine in her hour of need? Or was I really trying to ease my own guilty conscience by doing something for her?

Seraphine began to unravel her braid. She ran her fingers through her hair carefully, teasing the strands apart. "Did you know that the fairies come and steal little children?"

Hannah recoiled. Unconsciously, she placed one hand over the swell of her belly. Was Seraphine trying to frighten her?

Seraphine nodded knowingly. "It's true. They do. That's why my father hung a pair of scissors over my bed for many years, to ward off the fairies." She sighed. "He was afraid that they would come and take me back. But I would not have minded at all if they had stolen me away. I am only here at all because of a mistake, you know."

Hannah did not know what to make of that. A slight shudder ran through her. The girl was insane. Her behavior could not be explained any other way. How had Helmut ever dealt with such a strange creature? Seraphine was like a butterfly spun inside a cocoon—did she even realize that Hannah was there in the room?

Seraphine went on in the same distracted tone. "The star fairy brought me here. But she did not look very closely when she laid me in this cottage. I don't belong here. I belong . . ."

I, I, I—it was all Seraphine ever said! Hannah stopped listening and slid forward on her smooth chair. She had had enough of fairy stories. Seraphine was scaring her.

"Why didn't you go with your father when he went on the road?" she asked, her tone provocative, her eyes squinted. *If she had, Friedhelm Schwarz would probably still be alive today,* she added silently. That ought to drive out all the drivel about elves and fairies!

Seraphine looked at her in horror. "On the road? Me? I had to make my wedding dress . . ."

Hannah's shoulders rose and fell in resignation. The world really seemed to revolve around Seraphine, who had now jumped to her feet. "My wedding dress—would you like to see it?"

For heaven's sake, anything but that! Hannah stood up so quickly that her chair tipped backward.

"I have to go. I'm sure Wilhelmine has started to worry. She doesn't know I'm here . . ."

Seraphine laughed then. Thin, humorless. "You're scared, aren't you? You poor fat little lamb." She went to the door, and stood in Hannah's path. "There's one thing you should know: Helmut and I, we belong together. You're having his baby, you have his name, but that means nothing. Our love . . . our love is something unique. Even if I wanted to, I could not explain it to you. It's the same for Helmut. So your fear is unfounded, you see? You can't lose Helmut because you don't possess him, and you'll *never* possess him. Do you understand?" She smiled gently.

Without another word, Hannah fled the house.

Chapter Nineteen

It was surprisingly warm for the end of March. Helmut and Valentin had taken off their jackets and spread them on the ground beneath them while they rested. Chewing on grass stalks, they gazed up at the gleaming dome of sky overhead. Families of ducks paddled about on the pond in front of them, and now and then a fish leaped from the water to snap at an insect.

They were close to Ulm, and in two days they would be home again. The idea of their imminent return had left them both silent, and for some time the only sound was that made by the two horses, tearing at grass on the meadow beside them. Occasionally, one of the brothers would cast a glance toward the horses, which, like Helmut and Valentin, waited patiently for their owner, Heinz, to return.

Helmut turned to one side. "I'd like to know how much longer Heinz is going to be." He snorted derisively. "A girl in every village . . . It's a miracle he ever finds time for the actual work!"

Valentin frowned. Who was Helmut to talk? But he did not say as much, and instead said, "It's more a miracle that Heinz is able to keep track of them all. Just wait until we get home and he suddenly calls his wife Karla. Or Ingrid."

"Or Lucia!" Helmut added, laughing.

Since meeting up again with Heinz in Regensburg, hardly a day had passed without Heinz leaving them to attend an "urgent appointment." And that had not changed even out in this wilderness. If they could at least have waited in an inn somewhere . . .

Valentin nodded in the direction of the remote farmstead into which Heinz had disappeared. "What's he going to do if the farmer comes home early?"

Helmut screwed up his face. "Grab his stuff and run like hell, I assume. I know I wouldn't like to be in his shoes in a situation like that."

"Well, that isn't going to happen, is it?" Valentin replied. "Nope. You've been a picture of virtue this time, if I may say so." But he could not keep a trace of mockery out of his voice.

Helmut frowned. "Are you pulling my leg? You used to complain when I went off for a bit of fun, but now—"

"All right, all right," Valentin interrupted him. "It was just a joke."

Helmut glared a moment longer, but then his face transformed into a broad grin.

"You know, when you've got someone waiting at home as pretty as the girl waiting for me, the world looks very different than it did before. Anticipation makes the waiting worth it, as they say. Hannah will hardly be able to wait, too."

He swatted at a persistent fly, then stood and went to the horses.

"The brown's a bit skittish," said Valentin after a quick glance at the two animals, and he made calming sounds to it as he also stood. He was not at all prepared for the shove that Helmut gave him a second later.

"You'll have marital bliss waiting at home for you too, soon enough. You and Seraphine . . ." Helmut shook his head.

Valentin said nothing. It was the first time that their conversation had turned to Seraphine. The entire trip, he had waited for Helmut to say something about his sudden plan to marry, but in vain. And he had consciously avoided the topic himself. He did not know why, but deep inside, he felts the pangs of a bad conscience. As if he had stolen Helmut's wife, which was nonsense, of course.

"Really, though, the whole thing with the two of you, I think it's fine," Helmut said airily. "It means the girl will join our family after all, right?"

The muscles of Valentin's jaw tensed. How could Helmut talk about Seraphine like that? As if she were some kind of object to be passed on. All Helmut had to do now was mention how the compensation they had paid would also be coming back to the family.

Valentin led the horses, still pulling the cart, down to the pond. They had not taken the trouble to unhitch the animals—Heinz had promised he would not be away very long.

"Best to water these beasts now. Don't want to lose any time when Heinz comes back," he said.

Helmut nodded absently. "It came as a surprise, of course. Seraphine was *my* fiancée, after all. If Hannah hadn't come to Gönningen—but let's not start with that! I think you've acted exceptionally honorably, actually, jumping into the breach for me like that. I had a bit of a bad conscience, you know, about Sera, but that's gone now. Not every man would do that for his brother."

Valentin let go of the horses' lead rope and stalked toward Helmut. He knew the look in his brother's eyes: that sparkle beneath half-closed eyelids was always there when Helmut felt like starting trouble.

"What's that supposed to mean? You don't seriously think I'm marrying Seraphine to ease your guilty conscience?" he said. "I love Seraphine!"

"Oh, really?" Helmut shot back. "That makes me wonder how *long* you've loved her. And what you two were getting up to when my back was turned."

"You . . . I'm not going to put up with that." Valentin jumped at his brother, and they both landed hard on the grass. Without looking where it landed, Valentin landed a blow on Helmut's head, took one in return. In seconds, they were a knot of arms and legs.

Neither of the brothers noticed that their tussle was taking them dangerously close to the horses, which had finished drinking and were grazing by the water. When Helmut's back bumped against the hind leg of the brown, the horse reared as if stung by a hornet, then leaped forward, dragging its whinnying companion with it. The next moment, both horses were standing up to their bellies in the pond, snorting and snuffling, eyes rolling. The cart, which carried not only their baggage but also their seed sacks with all their earnings, had rolled down the slippery bank behind the horses. If the front wheels hadn't caught in the tangle of reeds at the water's edge . . .

"Helmut!" Gasping, Valentin freed himself from his brother's headlock, jumped up, and tried to get alongside the horses in the water. The reins! He had to get his hands on the reins. He lost his footing on the bottom of the pond. Beating his arms wildly, panicking, he tried to keep his head above water. Valentin could not swim. Neither of the brothers could.

Helmut was pulling at the back of the cart but losing his footing on the slippery earth. He fell, scrambled up again.

The horses trampled on the spot, sinking deeper and deeper into the muddy bottom of the pond.

In his desperation, Valentin clung for his life to the brown, kicking with his feet, trying to push his weight against the horse's chest. As if by a miracle, the horse responded and took a step backward.

"Pull! Pull!" Valentin—choking, his mouth full of muddy water—cried to his brother. He had managed to catch a rein and held onto it tightly, using his other hand to bat at the chest of the white, which was still out of its mind. "Go back, you stupid beast!"

Exhausted, soaked to the bone, the two brothers lay on the grass. They had tied the horses, still hitched to the cart, to a birch tree a safe distance away.

"That was close." Valentin was breathing hard. His chest hurt, as if he had a hundred-pound barrel pressing on his ribs.

"Close, but we managed it," said Helmut, gasping and coughing. He sneezed, sniffled back water and snot. "Females! Nothing but trouble!"

"What do you mean?" With the last of his strength, Valentin rolled over and looked at Helmut. "They're geldings, aren't they?"

Helmut sighed dramatically. "Were we fighting about the horses?"

A few scraps of pond weed were stuck between his nose and mouth, forming a kind of strange moustache, a sight so out of the ordinary that, despite his weariness, Valentin had to laugh. He gave his brother a friendly jab in the side, and Helmut winced in pain. "Right you are! Females!"

On Easter Saturday, Gottlieb Kerner finally returned from Alsace. Wilhelmine threw her arms around him before he even crossed the threshold, kissing and hugging him. Hannah, who was up to her elbows in a bowl of yeasty dough, smiled at them from the kitchen door. She would not have believed her mother-in-law capable of such a display of emotion. And Gottlieb, too, otherwise not above finding fault with this wife, was obviously happy to have Wilhelmine in his arms again.

If only Helmut were back! Hannah sighed deeply. Her anticipation for his return was mixed with worry and caused her almost physical pain. At the same time, it was a feeling that, at some strange level, she enjoyed. It bound her to Wilhelmine and all the other women who had stayed behind in Gönningen and who yearned for their men. She lifted the dough out of the bowl and began kneading it powerfully. When Helmut was finally here again, she wanted to be able to serve him the finest cakes and bread.

On Sunday, just before the Easter church service was due to begin, it happened. Helmut and Valentin's arrival was heralded by the squeals of joy of children, who in recent days had spent hours waiting in the streets of Gönningen for homecoming travelers. They were not disappointed: laughing and romping along, the Kerner brothers handed out caramels and all sorts of other candy.

Hannah, who had been combing her hair, raced down the steps with the comb still in her hand, threw herself into Helmut's arms, and launched into a monologue about her lonely weeks in Gönningen. Since her visit to Seraphine, she had not slept very well at all, and now she was overcome with a mix of relief and exhaustion. Tears rolled down her face, and she tugged at Helmut's sleeves and did not want to let go of him even for a moment. Only when Wilhelmine wedged herself forcibly between them to greet her returning son did Hannah manage to calm down a little.

Helmut, overwhelmed by the reception, galloped off to the inn a short time later to drink to the safe return of himself and the others coming home. Valentin did not go with him; shortly after their arrival, he had gone to see Seraphine.

Looking back, Hannah was annoyed at her own tearfulness. It was not how she normally was, and besides, she was a seed merchant's wife now and needed to have more self-control. At least she hadn't blurted out anything about her encounter with Seraphine. Still, her heart was heavy.

Even with Emma, Hannah could not really unburden her soul. Unlike the other traders, who were able to enjoy a little idleness after their return, the innkeeper and her daughter went straight back to work. They had a lot to do to get the inn ready for the expected onslaught of guests with full pockets and generous spirits. Still, Hannah turned the conversation to Seraphine at the next chance she got, and asked Emma if the girl had always been a bit peculiar.

"Peculiar?" Emma replied, her broom in her hand. "I would not call Seraphine peculiar. The girl just carries her nose a little too high in the air. Sometimes so high that her feet lose touch with the ground."

Hannah had to content herself with that, and she soon became convinced that she had simply read the entire situation wrong. Good Friday, plus the gruesome story with the daffodils growing from the dead man's trouser pocket, the visit to Seraphine in her gloomy cottage—all of it together had probably clouded her judgment a little, and she had ascribed undeserved importance to offhand words: *"You can't lose Helmut because you don't possess him."*

The dark clouds that had accompanied Hannah since that Friday did not dissolve completely. Seraphine *was* peculiar—and if she hadn't fully realized it before, she certainly did on the day that Wilhelmine invited her future daughter-in-law to discuss the final details of the wedding.

How indifferent she was. How apathetic. When Wilhelmine asked her if they should make garlands of flowers for the pews in the church, Seraphine merely shrugged. But they had flowers in abundance all around them! Whenever Hannah could spare the time, she went walking in the meadows around Gönningen, returning every time with a huge wildflower bouquet. If she could have, she would have had all the flowers at her own wedding, but in the winter, the best they could scrape together were a few boxwood wreaths.

Seraphine didn't show any more interest in the guest list. In the end, Wilhelmine took matters into her own hands and wrote the names of everyone she knew should attend.

When it reached that point, Hannah, who had been growing more and more fidgety by the minute, could not hold herself back any longer. It was supposed to be the most wonderful day of her life. "Don't you at least want to invite your friends and their husbands?" she asked Seraphine in disbelief. In reply, she got: "I don't have any friends."

A young woman who had spent her entire life in the village had no friends here?

In Hannah's eyes, that was more than peculiar. And the thought that she would soon be living under one roof with Seraphine made her more and more uneasy.

Who knew, she tried to reassure herself. Maybe it was no more than Seraphine losing her nerve, so close now to the big day. Like a filly shying at its first fence. If she thought about how excited *she* had been, this was the only logical explanation for the girl's strange behavior.

Chapter Twenty

April came, and Hannah was so busy with various festivities that she rarely found time to brood about Seraphine. She let herself get caught up in the day-to-day goings-on of Gönningen and enjoyed every minute. The Sunday after Easter, Gottlieb was elected to the local council, and Mayor Schultheiss delivered a glowing speech about the new councilor's merits and about the hopes people were putting in him. Gottlieb's entry into the town hall was celebrated in Gönningen like a royal coronation.

The weekend after that was Valentin and Seraphine's wedding.

When Valentin, beaming as if his face might break, said to Seraphine, "Now we belong together, forever and ever!" and the bride repeated his last words, only a few noticed that Seraphine's eyes were not on her husband but on his brother. Hannah was one of them, and her grip tightened on Helmut's arm.

"We're going out to the fields later," said Helmut, with a look out the window. "I hope the weather holds. I don't want to go digging around out there in the wet."

"If someone had told me it needed to be done and showed me how, I would have had the potatoes in the ground long ago. We've had enough nice days in the last few weeks," Hannah replied, and she took a bite of toast and marmalade—her breakfast. And she'd been bored enough to do it, too . . .

She looked over at the windowsill, where, since the end of January, all kinds of young plants had been sprouting. Not even a thimble could have fit in between the little pots and bowls. And all those plants also had to be planted out at some point. She had asked Wilhelmine several times why they hadn't already done so. Too early, too early! We have to wait until the night frosts are over, Wilhelmine had answered every time. "The planting out is only done after the Ice Saints festival." Which meant waiting until the middle of May. And now, finally, the time had come.

While Wilhelmine was busy carrying the men's plates to the sink, Seraphine swept in like an arriving ghost. And as so often, Hannah started at the sight of her. She still had not gotten used to Seraphine living under the same roof. How could anyone sleep so late? she wondered. Seraphine was always the last at the breakfast table and managed to hold up the entire family. Hannah gazed demonstratively at the clock on the wall, which just then ticked to seven.

Gottlieb patted Hannah's arm. "You're a hard worker, and no one can say otherwise. But around here, the potatoes are always planted after the Ice Saints."

Wilhelmine nodded from the sink. "It's always been that way. The harvest is a bit later than elsewhere, that's true, but now the ground has warmed up a bit, and that's good for the potatoes."

Hannah said nothing. Others in Gönningen had planted their potatoes long before. She had seen them herself. She stroked her swollen belly and sighed. A few weeks earlier, she would have been lighter on her feet and able to do her share, but working in the fields today would certainly not be so easy. But if it had *always* been that way . . .

"Now don't go looking so down in the mouth, darling. If you're not careful, our child will be born with the same face!" Helmut laughed and jostled her lovingly.

Hannah forced a smile. "And you'll really let me plant out my own vegetable patch, with anything I can find in the packing room?"

"If it's so important to you, why not?" Helmut replied with a twitch of his shoulders. "It isn't really necessary, though, you know. We plant more than enough of everything as it is. But we'll find a corner for Hannah's Field somewhere."

Hannah's Field—who would have thought, a year before, that she would ever become a real farmer? If she wrote that to her mother . . . the very idea cheered Hannah. She slurped down the last of her coffee noisily and rolled her eyes in pleasure. The brothers had returned home with their wallets bulging and with all kinds of delicacies, including the best roasted coffee beans Hannah had ever tasted.

"I think it's good, what you're doing." Valentin, who had not missed her look of ecstasy, refilled her cup. "It's a miracle, of a sort, isn't it? You put a little seed in the earth, pour a little water on it, and some weeks later you pull a vegetable out of the ground at that same place. And if, like you, the person who planted the seed comes from the city, then all the better, and all the more important it is to see this miracle for yourself." He took Seraphine's hand. "Why don't you help Hannah with the planting?"

Seraphine pulled her hand away but said nothing.

"The miracle of the seed! Don't go getting philosophical," Helmut teased. "Hannah is experiencing the same miracle with her own body, after all."

"Helmut!" Wilhelmine cried in horror, her face flushing bright red.

Hannah jabbed Helmut sharply in the ribs.

Seraphine sat motionless, pale as a linen tablecloth. "And what happens to a seed planted in poor soil? Or one that isn't watered properly?

What miracle does that seed have to wait for?" She swept a few bread crumbs from the table.

Valentin, confused, let out a laugh, but had no answer. Helmut frowned.

"That one will wither. Only a plant that can adapt can survive," said Hannah in the sweetest voice she could manage. "*It's always been that way*, hasn't it, Wilhelmine?" She could live without Seraphine and her strange remarks today.

Everyone else was in such high spirits and so satisfied with themselves and the lives they led that there was no better point to tell them what was going on in her head. Hannah took a deep breath.

"I have been meaning to ask you all something for a long time." She looked around at the family sitting at the table, her eyes finally coming to rest on the men. "Why don't you do what Emma Steiner does and send order cards to your customers in autumn? She doesn't have to go journeying at all then, not until January, when she goes out to deliver the orders. I think her method has a lot to recommend it."

"Time for me to go. Work is waiting!" Gottlieb's chair scraped loudly as he stood up. "And you lot better not waste much more of the day with useless blather!"

Hannah gritted her teeth as her father-in-law left. *Just stands up and doesn't even bother to give me an answer?* She put her bread down and looked at Helmut. But it was Valentin who answered first.

"For someone new to the business, the way Emma does things might sound tempting. But for most of us here, it is simply impossible, or others would have done the same long ago. Emma's fine customers around Schwäbisch Hall might be able to read, but many of the people we visit can't. What are they supposed to do with an order card? And even if they can read and write, I'd be worried that they might order too little or check the wrong kind. And there's another thing: letters get lost. It doesn't happen often, but it happens." He shook his head. "New ideas are good, but they need to be viable and—"

"And just think of all the effort you'd have to put in," said Seraphine now. "Someone would have to write out the order cards, and with all the different kinds of seeds that the traders have, that would be no fun at all. And how would you print them? There might be a printing house on every corner in the city you come from, but out here in the country you won't find one anywhere. And *that* means that the women would have to write out hundreds of lists by hand. Paper is expensive. I see that every time I need a new drawing pad. One has to be sparing with paper."

"But—" Hannah began, but she was interrupted immediately by Helmut.

"A piece of paper to replace a personal visit by the trader? Never! Do you know how happy the people are when we come?" he said. "Some of the regions we travel to are rarely visited by anyone else. They have no market days, no newspaper for the people to learn what's happening elsewhere. They can hardly wait for us to arrive sometimes. They ask us questions until our ears burn, want to know everything, and in detail. And they themselves want to talk, too. When we sit down at their table, we don't just talk about their orders, but about the last harvest, the latest news in the village, the troubles with the neighbors . . . about anything and everything. That's part of it."

Valentin laughed. "As a good salesman, you persuade your customers to buy a little more of this or that, of course. Or you encourage them to try a new variety. Like that, you put together much larger orders than you would get if you left it up to the customers alone. Oh, that would really be a sad way to do business."

Seraphine spoke again, her voice like needles. "Besides, orders have always been placed in autumn and the seeds delivered at the start of the next year. That's the rhythm we all live by. But an outsider like you can't be expected to know that." She turned to Helmut, and her voice turned to honey. "I can understand how you are drawn out into the world. You have to be among the people. You can give them so much more than just seeds."

Silly cow! The way she flattered Helmut was disgusting. Hannah shook her head as if to shoo away a fly, but her mind was hard at work.

The personal contact with the customers . . . she had not considered that side of the matter. Emma and Käthe did not seem to lack personal contact, even though they only went out once a year. The opposite was true, she thought, remembering how much they were looking forward to seeing the salt baroness.

Hannah tried hard to think what to say next. Despite all the counterarguments, she was not yet willing to give up on the idea of being separated from her husband only half as long in the year ahead.

She drank a mouthful of coffee.

"The autumn visit is important, I can see that now. But traveling the same route again at the start of the next year?" Her brow furrowed. Somewhere, far back in her mind, a thought was making its presence felt. An important thought. A good thought. All she had to do was bring it to the front somehow.

"Child, the men have explained it all already," Wilhelmine said, shaking her head. "It isn't so hard to understand." She and Seraphine exchanged a look.

"When you go out the second time, you send all your seeds ahead with the horse and cart, don't you?" she said to Helmut, ignoring her mother-in-law for the moment.

Helmut twisted his mouth to one side as if he'd bitten into something sour. "You know that. The horse or maybe the train takes everything to an inn that's as central as possible to the particular territory. When we get there, we pack the individual orders, then deliver them personally to the customers, which all takes quite a long time. But honestly, I don't understand all the questions. What's wrong with how we do things?" he added, sounding rather aggrieved. "Are you suggesting we carry the heavy crates on our backs all the way to Bohemia and save the cost of having them carted there?"

"Emma doesn't do it any differently," Valentin interjected. "She has all her seeds and bulbs sent to Schwäbisch Hall, and she distributes them from there. Most of the people in Gönningen do it like that, except those who work on a smaller scale and carry everything with them in their seed sacks."

Hannah waved her hand dismissively. "So the goods travel without you. You receive them at the other end, repack them, and deliver them," she repeated, realizing as she did so that everyone at the table must think her extremely dim-witted. "On your second visit, you don't spend as long with the customers, do you?"

Helmut rolled his eyes. Again, it was Valentin who answered.

"They need the seeds at the start of the year for planting. The soil has to be plowed, the cows taken out to the fields, and everything else. People don't have the time to chat for long, not even with us. So we deliver, get paid, and leave. But what do you—"

There it was! The thought! "Then your second visit is really just a formality," she burst out, before the thought could vanish again. She slid forward excitedly, and her belly bumped against the hard edge of the table. She looked around triumphantly. "We could just as easily pack the orders here at home and send them out with the mail. Or by cart. It wouldn't take any longer than if you went out on foot from the inn. And you would save yourselves three or four months!" She looked breathlessly at the brothers.

"How is that supposed to work, child? We don't even have a post office here." Wilhelmine spoke patiently, as if she were talking to a youngster who was having trouble grasping a new concept.

"That doesn't matter. We would take the packages to the post office in Tübingen, like we already do with letters. And it would be so much more convenient to pack the individual orders in the packing room here than to do it in some inn in God-knows-where."

Helmut bit his lip, considering it. "When I think about all the dumb looks we get sometimes, when we unpack our little spoons and start measuring out the seeds—and I have to say it really isn't very pleasant. If you look at it like that . . . but still, the cost! It isn't cheap to pack and send packages."

"Traveling costs money, too," Valentin said before Hannah could. She smiled inwardly. Valentin looked intently at his brother. "If we follow that through . . . wow! It would open up all kinds of possibilities. I'm thinking Russia . . ." His last few words were little more than a murmur.

Helmut, who was still chewing on his lip and deep in thought, froze. He blinked in the direction of his brother, and his eyes sparkled slyly.

"If I think about it like that . . . Hannah's idea is really just a development of what we've been doing all along."

The next moment, he pulled Hannah to him and kissed her enthusiastically on her lips.

"It would have been only a matter of time until we changed our process, wouldn't it, Valentin?" His brother responded with vehement nodding. Helmut went on. "But I must say, I'm impressed at how fast our 'outsider' got her head around our business!"

"But, Helmut, you can't be taking this nonsense seriously! I mean to say—" Wilhelmine began, but Hannah interrupted her.

"Just wait, your *outsider* might have a few more good ideas in her bag of tricks." She practically basked in the brothers' enthusiasm and ignored Seraphine's scowl. Her sister-in-law would thank her one day. After all, she would also profit from Hannah's suggestion, with Valentin, like Helmut, spending more time at home.

Chapter Twenty-One

It was a sunny end-of-May day. Seraphine had spread out her painting supplies on the table in the garden. An occasional apple blossom drifted onto the paper in front of her. Sometimes the gentle wind puffed a little harder and blew up a cloud of yellow pollen, and Seraphine had to cover her work with her hands. She would have preferred to paint in the house, in the room that she and Valentin had moved into after the wedding. But the risk of being disturbed was greater inside.

Someone always wanted something from her. Brush down her father-in-law's black jacket or cut Aunt Finchen's toenails or, or, or . . . there were voices everywhere. Strict and domineering whenever Wilhelmine complained about something. Sonorous and self-important when Gottlieb received guests in his office. Quivery and brittle if the old aunt tried to say anything. And loud, terribly loud, whenever Hannah laughed.

But hardly anyone came by the very back of the garden.

Seraphine opened the box of watercolors carefully. She dipped a brush in the water glass, but took it back out immediately when she saw how her hand shook. She could not paint like that! She did not even want to try. When she placed her brush and paint on the heavy paper, she wanted love to flow from her, not this terrible chaos that raged inside her like a summer storm.

Please, star fairy, make me calm. Give me silence.

As silent as the wall where the first little lizards warmed themselves in the sun.

As silent as the apple blossoms that could go to sleep again once the bees had done their work.

As silent as the little rosebush, its leaves shining silver in anticipation of the flowers to come.

But the silence did not want to come.

Her new life was different than she had imagined it. And this difference kept her awake nights. It made her crush her pillow, made her roll from side to side, ever mindful not to wake Valentin, because his concern would overwhelm her completely. "Do you feel sick?" "Are you too warm?" "Are you too cold?" "Should I get you a cup of milk?" Those kinds of questions were the last thing she needed. But calm, quiet, time to think—that was what she wanted. And there was never enough of it.

Driven away, forced to flee. By the raucous, restless family. By the terrible Hannah. By Valentin. Why couldn't he simply leave her alone?

Her dreams were gone. Her dream of happiness with Helmut—at times she found it difficult to evoke her memory of it. The star fairy was gone.

She dipped her brush despondently into first yellow and then red. With the orange she created, she began to shade in the aster she had sketched in pencil previously. Despite her dejectedness, her hand grew stronger with every brushstroke, and soon the flower seemed to glow from the inside.

Adonis roses, begonias, phlox, petunias, autumn asters, oxeye daisies—she had already collected at least twenty different flowers in her sample book, and planned on painting at least that number again. Unlike vegetable seeds, selling flower seeds was not always easy. You could eat beans. You could eat turnips. But asters and daisies were only food for the eye, and not everyone was willing to pay for that.

Seraphine had spent weeks working on her sample book, and she pictured Helmut taking it out of his bag on his next journey. None of the other seed merchants could boast anything like it. The beautiful, colorful illustrations would no doubt have Helmut's customers placing large orders.

When Seraphine had finished with the flowers, she began to paint in the deeply serrated leaves.

Every day, Helmut would hold something of hers in his hands. Looking through the book, he would know that every brushstroke, every line, had been applied with love. He would be with her in his thoughts, just as she would think of him every single day.

Abruptly, in the middle of a brushstroke, Seraphine paused.

How had things gone so far? To the point where here she sat, in the middle of May, wishing for Helmut's departure in autumn? Because when he was gone, he could think of her . . . She sighed deeply. God knew, she had not married Valentin for this. She had married Valentin to stay close to Helmut, very close!

But instead she felt further from him than ever before. She rarely found herself alone with him for even a minute. There was always someone pushing between them. Indeed, Seraphine sometimes had the feeling the others were trying to prevent them from being together at all costs. Whenever she followed him into the packing room to have a few minutes alone with him, Valentin or Wilhelmine would suddenly appear a moment later. The only one who did not seem to care how much time she spent with Helmut was Hannah. Hannah was stupid. Or was she? Perhaps she was smart enough to see that an invisible, inseparable cord bound Helmut and Seraphine together.

Seraphine smiled at the thought. The others, too, must feel the bond between Helmut and her, or they would not need to constantly keep them apart.

If only this life were not so strenuous. It took so much out of her, and so often she was exhausted by fury and grief.

That bumptious Hannah! Always turning the conversation to herself and pressing Helmut for answers. Poor Helmut could hardly eat breakfast in peace. And all those strange notions she came up with! Mailing everything—ha, that was too much even for her father-in-law. But why did he not just put the girl in her place?

"'You're a hard worker,'" she mimicked Gottlieb, speaking softly to herself. Working hard at having a child, maybe. Working hard at luring her husband into her trap. Seraphine snorted. The way she carried her fat belly around, smug as you like. And she stuffed down so much food, eating like there was no tomorrow. Her belly grew and grew, to the point where no one could possibly miss it. And instead of staying in the house, she just *had* to go out and make sure everyone saw, even out in the fields. In her mind's eye, Seraphine saw her playing the farmer, digging in the earth with her bloated fingers. As if that would impress Helmut.

She didn't like to think about Valentin, either. "'It's good to see you exploring the miracle of life . . . ,'" she muttered, aping his words. He was never that poetic around her.

Seraphine rinsed her brush in the water glass, then chose the lighter of two shades of green and went to work on the aster stalks.

Another thought struck her, and she stopped again. Was she not herself like a delicate plant, her seed sown in barren earth? Even here in this lovely house? Who was there for her? Who had time to take care of her now that Hannah was drawing all the attention with her loud laugh and dumb ideas? Where—

"Ah, here you are!"

Seraphine jumped. A shadow fell over her.

Valentin. Her brush twitched over the toothed edge of a leaf. Seraphine made a face.

"What do you want?"

"Hannah forgot the kohlrabi seedlings." He held the small planter for her to see. Hannah, Hannah, Hannah—even Seraphine's own husband danced when she whistled.

"Those who can't use their head must use their back," Seraphine muttered.

"And what did you forget?" Valentin smiled and lifted her chin. "I thought you were at your mother's. Don't you think she'd enjoy a visit? You haven't been to see her for ages."

"Mother—she forgot about *me* long ago." Seraphine avoided thinking about her old home. Gottlieb had granted her mother the right to live for the rest of her life free of charge in the little cottage, and he had written off the debts incurred by Friedhelm before his last trip. Now she sat there among her sewing like a pig in straw. Seraphine's marriage had killed off two birds with one stone: the threat of poverty had been averted, and she had gotten rid of her daughter to boot!

"You're her only relative here in Gönningen. People are already starting to talk about how little time you spend with her."

"Then let them talk. What do they know?" Seraphine hissed. What had gotten into Valentin, trying to tell her what to do?

Valentin looked at her dejectedly. "And you don't come out to the fields with us, either, though we could use every helping hand we can get. You'd rather watch Hannah toil, and in her condition, too. Sitting here all by yourself . . ." He sighed. "It isn't normal to shut yourself away like this. Hannah would have been happy if you had helped her lay out her garden."

"Oh, I'm sure she would have," Seraphine shot back. "Then she'd have one more fool dancing to her tune!" She glared furiously at the paper in front of her. Too much green, too bushy. Helmut's customers would think asters were all leaf and not enough flower. She bit her lip, thinking . . . Maybe she could still paint in a few more blooms.

Valentin leaned over her. His shoulder brushed against her hair. "You smell so good."

She shook her head as if a mosquito were buzzing around. Valentin instantly jerked away from her.

Seraphine laughed inwardly. So this was her husband. A coward, not man enough to accept her as she was. By day or by night. At night it was she who had to take the initiative. She imagined, there in the dark, that it was Helmut who held her in his arms. And when she opened her legs for Helmut, it was Valentin who moaned with lust. How stupid he was, Seraphine thought sometimes, in those moments.

The nights belonged to her. Her and her dreams. And as long as Helmut was not free to be with her, she would have to make do with Valentin.

She glanced over her shoulder sourly, saw her husband still standing there, shifting his weight uncomfortably from one foot to the other. She was sure he was only waiting for her to ask him to sit down with her.

But she had promised him nothing. He knew what he was letting himself in for. She had never made any secret of the fact that her heart belonged to Helmut. He wanted to give her time, Valentin had said many times, most recently just the day before. Time for what? she had asked, but not aloud. And still, he lurked. Watching her, every stirring of emotion, every move she made.

"That will be very pretty. And so lifelike. Considering how little time you spend outside, you've done really well with all the different kinds." Valentin picked up the finished pages and fanned them out in front of him.

"If you have enough imagination, you don't have to stand in the garden all day with a watering can in your hand. Give them here, you'll ruin them," she said, taking the pages back. She did not want to fight with him. She wanted . . . nothing with him, nothing at all.

Valentin laughed. "They will have to survive a little handling. If we're supposed to use your sample book, I'm going to have to hand it over to my customers to look through for themselves."

Seraphine pressed the pages to her chest protectively. "The sample book is for Helmut. He . . . he . . . what do you mean?"

How he looked at her, and how his eyes gleamed! Seraphine shuddered. She knew that look. It was a trait of the small-minded. Envious, jealous people. People like Hannah. People who tried and tried and tried again to destroy the love between her and Helmut. She breathed in and out slowly.

"He is the elder brother, after all," she said quietly, justifying herself. "So it should be his. Now let me get on with my work." She dipped her brush in the red paint. The next moment it skidded from red to green, then into brown . . . Her hand was clenched in Valentin's iron grip.

"Listen to me when I talk to you! I am your husband, though you like to forget it. So when you paint something, it belongs to me." Valentin's Adam's apple bobbed violently. "What makes you think you can fritter away your time painting pretty pictures for Helmut while the rest of us are breaking our backs? If I'd known that, I'd have hounded you out into the fields, and you had better not forget it! I—"

Seraphine cried out. "You're hurting me!" She twisted her hand out of his grasp and rubbed her reddened skin. "You always *want*," she hissed. "Me, me, me—I never hear anything else from you. You never think of me, never think about my feelings."

He laughed at that, mockingly. "Oh, look who's talking. Do you think I don't see how you still idolize Helmut? You're making yourself a laughingstock with all your pouting and posturing, and me with you! He chose Hannah. And if you ask me, he's made himself a damn good catch!"

"How can you say that, you . . . ogre! You don't know anything about it," Seraphine screamed, frightening herself at her vehemence. She so rarely raised her voice. But now she found the strength of a lion—for Helmut.

Valentin's face had turned chalk white. His lips trembled. "Oh, you don't want to hear that, do you? But Helmut is happy, happier than he's ever been in his life. And anyone with eyes in their head can see it. Except you, of course. And do you know why?"

Valentin's shouting had scared all the little lizards back into their hiding places in the wall. Seraphine stared at the gaps where they had vanished. She wanted the silence to return. The silence of the wall. The silence of the apple blossoms and the little rosebush.

"You've stuck Helmut in a shrine, and now you pray to him like he's a saint. And you can't even see that he's not worthy of your prayers. He's a normal man, no better than me or the next to walk past! But you, you can't even see what's true anymore."

The truth, the truth, the . . .

Concentrating hard, Seraphine swirled a drop of water into the brown. A few tiny veins and the stem would be finished, and she could start on the next flower.

"You are nothing but a hypocrite!"

She did not have to answer him. She did not even have to listen to him, not if she closed her ears tightly enough . . .

Hannah half crouched at the edge of her garden. She had to stop regularly to rub her stiff back. Since early morning, she had felt a tugging sensation in her belly, sometimes more a stab. Was the work too strenuous for her? Should she have stayed at the house? Emma had calculated that the baby would still be at least four weeks coming. And in such matters, Käthe assured her, Emma knew what she was talking about.

Carefully, Hannah lowered herself onto both knees. Ah, that felt better! Breathing deeply, she poked her index finger into the soil, creating several little hollows. Helmut had given her a small shovel and a stick that she was supposed to use to dig the holes for the seedlings, but she preferred to use her hands. If only her belly weren't constantly getting in the way!

"So where is *your* field?" she had asked Helmut when the three of them reached the edge of the village. She had noted the look of incomprehension that crossed his face, but did not know what to make of it. Then they had turned onto a series of narrow paths that cut between plots of every shape and size. All around them, the people of Gönningen were hard at work, and the brothers exchanged a few words with all of them. Finally, Helmut had stopped at a patch of unplowed ground between two orchards and had told her she could lay out her garden there.

Such a small patch of land for a family as large as the Kerners . . . Hannah had eyed the field doubtfully. "Where do you plant the potatoes?" she asked.

"The potato field is quite a bit farther, close to our orchards. If you need anything, just shout loudly. I'll hear you." And with that, the two brothers had disappeared in the direction of Rossberg.

Hannah sighed. She had embarrassed herself yet again with her questions.

She knew so little about Gönningen, she realized. It was not the case that every family had a single large patch of ground to call their own. Instead, each owned a block here, a meadow there, and perhaps a small field farther up the valley. Everything was disconnected and far apart, and rakes, shovels, and seeds had to be carried great distances. For Hannah, coming from big-city Nuremberg, this was a disappointment. She was not looking forward to laboriously harvesting all those little scattered plots. This was not her idea of life in the country.

The plot boundaries around Gönningen had been butchered by generations of divided estates, Helmut had explained, but it was also a fact that there was simply not enough available farmland for the village's constantly growing population.

"That's the basic problem. More and more Gönningers have to share the limited acreage. If we had enough farmland and we could all fill our bellies by farming grain and vegetables, our forefathers never would have thought of going out into the wide world to earn their money. But at some point, they turned necessity into a virtue."

Happy with her work, Hannah surveyed her rows of kohlrabi seedlings. She picked up the scrap of packing paper that had been lying beside the little plants. "Kohlrabi, crisp and delicate, fast-growing," she read. Then she looked at the flat slivers of wood that Helmut had left for her, along with a pencil. She was supposed to write on the slivers, then stick them into the earth so that anyone could read what was growing in which rows. But "Kohlrabi, crisp and delicate, fast-growing"? By the time she had squeezed all of that onto a wooden sliver, she could start harvesting! Instead, she wrote, "Kohlrabi, quick-pick." That was the way to do it! Pleased with herself, she picked up the next sliver, and instead of "Salad cucumber, medium-long, pale flesh," she wrote, "Green snakes." That conjured up a pretty picture! Then the next: for the rows of frisée that Valentin had described as "frizzy" and "quite tough" she wrote "Gönninger rogue," and for a second lettuce that the brothers had told her was particularly bountiful, she wrote simply, "Lettuce, full bowl."

She was having so much fun making up names that she was able, at least partly, to ignore the pain in her belly. "Full bowl . . ." She had to watch out that she did not go too far. Even so, on the sliver she used for the peas she had just planted, she wrote, "Green nonpareils." Suppressing a giggle, she tried to imagine Wilhelmine's face when they would go out together to pick green nonpareils. Helmut's mother was not what one would ever call a smiler. Aunt Finchen, however, was much merrier, although in Wilhelmine's presence she kept her natural gaiety in check. Hannah sighed aloud, then tried to think of a particularly daring name for the beans she was just about to plant.

A little later, she rocked back on her haunches, inspecting her work with satisfaction. She felt something warm and wet between her legs. She looked down in shock at the patch of dark-brown, muddy earth in front of her. Her water had broken and had doused several seedlings in the process.

"My God, the child is coming! Helmut!"

Chapter Twenty-Two

They called their daughter Flora. It was Helmut who suggested the name. A child that came knocking on the door of the world, so to speak, in the middle of a field, among burgeoning trees and vegetable beds, could only be named after the goddess of flowers. Besides, Flora was perfect for the daughter of a seed trader, he persisted—it took some time to convince his parents, who found the name unusual. Girls in Gönningen were named Klara, Martha, or Liesel. But Flora? "What about Seraphine's name?" Helmut retorted, but his parents just shrugged.

Hannah followed their exchange wearily but happily from where she sat on the long bench in the kitchen. She had not known that Flora was the name of a goddess. Nor had she ever heard of a father arguing so vehemently for the name of his child. Helmut seemed to be at least as overjoyed about the birth of a daughter as he would have been about a son. Unlike Hannah herself. She had been so certain that she was carrying a boy. But her disappointment was short-lived, and Flora won her heart from her first moment.

She was an undeniably beautiful child. Just after her birth, one could already see the fine structure of her face, and even her eyes were bright and alert. She was born not without hair on her head, like so many infants, but with black hair like her mother's. Hannah could spend hours just looking at her daughter. For her, it bordered on the miraculous that she and Helmut could have created such a beautiful being. Flora was something special. A rose growing in a field of dandelions. A holiday roast among dishes of turnips and cabbage. A thoroughbred among swaybacked nags. Hannah thought better of voicing such thoughts aloud, partly afraid of tempting fate with her motherly pride, and partly afraid that others would simply laugh at her. But when she and Helmut were alone with Flora, they outdid each other with compliments for their daughter.

Flora was not only a beautiful child but also an undemanding one, too, who only ever cried when she was hungry. As long as she was around people, she was happy to lie in her crib and watch everything going on around her for hours. She would let anyone hold her, but also did not complain when she was put down again, normally falling asleep within minutes.

Wilhelmine and Hannah's mother, Sophia—who traveled to Gönningen for Flora's christening and stayed for several weeks—agreed that they had seldom seen such a well-behaved child. And that was good, because with the seed trade as busy as it was, Hannah did not have much time to tend to her daughter.

For Hannah, the spring and early summer of 1850 was a time of joy: she savored to the full every minute that her mother was there. They strolled through Gönningen together, and she proudly showed her the garden she had planted, from which the first vegetables were already ripe for harvest. And Sophia Brettschneider, for her part—and as expected—complimented Hannah's gardening talents effusively, called Gönningen an exceptionally pretty village, and praised Helmut's qualities as a husband. She was greatly impressed by Emma and Käthe Steiner, two women who had managed to assert their place in the hard and usually masculine world of innkeeping. She thanked Emma from her heart for being a friend to Hannah in her time of need. Gönningen was a good place for Hannah, Sophia declared soon after her arrival. A place with friendly, open people, modest wealth, and enough intrigue to banish Hannah's longing for the more populous Nuremberg. She could hardly believe that, as Hannah described it, come the fall, Gönningen would once again be all but lifeless.

It was one of the hottest days of the year, and not yet the middle of June. Wilhelmine was in bed with a headache, Aunt Finchen had lain down as well, and Hannah was by the Wiesaz with her mother and Flora, cooling her feet in the water. Gottlieb, as he did every morning, had gone to the town hall early, and Valentin had gone with him. Father and son were planning to go to Tübingen together later to pay a visit to the regional administration.

Seraphine stood on the last step, holding her breath. Everything was quiet. The only sounds came from Gottlieb's old office—soft scratching sounds, and now and then a muttered curse. Seraphine smiled.

In contrast to the others, who already seemed rather dazed and exhausted by the time they finished breakfast—their clothes soaked through with sweat, hair stringy, skin shining—Seraphine felt cool and fresh. She smoothed her sea-blue dress a final time, hid the sample book that she had wrapped in brown paper behind her back, and knocked softly.

"Yes?"

"It's me." She slipped inside and closed the door behind her. All the shutters were closed in the office. Seraphine blinked once or twice to get used to the darkness. "You'll ruin your eyes if you sit at the books too long," she said, admonishing him.

Helmut snorted. "If I don't close everything up, the room heats up like an oven. In weather like this, I could certainly imagine better ways to spend my time than sitting here. But someone has to earn the money, after all." He grinned crookedly. "I just wish the orders would not take up so much time."

"I could help. You only have to show me what to do." Seraphine pulled an extra chair over and sat down next to Helmut.

He shook his head. "No, I won't have you slaving away in here on such a beautiful day. But what is it you want? Valentin isn't here. He's—"

"I know," Seraphine interrupted him. She stroked a few strands of hair out of his eyes. He looked overheated, a little irritated, as if she had disturbed him in the middle of something important. She peeked surreptitiously at the papers spread across the desk. If he really was as busy as he looked, perhaps it was not the right moment to present him with her gift. Or maybe it was? She laid the packet on her lap, beneath the table and out of sight.

Helmut frowned. "Hannah isn't here, either. She's with her mother and Flora, down by the river."

She could be in hell for all I care, Seraphine thought, but she said instead, "It's a wonder that they are finally treating themselves to a bit of peace and quiet together. They've made your mother quite nervous, you know, with all their frantic activity . . ."

"Ah, do I detect a touch of accusation there?" he said, giving her a teasing poke in her ribs. He had put down his pencil and no longer seemed in as much of a hurry to get back to his work. Seraphine was annoyed at herself for not thinking to bring along a glass of wine. A little refreshment would have done him good.

"My esteemed mother-in-law happens to be a very hardworking woman," Helmut said. "She's not used to being waited upon, as I've also explained to Mother. Sophia's intentions are nothing but good when she tries to be everybody's helper. And at the same time, she really ought to sit and put her feet up more. I'm sure she never gets the chance to do that in Nuremberg." He smiled. "And here we thought that our Swabian girls knew all about hard work . . . I think Sophia is a very nice woman, don't you?"

Seraphine shrugged. In her eyes, Sophia Brettschneider was about as common as a woman could be: excessively informal, with the same vulgar laugh as her daughter, and with only the most simpleminded of interests.

Silence settled over them as Seraphine thought frantically about how to turn their conversation to her gift. Helmut watched her for a moment with an absent smile, and then he picked up his pencil again and began to enter numbers into a list.

Seraphine frowned. Why was she always so self-conscious around Helmut? Why did she have so little to say to him? Of course, they understood one another perfectly without words. In fact, it was an intimate silence that bound them together. But why couldn't she just ask him how he felt? Whether he was happy to know that she was at his side, despite their star-crossed situation? And why didn't he ask *her* these things?

There had been days when Seraphine could have screamed in fury, frustration, and disappointment. She could have slapped the nearest person, hurled things, destroyed others. Of course, she did none of that. It would not have helped her or Helmut, neither of whom had chosen this life for themselves. So she smiled instead, became a picture of gentleness, never raised her voice as Hannah, so easily irritated, was apt to do. No, Seraphine put on a brave face until her face muscles threatened to freeze. And all of it was so exhausting that there were times when she was so tired she could barely lift a quill. She imagined herself a free-ranging animal trapped in a too-small cage.

Only in the seclusion of her room, when she and Valentin were alone and the night her only witness, did she give her feelings free rein. There in the dark she could do all the things that she had to renounce in the light, could give herself over to the turmoil she felt inside, and scream, moan, sob. She did not call it love. She had no word for it. All she knew was that, without that physical release—born of the deepest pain, from wrath and boundless despair—she would not have been able to go on living.

Valentin—he understood nothing. Or, really, he understood everything the wrong way. He actually believed that she would passionately give her love to him. Sometimes, if they were alone during the day—which, thank God, did not happen often—he searched for words for what happened between them at night. But Seraphine did not want to hear it.

"What . . . um . . . why are you actually here?"

Seraphine jumped. She had been so deep in her thoughts that it took her a moment to rediscover the weight on her lap.

"I have something for you. A present." With shaking hands, she laid the parcel on the table.

"For me?"

She nodded. "Open it."

"I don't know what I've done to deserve a gift."

Seraphine held her breath and watched him turn the pages one at a time. Why didn't he say anything? Did he not like it?

Finally, he closed the book and put it on the desk. "It is beautiful. And so well done . . ." He looked away from her.

"But . . . ," Seraphine said, continuing his unfinished sentence.

"But what am I supposed to do with it? If you want to make a gift of something as lovely as this, then you should give it to Valentin—"

"Valentin, Valentin," Seraphine interrupted him harshly. "He can't appreciate anything like this. Besides, you're the older brother—you're the one who makes the decisions when you talk to your customers. He even says that you're the cleverer one."

"Which is exactly why you should offer something as useful as this to *him*," Helmut said. He raised his hand before Seraphine could say anything. "On our next trip, *both* of us have to be at our best, and when it comes to selling, it's true that he is sometimes a little reserved. But that won't get us very far in Russ—" He broke off. "Oh, forget I said anything! Take the book and give it to your husband!" Helmut turned to the bookshelf and picked out a file of papers.

"You don't even talk to me anymore," Seraphine said, her voice quavering. She had not pictured things going this way. All the work, so much love, cast aside like trash.

"Oh, Sera, I didn't mean it like that. It's just . . . damn it!" He took a deep breath. "Valentin and I agreed not to say a word about our plans. But maybe it's good if you know." Helmut looked at her inquiringly. When she said nothing, he went on. "You must have noticed that we haven't made any plans for the Jakobi trade this year."

Seraphine nodded, although she had not noticed anything of the sort. The Jakobi trade was what they called the extra trips the Gönningers made every year after July 25—the feast day of St. James—to sell dried pear and apple. Seraphine tried not to think of how her father had gambled away her family's profits the year before.

"Well, this year we're going to miss the Jakobi trade. Valentin and I have decided to send the entire harvest to Rudi Thumm."

"Rudi Thumm? But . . . he lives in America now." Now Seraphine was completely confused. Was it actually worth it to send dried apple so far?

Helmut nodded. "Right. Good old Rudi, longtime friend of Valentin's, the very same Rudi who immigrated to America three years ago. He and Valentin have been exchanging letters since he left, so we know what he's up to. Rudi is convinced that our Swabian apple slices would sell well in his mostly German district over there. I was skeptical about sending dried fruit on such a long voyage, I'll admit. But the costs are acceptable, and if we pack it all up in solid wooden crates, then it should reach the other side safely. And a consignment like that means all sorts of paperwork, but if it pays off, it will be well worth it." Helmut patted a pile of customs and export documents.

Valentin was writing letters to a man in America? Seraphine considered the idea only briefly, because the next moment the consequences of what Helmut was telling her became clear.

"But that means you'll be staying here until the fall! That's . . . wonderful!" Spontaneously, she threw her arms around his neck and kissed him on his cheek. What a lovely surprise! And she was the first to find out about it. *Thank you, star fairy, thank you!*

Reluctantly, she let go of him again and composed herself.

"Well . . . that's true, but it's only one side of the coin." He shrugged. "The other side . . . I'm not sure that Hannah or you will take the other side nearly as well. The fact is: Valentin and I need the summer to prepare for our next journey. We won't only be going to Bohemia in the fall as we have for so long. Afterward we will continue on to Russia. To Odessa, to be exact. One of Father's cousins lives there, and he, Leonard, has been asking us for years to pay him a visit. A house to stay in in another country, for free! That's really something, isn't it? And someone who knows his way around over there, who speaks German and Russian—you can't get a better opening to do business. In the past, Father spoke about going off to Odessa, but he never managed to do it. Nor will he, now. But Valentin and I—we're really doing it! We're going to Russia!"

Seraphine's smile died while Helmut spoke. "Oh," she said in a soft voice, as Helmut's words settled onto her skin like a frost.

Helmut seemed unaware of the change in her mood. He chattered on cheerfully. "We won't be taking any vegetable seeds to Russia. They've got enough cabbages and turnips of their own." He laughed. "Cousin Leonard wrote that there are a lot of big estates around Odessa, and rich owners willing to spend a lot on their gardens because they're all trying to outdo each other. So Valentin and I will be specializing in flower seeds, and your book will be just what we need. It's like you knew where we were planning to go . . ." He fell silent for a moment. "Tulip bulbs wouldn't be a bad idea, either, but we might not even get there before the beginning of March, which is far too late to plant bulbs. So that leaves the seeds—and I've ordered only the very best from our suppliers. And we'll take a few roses, too. There's good business to be done!" He rubbed his hands together.

Seraphine nodded, but she was thinking: *Tulips, roses . . . I didn't even paint those!*

"God, I'm glad you're taking the news so well. I mean, you're the first to find out. Father knows, of course, but it took a lot to talk him into it." Helmut let out a harsh laugh. "But apart from him, we thought it would be for the best to keep our plans to ourselves for the time being. Mother will be so worried about us that she won't stop praying. And you know how talk gets around the village . . ."

A trip to Russia? Gradually, his words began to penetrate Seraphine's consciousness. Russia. That was . . . dangerous! Few from Gönningen had ever risked the long journey, and not all of them had come back. And Odessa, of all places! Just five years earlier, a neighbor had gone to Odessa. Johannes Wagner died miserably there, of consumption. His widow, Anna, had not been the same since, talking nonsense and sometimes wandering around the village like a madwoman. Grief drove her insane, the people said. Why couldn't Helmut just go to Bohemia, like he did every year? And if he absolutely had to go somewhere else, then to Alsace. What was the point in visiting a distant relative in Odessa? He didn't even know the man. *Stay here, I beg you! I love you. I can't survive long without you.* Seraphine's stomach tightened into a knot, but outwardly, she remained serene, plucked a bit of fluff from a sleeve, stood up, and opened the window.

What good would begging him do? Helmut trusted her so much that she was the only one he had told about his plans. In the face of such trust, how could she now burst into tears like a child? She couldn't. And one look at his face told her that all the begging in the world would be in vain. The ambition she saw there! The longing . . .

"Odessa," she repeated flatly. As if he had really said "Golgotha."

Helmut nodded. "Isn't it fantastic? Down the Danube on a ship—I can still hardly believe it. This is going to be such an adventure!" He wore a rapturous expression, as if already picturing the expanse of the Black Sea in front of him. "And we owe it all to Hannah. If she hadn't come up with the idea of sending the seed orders by post, then we would have to travel to Bohemia a second time. But like this, once we're done there we can head straight for Russia and be back again by May. Of course, this means more work for the rest of you, starting in January. I only hope you'll be able to get the orders packed and shipped on time." Helmut laughed. "Time for the women to roll up their sleeves for a change!" He did not sound terribly worried.

Hannah! All she ever heard was Hannah! *She* was the one driving Helmut away from home. She was to blame for putting this obsession into Helmut's head. He called it a dream. If he were married to her, Seraphine, then he wouldn't have to look for escape in dreams. She would have given him heaven right here on earth.

"Hannah really doesn't know about your plans yet?"

He shook his head. "Frankly, I don't know how I'm supposed to tell her. She . . ." His voice suddenly sounded pained.

Seraphine nodded. "I know what you want to say. Hannah would try to keep you here. She doesn't even like it when you men go off to the tavern. And she's so dependent on us all the time, so clingy—she simply isn't one of us, so how should she know that one has to let one's beloved husband go, and do so again and again? Will she ever learn it . . . ?" Seraphine surprised herself, talking like that.

Helmut frowned. "Saying goodbye is also hard for me. And Valentin, too, of course," he hastily added. "But you're right. Traveling is simply in our blood, and it has always been." He rolled his eyes. "God, I'm starting to sound like Mother."

Seraphine smiled. The layer of frost on her skin began to thaw. Maybe everything wasn't so bad after all. *She* was the daughter of a seed merchant. *She* understood Helmut. He could confide in her. And when he went to Russia . . . then she would have to be strong. As she already had to be strong, every day. Her gaze stroked Helmut's gleaming face.

He took her hand in his. "My heart feels lighter, knowing that you know," he said. "It's probably for the best if I tell Hannah, too, and the sooner the better. She simply has to get used to the idea of getting by without me around."

"Don't do it," Seraphine said. She held his hand tighter. "I mean, Hannah would fret about it every day. She'd complain and reproach you and try to talk you out of going to Russia."

His frown deepened, and Seraphine went on hurriedly. "I'm sure she doesn't mean it badly, but you won't have a free minute after you tell her. And you need the time to prepare for the trip." She turned toward the table covered with paperwork. "It is best to keep Hannah in the dark about Russia as long as you can. Once you're gone, she will have enough time to get used to it. And I'll still be here to help her, however I can." Seraphine was especially proud of her last sentence, though it all but made her retch.

Helmut looked at her pensively. After a moment of silence, he said, "I think you're right. I don't want her to get upset so soon after the birth. Maybe it really is best if she doesn't know about it. Not yet."

Chapter Twenty-Three

When Sophia Brettschneider left at the end of June, Hannah cried for a long time; she had no idea how long it would be before she saw her mother again.

Her sadness at Sophia's departure was short-lived, for just a few days later Helmut asked Hannah if she had heard of the Jakobi trade. She had, but she had not realized that the travels that followed the Feast of St. James at the end of July were as fixed a part of the calendar as the journeys in autumn and winter. Another trip? Another separation? She burst into tears again. But Helmut said that Valentin and he had decided to skip the Jakobi trade that year. Instead, they were going to send all the dried fruit from the last harvest to America by ship. Of course, it meant a lot of documentation had to be completed, but they would save an entire sales trip. When she understood that, at least this year, she had escaped this particular fate, her tears became those of joy.

In the weeks that followed, she spent as much time as she could with Helmut. Once, they visited Reutlingen together, and another time went off to Tübingen. They worked well side by side, too, whether they were getting the packing room into shape or toiling out in the fields. They had a similar rhythm and complemented one another instead of getting in each other's way. For the more labor-intensive tasks—for example, the late-summer harvest—Valentin and Seraphine were also involved, of course, and even Wilhelmine and Aunt Finchen helped some days. But Hannah and Helmut filled baskets with apples and pears faster than any of the others, laughing as they did.

Little Flora was with them constantly, either wrapped tightly against Hannah's chest or lying in the same high-wheeled carriage that Wilhelmine had used for her own children.

When there was no work to do in the fields, Helmut spent hours in his father's office or in the packing room. Hannah was amazed at the countless letters that went back and forth between seed growers, gardeners, and the Kerners. Besides the suppliers, there was correspondence with the customs union, cards listing train times and connections, and information about ship traffic on the Danube. Hannah had never suspected that so much went into the preparations before a seed merchant even went out with his or her seed sack.

When late summer began to cool toward autumn, the men were more on edge. It seemed to Hannah that the brothers lived for nothing but the day when they could finally pack their things and get on the road. It saddened her to think that Helmut was so lighthearted about leaving her and Flora behind. And at the same time, it increased her resolve to enjoy every moment they had together until his departure.

She would gladly have joined Helmut in the office more often when he had to deal with his paperwork—simply to spend more time with her husband. But usually Seraphine was already in the second chair in the office, filling out a list or sorting papers into thick files, trying to look as important as she could. Hannah did not know when Seraphine had started to do office work. Probably sometime in the weeks Hannah had spent so much time with her mother . . . It was not that Helmut and Seraphine ever made her feel that she was not wanted in the office. More than once, Seraphine even offered to induct her into the complicated ordering system. But Hannah thanked her and left again, acting as if she had countless other exciting tasks to take care of. When she saw the two of them sitting so close, side by side, with Seraphine's silver-blond hair next to Helmut's unruly mop of hair, she could hardly contain her jealousy. But there were also days when her heart was more generous and she could say to herself: Let Seraphine have her fun! What was she doing, after all? Just helping Helmut with the office work.

Occasionally, Helmut and Hannah walked to the top of Rossberg, sometimes before the day's work began, sometimes at dusk. Hannah liked the evening walks the most. When every stalk of grass seemed to hide a chirping cricket and when the earth underfoot was still warm from the sun, she felt more bound to the burgeoning natural world all around than at any other time. Up there, on the mountain, so much closer to the sky, they talked more intimately. Up there, Helmut could open up about how angry it made him to have to work so hard to convince his father about any new idea. Up there, his voice took on a strange timbre whenever he talked about setting off for the new shores he longed so much to see. Hannah did not always understand what he was talking about, and sometimes his words frightened her a little. When that happened, she took his hand in hers and listened in silence.

Up on Rossberg, Hannah could tell him about the strange observations she had made about Seraphine. Once, she had found her sister-in-law in her and Helmut's bedroom. When she had asked Seraphine what she was doing there, Seraphine had answered that she had gotten lost. Gotten lost! In her own house! Hannah confided to Helmut that she felt uneasy seeing little Flora in Seraphine's arms, because she was afraid her sister-in-law might do something bad to the child. And even though Helmut dismissed Hannah's fears as nonsensical and even defended Seraphine, it lightened Hannah's heart a little to talk about her fear.

Then, abruptly, summer disappeared. The spiderwebs that, the day before, had been shining and silvery in the sunlight now hung heavy with raindrops. The birds stopped singing, and fog filled the valley around Gönningen. The trees, freed from their heavy loads of apples and pears, once again stretched their branches skyward. Some were already losing their leaves.

Departures and farewells hung in the air, and a peculiar mood spread through the town.

⚜

Seraphine pressed the pillow to her face and breathed in deeply. It was still a little warm. How good it smelled! Of a man, of earth, as warm as if it had trapped the last rays of the summer sun.

With a sigh, Seraphine put the pillow down again. Her eyes roamed across the room and came to rest on the colorful patchwork carpet that lay at the end of the bed. It made her think of the carpet she had woven herself. She had gotten the brown and white wool for it from Wilhelmine. She had changed the threads in the weft again and again until they seemed to run into each other like paint on wet paper. Her work was so much finer, so much more elegant than that ugly, colorful thing.

If Helmut had become her husband, she would have given him beauty. But Helmut was not her husband. And this room was not her room but instead Helmut and Hannah's.

She could not have explained to anyone why she kept returning to the room. Once, Hannah had even caught her.

She ran her fingertips over Helmut's clothes, which lay on a chair, thoughtlessly cast aside. The smell of him was even stronger in his shirts. With one ear listening for any sound out in the hallway—everything was quiet upstairs; the others were already eating breakfast—she stuffed one of the shirts inside her cardigan. She would place it under her pillow like a talisman.

Seraphine turned to leave, Helmut's shirt pressed firmly against her chest, when a stack of documents on the bedside table caught her

169

eye. Weren't those the shipping papers meant for the supplies already put aside for Odessa? Wasn't he afraid that Hannah would find them? Looking more closely, she saw that Odessa had not yet been written in as the destination. Relief flooded her—so Hannah truly did not yet know.

Hadn't Helmut said that he wanted to deliver the papers to the customs office in Tübingen that day? Hadn't he talked about special import regulations that he had to find out about?

Seraphine had the papers in her hand. She couldn't do what she wanted, which was to run downstairs and give them to him. Instead she crouched, then went down on her knees, slowly, as if each movement was momentously important.

An accumulation of fluffy dust balls stirred beneath the bed—lazy housekeepers' favorite pets. Seraphine sniffed disdainfully, carefully raised a mass of dust with one hand, and pushed the stack of papers underneath it.

Then she brushed her hands clean on the dress Hannah had slung over the back of the second chair and left quickly. She had to get Helmut's shirt safely to her room.

Minutes later, wearing her nicest smile, she joined the others at the table.

✕

"Blast it, where are the papers?" Pushing his fingers through his hair, Helmut strode through the bedroom, rummaged through the things on the chair, looked in the wardrobe. "I could have sworn I put them down here on the table, but now I don't know anymore. They're certainly not in the office . . . damn it all!"

"What's so important about the papers?" Hannah asked. She was standing in the doorway with Flora in her arms. "Why are you making such a fuss?" She went over to him and tried to kiss him on the cheek, but he brushed her off impatiently.

"You don't understand. I need them!"

"If I don't understand, maybe it's because you never explain anything to me," she replied, more sharply than intended. For days, Helmut had been as grumpy as an old bear—tetchy with her and with hardly a moment to spare for Flora. She had tried to believe that he was acting like that because his impending departure and their separation was as hard for him as it was for her. But what she truly felt was that, in his head, he was already walking along a road somewhere else. Hannah swallowed, fighting down the lump rising in her throat that would soon turn into tears. *You old crybaby!* she silently chided herself.

"Aren't you coming?" Valentin poked his head in the door. "If we don't get going now, we'll get to Tübingen just in time for Mr. Krohmer's two-hour lunch break."

"The papers are gone!" Helmut threw both hands in the air helplessly.

Valentin frowned. "What do you mean, the papers—"

"They're gone! I can't find them!" Helmut yelled at him.

"If we all look, maybe we'll find them." Hannah did her best to placate him. She laid Flora on the bed and looked around. But she really had no idea where to look.

"My God, Helmut." Valentin rolled his eyes. "If we don't take care of it today, it'll be too late. Today is Krohmer's last day. By the time his successor's found his feet, we'll already be in Russia, but won't have the right import papers!"

"Valentin!" Helmut hissed.

For a moment, all three froze like statues. Hannah was the first to break the paralysis.

"Russia?" She shook her head. *"Russia?"*

Helmut groaned. He glared furiously at Valentin. "Thank you so much, dear brother. Now Hannah has to find out about it like this."

Valentin, chastened, scratched at his chin, then left the room without another word.

Hannah gaped at her husband in disbelief. What was going on?

"I wanted to tell you about it long ago, but . . ."

"*What* did you want to tell me?"

"Hannah . . ." Helmut stroked her hair, but to Hannah his hand felt like a stranger's. "Now don't cry. I'll be back for Flora's birthday at the latest."

Hannah threw her hands over her face and shook free of him. Her body quaked with her silent sobs. For Flora's sake, she pressed her lips together tightly to stop from bawling out loud.

Russia . . .

He would be gone for half an eternity. What if something happened to him? She would not survive that.

Suddenly, a thought occurred to her. She lowered her hands and fixed her eyes critically on Helmut.

"So when were you planning to let me in on your plans? I mean, you're leaving on Monday." The icy tone in her own voice scared her.

He sighed. "I wanted to tell you long ago, truly, but it was never the right moment. And then . . . well, I know you . . ." He was the one who broke eye contact first.

"And the others already know, don't they?" Hannah could not stop her voice from breaking at the end.

"Yes. No! I mean . . ." Helmut twisted his mouth. "Father knows, of course. We couldn't finance the trip without his permission. And Mother . . ." He shrugged. "She always frets and worries so much that we didn't want to upset her unnecessarily early."

"Seraphine . . . well, she . . ." Like a schoolboy pressed for an answer he doesn't know, Helmut shifted clumsily from one foot to the other. "She's one of us, after all, so—"

Hannah cut him off with a snort. One of us! And what did that make *her*? "Then that makes me the only idiot in the house, at least aside from your mother." Before she could do anything to prevent it, she was overcome by another fit of crying and once again hid her face behind her hands.

Why did he have so little trust in her? Why did he go out into the big, wide world when he had a wife and child? Was she such a terrible wife? She tried so hard.

Helmut's attempts to calm her down were in vain.

"See?" he cried, suddenly upset himself. "That's why I didn't say anything. I knew you'd react like this! But not Seraphine, oh no, she reacted very differently. Composed and calm, though I'm sure she's not happy to be losing Valentin, either. But she understands that a man has to do what has to be done."

With a groan, Helmut went down on his knees.

Hannah watched him from between her fingers. *No, I won't forgive him. I don't care how long he kneels there,* she thought bitterly.

But Helmut was busy with something else. He propped himself against the bed frame with one hand and rummaged under the bed with the other.

"Now look what we have here . . ." He pulled out the dusty stack of papers, blew off the dust, and shook his head. "Never in a million years did they slide under the bed by themselves." He turned toward Hannah, who had picked up Flora—who had also begun to cry—and was rocking her in her arms, sniffing hard all the while to stop her nose from running.

Helmut narrowed his eyes at them. Then he let out a dry laugh.

"Why look at me like that?" Hannah flared, furious and miserable. "Am I also to blame for your mess now?" He could travel all the way to hell for all she cared.

Helmut abruptly turned and walked away, but he turned back in the doorway.

"If it weren't so hard to swallow, I would say that this"—he brandished the papers in the air—"is your handiwork. Because you don't want me to go away. Because you would rather sit on me like a brood hen on her chick. But I'll tell you this: You can't tie me down! Not with your tears and not with ridiculous tricks like this!"

Hannah grabbed the nearest object—of all things, it was the Bible on the night table—and hurled it at Helmut's head.

Chapter Twenty-Four

The brothers were in a more muted mood than usual on the way to Bohemia that year. Instead of the anticipation he normally felt, Helmut was in low spirits; the incident with Hannah just before he left was still playing on his mind. But Valentin's gloom stemmed from Seraphine's excessively cool goodbye, which had not extended even as far as a kiss.

A kind of weariness had crept in stealthily, too, something new for both of them. They knew the route, they stayed in the same inns they always did, and the customers were the same as always. Even the ride on the horse-drawn railway from Budweis, which had always been one of the high points of their journey, left them cold. In truth, Helmut and Valentin were anxiously looking forward to their great Russian adventure.

The business they had to do ran smoothly enough, although Helmut and Valentin had to work hard to convince some of their customers about their new order-delivery process. What other choice did the customers have than to accept the new system? They needed the seeds, and they needed them at the beginning of the year, which wasn't really all that far off.

At the end of December, in good health and energized—their excitement about Russia was a huge motivation—the brothers, with a full order book, made their way to Ulm, fifty miles east of Gönningen, where they would embark on the long journey by ship.

While still in Bohemia, they had debated at length about whether they should pick up the goods they needed for Odessa in Gönningen. They had already been away for a couple of months, and it would have meant seeing their family again for at least a few days, but the trip would have taken at least a week. Besides, leaving again after such a short visit would have been exceptionally hard on everyone.

In the end, they decided against it and sent a letter to their neighbor Matthias asking him to take the three wooden crates, already packed and marked for Russia, directly to the ship in Ulm with his horse and cart. There, they gave him a bundle of letters for the family as well as a thick envelope that contained the order book. Every page of the book contained a single order, and for every order Helmut and Valentin had written explicit instructions so that the women would have no trouble assembling the seed packets and getting them in the mail.

The ship that would take them from Ulm as far as Galati was called *Malinka*. By the time they reached Galati, they would already have a big part of the journey behind them, and from there to where the Danube emptied into the Black Sea was only about a hundred miles. In Galati, they would have to transfer their cargo onto a larger ship than the one that would carry them downriver.

But first they had to find the right ship in Ulm. While Valentin kept watch on the crates containing the seeds, Helmut picked his way along the narrow quay among hundreds of people, stacked crates, and baggage.

How unfamiliar everything around him was! The noise and shouting were deafening, and the excitement among the people all around hung overhead like something palpable and almost physically within reach. Dozens of ships' hulls pressed close like a pod of whales. When Helmut finally spotted the *Malinka* sandwiched between two larger ships, he let out a sigh of relief.

They would sail downriver as part of a convoy with seven other ships, the captain explained to him. Departure was planned for around midday, and all the cargo had to be loaded by then.

The brothers watched nervously as the crates and their valuable cargo of seed were stowed in the belly of the ship. What if the ship leaked and the seeds got wet? What if vermin ate through the wood crates and damaged the goods? Helmut and Valentin would gladly have stationed themselves in the hold and watched over their cargo like shepherds guarding their flock. But that was prohibited, so they had no choice but to make themselves as comfortable as they could on deck and do their best to forget about the crates during the long trip down the Danube.

"You're lucky," said a man who settled onto the bench beside them a little later. "Our captain knows what he's about." Like the brothers, he, too, was wrapped warmly against the winter chill. He wore two coats, one over his obviously thin frame and another over the top, plus a huge fur cap on his head and a scarf that he had wrapped until it covered his chin. His face was barely visible, but Valentin guessed he was in his fifties. The man said, "His name is Mariusz Dobrez, and they call him the old wolf of the Danube. This is his twenty-eighth year on the stretch from Ulm to Galati, and so far he's only lost five ships. And stayed alive, to boot!" He laughed so hard that he shook from head to toe. Then he introduced himself as Herbert Richter and told them he was a businessman, but did not go into any details.

The brothers exchanged a look. "He's lost five ships?"

"Don't worry. It's no more dangerous to travel now than at any other time of year. Just colder," Richter replied calmly. "Although it will probably get a little more difficult once we get past Pressburg. Last summer was dry everywhere, and the Danube is low, so we'll have to watch out. But we can rely on the Danube wolf and his crew."

"How do you know all this?" Valentin asked. He turned and looked out over the silvery, smooth-flowing waters. The *Malinka* would lead the convoy, which meant they would have a good view of the river ahead. But wouldn't it be less dangerous to sail as the second, third, or fourth ship?

The man grinned. "I'm an old Danube wolf myself. This is my seventh trip to Vidin, but I've been to Galati, too. Worked with the Turks there—business . . ." His last words were reduced to a whisper while he cast a disgruntled look at a man with his wife and six children who, along with a huge pile of blankets and a lot of noise, made themselves comfortable beside them.

"Immigrants. On their way to Izmail, near Odessa, I'll bet," he murmured in a slightly contemptuous tone. Then he said loudly, "So where is your road taking you?"

While Helmut told Richter about the invitation to Odessa, Valentin leaned back and thought about the way ahead.

They had done it! They were following the river that meant so much promise to so many people. The Danube wound its way through many countries, changing its name as it went. Donau in Germany, then Dunaj, Duna, Dunav, Dunaja . . . only to empty into the Black Sea after a journey of nearly two thousand miles.

A strange melancholy rose in Valentin, and he wondered where it came from. Was it because they were stepping off their old, familiar routes? Was it homesickness for Gönningen, so close to Ulm and yet still out of reach? Or did it come from fear of the unknown ahead of them?

Sometime in the future, no later than the end of spring, they would once again pass all the churches, ruined castles, and pretty towns here, but from the other direction. Would he and his brother have changed then? Valentin smiled. The best he could hope for would be for them to return home better and wiser—and rich, too.

They had found a good traveling companion in Herbert Richter. He showed them points of interest along the way, and knew the names of the towns and villages they drifted past. But he could sit and be silent, too. He shared valuable information with them—for instance, it was better to replenish their provisions in Vidin, where it was much less expensive, than in Orsova, where most travelers stocked up.

From Vienna, the journey continued on to Pressburg, where the convoy drifted with the strong current around the castle. At that speed, they calculated that they would make the journey in less than five weeks. But Helmut and Valentin had rejoiced too soon. Just after Pressburg, small hills rose above the river's surface, sometimes overgrown with reeds and willows, and sometimes covered with stones and gravel. The ships had to pick their way carefully through the confusion of water grasses and low-hanging willow branches. Until they passed Komárno, Richter told them, they had to sail with the utmost caution. Many a ship had been stranded on one of those little islands, and more than one had ripped open its belly on sharp gravel.

While the ship crept slowly past the islands, hundreds of cranes, cormorants, and bustards rose from the reedy watercourse, circled high, and dived at schools of fish, only to have part of their booty snatched away by the storks that lurked at the water's edge.

"Not very bright," Valentin said, and the brothers laughed, watching the birds. "Letting the storks steal the fruits of their labor."

Richter grinned. "No more foolish than some who go to Russia, if I may say so. You'll have to keep an eye on your belongings, especially in the harbor at Galati. There's no shortage of crooks there just waiting for an unsuspecting traveler to rob!"

"Thank you for the tip," Helmut said. "So far, we've had a good nose for dangerous places—nothing has happened to us yet. And besides, there are two of us . . ."

The days passed and became weeks. January 1851 would soon come to an end. The brothers had grown accustomed to the rhythm of life on board, which was not nearly as monotonous as they had imagined it would be. Customs officials constantly came on to check passports and cargo, and in a few of the more perilous stretches, the captain brought pilots on board—watching them work was always exciting. The brothers had become friendly with some of the sailors and their fellow passengers, and time was spent singing and playing cards, and occasionally bickering with one another. The journey itself constantly surprised them: in Hungary, which the brothers traditionally thought of as flat given the extensive Pannonian plains, the river actually wound between two towering mountain ridges and grew very temperamental. Valentin, who thought they were passing through the notorious Iron Gates, was corrected by the captain—the Iron Gates were still at least five days away.

It was the start of the fifth week on board. They were due to tie up in Orsova that evening, where passengers would disembark and others would come on board. In front of them, strangely clefted stone walls thrust skyward. It looked as if the Danube was flowing directly toward those towering cliffs! Somehow, they would find a path through—they always had so far, Helmut thought, trying to calm himself. He gave Valentin a sharp jab, waking him from a doze.

Valentin grumbled, but then pulled himself together and straightened up from his half-reclined position. "What's the matter?" He yawned.

"The current's suddenly extremely strong. And look how narrow the river is!"

"My God, we're sailing straight into the rocks!"

It had become as dark as the bottom of a ravine. Barely an arm's length away, steep crags jutted from the water, which foamed and swirled as if boiling.

"God save us," Valentin murmured. "This is bad."

There they were, in the grip of the Iron Gates.

Would the most dangerous stretch of the entire Danube be their demise? *I don't want to die!* Helmut thought, panicking. *What will become of Hannah and Flora? I want to go back to Gönningen.*

In his mind's eye, he suddenly saw his old teacher, Grimme, unrolling a map of Europe and tracing a snaking line marked Donau with his stick. Helmut and Valentin had loved their geography lessons, and they had listened reverently to old Grimme's stories about the treacherous narrows and the perpetual battle between water and rock. The Southern Carpathians. The Balkan Mountains. And between them the mighty Danube. Courageous men challenging the Iron Gates in their ships. Even when the lesson had finished, the brothers could not drag themselves away from the map. At night, they had dreamed of the wild river, and what it would be like to sail down it themselves one day.

And now . . .

A paralyzing fear coalesced into a ball in the pit of Helmut's stomach. The old Donau wolf—why didn't he do something?

So this is what it feels like to die.

He closed his eyes and waited for the death he felt was certain, waited for the ship to be smashed to smithereens against the rocks.

A few moments passed, and through his closed eyelids he saw a brightness and felt a warmth. He blinked tentatively and saw sunlight. That was it? Was he already in heaven? It was that simple? No pain, no agony . . .

"Made it!" he suddenly heard, a voice in his left ear. A hand came down on his shoulder. Trembling, he turned around. "Those rapids are a vision of hell, aren't they?" Richter laughed. He had been up the entire night playing cards, and he looked more tired and gaunt than usual, but his mood could hardly have been better.

"What would you say if I were to invite you two to a jug of decent wine tonight in Orsova?" Richter shook his money bag, which hung heavily from his belt. "Early tomorrow, we'll reach the Iron Gates, and when the captain picks up the key to unlock them"—he laughed at his metaphor—"it is useful for us passengers to be not entirely in possession of our senses."

"What?" Helmut cried in horror. "That wasn't the Iron Gates?"

They were in luck: the key to the Iron Gates fit perfectly. The pilots brought the *Malinka* through safely, and the rest of the convoy also made it through that stony gorge unscathed.

Once they were past the Iron Gates, the river grew more placid, and the brothers' tensions eased.

Richter left the ship in Vidin to pursue his business there. The brothers restocked their provisions for the next leg of the journey.

The wild ride of the past few weeks had made the Danube sleepy, and it wound on sluggishly toward the Black Sea.

At the end of the fifth week, the *Malinka* finally berthed in Galati. For Helmut and Valentin, it meant they had to watch over the unloading of their crates. They also had to look for a new ship for the journey onward. The ships that sailed into the Black Sea were larger than any of the ships they had seen so far.

Beyond Galati, the land was lush, overgrown, and impenetrable. Forests of trees unlike any they had ever seen lined both banks; impregnable walls of dense-growing reeds and rushes that blocked any more distant vistas opened up only to reveal an occasional small village, and the sea, now close, gave the air a briny taste. The Danube split and then split again, the central branch of the river taking them to Sulina, where the ship docked to take on freight. One of the sailors pointed out a sign attached to a towering lighthouse: a large black zero painted on a white background. It marked the end of the Danube, where it spilled into the Black Sea.

Seeing that gave Helmut a strange feeling. They had grown so used to the rhythm of the Danube, and had met so many interesting people—ship captains, pilots, customs men, passengers—and called in at so many unfamiliar ports. Now, the journey took them out onto the open sea. God willing, they would tie up in Odessa the following evening.

Helmut and Valentin looked at each other and laughed. Odessa had been calling, and they were finally answering that call!

Chapter Twenty-Five

It was already dark when the ship moored in Odessa harbor. And one last time, the brothers had to unload their crates. Then, on unsteady legs, they wandered through the free port, where the goods they had brought with them would be stored for now.

They were no longer in any kind of hurry. Silently, they stood on the quay and gazed across the black waters, lit here and there by the lamps of a ship.

Finally, Helmut gave himself a shake and stretched one arm across his brother's shoulder. "Shall we?"

"We certainly shall, dear brother!"

Both spoke with more confidence than they actually felt.

After a half hour's march through the city, they finally found their way to Leonard's house. Was this really the place? This huge house? Helmut rapped with the door knocker—an enormous brass lion's head—hesitantly.

Leonard and his wife, Eleonore, dragged the brothers inside like long-lost sons, embracing and kissing them effusively although they had never met. For the brothers, such an outpouring of emotion felt very strange indeed. Back home in Gönningen, such a welcoming would have been unthinkable.

Then Leonard and Eleonore's five daughters with their husbands and children came pouring in, and Helmut and Valentin were greeted by them as wholeheartedly as by their parents. The circle grew to include the neighbors, and in a short time it seemed that half the district had gathered in the house to share in the welcome. The brothers, exhausted from their trip, would have liked nothing more than to sneak off somewhere quiet, but for the next few hours escape was out of the question. They let themselves be led through the house, where glasses of vodka were pressed into their hands. They pulled from their packs the gifts they had brought: damson plum and pear brandy for Leonard, the finest Swabian linen for his wife, and sweet tidbits from Bohemia for the daughters. Eleonore especially seemed overjoyed at the fine fabric. Even after thirty years away, she had not completely shaken off her homesickness for the old country, she admitted tearfully to the brothers.

After the spontaneous welcome party that went on long into the night, Helmut and Valentin finally slumped into their beds and fell asleep in seconds.

The next morning, Helmut asked Leonard to show them the way back to the free port. They wanted to make a detailed inspection of everything they had brought. Although Leonard wanted to show them around the city, they were not to be dissuaded. They first needed to know how well or badly their sensitive cargo had survived the long journey.

"I can hardly believe it," Helmut murmured to himself, his eyes gleaming as he opened the second crate. "If the roses look as good as everything in here, we're saved!"

Valentin was still poking through the first open crate. "The lily bulbs look as if they've just come out of the ground," he said. "They're not shriveled at all, not the slightest bit dry, even on the outermost parts—and after coming all this way!" He swept his arm out wide in a gesture meant to encompass the enormous storage area but had to quickly pull his arm out of the way of one of the countless horse-drawn carts. "It's a miracle that anything in this madhouse is where it ought to be." Valentin looked respectfully toward the customs officer observing them. "The guys here seem to really know what they're doing."

"And nothing's disappeared," Helmut went on, keeping his voice low. "When I think how uneasy I felt yesterday evening, just leaving the goods here, where we could not watch them, but everything is here, and it's all in perfect condition!" He couldn't stop grinning his lopsided grin. "When we write home about this . . ."

Wearing a triumphant expression, Valentin looked up from the third crate. "The roses are also in excellent shape!" He lifted up a bare rosebush, its roots wrapped in a scrap of sackcloth. "No dehydration and no trace of frostbite!" The next moment, a hand clapped him solidly on the back.

"Well, everything in order?" Leonard was smiling so broadly that the ends of his moustache bobbed upward. "Your goods are as safe here in the free port as they would be in the vaults of the Vatican. No one can get near them without the right papers."

Helmut threw a companionable arm across Leonard's shoulders. "This is such a load off my mind. Nothing has been damaged at all. And if that isn't a good sign for the business we want to do here . . ." He realized he was shouting just to be heard in the rising din of voices in the warehouse.

"I suggest we leave the crates in the care of this gentleman awhile longer and find our way back into the city. We need to raise a glass to your business!" Leonard shouted back.

"What about paying the customs duties? Shouldn't we get that behind us as soon as we can?" Their Russian business was off to such a promising start that he did not want to make a mistake now. Besides, he was worried about the cost of the storage.

Leonard dismissed the idea with a wave. "We have a free port. You only pay customs duty when you sell the goods. As long as they stay here, they won't cost you a ruble. So, time to go. I know a little tavern where they can fill our glasses with the best wine in the region!"

Happy and lighthearted, the three men made their way to one of the steep stairways that connected the harbor with the city proper, situated at a higher level.

The rest of the day passed as it had begun: Helmut and Valentin overcome by a flood of emotions, mixed with a certain pensiveness.

Leonard had told them about rich estates with beautiful parks, located along the coast around Odessa. And in every one of his letters, he had dangled the prospect of the good business to be done in the city on the Black Sea. But the brothers had never entirely believed him. Good business—that was always a question of perspective. Leonard had also written that through his work as a doll maker he had achieved his own modest wealth.

Modest wealth?

The first shock of the day came with the realization that his modest wealth was an enormous understatement. The evening before, they had been so tired that they had barely registered the sheer splendor of the huge house the extended family shared. When they saw it for the first time in daylight, it took their breath away. Situated high in the western part of the city, with a magnificent view over Odessa Bay, the house was furnished as sumptuously as a czar's palace. The windows reached from the floor almost to the ceiling, and the streaming sunlight lent the rooms a depth that made them appear even larger. Instead of a garden, there was an enormous inner courtyard, in the center of which a large fountain spouted water high in the air from a dozen nozzles.

A fountain? In February? Valentin asked Leonard if it sometimes froze, and Leonard replied that while certainly Odessa suffered from the icy east winds, winters were otherwise very mild, and the temperature seldom fell below freezing.

A mild winter? For the brothers, that description had as little to do as anything else with how they had pictured Russia.

Russia . . . in Helmut's and Valentin's eyes, Russia meant little more than poverty. Small wooden shacks that barely stood up to the Russian winters. Haggard farmers squeezing the last drop of milk from the udder of their only cow. Faces deeply grooved by gloom and a life-time of deprivation. *That* was what the few Gönningers who had been to Russia talked about in the taverns.

Those who had visited Russia in the past had always gone to see relatives, just as Valentin and Helmut had. And the relatives they had gone to see invariably had emigrated during the famine thirty years earlier, hoping to find a better life in Russia. But that better life eluded many of them. "Death for the first, dearth for the second, bread for the third"—it was a saying often repeated when conversation turned to the émigrés, and it meant that at least three generations passed before one could even find one's footing in that land. No one said a word about anyone like Leonard and his wife and the wealth they had amassed.

Leonard, his chest swollen with pride, led them through his Odessa. They strolled past palatial company buildings, and Leonard had a story to tell about every one of them. It seemed that Leonard knew every-body they encountered, and that everybody knew him. Every few steps he stopped to exchange a few words with this or that elegantly attired gentleman or to kiss the hand of a well-to-do lady.

They crossed broad streets so busy that they had to wait for a gap among the many horse-drawn carts, droshkies, and sulkies to make it safely across. A babble of Russian, German, Polish, and Armenian spilled from the countless cafés and bars, streamed from the many small markets. Even the droshky drivers who stopped to ask if they were in need of a ride spoke different languages. When Helmut remarked on this, Leonard screwed up his nose.

"All the immigrants are starting to become a problem. They're all hoping for their lucky break, but few want to work for it. If things keep on like this, we won't be able to fend off the beggars in a few years."

Helmut and Valentin exchanged a look. Words like that from a man who was new to the country himself just a few decades earlier . . .

They were also amazed at the many large parks that linked the sections of the city. All of Gönningen could have fit in one of them five times over! *The Odessites appear to be true garden lovers,* Helmut thought as they walked along another tree-lined path.

Leonard, who had noticed the way Helmut looked around in the parks, said, "Just wait until they get their leaves again. Then wherever you go in Odessa you feel like you're walking beneath a green, shady parasol—it's magnificent. Did you know that they have planted more than forty thousand trees inside the city in the last twenty years? Some of them died off within the first few years—the summers can be bone-dry—but most of them have managed to pull through and have adapted to the conditions. They don't have much choice, do they? Adapt or die!" Leonard laughed gleefully.

Again, the brothers exchanged a look. Each knew what the other was thinking: forty thousand trees—the people of Odessa dealt on a different scale altogether.

How would the flowers and rosebushes they had brought with them cope with the icy winter winds and the dry summers?

Adapt or die . . .

Despite Leonard's belief that the city only revealed its true magnificence in spring, on that sunny winter's day Odessa looked as fine as a woman dressed up for a ball. How would they sell their paltry seeds here? They had assumed all along that they would be offering the Russians something special, from the wealthier world. But now, looking at the prosperity on display, they had their doubts. In Bohemia, they were important men, whose opinions and advice were taken seriously. But here . . .

When they were finally sitting in the tavern, Leonard ordered wine and food for them in fluent Russian—or did Odessa have its own language? When the waiter left again, it was Valentin who first voiced his concerns.

"I'm a little worn out, to be honest. They say that we seed traders are born to walk, but I've learned otherwise just on our walk through Odessa. This city is . . . huge!"

Leonard nodded but was distracted by the platter of food the waiter carried. With great enthusiasm, Leonard announced, "Blini and caviar" as soon as the platter was set down. He took one of the small pancakes, scooped onto it some of the red roe from the center of the platter, and pushed the whole construction into his mouth.

Another exchange of glances between the brothers. Caviar! In an establishment as fine as this, they had counted on cutlery, or at least a spoon. Were things really so different in Odessa?

Valentin looked at Leonard almost in desperation. "And the wealth here! Everywhere you look! How can it be that the streets here are practically lined with gold?"

Leonard's brow furrowed, giving him the countenance of a wise old man. "Who says the streets of Odessa are lined with gold? No, no, my boy, in Odessa one has to work just as hard as anywhere else, if not harder."

Abashed at being corrected, Valentin turned away.

Helmut leaped into the breach for his brother. "But what about you? I mean, you came here with nothing yourself. And look at you now. Your wife and daughters are dressed like princesses. Your house is practically a palace, and you are a respected businessman. How can a simple doll maker prosper like that?"

Leonard stopped chewing, then half choked on his blin and began to cough loudly. Morsels of food landed on the tablecloth. His coughing fit transformed into braying laughter that went on for a long time, and very soon all eyes were turned toward them.

Embarrassed, Helmut looked down at the floor. His relative's behavior was incomprehensible to him.

After a bit, Leonard calmed down. "The doll maker!" He was still grinning broadly. "Do you seriously believe I earned my money with dolls?"

Helmut shrugged. He was beginning not to care at all about how Leonard earned his living. He just wanted him to behave a little more unobtrusively.

"You wrote yourself that you were a doll maker," Valentin said, frowning.

"Yes, but only because . . ." Leonard began to laugh, and again it took him some time to compose himself. "Because that's what the people here call me! Five daughters! Five daughters and not a single son! That's why they call me the doll maker!" He shrugged casually, but his moustache was still hopping with glee.

For a moment, there was absolute silence at the table, then laughter rang simultaneously from all three throats, and neither Helmut nor Valentin cared how much attention they drew in the upscale tavern.

When they were finally done wiping the tears from their eyes and cooling their throats with a fresh glass of wine, Leonard grew serious.

"I think it's time I told you a little about my life."

Chapter Twenty-Six

"The first year here was not as hard as I'd imagined," Leonard began. "Although, admittedly, I might be the only one who can say that . . . Most of those who immigrated regretted their decision bitterly. My first wife—God rest her soul—had the idea to open a small shop, and we did that."

"Here in Odessa?" Helmut asked.

Leonard shook his head. "No. We were in Carlsthal, about four hours from here. I obtained all my goods from Russian tradesmen: baskets, boots and saddles, ironware, grain and seeds. Our countrymen were happy that they could talk to me in German. Many of them found the Russian language hard to learn, you know?"

Valentin nodded. "In Bohemia, we could get by with German, but here—"

"I had no problem with it," Leonard interrupted him. "Seems I have an ear for Russian. And the people came from far and wide to shop at Leonard's. Those were good times!" He reached for another blin.

"Then you got a taste of success early on." Helmut looked admiringly at him.

Leonard grimaced. "Well, just so I didn't get too comfortable, fate threw a hard test in my path." He furrowed his brow. "Didn't your father ever tell you anything about this?"

The brothers shook their heads.

Leonard sighed. "It's been a long time since I've talked about it. It was like this: My first wife died in a terrible fire. Our son with her. Everything went: the shop, all our stock . . . the lot. Lea was just a toddler then, and she and I were the only ones who managed to get out."

Helmut tried to connect the name Lea to a face from their first night. Then he remembered: red hair like her father's, pinned up elaborately, uncommonly tall for a woman, exceptionally elegant. She was married to the musical director of Odessa's philharmonic orchestra.

"We had friends who put us up, and everyone in the village helped us rebuild the shop, but it just wasn't the same after that. All the joy was gone. I was a widower. I had no money. Everything I had I paid for on credit." He closed his eyes and, for a moment, seemed very far away. Then he straightened his shoulders, and the sadness disappeared from his face. "I only really got back on my feet again when Eleonore came here from Germany. She was the one who laid the foundation for our prosperity today."

"What? How?" the brothers said simultaneously. "A woman?"

Leonard smiled. "She suggested we move here. It's a lively city, and she said Odessa reminded her of Stuttgart. Carlsthal held so many bad memories for me that I was happy for a new beginning. And it was worth it: with her confectionery skills, Eleonore conquered the city, so to speak."

"Confections . . ." Helmut frowned. He was slowly starting to wonder how much credence he could put in Leonard's story. It did not sound particularly convincing.

"Eleonore was a famous confectioner at the royal court in Stuttgart. She was offered five permanent jobs within a month of us moving to Odessa, and in the finest houses! Eleonore was determined to continue independently. We spent long nights in a small, rented kitchen. And during the day, we had to look after little Lea, and Eleonore was pregnant with Bettina. Those were hard times. At some point, the demand for Eleonore's confections was so large that we couldn't keep up with it by ourselves."

"So you took on employees," said Helmut, who had actually been hoping for a more exciting story.

"Wrong!" said Leonard triumphantly. "Eleonore decided to open a school for confectioners and pass on her talents. The school was a resounding success. Every blue-blooded woman in the city took the view that it would not hurt for their daughters to learn practical skills along with music and arts. The way to a man's heart is through his stomach—that's as true for Russians as it is for Württembergers. Eleonore's cakes and confections boosted the marriageability of more than one young lady."

All three laughed.

"A mad story!" Valentin said, shaking his head. "What became of the school? Does it still exist?"

"Certainly. And it's expanded to teach even more than cooking and baking. Eleonore is still there, and Bettina, Margarete, and Maria are employed as teachers. Personally, I have nothing to do with it."

Leonard gave a shrug that suggested he wanted to downplay his role as much as possible. But the next moment, his eyes lit up and he puffed his chest again.

"My world is down there." He pointed his chin in the direction of the free port. "After it opened in 1819, I quickly saw my opportunity . . ."

"Can you tell us what that opportunity was?" Helmut said.

"To do that, I have to tell you a bit about Odessa's history. The port was the breakthrough for our city. It was the realization of Catherine the Great's dream to make Odessa a window to the south. The duty-free port attracted a vast number of foreign investors. Goods came in from all over the world, and those goods had to be sold!" Leonard rubbed his hands together as if he were still pleased with the successes of those days. "Leonard's became a big wholesaler." He paused for a moment and sighed deeply. "But as the years passed, it got harder and harder for the local tradesmen to sell their own products. Who wanted badly forged knives when ships were bringing in high quality Solingen blades by the ton? A blessing for one, a curse for the other—that's how things will probably always be. There are many who would love to see the free port close, and the sooner the better."

Propping his elbows on the table, Leonard leaned forward. "Enough about me. I can see in your eyes that you're ready for a slice of the Odessite cake yourselves."

Helmut laughed. "Oh yes! Let's talk about the seed trade in Odessa."

They spent the rest of the afternoon doing so, continuing the discussion at Leonard's house, with Eleonore and Lea joining in. Both had close contacts among the city's wealthier families—Eleonore through her school and Lea through her husband—and they were familiar with the finely tuned mechanisms of Odessite society. Odessa was an uncommon city with uncommon inhabitants. If you wanted to do business there, it was good to keep that in mind.

The free port had not only brought a lot of money and goods with it, but also introduced new culture to the region. Suddenly, the Russians began to look beyond the familiar, Eleonore said. In modern Odessa, it was important to live a cosmopolitan lifestyle. For those who could afford it, this philosophy extended to the garden.

Valentin said that they had seen for themselves that the people of the city were garden lovers. Even now, in winter, the gardens looked well tended.

Eleonore nodded. "And you haven't even seen any of the landed estates yet. I think you will be very happy indeed to see those."

Valentin cleared his throat. "Why do so many rich people live *here*? In Odessa?"

Leonard smiled. "Look around you! I suspect our Lord above created very few places more beautiful than here." He nodded out toward the Black Sea.

"Papa," said Lea, "don't you think Valentin and Helmut deserve a more precise answer?"

"Odessa is like an island in the middle of a very restless ocean. A beautiful, calm, safe haven. This is not something one can say about Saint Petersburg or wherever else our esteemed czar might be visiting. The saber rattling in other places is so loud it hurts your ears."

"Political reasons, then," said Helmut.

"I won't say a word against the czar!" Leonard raised his hands defensively. "Still, one could wish the man were blessed with more political skill. He would rather rule with a hard hand and pour prodigious sums of money into his million-strong army. In their smart uniforms they certainly look impressive, but with their outdated weapons, they couldn't even hold their own against a horde of Cossacks." He sighed despondently.

"But I still don't understand. What does that have to do with the estates around Odessa?" Valentin asked.

"Czar Nicholas suspects subversion hiding behind every bush and tree. His nervousness has increased in the last year or two, with unpleasant consequences for those close to him. The saber rattling, you know? He demands justification for every step any of his followers makes. Many people do not like that, so they retreat to their country estates, where they can throw their parties and conduct their business without interference."

Lea, whose husband owned such a country manor, nodded her agreement. "Practically everyone around here is related to the Romanovs. Money and influence are tangible forces in our city. But let's come back to your seed trading. The people here will pay a lot of money for good quality. Your advantage is that you come from Württemberg. The Russians trust German goods."

"They certainly should. And our prices are good, too," Helmut said pompously.

Lea shook her head. "The prices are not important. If you are knowledgeable and prepared to put in time with your customers, and if you have imagination and style, you will have them eating out of your hand."

Chapter Twenty-Seven

February 4, 1851

We finally arrived in Odessa, safe and sound, two days ago. The first thing we did, of course, was check the crates, and we were overjoyed to see that everything had survived the long journey well.

"The entire shipment safe! Thank God!" Wilhelmine said, interrupting Hannah.

Hannah looked up from the letter.

"Why does he always have to talk about business?" she said, exasperated. "Not a single word about how he and Valentin are or if he's even a little bit homesick or if he misses his daughter . . ." Or me, she silently added.

Wilhelmine laughed. "Child, you really have a lot to learn. Our men don't go out traveling for fun. It's all about the business. Or would you prefer him to babble on about how he's keeping himself entertained while he's gadding about out there?"

Hannah screwed up her face. "Of course not."

"Helmut is just a practical man. Writing is not exactly his passion, is it?" Seraphine hissed through her teeth: she was holding the loose end of a length of string tightly between them while she wound the other end around a package.

Hannah read the last few lines aloud and then handed the letter back to Wilhelmine, who snatched it from her greedily.

"You don't need to tell me what kind of man Helmut is," she snapped at Seraphine. "I'm married to him, aren't I?" she added, feeling rather childish even as she said it.

Seraphine raised an eyebrow.

Hannah had been so happy when the mailman arrived with the large envelope. What had become of her happiness?

She tried to focus on the dozen small seed packets on the table in front of her. Did she have everything that Mr. Stanecik had ordered? In the right quantities? Had she already added a few sunflower seeds as a bonus? After she had once again compared everything with the page in the order book, she pushed the packets across to Seraphine, who was responsible for the final packing and addressing. Hannah hoped her sister-in-law's fingers would cramp while trying to write complicated Bohemian names like Zdenek Stanecik or Bohumil Dolezil!

Hannah turned without enthusiasm to the next page in the order book. Her eyes wandered over to the cradle by the window, where Flora was slumbering away peacefully. If only the little one would cry! Then she could pick her up and have an excuse to get out in the fresh air and escape the feeling of suffocating inside.

Since Helmut's order book had arrived some weeks earlier, the three women had spent every day in the packing room, filling the orders. They had already driven a neighbor's horse and cart to the post office in Tübingen three times, each time sending off a cartload of packages. Today they wanted to finish the rest.

Hannah enjoyed the work itself. She loved folding and labeling the little paper packets, measuring the individual varieties with the different spoons, even the physical feel of the different kinds of seeds in her hand, some thick and round, others long and thin, some so delicate that Hannah had trouble even imagining that they would one day transform into a carrot or radish. And despite minor differences of opinion, she was happy to work with Seraphine and Wilhelmine. Real work meant a change from the usual tedious chores.

But in the last few days, nothing had given Hannah much pleasure at all.

She pushed another order to Seraphine.

"What did Valentin write?"

Without waiting for Seraphine's reply, she grabbed the envelope, which was in the middle of the table. "You haven't even opened it yet!"

Wasn't Seraphine interested in what her husband had to say? Carefully, Hannah began to open the thin paper with her index finger.

"Hannah! You can't just go opening other people's letters," said Wilhelmine.

Hannah shrugged. "Why not? Seraphine does it all the time."

Three times, in fact, Seraphine had opened one of Helmut's letters. "By accident," she always said. Hannah had not believed her. Her name had been written in large, clear letters on the envelope, just as Seraphine's was on the one she now held in her hand. One would have to have been struck blind to open the wrong letter by accident!

"*Dearest Seraphine,*'" she began to read aloud. "*I hope you are safe and well as you read these lines. The long trip to Odessa has taken less out of us than we feared, and we are now enjoying the generous hospitality of our distant cousin Leonard. The cakes and confections that his wife, Eleonore, makes have long since made up for the meager fare on the ship. If things go on like this, we will come home as round as barrels! Oh, Seraphine, so many times have I thought of you here in this city! The splendor and the beauty on every corner—your artist's eye would rejoice to see it.*'"

Hannah lowered the letter. Why couldn't Helmut write like that? Surreptitiously, she glanced over at her sister-in-law, who seemed unmoved by Valentin's words and did not interrupt her work to listen. Didn't Seraphine appreciate Valentin's heartfelt words? Ungrateful creature!

"'As for business, Odessa is anything but an easy city. Oh, there are more than enough rich people here, but their expectations don't exactly correspond with what we have brought with us. Just yesterday, Helmut said that he—'"

"Helmut? What did Helmut say?" Seraphine jumped to her feet as if a spider had bitten her.

"What does he mean, the customers' expectations don't correspond with what they have?" Wilhelmine's brow furrowed.

Hannah quickly scanned the next few lines. "He doesn't say anything more about it. He just says that Helmut is getting annoyed with everything and that the two of them are slowly losing their enthusiasm for selling." She shook her head. "Strange."

"That's not how I know my boys at all." Wilhelmine sighed elaborately. "Oh, I can't tell that to Gottlieb. He'd just go on about 'If the boys had only listened to me!' And he would not be entirely unjustified. Gottlieb's profitable old territory in Alsace has been abandoned while those two traipse around somewhere in Russia."

Seraphine snatched the letter out of Hannah's hand and skimmed it rapidly.

"Russia clearly is no good for them. But is it any wonder? If only things hadn't gone this far! Well, we all know who to thank for that." She glanced poisonously at Hannah. "And poor Helmut can't bring himself to say how worried he really is," she murmured, more to herself.

"'Poor Helmut!'" Hannah cried. "Helmut is not *poor* anything. He *wanted* to go to Russia. That was his dream! And Valentin's, too. Before they left, you acted as if you understood that. Now that things don't seem to be going very well, he's *poor* Helmut. I can do without that kind of prattle, thank you!" Hannah breathlessly swallowed down the spittle that, in her anger, had gathered in her mouth, like poison to be spat.

"What's she taken the wrong way now?" Seraphine said, turning to Wilhelmine and shaking her head.

Hannah could not overlook the superiority in her voice. As if she were talking about an ignorant child, the witch!

Wilhelmine took Seraphine's side. "There's really no reason to get upset!" she chided Hannah. "And now you've woken the child with all your shouting." She was about to get up and go to the cradle when Hannah placed her hand on her shoulder.

"No. I'll take care of Flora," she said icily. She maneuvered the cradle out of the room fiercely and let the door slam shut behind her.

They could all go to hell!

With a scarf wrapped around her neck and ears and a heavy sheepskin over Flora's carriage, Hannah walked through the deserted streets of Gönningen. There were lamps burning inside some houses, while others waited dark and lonely for the return of the people who lived in them.

Tears streamed down her cheeks. She could not remember ever being so weepy back in Nuremberg. When had she become like this? She hated herself for it.

Her gaze turned toward the high, steep mountainsides that cast their long shadows over the valley. Although it was still early in the afternoon, the daylight was almost gone. It was late February, and the days were growing noticeably longer.

One has to be gloomy here, she thought grimly. At the same time, she knew that it was not the winter itself or the short days or even the looming Swabian Mountains that were to blame for her gloom.

It was Helmut. She missed him so much. If only she did not love him so much. Then she would not be so fearful. Fearful that his scent might fade from his pillow and disappear once and for all. Fearful that she might forget the sound of his voice, his laughter.

Fear made her sad and angry, and Hannah hated it. And she hated Gönningen with its terrible seed trade!

Why couldn't she have ended up in a village whose inhabitants lived from planting crops and raising animals? Where the men came home in the evening and ate a decent dinner with their families? Where they had festivals and parties, and people danced and celebrated? Instead, Gönningen was impregnated by the rhythm of the journeys of trade. In January, she had experienced for herself how much that rhythm affected her life.

It had been their first wedding anniversary, and her husband was thousands of miles away. Nobody said a word about it. In the Kerner house, they never made much fuss about such matters. Hannah had taken Flora and marched to the summit of Rossberg, where she spent a long time gazing in the direction of Russia. Then she lit a small candle and prayed for Helmut's early, healthy return. Was Helmut thinking of her, too, then? She did not know.

And before that, Christmas had also been a less than joyous occasion. Like an old maid, she had spent it with Wilhelmine and Gottlieb. Helmut's sister had traveled from Reutlingen with her husband, and although the two had spent the entire time fighting and firing venomous remarks like arrows, Hannah envied them. Better a husband there to fight with than no husband at all.

The previous Christmas, when Hannah had sat alone and lonely in her guest room at Emma's inn, she had pictured in her mind how beautiful her future could be.

"Dreams are smoke," she murmured to herself now, and smiled at Flora, who was looking all around with interest.

None of the others seemed to notice how sad everything was. Wilhelmine and Gottlieb acted as if it were the most normal thing in the world to celebrate Christmas without their sons present—and to live day after day like that. Wilhelmine visited her old people and looked after Aunt Finchen. Gottlieb had thrown himself wholeheartedly into his new job with the parish council. And Seraphine? She had adopted an air of insufferable smugness to the point that one could imagine that she was happy to be rid of Valentin. Since his departure, she seemed less tired than usual. She busied herself with tasks around the house, and she spent a lot of time painting or reading and writing poetry. Once, Seraphine had accidently left the book in which she wrote her poems in the front room, and Hannah could not stop herself from looking at it. There was quite a bit about a "star fairy." Hannah did not know if she should laugh or cry at all the lines that contained such words as "yearning," "pain," and "pining." Ha! She knew exactly what her sister-in-law was pining for: her old love!

When she told Emma about her discovery, Emma asked if Helmut's name appeared in any of the poems. Of course not, Hannah had said. Seraphine wasn't stupid. Then, Emma asserted, it didn't prove that Seraphine's heartbreak was about Helmut at all, and that Hannah could well be imagining things.

Whatever Emma thought, Hannah had no interest in spending her time painting, reading, or composing poems. It was all so *boring*. She missed the hustle and bustle of her parents' inn in Nuremberg so much. Passionate discussions, music, laughter, people kicking up their heels— life could be so beautiful! Of course, she still would have missed Helmut if she were in Nuremberg—but not day and night, not every minute.

Hannah sighed deeply. Why couldn't she be satisfied with what she had? Why did she always want more and more from life?

She paused for a moment and watched her sighs vanish in the air in little puffs of vapor. If only all her cares would dissolve like that.

Suddenly, she found herself standing in front of The Sun. She must have followed the street in that direction without even realizing it. She hesitated, wondering whether to go in, when the door was jerked open from inside.

"Hannah! How lovely! And with little Flora, too."

Before Hannah could say a word, Emma reached into Flora's carriage, lifted her out, and disappeared into the inn. Hannah laughed and followed.

"We're off again tomorrow—we've never left as late as we're leaving this year!" said Emma, making herself comfortable at a table and nodding toward her bags. "Off to Hohenlohe!"

Hannah sighed. "How am I supposed to put up with Gönningen without you?"

Emma smiled understandingly. "A year flies by so quickly, doesn't it? It feels like just yesterday that we sat together here and I told you about our traveling habits."

"And now I'm sitting here again!" Hannah could not keep the bitterness out of her voice, although she had been determined to let nothing of her mood show on the outside.

"Time doesn't stop." Emma laid one hand on Hannah's arm. "We'll be back long before Flora's birthday. You know what? We'll celebrate Flora's first birthday here in the restaurant! Does that sound like fun?"

Hannah nodded listlessly. Normally, Emma's offer would have thrilled her, but today . . .

"Oh, don't look so down in the mouth. Any news from Helmut and Valentin?" She pushed a plate of *Hefezopf* toward Hannah.

Hannah told Emma about the two letters that had arrived that morning. "Seraphine hadn't even bothered to open Valentin's letter."

"She's a strange girl," Emma conceded. "But you don't have much choice. You have to accept your sister-in-law as she is."

"Sister-in-law!" Hannah sniffed. "The way she's acting, anyone would think *she's* the one waiting for Helmut to come home. She talks about him as if he is *her* husband. Much as I'd like to, I can't prohibit her from speaking." She banged her fist on the table, and Emma frowned. Hannah leaned toward her. "Just yesterday, I caught her rummaging through our wardrobe. She said she wanted to go through Helmut's work aprons to see which ones needed to be mended."

Emma laughed. "Is that a problem? Then send good little Seraphine here. I'm sure I can find some clothes for her to mend!"

"You don't understand. If Helmut's clothes need to be mended, then that is *my* job, even if the seams split again after the first time he wears them," Hannah said. She was sorry for her tone, but then her expression turned fierce again. "The worst part is that Seraphine is always acting so falsely friendly. She wanted to do me a favor, she said. Because she knows how much I dislike sewing. What am I supposed to say to that?" Hannah lifted her hands in a gesture of helplessness. "She's constantly driving me to the point where I feel childish and stupid, and at the same time, she makes herself look good. If she is trying to drive me out of the house, then she might as well knock her head against a wall. I don't give up so easily."

"You talk as if you're in a war with her, but it can't be all that bad, can it?" Emma's eyebrows rose inquiringly.

Hannah glared at her. "Don't you go looking at me like that! You think I'm being childish and stupid, too!"

Emma smiled. "No, that's not what I think. You're jealous! That's a different thing altogether, and normal for a young married woman. The question is really whether you are doing yourself any favors like that. Isn't your jealousy completely unfounded? I mean, Helmut married *you* . . ."

Yes, Helmut married her. And yet he had entrusted Seraphine with the news about the trip to Russia before telling his own wife. That lack of trust still hurt.

Emma stood up and laid Flora, who was gurgling happily to herself, in Hannah's arms.

"You're welcome to stay a little longer. I'll bring you a cup of tea if you like. But I have to keep packing. Käthe has gone off to buy our provisions. If I'm not finished by the time she's back, she won't let me hear the end of it! She'll call me old and infirm, and that's not what I want to hear." She smiled impishly.

"I'm sorry. I didn't mean to keep you," said Hannah, contrite. She quickly stood up. "I'll come by early tomorrow to wish you and Käthe bon voyage. Thank God the ground is still frozen and you can walk with dry feet."

"I'll take whatever mercies come my way!" Emma said. "You're finally starting to think like a true seed merchant's wife."

Hannah laughed drily. "Let's hope I *act* like a true seed merchant's wife one day."

Chapter Twenty-Eight

Although the sun was shining, Countess Ludmilla Voraskova was wrapped head to toe in heavy furs. She had been leading the brothers through her garden for more than an hour. Her garden was more like an extensive park, with small temples, grottoes, and other structures that served no purpose other than spiritual edification.

The countess stopped and pointed off to the right, where a squad of men was digging in front of a small patch of woods. "I'm having the straight paths replaced by winding paths. At first, I considered adopting an old principle and overlaying a network of winding paths onto the fixed grid of straight ones, but I found the idea fundamentally unthinkable."

"Unthinkable," Helmut agreed, giving Valentin an inconspicuous nudge at the same time.

"And then perhaps not so unthinkable after all," the countess went on, and Helmut wondered whether she had perhaps noticed a sarcastic undertone in his voice. "Batty Langley spent a lot of time on exactly this question in his book *New Principles of Gardening*. A classic. You must know it."

Helmut hastily told her no, that he'd never heard of him. He thought for a moment, then said, "Keep in mind, my lady: you won't see a straight line in nature—not in any forest, creek, or lake. If you want to create a natural space, then you are certainly thinking along the right path."

"A fitting play on words," the countess said, looking at him intently, as if wondering whether she could trust him.

Valentin forced himself to smile. He was trying to count how many men were slaving away at the cold earth, poorly dressed and some without shoes, to bring the countess's latest whim to fruition. A simple man was not worth much in the countess's circle, and Valentin did not want to do business with people like her.

On the other hand, Countess Voraskova was very friendly to them. She asked for their advice when others had simply laid out their high-flown garden plans. And it was better to sell their seeds than toss them in the Black Sea, wasn't it?

Valentin breathed in deeply, then exhaled. "My lady, forgive me an ignorant question, but to understand your gardens, I am prepared to make a laughingstock of myself . . ." He was close to bursting into laughter himself. *If we don't manage to sell our seeds, we can always go on stage,* he thought.

"Yes?" the countess said, from behind her high fur collar.

Valentin pointed toward the bridge off to their right that crossed a small lake. Black swans swam picturesquely on the green, shimmering water.

"Where does the bridge lead? I mean, your main estate lies farther to the right, unless I am disoriented."

The countess laughed brightly. "Where the bridge leads? Oh, how priceless! Nowhere, in fact! But tell me: Wouldn't something be missing if there were not a bridge right there?"

The brothers murmured their agreement while the countess explained that the lake was not a true lake but a creek that had been dammed.

"So, we've arrived." The countess gazed out over a grassy area that stretched beyond the bridge and small lake. The grass was broken up at

209

regular intervals by strange-looking circular and winding excavations. Valentin frowned.

Countess Voraskova did not miss the look on his face. "Just last year, this lawn was practically covered with what I can only call embroidered flower beds. It was a disgrace, and I had it all removed. Dressing up the earth like a wedding dress with lace borders is so terribly passé, don't you think?"

"Well, such fashions are certainly still to be found in France." Helmut cleared his throat affectedly. The countess turned away from them, and he whispered to Valentin, "If everyone thought like her, we'd go bankrupt in a week."

Valentin suppressed a giggle by turning it into a cough. Helmut, the show-off!

"So this fine lawn is your latest project?" Valentin said. "Though it's still winter, as far as I can tell, it is already close to perfection. No weeds, no molehills." And no business to be done, he thought, annoyed. They did not have grass seeds. If they had known that that was what this was all about, they could have saved themselves the long walk out here.

"That's exactly the point!" the countess cried. "The lawn is too perfect. Have you ever seen nature produce such a well-groomed patch of grass?"

"Then what do you have in mind to do with it?" Valentin asked.

"Back to nature! I want to transform this expanse into a flowering meadow. Which means that your seeds have arrived at the right time. March and April *are* the best months to sow most flowers, aren't they?"

Helmut gulped. "Please excuse me for speaking so plainly, but do you realize how much labor a project like that would involve? Of course, we have the right kinds of seeds—English violets, veronica, daisies— varieties that would make your garden perfect. And it would be the ideal time to sow them. But the lawn would have to go. Throwing the seeds onto the grass and hoping they will sprout would be a waste of time and effort."

"That's right," Valentin confirmed. "The lawn would have to removed completely and the soil built up again with loam and peat before any seeds could be sown."

"Then that's just what we'll do. Don't worry about the work. I'm happy if I can keep my people busy. Thank you for the little tip."

For a moment, the brothers did not move, at a loss for words.

"Come along! I can't wait to work out the right mix of seeds with you!"

"Better than expected!" said Helmut. He and Valentin were at an inn, each with a glass of wine. "I didn't think we'd sell her a single seed."

Valentin grinned. "We did a good job of it, didn't we? Your idea to talk up our daisies as 'especially natural' was inspired."

Helmut frowned. "Yes, but things can't continue like this. This has nothing to do with the seed trade anymore. I'm starting to feel like a mix of circus monkey, professor, and simpleton, and I don't like it at all."

Valentin raised his glass. "I'll drink to that! And then I want to order something to eat. All the talk has made me hungry," he said.

Leonard had kept his word and gotten them into the finest estates around Odessa. Their first visit had been to Count Tscherkov. The memory of his garden still made one of Valentin's eyelids twitch. It was overloaded with marble benches, angel statues, fountains, and assorted objects. There was not a single bush that had not been tortured into the form of an animal! Not a turn in the path that did not lead to a surprise. And some of the surprises—like the maw of some monstrous beast, carved in stone and spewing a jet of water—were so grotesque as to be positively frightening. Water was the repeating element in Tscherkov's garden: fountains, babbling pools inside artificial grottoes, canals. Beds of flowers and perennials were of secondary importance. Tscherkov had explained that his garden harked back to the centuries-old tradition of Mannerist gardens.

Some of the estate owners did not even have interest in meeting the brothers themselves; instead, they had their gardeners meet them. The gardeners led Helmut and Valentin through enormous greenhouses where lilies, roses, and rare orchids were raised or, at least, spent the winter. In those places, seeds were in demand, but the negotiations were far from straightforward because the gardeners insisted on every last detail about what they were buying. The way the brothers were treated at those estates was not to their taste at all, but they sold most of the seeds they had brought with them. After the countess, all they had left were most of their rosebushes.

"I think we need to forget the big places and try to sell off what we have left a little farther down the market," said Helmut. He tore a juicy chunk of chicken from a drumstick with his teeth, and fat dripped onto the tablecloth beside his plate. "There are enough business owners in Odessa with smaller houses and gardens than the ones we've seen so far."

Valentin nodded. "Not a bad idea. I mean no disrespect for Leonard's willingness to help, of course. He only wanted to do us a favor by introducing us to the best houses, but—"

"Do us a favor!" Helmut interrupted. "He just wanted to show off!"

"I don't believe that. He and Eleonore are at home in those circles. Their daughters, too."

"Well, I have had all I can take of pompous blowhards," Helmut said. "Tomorrow, we'll sell our roses, and then we'll look for the first boat back home." He smiled, suddenly dreamy. "I can hardly wait to hear someone speak decent Swabian again."

"And to be around normal people," Valentin added.

"And to eat somewhere that doesn't have a tablecloth to get in the way," said Helmut, picking up his side of the starched white cloth, now stained with fat and gravy.

"I'm looking forward to seeing Seraphine again!" Valentin breathed deeply in and out. "I think about her every night. It's good to know that she is waiting for me at home."

Chapter Twenty-Nine

They were in luck. Three days later, the next ship was leaving Odessa for Galati.

Leonard and Eleonore accompanied the brothers to the harbor. Both were unhappy to see their Swabian relatives go, and Eleonore had been crying sporadically ever since Helmut had announced that they would be returning home as soon as possible. To distract herself, she had bought gifts for her unknown relatives in Swabia.

Although they had grown fond of Leonard's family, after many weeks in Odessa Valentin and Helmut were looking forward to their return to Gönningen so much that they found it hard to feign any sorrow at leaving the city. But when they embraced their relatives a final time, the tears flowed down their cheeks, too.

"We will come again," Helmut whispered in Eleonore's ear as she held him tightly, and in that moment he truly believed it.

"Say hello to the homeland for me," Eleonore whispered through her tears. "And remember your promise to go to Rotenberg and lay flowers on the grave of Queen Catherine for me."

Leonard freed Eleonore's hand from Helmut's arm and drew his wife lovingly to his side. "Go, you lucky men, go! Home is home. That's just the way it is."

"What Leonard said earlier . . . I can't get it out of my head." It was Valentin who broke the long silence between them.

Helmut raised his eyebrows inquiringly.

"Oh, about home? We really are lucky, you know. Wherever we go, to Bohemia, Alsace, or farther afield, we seed merchants are always on our way home. Whether we're ten miles from Gönningen or a thousand—the road always leads back home. That's a comforting thought."

They had only been on the ship a few hours, and already a strange mood had settled over them. Another new ship, a captain they did not know, the passengers all strangers—everything exciting, strenuous, interesting, but still . . . the new had become old. They would have loved to have a magical incantation that would transport them home in an instant. Instead they were faced with weeks on a ship, and the time spent in the foreign climes had worn them down. Perhaps that was why they could, for now, find little joy in the success of their Russian adventure. They were heroes, actually. They had succeeded where so many before them had failed. They could have spent their time aboard telling stories, but instead they crawled like snails into a house of silence.

Other than a violent thunderstorm just before Pressburg, the upriver journey passed uneventfully. Almost too uneventfully for Helmut. Idly sitting around made him irritable. Bored, he provoked unnecessary arguments with fellow travelers, played cards, or tried his luck with dice. When they finally arrived in Vienna after weeks that felt endless, Helmut was more restless than he had ever been in his life.

"Tonight we celebrate!" he said to Valentin, even before they had docked. "Let's go and find something to drink. The best wine. Or beer,

I don't care. I want music, and I wouldn't say no to a dance. Haven't we earned it?"

Valentin laughed. "Let's at least drop our bags at The Neidler first."

"Deal!" Helmut clapped his hand loudly against Valentin's back. "And then the night is ours."

When they deposited their bags in their room, the innkeeper assured them that everything would be safe and that no one would get past her without permission. Considering the woman's size, the brothers were quite willing to believe her, but they still could not bring themselves to leave their money there. When they went out, they carried it as they had since leaving Odessa—divided among the purses on strings around their necks, the pouches sewn into their trousers, and the crotch bags. Leonard had insisted that Eleonore sew the special crotch bags that hung between their legs. "A purse around your neck can be snatched away in a heartbeat, but it takes a brave thief to go for your balls!" Leonard had said with a laugh, although he meant it seriously.

Apart from their own, only three tables were in use at the tavern. The food was as tasteless as what they had eaten on the ship, instead of music they had to listen to the cook scolding the kitchen boy, and the beer was flat and watery. The room stank of floor polish, and Valentin sneezed several times.

"Can't pour a proper beer and can't cook." Helmut stared at his soup, a single pathetic scrap of meat floating on its oily surface. He lifted a spoonful to his lips, then threw the spoon onto the table. "Come on. Let's go somewhere else." He threw a few coins on the table and abruptly stood up.

Valentin grabbed him by the sleeve and pulled him back onto his chair. "We stay," he hissed. "That's what we agreed, remember?"

"Don't get upset! I don't want to tour the city, just see what's a few doors down! There has to be a bit of life somewhere," Helmut snapped back. As he spoke, the door opened. "Just next door, I saw . . ." He fell silent.

Valentin turned to see what his brother was looking at. Four young women sat down at the next table with mugs of beer. They were nicely dressed . . . too nicely for that place, Valentin thought. He pulled Helmut closer.

"I have no interest in getting knocked over the head in a dark alley somewhere. We'll drink another beer, maybe two, and then we go back to our room. We can celebrate once we've got the money home safely."

"All right, all right." Helmut rolled his eyes. "So what do you think four pretty girls are up to, going to a bar by themselves?" he whispered. One of the young women, who had clearly seen Helmut looking at them, lifted one hand in a friendly wave. "They don't look like whores . . ."

Valentin shrugged. "Just because a woman goes to a bar by herself doesn't make her a prostitute, or you could say the same thing about our women in Gönningen." He couldn't care less about the women, but if their presence meant that Helmut was content to stay in one place, then he was happy with that.

Putting on his most winning smile, Helmut turned to the next table. "Could I buy you ladies the next drink?"

Valentin sighed. He'd seen this coming.

One of the women beckoned Helmut closer. "*One* beer in this dump is enough," she whispered. "The barwoman is my aunt, so we can drink cheaply. But as soon as we've finished this, we're going somewhere else." With a casual shrug, she turned back to her companions.

"There, you see? They can't stand this place, either!" Helmut said, narrowing his eyes at Valentin.

The woman at the next table cleared her throat exaggeratedly. "If you gentlemen would like, you could invite us for a glass of wine at another spot. A friend of ours runs an outdoor bar close by, and another friend is playing there with his band. It should be fun."

"More fun than this place," giggled one of the other young women.

"And it's a warm night," added a third.

"Sorry, but—" Valentin began.

"Why not?" said Helmut at the same time.

The young women told the brothers they were actresses from the royal court theater. While Helmut entertained the women with stories, Valentin stomped along grumpily behind them. He did not like the way one of the women batted her eyelids at Helmut. She was walking directly beside him, their shoulders brushing as if by accident. How brazen could she be? He knew his brother well enough to know that he had a lot more in mind than just a glass of wine, but he was a married man!

Valentin's hand instinctively checked each of his money bags. They were carrying too much money on them to go strolling through an unknown city in the middle of the night. The streets there were still well lit, and the area did not seem particularly dangerous. Still, it would be best to turn around, go back to their inn, lock the door, and not tempt fate, which had been so good to them so far . . .

He walked faster until he came up level with Helmut, and then he pulled his brother away from the women.

Before Valentin could speak, Helmut hissed into his ear. "I know that look. You've got something against me having a little fun, again! I spent weeks in Odessa dancing to other people's tunes, and tonight I'm going to do whatever I want." He jerked free of Valentin's grip and rejoined the women. "So, ladies, how much farther to your fabulous bar?" And Valentin had no choice but to follow.

Chapter Thirty

"We've been robbed! Our money . . . it's all gone!"

Valentin, his hands shaking, pulled his pockets inside out. He could not stop a sob escaping from his throat. He tried to regain his composure.

"Now one thing at a time, gentlemen! First, your details—passports, if you please." The gendarme held his hand out across the counter.

Valentin plucked the two passports from the pocket of his shirt. "Thank God they didn't steal these."

While the gendarme slowly recorded the information from their passports, Valentin looked down at himself. His shirt was shredded and filthy, the buttons ripped off, and his trousers were torn where the thieves had cut out the special pouches. They had cut the pouches from Helmut's pants, too, and the purses they had worn around their necks were gone also. All they had left were the two crotch bags that Leonard had insisted they wear . . . a poor consolation, barely one-third of their money. Enough to pay for the remainder of their journey home, but not much more.

This can't be true. It's a nightmare! Please, God, let me wake up. Valentin ran one hand over his face anxiously. His skin was raw.

Helmut, sitting beside Valentin and mired in his own thoughts, looked no better. Worse, in fact. The left side of his face was smeared with blood from a cut beneath his eye. He was holding onto his head as if he was in pain. Had he been beaten? Valentin gave himself a shake, trying to reconstruct what had happened.

All he could remember was before the robbery. They had walked for no more than ten minutes when they reached the outdoor pub that the women led them to. It had an unusual name: The Gilded Hen. There, too, there were no more than four tables occupied, but the atmosphere was merry and loud and the wine good.

A Hungarian man had played his fiddle loudly and not always well, and the sound of it still scraped in Valentin's ears. They had danced, too, Helmut with a woman who called herself Rosi, and he with . . . he had forgotten the name of the woman. But then a breeze had blown up from the Danube, and the air grew damp and chilly, making his limbs stiff, making it hard to dance. He wanted to leave and head back to their inn—

"Right, let's hear what happened." With his pencil poised and a bored expression, the second gendarme looked from one brother to the other.

Helmut managed to pull himself together a little. Haltingly, he described the events of the evening. How they had gone from the first bar to another one in the company of the court actresses and—

"Actresses? From the royal court?" The man's bored expression vanished, and his pencil clattered onto the table and rolled to the edge.

Both brothers nodded. "Real ladies *they* were!" Helmut spat. The two gendarmes exchanged a look.

"Keep talking."

Helmut raised his hands helplessly. "They must have put something in the wine, a sleeping powder or . . . I don't know. My head hurts, and I've got a bump on the back of my head. Maybe someone knocked me out. I can only remember up to a point, and then . . . no more. Everything goes black."

"I woke up because I was freezing," Valentin said. His mouth felt dry. "When I looked around, I didn't know where I was or how I got there." He had been so miserably cold, and still was. He felt as if he would never be able to get warm again.

The money we earned . . . gone! Our work . . . a waste of time.

He threw both hands over his face.

"Let me guess." The older gendarme sighed. "When you woke up, you weren't at The Gilded Hen anymore?" He said the name of the bar in a cynical way. Helmut shook his head and the man went on. "No. You found yourselves in an alley somewhere, and you'd been robbed. Did you try to find the place the ladies led you to?"

"Of course we did!" Helmut cried. "That was the first thing we did when we came to!"

Their minds still foggy, they had wandered in a daze along the Danube, but in the dawn light they could not find the sign with the gold hen that they had seen the night before. Everything looked different in daylight, and they had argued: Had they turned left or right at this corner? Helmut did not think they had walked so far, but Valentin believed they had gone much farther. In the end, they had given up and gone in search of the nearest gendarmerie station.

The gendarme leaned back in his chair, his arms folded on his chest. "How much money did they get?" When Helmut told him the amount, the gendarme let out a whistle. "We will do everything we can, of course. But barring a miracle, you have to get used to the idea that you won't see the money again."

"What? But—"

"You're the victims of a notorious gang of thieves. This is the second spring in a row that they've been up to no good in our beautiful city. They were in Pressburg before they came here. So far, they've eluded us." The gendarme looked away, as if he were personally responsible for that failure.

"But the bar, The Gilded Hen! The women are known there! And the first bar we were in, where we met them . . . the barwoman there is the aunt of one of them. All right, I know that they're not actresses, but—"

"Your Gilded Hen does not exist, and the barwoman probably saw her alleged niece for the first time last night," the second gendarme interrupted Helmut harshly. "The whole thing was a show. If you look at it like that, then the women *were* actresses."

With blank faces, the two brothers heard what the gendarmerie knew about the workings of the gang. The story was always the same as the one the women told the brothers, and it was how they got their future victims to the next bar. This outdoor bar was set up by their accomplices in the garden of one of the many empty summer residences along the Danube, and would look like the real thing, complete with a sign, tables, benches, and music. The next morning, the entire setup would have vanished, like magic.

"The guests, the fiddler—all of it was just a show?" Valentin said in disbelief. The situation was so incredible that for a merciful moment he forgot the sad role that they themselves had played in it.

The gendarmes nodded. What happened next varied from victim to victim. Some said, like Helmut, that they had been knocked out from behind, while others believed they'd been drugged. The result was the same, however: once the victims had been cleaned out completely, they were dropped off in an alley somewhere. By the time they woke up, the thieves were long gone and maybe even preparing their next performance.

"We call them the Spring Thieves because they are only active at this time of the year and only when the weather is good," said the gendarme, and he chuckled. "If it had been pouring rain yesterday, you'd still have your money today."

"And if you'd come to Vienna a month or two from now, the same," the other added. "Then the people are back in their summer residences and the thieves lose the backdrop for their charade."

"Don't say anything," Helmut croaked as soon as they left the gendarmerie station. "Every accusation you can throw at me I've already thrown at myself, two or three times over. If only I'd listened to you. I just wanted a bit of fun—well, we've got it now."

Valentin nodded morosely. He had no intention of accusing Helmut of anything. He was too busy accusing himself. If he'd insisted on staying close to their inn . . . He swallowed back a sob and fought hard against tears. If he started bawling like a baby now . . .

"None of it would be any use." He placed one arm across Helmut's shoulders, and Helmut returned the gesture. "All we can do now is think about how we get home, and—" Valentin broke off with a sigh.

"And how we explain our stupidity when we get there," Helmut said.

Chapter Thirty-One

"It was like they came from nowhere! Five at once! Or was it more?" Helmut turned to Valentin, who only shrugged. "They grabbed us from behind, and one of them held a knife at Valentin's throat." He swallowed.

Wilhelmine, horrified, fluttered one hand at her throat as if she could feel the blade pressed into her own skin.

"They bashed me here, in the eye. You can still see the mark." Helmut tapped his index finger under his right eye. "Dangerous men, each and every one of them! Ready for anything."

"We didn't have a chance." Valentin stared gloomily into his beer. "All the money, five months of work, all gone. All except what . . . what was hidden in our crotch bags."

"Well now, it really could have been worse," Hannah said, trying to lift the brothers' spirits.

Helmut snorted. "It leaves a big hole in our finances." For that, he earned a sharp jab in the ribs from his father. Hannah sighed. Gottlieb did not want such private matters discussed publicly—and she would just have to accept that.

She looked over toward the crib that Emma had had specially brought into the restaurant. Flora was sleeping blissfully by way of celebrating her first birthday.

What a lovely day it could have been . . .

Hannah smiled at Helmut. "Tell us again about the beautiful houses in Odessa."

Helmut cocked his head and looked at her, then seemed to gather himself and said, "Houses! They were more like palaces, beyond compare! The people in Odessa know how to live. Distinguished people, very elegant and refined." He looked at those gathered around. "There was one count whose garden—a veritable park, really—had fishponds, apple orchards and vegetable gardens, and four—four!—greenhouses just for orchids. And more greenhouses for his other plants during the winter. Mad for flowers, he was."

Hannah smiled. She'd been able to lift him out of the dumps again.

Emma had kept her word and invited the Kerner family for lunch on Flora's birthday, which had initially led to some discussion. Wilhelmine was against going. "Who feels like celebrating anything now?" she asked, her eyes red from crying.

"Right now is when the men need a little cheering up," Hannah had argued, and Wilhelmine, finally, saw that she was right.

The afternoon had now worn on somewhat, and more of Gönningen's seed merchants had joined the family. The brothers' return from distant Russia and the terrible robbery in Vienna had been the talk of the village, and everyone wanted to hear the story directly from Helmut and Valentin.

Gradually, Hannah relaxed. She had never known Helmut to be as moody as he had been since his return. Silent and brooding one minute, loud and full of self-reproach the next. At the start, Hannah had tried to console him, telling him it could have happened to anyone, that he was not to blame for the misfortune that had befallen them.

He had cut her off abruptly, and she had turned away from him, feeling insulted. Since coming home, he had generally been more aggressive toward her, as if *she* had personally hired the thugs who had robbed them. Even in the privacy of their bedroom, he was different. The first night after his return, he had taken Hannah so roughly that she had almost cried out in pain. But she sealed her lips, pressed her teeth together. She could imagine what he was going through. The fruit of so many months of labor, gone in one night! It was about more than the money. For the brothers, the entire affair was a tremendous personal failure. Instead of being able to toss the profits from their Russian adventure onto the table with pride, they had come back to Gönningen as beggars.

She was, therefore, all the happier to once again hear the swaggering words, the eloquent storytelling she knew from before. And the Gönningers did him the kindness of listening with open mouths and wide eyes.

And she had really been a little afraid of how the people in the village would react. Schadenfreude was the last thing either Helmut or Valentin needed. In the time she had been in Gönningen, Hannah had come to realize that there were some who envied the Kerners their success. People like Lothar Gmeiner, a merchant the same age as Helmut, who had never been farther than Bavaria. Hannah looked critically toward him now—he was the only one, so far, who had made any kind of snide comment. Luckily, Helmut had not noticed because just then Emma had arrived with fresh mugs of beer. Apart from Lothar, the brothers had garnered only understanding nods, a pat on the shoulder here, an encouraging word there. And from the stories being told around her, Hannah gathered that other villagers had also fallen victim to such crimes. Small consolation . . .

If there were only some way I could help him, she thought. *Take the burden off his shoulders* . . . She knew that the Kerners paid out more than three thousand gulden for seeds every autumn. A certain proportion—two or three hundred guldens' worth—were resold immediately to smaller dealers. But it was the Kerners who first had to put the money on the seed producers' tables. The profits from the Russia trip had been calculated into those purchases, and now the family had to dip into their savings to make up for the shortfall. It would certainly not drive them to the brink of ruin, but it would still hurt.

For Helmut and Valentin, it was not just the lost money. Hannah sensed that the injury to their honor or standing or whatever they might call it weighed on them more heavily.

Emma came to the table with a large bowl of cookies. "That's very fine fabric you're wearing," she whispered in Hannah's ear, stroking one hand over Hannah's back. Only then did Hannah realize how tense she was. She shook herself like a wet puppy.

"You think so?" Hannah whispered back. "It's from Odessa. Leonard's wife helped Helmut choose it. He thought the red would suit my black hair. Seraphine's dress is the same, but pink. Pink—ugh!"

Emma glanced over at Seraphine, perched sullenly between Valentin and her mother-in-law.

"But her dress fits so much better," said Emma. "Don't take this the wrong way, child, but somehow . . ." Emma plucked first at a fold in the cloth beneath Hannah's right breast, then at the seam between the upper part and the skirt. "It may be the fashion in Russia, but here I can only call it poor workmanship."

Hannah's expression darkened immediately. "It's Seraphine's work! The dress was too tight for me. Since Flora was born . . . I don't know, I'm so hungry all the time." She looked down at herself unhappily. Where her once-slim waistline had been, there were now small rolls of flab, and her thighs rubbed together. Helmut had noticed her extra weight, too, and had remarked to the effect that idleness seemed to agree with her. Idleness! She spent the entire day on her feet!

"Sera let out the dress a little for me. She said it was no trouble. You know that sewing isn't exactly my favorite thing. Does it really look so dreadful?" Hannah suddenly did not know how she ought to sit anymore. She felt fat and unshapely and tried to push her shoulders forward to disguise her supposed corpulence.

Emma looked over at Seraphine disapprovingly. "Bring the dress to me tomorrow, and I'll see what I can do."

"So have you given up on traveling now?" asked Lothar Gmeiner. "Or set your sights on America next?" The mockery in his voice was unmissable.

Lothar! How could he even mention leaving again when the men had just come home? Instinctively, Hannah edged closer to Helmut.

He patted her hand. "I have enough to keep me busy here for a while. Hannah has taken care of our fields and orchards, and most things look in good order, but there are some things only a man can do. And then"—his shoulders slumped and he looked down at the table—"we'll have to make up for the lost money somehow."

For a moment, no one said a word.

Gottlieb slapped the table. "Your old father is still around, you know! I'll go out again in autumn if need be. Frankly, I miss the open road. I'd love to smell someone else's apple trees again and rinse my feet in a different stream. Meet people who have something new to tell me . . . And then there's the business, oh yes, the business!" He swallowed hard, and his Adam's apple bobbed. "Some of my customers have even written to me to ask when *their* seed merchant is coming back . . . and I actually had in mind that the two of you would make the trip to Alsace this year." He looked reproachfully at his sons. "But it would probably be for the best if you concentrated on Bohemia. Alsace would mean trying to do too much at once, and that won't fill our empty coffers, either." He sighed heavily. "The open road . . . if only there weren't so much to do in the town hall this year."

"Any progress on getting a post office for Gönningen?" Matthias asked. "Tübingen must see that we are in dire need of our own office here."

Gottlieb nodded. "My sentiments exactly. But these things take time. We need advocates in the right places, and it's just that . . ." He launched into a lengthy monologue about all the letters he had already sent off to Tübingen, and that he was now planning a trip to Stuttgart in the hope of being able to garner support there.

Hannah was getting sick of all the talk. The afternoon sun was shining, the last fruit trees in flower were snowing white petals, and the scent of lilac drifted in through the open windows. She would have loved nothing more than to go for a walk with Helmut; perhaps that would drive out some of his gloom, and her own with it! Out of the village, across the fields and meadows, there where the sky was huge and not bordered by any rooftops. Hannah sighed longingly, and the next moment realized—with a little derision—that she was thinking like a seed merchant, like someone drawn to open spaces, drawn away from home despite the dangers lurking out there.

And then something else came to her, something so daring, so frightening, so new . . .

What if I went out as well? What if I became a merchant? If I did that, I could help him. But what about Flora? she immediately thought. *I can't leave my child here alone. Lord, how could I cope without her?*

And with whom was she supposed to go out? She would not trust herself to go out alone, and besides, it would be far too dangerous. Maybe she could convince Gottlieb to go with her? No, he had his tasks in the town hall to take care of. Wilhelmine? Lord no! Hannah could not imagine going on any kind of journey with her mother-in-law. Seraphine?

Hannah looked down at her ill-fitting dress. She was now convinced that Seraphine had deliberately cut it wrong. And she was considering going on the road with someone as mean as that? No, that was too much!

She would have to come up with another way, any other way, to support Helmut. But then again . . . in good times and in bad—that was part of the oath they had sworn, wasn't it? If she could really overcome her aversion to Seraphine and go traveling with her, then Helmut would know that he was not alone—and *that* would be good for him.

Before she lost her courage, she said, "What would you think if *I* traveled to Alsace? Seraphine could go with me. I'm sure we could manage a sales trip together."

Gottlieb and the rest of the group fell silent.

"What do you mean . . . you and Seraphine?" Helmut asked, a crease deepening between his eyebrows.

"I mean just like any seed merchants! With seed sacks and a good load of seeds to sell. Or don't you think I could do it?" She glared at him—let him say that in front of all these people! The more she thought about the idea, the better she liked it. Flora would be all right with Wilhelmine to look after her, and she would only be gone for a few weeks. She simply would not take Seraphine's petty cruelties to heart. Perhaps Seraphine was not being as nasty as Hannah thought. Maybe she was being overly sensitive about her sister-in-law. Hannah did not want to think too much about that. It was much nicer to think about traveling rather than sitting around the house through the autumn and winter, waiting for Helmut to return.

"Out of the question!" Helmut burst out. "Neither of you has any experience! And besides . . . man, Valentin, help me out here!" Red blotches—which had not been there a moment earlier—had appeared on his cheeks.

Valentin nodded vigorously. "Your offer does you credit, Hannah, but we made our bed, and now we have to lie in it."

"Lie in the bed you've made? What rubbish! You're acting as if you *let* yourselves be robbed on purpose. It was simply bad luck. It could have happened to anyone, which is why I think it's only right if Seraphine and I contribute to the business, too. Sera, you must see things the same way, don't you?" Hannah looked encouragingly at her sister-in-law, a look that Seraphine returned with a venomous smile. *Then why doesn't she say something, the stupid cow?* Hannah thought.

Helmut slammed his fist on the table, making the beer mugs jump. "Out of the question, I said! And now I don't want to hear another word about it. If things get so bad that we need a woman to help us out of a sticky situation . . ."

"And why not?" said Wilhelmine. "It really would be a help, deny it all you like. And Alsace is not a dangerous corner of the world, after all. It's just right for women."

"My *Samenstrich*? For women? Wilhelmine!" Gottlieb nearly choked with indignation. "I have a word or two to say to you about that. At home," he muttered.

Hannah, seeing support from an unexpected corner with Wilhelmine, ignored Gottlieb. "With a little preparation, we can do it! We still have the whole summer ahead of us, plenty of time to learn what we need to know about the different seeds." She tried to take Helmut's hand in hers, but he jerked it away. She turned away from him, insulted. Did he really think she couldn't do it just because she was a woman?

Lothar Gmeiner gave Hannah an approving look. "If Sera had suggested it, it would not have been anything special. But I have to say I would not have expected it from you."

All eyes—all but those of the two brothers—looked at Hannah with newfound regard, and she liked the way it felt.

Chapter Thirty-Two

It was a quiet summer morning. At six, the sun was already streaking the bedspread brightly through the gaps in the shutters.

Valentin loved summer. He loved the long days that never seemed to come to an end. He loved getting up early and working late in the fields.

Another one of those days was beginning. All he had to do was swing his legs over the side of the bed and pull on a thin shirt and shorts. But he allowed himself a moment longer in bed.

Propped on his right elbow, he studied his wife. It was something he did often, and gladly, especially in the mornings, when Seraphine was still asleep. She was wearing a white nightdress with pretty eyelets around the neckline. In the heat of the night, most of her hair had worked loose from the tight braid that she had woven it into the night before, and her hair now circled her pale face like a halo. Her eyelashes did not flicker, nor did her cheeks or even the delicate sides of her nose betray any sign of motion, so low and steady was her breathing.

She looked as if she were dead, Valentin abruptly thought. The flawless beauty, the coolness . . . He could not resist the impulse to stroke a few strands of hair clear of her face. Seraphine was so much finer than anyone else he knew. So much more sensitive.

And now this beautiful, delicate creature was supposed to travel with Hannah to Alsace to sell seeds? What was his mother thinking, supporting Hannah's suggestion? "Each in her own way is a good and likeable woman," his mother had replied, when he expressed his doubt about Seraphine's suitability for such an enterprise. "But here at home they are like two chickens who can't stand the sight of each other. You know yourself what it's like to go on the road together: you have to learn to get along. It will do both of them good, and maybe we'll have a little more peace in this house afterward. It will help financially, too." Valentin had looked away, ashamed of himself—things had gone so far that the women had to help make up for his and Helmut's idiocy.

He looked at his fingers, which had just touched the silvery strands of Seraphine's hair. Suddenly, Seraphine opened her eyes, instantly awake. "What do you want?" Her voice was as clear as water and as chilly.

Valentin flinched. How long had she been awake?

"Nothing. I—"

"Why are staring at me, even in my sleep? Can't I even rest in peace?"

"I'm not doing anything to you!" Valentin defended himself. Wasn't it completely normal for a man to look at his wife in a quiet moment? He sighed.

"I slept badly, but of course *you* didn't notice that at all," Seraphine hissed. "You're to blame for this ridiculous Alsace trip! Every time I think about it, I have nightmares."

Valentin jumped out of bed as if it were suddenly on fire.

"Excuse me for being stupid enough to let myself be robbed!" he shouted at her. "I'm just not man enough to give my wife a carefree life. But there's one thing you should know." He narrowed his eyes. "You can thank my wonderful brother for everything. If he hadn't insisted on going off with those women—"

He broke off. What had gotten into him? They had promised each other never to say a word about that.

"What . . . what women?" Seraphine frowned.

"Oh, you don't want to hear that part of it, do you?" He laughed bitterly. "Forget what I just said."

His legs were as heavy as lead as he trudged down the stairs to the kitchen. Over his shorts and shirt he had pulled on his coat of loneliness.

All his joy at the beautiful day was gone, and his mind was filled with gloomy thoughts. What was wrong with her?

At night, her passion nearly killed him. She showed him things he did not even know lovers could do. At night, he felt loved. In those hours, they belonged together, were closer than he had ever dreamed possible. His loneliness vanished, extinguished by a fire that burned away the wretchedness of his days.

But during the days . . . Seraphine wanted nothing to do with him. He had tried several times to ask her why things were as they were. Why she practically ate him alive at night, and during the day would not even hold his hand. In response, she looked at him as if she had no idea what he was talking about.

Sometimes she was cold and dismissive and said hurtful things, as she had just now. But most of the time she seemed to live in a world of her own. In her gaze, he could see that she often was somewhere else. And sometimes, even in the middle of the day, her eyes were closed, as if life itself exhausted her.

Valentin had tried everything he knew. He tried to be gentle and loving, tried to predict what she wanted before she knew it herself. He had bought sketchbooks for her, and new watercolors. And she had taken them without so much as a word of thanks.

Other times, he was rough with her, rougher than was in his nature. She was his wife, after all, and he could demand that she act reasonably with him. His outbursts brought none of the change in her that he wanted—Seraphine was as indifferent to his gestures of love as to his boorishness.

Because I mean nothing to her, he thought sullenly.

Helmut, however, only had to crack one of his dumb jokes, and Seraphine would open up like a freshly watered flower.

Why couldn't she be at least a little like Hannah, who laughed so resoundingly that he could practically look down her throat when she did. Hannah, who planted her lips to Helmut's cheek at every opportunity—often to the displeasure of their mother, who found such demonstrations of affection unseemly. Valentin could not remember ever seeing his parents embrace, let alone kiss. Maybe Seraphine was like his mother in that respect? He did not know if his parents loved each other, but they were still a married couple that had produced three children. That took love, didn't it? Or affection, at least . . .

Maybe, one day, it would be the same for them. Maybe a child would drag Seraphine out of her silence. And maybe make the thread that bound them at night visible in the daylight. A child—possibly even a son—that was his hope!

Valentin took a deep breath and pushed open the kitchen door.

What am I supposed to do? What am I supposed . . .

When Valentin left the room, Seraphine rolled onto her back again. Helmut and Valentin and some strange women in Vienna . . . what did that mean? Oh, if only she could slip out of her skin like a snake. But that was impossible.

She was pregnant.

She felt nothing at all for the child that lay like a tadpole some-where inside her. But she did feel something, of course: the child represented a problem for her.

She could not have a child with Valentin. Not because the child came from him—he was actually a nice enough man, and she *was* his wife, after all. But having a child was not why she was put on this earth. That was not the purpose she was destined to fulfill.

Sometimes, feeling melancholy, she regretted that it was so. Everything could have been so simple. She and Valentin could be parents, bound forever by the small being they had created. A carefree laugh here, a moment of married intimacy there . . . there were moments when she longed for no more than that.

But that life was not hers to live. At least, not with Valentin.

A child would destroy everything. Who would Helmut be able to turn to if she had to feed a wailing infant? She could already give him so little. Would he have sought the company of strange women in Vienna otherwise? How lonely he must have felt.

A child . . . I can't do that to Helmut.

Once she had realized that—and how simple and clear a realization it was—she let all her other thoughts run freely, like horses for which the gate has been opened.

What should I do?

The child had to go—it stood in the way of her love.

What should I . . . ? Of course she knew that sleeping with a man meant there was risk of getting pregnant. But she had underestimated the danger. She and Valentin? Unthinkable.

When she was younger, she had believed that a child could only be created when a couple were united in love. But ever since Hannah had come dancing into Gönningen with a baby inside her, Seraphine had known that love played no role.

And this child? How am I supposed to . . . ?

The year before, a woman in Gönningen had lost her child at the end of her pregnancy, and had almost died herself because of it. At the time, people said she had overexerted herself, out traveling with her husband almost until the last day.

Would her child die during the terrible journey to Alsace? Seraphine rolled restlessly from one side to the other.

Should I put my hopes in that?

It was still many weeks before they were due to leave. She might even be showing by then—a swollen belly would tell everyone. And what if the child survived the journey?

Perhaps if she fell? But what if she simply broke a leg? She could not risk that. After all, during the Alsace trip she had to prove that she was the better merchant. She was still annoyed at herself that she had not had the idea to go, and that Hannah had. On the other hand, Helmut seemed not particularly pleased with the entire situation . . . which was strange, she thought, not for the first time.

She sat up abruptly.

Of course!

Helmut had a bad conscience. Then Hannah presented her grand idea, and all she achieved was to make Helmut's conscience worse . . . How he must hate her for that!

Seraphine frowned. Why hadn't she probed deeper into the robbery story? If she had, she might know more, and could consider what it meant and how to react . . .

She had grown careless, had let her attention wander. She was too caught up in herself and not giving Helmut enough thought. No wonder he barely looked at her sometimes. She had believed so deeply that everything would be better once he came home from Russia, that he would see she was the right woman for him. Instead, all he had on his mind was money: the money that had been stolen from him, the money that they would have to earn on their next trip. Money, money, money—and no room left for compliments, a friendly word, a tender look.

If Seraphine had not known better, she could believe that she no longer meant as much to him as she once had. But there was still that invisible, unbreakable bond between them. She sensed it, Valentin sensed it, and Hannah sensed it most of all!

Seraphine smiled maliciously.

Maybe I should tell dear Hannah what I found out from Valentin. We'll see how thrilled she is about traveling after that.

It had taken Seraphine a long time to find a weakness in her sister-in-law—apart from her general commonness. She was hardworking, generally in a good mood, rarely insulted. All virtues that went down well with the Kerners. But Hannah was jealous—*that* was her weakness!

Maybe I'll keep this news to myself for a little while. I'm sure the right time will come to surprise Hannah with it.

The child . . . it had to go. It would destroy everything she had lived for until now.

Oh, star fairy, why didn't you watch over me better than this?

There were certain plants, she had heard, that would give a person terrible diarrhea and stomach cramps. Would they also get rid of the child? Which plants? And how much would she need to eat? She didn't want to give herself a lethal dose.

Valentin! He had done this to her, but this was something he must never find out about. He would kill her if he knew what she was planning. She felt a little sorry for him. He tried so hard, after all. Why couldn't she make an effort, too?

And if, for a moment, she thought seriously about the impossible? What if she actually gave birth to the child? What if she actually tried, as hard as she could, to love Valentin?

Impossible. Not as long as Helmut possessed her heart. And he always would. She punched the bedcover indignantly. This was no time to give any thought to Valentin or how he felt. But what was she supposed to do? Maybe there was some kind of magic . . .

Oh, star fairy, why couldn't you let my blood flow like you do every other month? If only everything were good again. If only the child were gone.

Maybe she could make her blood flow? Get the child out the same way it had gone in?

Experimentally, Seraphine pushed one finger inside herself, back to the cave where she suspected the child's nest must lie. Nothing. It must be deeper.

Maybe it was so small that she could not yet feel it with a bare hand? It took a long time, after all, before other people could see that a woman was pregnant.

She needed something else. Something long, pointed. The child would not give up its hold on her easily.

Seraphine looked around the room.

Her brushes. There they were, on the table.

Late the previous afternoon, she had started a new painting: the orchard in the meadow, the sun setting behind the apple trees. She had done a good job with the small, immature apples, but then her setting sun had been smothered by a mass of dark clouds, and she had torn the picture to pieces.

Creation and destruction were so close . . .

Seraphine stood and went to the table. Which brush should she use? She chose the biggest, then slipped back into bed.

The pain was bearable. She had experience living with pain. And mental or physical—what was the difference? She gritted her teeth and listened to her jaws grinding. That and her loud breathing were the only sounds in the room. She had to remember to breathe, she must not faint . . . for Helmut.

Star fairy, watch over me.

She felt something. Resistance, something soft . . . the child was a part of her . . . She did not want to think about that. She bored deeper. Everything became softer and softer, warm, wet. It hurt so very, very much . . .

She had not thought to lay an old cloth on the bed! If it worked, if her plan functioned, there would be a lot of blood. One might even see what was there . . .

Seraphine paused and set her tool aside. Half fainting with the pain, she staggered to the cupboard and rummaged around, looking for the rags she normally used for her monthly bleeding. Too late. Blood ran down her legs in a hot, pale-red stream.

Quickly, she pushed the whole wad of rags between her legs. That was good, or better. She made it back to the bed with the last of her strength, dropped the brush behind the headboard. No traces . . . she was clever. The thought that she had everything under control comforted and calmed her. She closed her eyes, gave herself up to the waves of pain that washed over her.

After a short time, she felt how the rags grew soft and warm. So much blood?

She had done it. She had succeeded in pushing the child out of its nest. Nothing more would grow there, nothing more, nothing but her great love . . . for Helmut.

An hour later, when Valentin, at his mother's behest, went to wake Seraphine—the women had arranged to go berry picking—he at first thought that she had fallen back into a deep sleep. But he was surprised when she did not react even to being shaken. Acting on impulse, he pulled back the blanket. What he saw frightened him half to death. Blood! Blood everywhere!

The doctor who came to Seraphine's bedside had never seen anything quite like it and was deeply concerned. He brought her around with smelling salts and sat while she explained that the cramps had begun in the night. Her period was due, and her bleeding was usually quite severe, she explained. Women's business, then . . . no need to worry . . .

The doctor patted her arm. She was a young woman; bleeding like that was to be expected when she was older. The blood loss together with the morning heat . . . and Seraphine was a pale creature at the best of times. It was perhaps not unusual that she had fainted, all things considered.

Seraphine smiled weakly.

The doctor made a few notes and wrote a prescription. He recommended that Seraphine drink beet juice, which he said was conducive to restoring the blood, and generally advised her to rest and not exert herself.

Valentin charged out of the house to get the tonic the doctor had prescribed. He would have liked a tonic to assuage his own conscience, too. *There I was thinking she looked like a corpse, and I didn't even ask her if she was feeling well!* he reprimanded himself over and over. Who knew how long she'd been suffering like that, month after month. Was it any surprise, then, for a woman to be cool and remote?

Chapter Thirty-Three

Summer began to falter, and autumn was just around the corner. Every day was filled with work. Apples and pears had to be picked, cored, and sliced into thin rings. The rings were then dried on special racks in the large oven—sweaty work, especially because it was still very warm for that time of year. And there was plenty to be harvested out in the vegetable fields, too. Seraphine was still recovering from her bleeding episode, so most of that work fell to Hannah, and it didn't bother her in the slightest. She was thrilled by every cabbage she cut from its stalk and every bean she picked: she had planted the seeds herself, after all. Every day, the Kerners' basement filled a little more: dried fruit, onions, potatoes. The sight of it filled Hannah with pride and satisfaction. Her parents had always bought the vegetables and groceries that they served the customers of The Golden Anchor at the market or from traveling merchants. Instead of a garden, her parents' inn had no more than a grim rear courtyard. If she had stayed in Nuremberg, Hannah would never have known how much fun it could be to plant her own food and watch it grow.

She did not tire of the earthy smells that hung over the fields—the slight odor of decay that rose from the cabbage patch, the sweet overripe apples in the orchards, and the intense aroma of cut lovage and savory.

The mixture of fragrances teased Hannah's nose, at once captivating her and making her a little sad.

As if by some secret arrangement, the good weather came to an end on Hannah and Seraphine's last day in Gönningen. The day they were supposed to depart, Hannah looked out the window to see a day as gray and gloomy as she felt inside. A chill wind blew small branches and leaves through the streets, and raindrops splattered onto the cobblestones. Wilhelmine's rosebushes cowered from the rain against the house well. There was not a soul in sight.

Hope germinated inside her. No one would expect them to leave in such miserable weather. She crept back into bed beside Helmut, who would be leaving with Valentin a few days later.

But an hour later the clouds parted, the day brightened, and the October sun reflected blindingly from the surfaces of puddles and wet stones.

Hannah's reprieve was over.

"How do I look?" Hannah straightened her green traveling dress one last time. She reached up with her right hand and touched her black lace bonnet, which she had fixed in place with hairpins. There was no outfit ordained for the women who went out from Gönningen as seed traders, but the black bonnet had become something to recognize them by. Hannah had been given hers by Wilhelmine, and Seraphine wore her own.

"Good," Helmut answered, but that was all. He was trying to keep a wriggling Flora in his arms. Then he seemed to think better of his one-word reply and added, "You and Seraphine will have the Alsatians eating out of your hands. You'll have sold the lot in no time, wait and see!"

Hannah sighed. She could certainly use the encouraging words, for she was far less sure of herself than her husband seemed to be. Several times already, she had regretted opening her mouth on Flora's birthday as she had.

"They'll probably lay us bare as pretenders in minutes . . . I mean, we don't know *so* much about farming, despite what we've learned this summer." She glanced over at Seraphine, who was standing in silence with Valentin a little way off—another way to say goodbye. Then she looked at the parcel of food for the road that Wilhelmine had given her earlier. Hard-boiled eggs, bread, a chunk of cheese. Abruptly, she turned away from Helmut, took a few steps back toward the house as if she wanted to go inside again, turned back to Helmut once more.

Helmut stood and watched this strange dance with a playful smile.

"I'm going to miss everything here so much! Rossberg, the Wiesaz, and all of you most!" Hannah threw her arms around Wilhelmine, who had just joined them. Her mother-in-law smiled and extricated herself from Hannah's embrace. She pinched Hannah's cheeks as if she were a little child.

"Who would have thought that someone from outside could fall so in love with our Gönningen? But keep in mind: it was *your* idea to go on the road."

Hannah nodded. "I'm terribly excited about going out, but when I think of little Flora . . ." Her heart sank as she looked at Helmut and Flora. If she did not control herself, she'd start crying and never stop. She wished her goodbyes were behind her already.

Helmut laughed. "Now you know how I feel every time I have to leave."

He set Flora down on the ground and picked up Hannah's seed sack.

"It's only for a few weeks, and who knows? Maybe you'll like traveling. If not, then you'll just have to grin and bear it!" Skillfully, he fastened the seed sack's straps under Hannah's arms.

Hannah looked up to see Gottlieb hurrying from the direction of the town hall.

"Did you pack my route description?" he asked loudly as he came to a stop. "Remember: when you stay at The Cobbler Inn in Herrenberg, you have to remind the woman who runs it about the special price that I—"

"We'll remember everything you've told us, no need to worry!" Hannah placated him. She rummaged in a bag and produced a thick writing pad. "All here, see?" she said, although she was not sure when she was supposed to read the pages of detailed instructions.

Helmut's father screwed up his face. "You know I'd love to be coming . . ."

Hannah stroked his cheek, which made Gottlieb jump back in shock. He was not used to such tenderness in public.

"Keep the pressure on those men in Tübingen and see that we get our post office here. We promise we'll do a good job with your *Samenstrich*." Hannah was surprised at how firm her voice sounded, but at the same time her knees were trembling.

Hannah straightened her shoulders. The heavy seed sack was already pressing uncomfortably into her back. In the meantime, Seraphine had also joined them. Valentin stood behind her, his face blank.

With a sob, Hannah threw herself on Helmut's breast, but he pushed her away gently.

"Go now. Saying goodbye gets harder if one drags it out."

They had not yet put the last outlying houses of Gönningen behind them when Hannah burst into tears.

"I can't do it . . . Flora!" Her whole body trembled, and the seed sack quaked on her back with every heaving sob.

"Don't worry now," she heard Seraphine say quietly. In the middle of her sobbing, Hannah was not certain that she had heard her correctly. Seraphine was trying to *console* her? She blew her nose loudly into a handkerchief.

Seraphine smiled. "That's better. And while we're at it, don't you think we should make peace? No more fighting. We need to stick together, don't we?" She tilted her head to one side like a squirrel eyeing a particularly attractive hazelnut. "The journey will be much easier for both of us like that."

Hannah stopped in the middle of wiping her nose. She looked suspiciously at the hand that Seraphine extended. What was this all about? Some kind of ill intent lurked behind it, Hannah was certain.

"All right," she said regardless, and grasped Seraphine's outstretched hand. All the time, a voice inside her was screaming, *Nooo!*

The passing wagoners were quick to pick up two pretty young women, so they made good time. Again and again, Hannah looked back over her shoulder to see if she could still catch a glimpse of Gönningen, but the village had long since been swallowed up by the hilly landscape. Until that morning, she had done no more than trace on a map the roads that led out from the seed merchants' village into the wider world—and now she was traveling those roads herself.

To escape her gloomy mood, Hannah began to repeat to herself the knowledge that she would need to know as a prospective seed merchant. "Cucumbers need warm earth and sunshine. They can only be planted when no more nighttime frosts are to be expected. Cauliflower needs to be well fertilized and the soil loosened up periodically. Runner beans don't like cool north or east winds, so consider that when choosing where to plant them. Kohlrabi . . . what was it about kohlrabi, again?"

Seraphine shook her head. "The people will already know all that."

"But what if they don't? Oh God, what do we do if someone wants to know about the different kinds of kohlrabi?" Hannah groaned dramatically.

"Then we can only hope that we come up with something clever to say," said Seraphine drily.

Hannah giggled nervously. "Forget the kohlrabi for a moment. Do you remember all the different kinds of leeks? And are you supposed to fertilize the soil for lettuce or not?"

"The leeks . . . hmmm . . ." But that was all Seraphine said.

Suddenly, everything was gone, everything that they had spent evening after evening for weeks learning by heart with their husbands, as if blown away on the wind.

"Well, aren't we off to a wonderful start? We're going to make complete fools of ourselves," Hannah said. Pessimistic she might be, but she was surprised to find that her mood had brightened considerably.

In Tübingen they quickly found someone who was traveling on toward Herrenberg. Neither woman had heard of the place he named as his destination, but a quick look at Gottlieb's old map told them that they would be going in the right direction. The man's wagon was full, so they squeezed beside him on the driver's bench. The driver turned out to be a garrulous fellow, and while he entertained Seraphine, Hannah tried to compare the route they were following with Gottlieb's descriptions in the writing pad—a fruitless undertaking, as it soon became evident. Nothing of what he wrote resembled the road they were traveling along. It seemed that there were several roads that led to Herrenberg. Disappointed, Hannah pushed the pad and the map back into her bag.

For a brief moment, an uneasy feeling came over her at the trust they were putting in this stranger. What if he was taking them somewhere else entirely? What if his intentions were sinister? She glanced covertly across at him and decided that he really looked completely harmless. He threw his energy into one story after the other, and was happy to elicit an occasional admiring "Incredible!" or a horrified "Oh my goodness!" from Seraphine. Even so, Hannah was determined that from Herrenberg onward, they would follow the route described by Gottlieb to the letter. And if they were unable to find a wagon to take them that way, then so be it—they would just have to go on foot. The decision allowed her to relax a little.

The sky was filled with fast-flying clouds, and between them the sky looked like a blue blanket. The sun peeped out from behind a cloud and doused the landscape in honey-colored light. And although the wagon was only rolling at a walking pace, the breeze was fresh and came from in front of them, causing Hannah's traveling dress to billow. And whenever they passed beneath low-hanging branches, tattered cobwebs brushed into her face. Oh yes, it was autumn.

Hannah watched a wedge of birds flying languidly southward.

The seed merchants are like migratory birds. They come and go with the same regularity.

Where had she heard those words before? It had not been long ago, but she could not match them to a person. All she knew was that she had heard the words in Gönningen.

Hannah smiled. A not unpleasant melancholy settled over her. Autumn was the season of departures, the season in which the Gönningers set off for other places, foreign lands. The only difference from the year before was that, this year, she, too, was starting out. Like a migratory bird . . .

Dusk was already starting to settle when the wagon driver stopped. They would part there. He had to go right toward the brewery where he would fill his barrels, but the way to Herrenberg continued straight ahead.

"In about three miles you'll reach a small patch of woods. Just as you leave the woods, you'll come to a track on the left that will take you into Herrenberg. That way is too narrow for a cart, and bumpy besides, but it's an excellent shortcut for anyone traveling on foot. It should be well trodden at this time of year, so you can't miss it." He added that Hannah and Seraphine would reach Herrenberg in two hours at the most.

"Finally!" The wagon was hardly out of sight when Hannah dashed into the bushes. She had been holding it in for hours!

When she was finished, she straightened her skirt and rejoined Seraphine, who was looking along the path in the direction of the woods.

"I wonder if it would be more sensible to go around the outside? It will be dark soon."

Hannah was also uneasy at the thought of passing through the unknown woods alone. She looked at her sister-in-law. "I don't think we have any choice. If we don't drag our feet, we'll be out the other side quickly enough." She put as much confidence as possible into her voice, but was secretly willing to entertain any objections Seraphine might put forward: *I'm too tired, I can't walk anymore, the forest scares me, why don't we wait for another wagon to come by and pick us up* . . .

But instead of lamenting their lot, Seraphine nodded. "Let's get going then," she said, and set off at a fast pace.

Perplexed, Hannah marched after her. What had gotten into Seraphine?

Chapter Thirty-Four

With every step, the forest grew denser. Beeches and oaks gave way to conifers. The little light that penetrated the foliage of the tall trees was absorbed by dark swathes of moss, and the women did not progress as quickly as they would have liked. The danger of slipping or stepping in a hole or stumbling over an exposed root was great.

For a time, only their heavy breathing could be heard. "It's as silent as a church here," Seraphine finally whispered.

"A church isn't nearly as spooky as this," Hannah murmured in reply, and added, "Why are we whispering, by the way?"

They both giggled nervously, listening to the low sounds—the normal sounds?—of the forest.

Hannah hoped that their entire route to Alsace was not as spooky as that little patch of woods. She was so nervous that her stomach muscles ached. How could Seraphine be so calm in this dismal wilderness? She was completely different from the Seraphine that Hannah knew from Gönningen.

One could almost describe her as . . . superior. She was, after all, a seed merchant's daughter at heart.

Hannah squealed and stopped in her tracks. Her hand flew to her chest as if to stop her racing heart from bursting out. Heavens, what was that?

Seraphine wheeled around. "What is it? Why did you scream?"

Hannah pointed to the right. "There . . . it just drops off. I can hear water, too."

Just inches away, right beside the path, the ground opened into a chasm. One false step and she would have tumbled into it! Hannah felt her skin prickle and the small hairs on her forearms stand up.

"Come on, Hannah. We must keep on while it's still light."

Hannah, dumbstruck, looked at her sister-in-law. *While it's still light* . . . If that gloom was light for Seraphine, what would darkness look like? Knees trembling, she put one foot in front of the other, while Seraphine marched ahead briskly.

Hannah was greatly relieved when the forest began to thin half an hour later. The shortcut that the driver had mentioned was actually wider than the path they had just followed, and in another half an hour they had put the forest well behind them. Through a thin veil of fog, they could see shimmering lights—a farmstead, or already the first houses of Herrenberg?

Pressing one fist against her aching back, Hannah walked faster. She was tired and thirsty and wanted to get the seed sack off her back. But she did not want to stop now, not at one of the many springs that bubbled out of the earth around them, or to rest her back. Soon they would reach the town and find the inn that Gottlieb had recommended. They would be able to drink beer, eat bread, pull off their tight boots, stretch their arms and legs, and—

She was so lost in her vision that she did not notice that Seraphine had suddenly stopped in front of her, and Hannah walked straight into her seed sack. Her sister-in-law grumbled and Hannah apologized.

Seraphine nodded toward the hazy lights in front of them. "That's definitely not Herrenberg. Not yet. Probably just an outlying farm. But I think we should go there and ask for directions. Strange that we haven't seen anything of the town yet. Maybe on the other side of that hill? Or more to the right . . ."

Again, Seraphine led the way. Admittedly, so far, they had ridden most of the way, and the journey had not been particularly strenuous. But Seraphine felt as if she could tear the dark trees in front of them out by the roots.

It was as if, by leaving Gönningen, she had left all her cares behind. As if she had shed her old scales like a snake and was traveling now through unknown lands in a brand new skin. With every step she took, she thought of Helmut. Helmut, to whom she wanted to prove, with this trip, that *she* was a true seed merchant's wife and not an outsider. She would not tire, and she would do her business cleverly—no doubt people would prefer to buy from a beautiful woman than from a plain one! In her mind's eye, she could already see Helmut's admiration when she returned home with a sack of money. The very thought energized her.

Seraphine looked back over her shoulder. A few steps behind her, Hannah was huffing and puffing along. She looked quite exhausted already. Would this be a good opportunity to tell her casually that Helmut had gone off after some whores in Vienna? No, she would save that for later.

When she had offered, that morning, to bury the hatchet with Hannah, it was not because her attitude toward her sister-in-law had changed. Quite the opposite. When she had seen Hannah's tear-drenched farewell to Helmut, she wanted nothing more than to drag her off him. But to offer Hannah her friendship seemed necessary. She wanted Hannah to think that she, Seraphine, was no threat to her. Let her think she held the scepter, as usual. She'd find out soon enough that times had changed. Here, far away from familiar surroundings, Hannah was no longer the big talker, no longer as loud and confident as usual. There! Was she actually whimpering? And there she was again, tripping over her own feet. *That* was how Helmut should see his wife!

With every step closer to the farm, the uneasy feeling in the pit of Seraphine's stomach grew. Her body stiffened, her hands clenched into fists, and she tried to swallow the hard knot forming in her throat. She walked down the final slope apprehensively.

If it were not for the light shining from two of the windows, she would have thought the farm abandoned. Half of the roof of the main house was missing, shutters hung strangely on their hinges, and some windows had actually been boarded up. Even in the gloom of early evening, it was clear that the two smaller outbuildings were in a similarly desolate condition. The entire property looked as if it could tell many unhappy stories.

Stories that Seraphine did not want to hear.

The house exuded poverty like sweat from feverish skin, and Seraphine, for a moment, was overcome by loneliness, at once terrifying and oppressive. Suddenly, everything she thought she had left far behind returned—the feeling of being in the wrong place, the sense of injustice, her mother's forbearance, her own silent fear before every new day.

The star fairy had rescued her from exactly these conditions, conditions that were no longer part of her life.

The thought should have been a solace, but Seraphine's expression hardened as they drew closer. She had no desire to scratch at that old wound, so prone to infection and pus.

Let's just go on. We'll find Herrenberg by ourselves, she wanted to say to Hannah just as her sister-in-law came up to her.

"Who would live here?" There was apprehension in Hannah's voice, too, as she pushed aside the overgrown hawthorn still between them and the farmyard. "Whoever it is, I have no desire to spend long here. We'll ask for directions, then—"

A strange rattling sound came from close by, at ground level. At the same time a dog began to bark loudly.

Before Seraphine could even turn to her, Hannah dropped to the ground. She cried out like a mortally wounded animal, and her face was twisted in pain. "My leg . . ."

Seraphine's eyes moved down, and she saw a rusted object of some kind among the hawthorn spines. She yelped in fright. "A trap! You've stepped in a trap!" Her eyes widened as she stared at Hannah's right foot, caught between the teeth of a steel fox trap. The teeth had buried themselves into Hannah's ankle above her shoe, and she was already bleeding.

Ignoring the hawthorn spines, Seraphine tried to open the trap with her bare hands. But as hard as she pulled and tore at it, the iron jaws did not move at all.

"Oh God, what do we do now?"

Seraphine looked at her hands. Her knuckles were scraped and bleeding, and blood ran from a cut on her thumb and mixed with the rust of the fox trap. Cold sweat beaded on her forehead. The effort and the fear had made her dizzy. She swallowed her spittle, but it went the wrong way, and she had to cough. Hannah's leg . . . it looked so horrible. Like a dead creature in an iron maw.

"You . . . have to . . . get help," Hannah muttered through clenched teeth.

"But where? I'm not going into that house by myself! Who knows who's there . . ." Tears sprang to Seraphine's eyes. She didn't want this! Hannah was supposed to suffer on this trip. She was supposed to go tumbling off her high horse and finally realize that she was no good as Helmut's wife, that she was preventing him from being happy. But not like this! It was horrible, just horrible. A nightmare . . . She wrung her hands in helplessness.

"Jesus Christ, pull yourself together!" Hannah screamed, still pulling desperately at the trap. "Your whining isn't going to help us now. Go into that house and get somebody out here who can open this thing. I can't get out of it by myself." Hannah gave way to tears herself, and the whites of her eyes glowed in the darkness. "Go, damn it! Go!"

Like a marionette controlled by a stranger's hand, Seraphine stalked off toward the house. As if with eyes in the back of her head, she could still see Hannah: tangled in the bushy hawthorn, her hair a mess, her face scratched by the thorns, her leg like something lifeless, unnaturally twisted. Oh God, why did this have to happen? *Hannah is helpless. She needs me . . .* Seraphine tried to concentrate on that thought.

An accident. On their first day. Something that none of them thought could happen.

Star fairy, is this your doing?

A fox trap. Bestial. Horrible. Something for which no one could be held accountable.

And it had to happen *here*, far from any town.

If she could only see something. But night had fallen completely now. Was it seven o'clock? Or eight, even? Seraphine had lost all sense of time.

In the dark, one could easily go astray and get lost, especially in an unfamiliar environment. Another thing to think about.

What if I can't find Hannah again? Would she survive the night alone?

Seraphine stopped abruptly. She frowned. Her fingers burned where the skin was scraped open. She licked her finger and dabbed the spittle on her cut thumb. What if Hannah bled to death? Or froze? She was already exhausted from their march through the forest. A long night out here alone, unprotected, injured—surely she would not live through that.

And what would Seraphine say when she got home again? *Hannah stumbled into a trap.* That's what she would say, but not in the strangely cheerful tone that she heard in her mind.

Hannah stumbled into a trap—wasn't that strange? Single-minded Hannah, of all people.

Before the horrified, uncomprehending eyes of the family, she would burst into tears and relate how she herself had tried desperately to fetch help. And how she had wandered helplessly through the night, and when she had found Hannah again the next morning, she . . .

Seraphine blinked and tried to think clearly. Wasn't she really in the process of getting lost just then? If she closed her eyes, where was forward? Where was back? Which direction had they come from? And where was Herrenberg? It was very easy to lose one's orientation. All you had to do was go a few hundred steps in the wrong direction . . .

Seraphine closed her eyes, stretched out her arms, and began to turn like a top.

The wrong direction . . .

Hannah. Out of my life forever.

Fast now. Faster.

If your legs could hardly carry you, then which way was forward and which way back?

Her dance was accompanied by the shrill barking of the chained dog protesting the presence of strangers on its territory. Seraphine smiled.

A penetrating buzzing sound filled her head. Thoughts dissolved, and she felt strangely weightless.

The wrong direction . . . an accident . . . terrible . . . no more cares . . . Helmut liberated . . . for her . . . finally . . .

"What do you want here?" Every word was the lash of a whip.

Startled half to death, Seraphine opened her eyes and almost stumbled into the outstretched arms of a woman.

"I . . ." She noted with horror the knife that gleamed in the woman's right hand. She instinctively lifted her hands. *I'm harmless!* she wanted to cry, but the words would not come out.

Star fairy, where are you?

"You tell me what business you have on my land!" The knife shimmered, silvery in the hazy moonlight. "If you think I've got anything to take, you're in the wrong place." The woman laughed hoarsely. "Others have already tried, and they got what was coming."

Seraphine stared at the other woman. She looked like she would not hesitate to use her weapon. Even in the dark, she could see that the woman's face was blotched with birthmarks and liver spots, and her hair was shorn back to the scalp—she looked almost as if she had death's head on her shoulders.

"I . . ." She flailed one hand vaguely behind her. "I wanted to get help. My . . . sister-in-law stepped on a trap." She tried as hard as she could to stand up to the other woman's contemptuous gaze.

"Get help? And what was that Saint Vitus's dance all about? Who are you trying to fool?" The woman snorted with derision. Without another word, she turned and started to walk back to her rundown house.

Seraphine gaped after her. "Stop! Wait! You can't just—"

The woman spun back to Seraphine like a dervish. "What can't I do?" Suddenly, she was so close that Seraphine felt her breath on her face. "What I do on *my* land is *my* business. I have a right to protect what is mine. If an intruder lands in one of my traps, then that's too bad!" She stalked away quickly to a shed that lay to the right of the main house and tugged at the door until it gave way and opened with a creak.

Traps? Did that mean there were more of them? Seraphine scanned the ground around her anxiously. What was this place?

The next moment, the woman returned and held out a curved length of iron. "You can use that to lever open the trap. And then go! Fast!"

Seraphine took the tool and stared at it in horror. "But . . . what do I do with it? I don't know where . . . or how . . ."

Cursing, the woman snatched the iron bar back again. "You still remember where the trap was, don't you?"

Seraphine nodded and took off, leading the way.

Chapter Thirty-Five

When they reached her, they discovered that the woman in the trap had slipped into unconsciousness. It took Evelyn only a few seconds to pry the trap open with the iron bar. The injured foot, meanwhile, had swollen considerably, and blood and rust were mixed into a sticky mass where the teeth of the trap had bitten into her skin.

What a mess! It was inconceivable that the two young women could travel on that night. And she could not leave the injured woman there, either. It was the start of October, and the nights were already quite cold.

Swearing to herself, Evelyn pushed her hands under the injured woman's arms and half dragged, half lifted her back to the house. The other woman followed behind with two huge sacks.

Inside, Evelyn deposited the woman on a wooden bench.

"Here, take these rags and wash her leg. You'll find water over there. Wash it well!" she said to the second woman, and then she went outside again. When she came back, she was carrying a bunch of herbs, which she quickly ground to a paste with a mortar and pestle. It would help prevent blood poisoning, she explained as she applied the paste to the lesions. While she was treating the wound, the injured woman came around momentarily, but passed out again from the pain and exhaustion.

And what now? Evelyn was not used to having visitors. What was she supposed to do with the other one? She did not want to spend the night with two women she had never met, but neither could she simply throw them out, especially after one of them had stepped in one of *her* traps. Stupid women! What were they doing creeping around out there anyway?

Reluctantly, Evelyn fetched apple juice and two cups from her cupboard and banged them onto the table. She noted the look of suspicion on the stranger's face.

"I'm not about to poison you, never fear," she mocked, pouring juice into both cups.

She watched as the stranger sipped cautiously, then gulped at the juice. Shining, silvery hair, eyes as big as a doe's, flawless skin. Not a freckle, not a wart to blemish her perfect complexion. An uncommonly beautiful young woman, like a princess. And there sat Evelyn, her head shaved, deep-set eyes, and a dress that hadn't been washed in weeks.

The princess and the witch—Evelyn guffawed at the thought. No wonder the girl was looking at her in such fright.

Supporting her weight on her elbows, Evelyn leaned across the table. "Right, now I want to know what business you have setting foot on my land."

The princess explained briefly that they were seed merchants. "All we wanted was to ask directions—but if you see that as a crime . . ." She shook her head with disgust and went on. "How can anyone put out a trap so close to a public path? You can almost guarantee that someone is going to step in it, sooner or later."

The stranger sounded angry and morose—but whatever fear she had felt at her first sight of Evelyn had disappeared utterly from her voice. There seemed more to this princess than a delicate, anxious girl. She recalled the stranger's bizarre dance: her arms out wide, her eyes closed, she had been spinning wildly, jerkily, as if trying to make herself giddy. What had that been about?

"As you may already have noticed, I live alone here. I have to protect myself," Evelyn said with no trace of remorse. "Seed merchants, you are? We get one of those through here once or twice a year. A man. Perhaps he's from your village." She shrugged. "Seems to me you must live a free life." An involuntary sigh escaped her. Quickly, she drank a mouthful of her juice.

"Well, not as free as you might think," the princess replied. "We have our regular traveling times, and the regions in which we are allowed to sell our seeds are generally fixed. We seed merchants all have our own trading territories, and we respect each other's rights in that regard."

Evelyn nodded. It was not as if the details of seed trading particularly interested her—but this stranger certainly did. There was something about her . . . something in her eyes that struck a chord in Evelyn. Mentally, she gave herself a shake. What did she care about this girl? Had she grown so lonely that she felt the need to make a stranger talk? The thought angered her. Even in her anger, however, she heard herself say, "But there is no husband to tell you what you have to do—that's what I would call freedom."

The princess creased her brow. "Gönningen women do marry, of course. But that does not mean that we are dependent. We have been traveling alone in our *Samenstriche* for hundreds of years—and there are many who would gladly have their husband at their side when they travel," she added, her face twisting into a grimace.

Evelyn had to laugh, and the stranger laughed with her.

So she has a sense of humor, too . . . Evelyn took a deep breath, looked closely into the princess's eyes for a moment, then stood up, opened a cupboard, and sat down again with a loaf of bread and a block of cheese. She began to cut thin slices from both with the same knife she had used to threaten her guest earlier. The entire situation struck her as so ludicrous that she had trouble withstanding the urge to burst into hysterical laughter.

Then she nodded in the direction of the sleeping woman. "You don't like her much, do you?"

"What makes you think that?"

Evelyn did not miss the horror in the stranger's voice—she had hit the nail on the head! She grinned. But she did not know herself how she had come to the realization. It was a feeling . . . the way the princess looked at the other woman. Not openly hostile, but not with the concern one might otherwise expect in such a situation.

"My name is Evelyn, by the way."

"And mine is Seraphine. Evelyn and Seraphine—not the two most typical names."

"Nor the most typical women, I'd say." Evelyn raised her eyebrows. She did not know if their sudden familiarity pleased her. At the same time, her fascination with Seraphine grew.

Normally, she did not care much about other people. But now, suddenly, with this unexpected guest, she found all kinds of questions burning on her tongue—the young woman seemed so . . . peculiar. What was going on behind that pretty forehead? What kind of life did these seed-merchant women lead? Evelyn decided to curb her curiosity, to wait and see if the stranger would open up by herself.

She did not have to wait long.

"She took my husband from me. He is the great love of my life."

Evelyn tilted her head and looked at Seraphine. That was all it took.

Haltingly, Seraphine began to talk about how the injured woman, Hannah, appeared in Gönningen one day and what happened after that. She corrected herself constantly, looking for more fitting words to express how she felt. She seemed unused to telling stories. Had she no friends there in her village? Was this Seraphine just as lonely as she herself was? Evelyn could not see the rhyme or reason in everything the girl said, and she had questions she wanted to ask, but the words were tumbling from Seraphine's lips now, and she did not want to interrupt.

"I hate her!" she finally said, and stopped speaking. The slight pinching around her mouth, which had nearly disappeared while she spoke, returned, more tense than ever.

For a moment, neither woman spoke. "You could have left her lying there," Evelyn finally said. "Out there, in the trap."

"I could have. Then I'd be free. Free for the love of my life." Seraphine sat up and straightened her shoulders as if that action would give her strength.

"But you did not." Evelyn's eyes narrowed, and she scrutinized her guest. "Because I came along?"

Seraphine shrugged. She broke her slice of bread in two, laid a piece of cheese on one half, and bit into it. A slight twitch beneath one eye was enough to show that Evelyn's question had ruffled her. It was a kind of answer. Then the girl began to speak again.

"I might have done it. But I might have been too cowardly, too. It doesn't matter, because you took the decision away from me. You with your knife and your venom and your traps and tools!" Seraphine suddenly burst out. "For the first time in forever, fate could have been kind to me. And then *you* came along! You—" She broke off, as if she could not think of a suitable term of abuse.

"Fate!" said Evelyn with a sniff of contempt. She was very close to taking the silly girl by the shoulders and shaking her for her arrogance, shaking . . . "What do you know about fate? A 'fateful' accident, and suddenly your adversary is out of the game! What would have happened after that? How would you have lived with what you'd done? Not well, I can tell you that, because—" She stopped abruptly. Good heavens, she was on the verge of incriminating herself.

"Because you've been through it," Seraphine said matter-of-factly. Evelyn blinked. Her coolness. Her expectant eyes!

"Yes. I've been through it," she said slowly.

"And?"

Incredulous, Evelyn stared at Seraphine. "You think I'd tell you about it?"

"I can see it in you."

Their eyes locked. Evelyn looked away first. She smiled, and did not hesitate long.

"I was married once, too," she began. But how does one summarize a life in a few sentences? "This place used to be a large farm, with a lot of acres of land. We grew hops and sold them to the breweries hereabouts for a good price. When I married into the farm, I was twenty-four. My husband, Kurt, was in his forties. Not the love of my life, but things could have been worse. I was never as pretty as you. At first, things went well enough, but then came the first bad year—the rains destroyed our entire crop. Money was tight. My husband hadn't put anything aside. Then came the second bad year; some kind of disease attacked our hops. Kurt mixed manure and fertilized, sprayed, cut back the plants, everything he could think of, all for nothing. No harvest, no money. No life. Suddenly, I was to blame for everything. Ever since I'd come to the farm, his luck had vanished—and this was a grown man talking! First, we sold the pigs, then our cow. But Kurt didn't buy new seeds with the money we got. He drove to Herrenberg—we still had our horse and wagon—and drank the lot. And when he came home, he beat me. I could not believe that he was treating me so roughly—I hadn't done anything bad at all! I blamed it on the schnapps. One time doesn't count, does it? At least, that's what I told myself. But it didn't stop with once. The second time, he broke my arm here"—she pushed up her sleeve and revealed a strangely malformed elbow—"and another time he hit me so hard in the back that I had to crawl on all fours for a week. I was pregnant then. The child was stillborn."

Evelyn stared into space, her eyes empty. *Stop talking, stop telling, it hurts so much,* screamed everything inside her.

"And no one helped you? Someone must have seen what was going on."

"Tell me who. And even if someone had, since when has it been a crime for a husband to beat his wife?"

Evelyn screwed up her face bitterly.

"A few months later, I was pregnant again. I was so happy to have another chance at a child, and I thought my husband was, too. As soon as we had an heir for the farm, I hoped he would come to his senses again. He'd been a hardworking farmer once, you know. To this day, I don't know why he changed. One or two bad harvests . . . that's nothing unusual. We all know what lean years are like, and the good years always come again. That's how life is.

"But we kept on fighting. Maybe I should have held my tongue more often, but when he was drunk, everything I did was wrong. If I said nothing, I was a pigheaded old goat, and if I answered back, I was an insolent bitch. He hit me, and he hit me. And every time he did it, I hoped that it would be the last time. That he would go back to being the man I knew before—an everyday, honest, decent man. Ha! I would have waited a long time for that. I did my best to protect my belly. I turned so my back took the blows. But one day . . ." She took a deep breath.

Every detail of that day was burned into her memory. She still recalled how the entire house reeked of sauerkraut. It had been foggy, too, one of those days that did not seem to want to brighten at all. The dog had gotten off its chain in the night and had come back from its hunt wet and filthy and with a bloody mouth. The dog had been the trigger for the quarrel, and her husband accused her of not chaining it up properly.

"He threw me down the stairs. It was just a few steps, but it was enough. I lost that child, too. I bled and bled for days. I wish I'd died that day. *That* would have been fate on my side. But I survived. I had to sit opposite him at this table day in, day out, cook his food, wash his ragged trousers. He never said a word about any of it."

Seraphine swallowed. "What happened then?"

"I took matters into my own hands. He disappeared one day, just like that. Fate!" She laughed.

Seraphine said nothing. She picked her bread into tiny crumbs. A sound came from the bench. Hannah sighed loudly in her sleep. At some point, Seraphine looked up. "It was too late, wasn't it?"

Evelyn nodded. "The cries of my unborn children followed me night after night. If I had done something earlier, if I had *not* just taken everything that monster did to me, one of them might be alive today."

Her cramped muscles loosened a little, and the knot in her throat hurt a little less. She had known that Seraphine would not pry any deeper. Disappeared? How? Why?

"The people around here think he just abandoned me and this place. With a wife like me, that was no surprise to them. He talked ill of me everywhere he went. Even my own father wants nothing to do with me now. I don't care. Let them believe what they want to believe. The constable stuck his beak in a few times . . . He wanted to know exactly what happened on the day Kurt disappeared. But not about any of the other days. No one wants to hear about those."

Lost momentarily in her memories, Evelyn stared off across the room. Then her eyes locked onto Seraphine's again and did not let go.

"If you want my advice, forget the man! And don't say another word about bringing fate to heel. Look at me—I chased an illusion for years, too. I simply didn't want to believe that the schnapps could sink its claws into Kurt so deeply that he could never escape. That nothing would ever be how it was before. Just like you don't want to believe that your Helmut doesn't feel anything for you anymore. I pleaded with the heavens above, and what did it get me? Not a thing. I should have snatched the reins of my own life. If I'd tried hard enough and long enough, I know my father would have let me come back to the farm. If not, I still could have run away, could have lived peacefully somewhere else. *With* my child. But I didn't do any of that. I held my tongue, and I did nothing—I left all the doing to him!" She laughed hoarsely.

"But it isn't true that Helmut doesn't have any feelings for me!" Seraphine cried. She looked over at Hannah, sighed, and then in a quieter voice, she said, "What you had to put up with was simply awful. That whole thing was horrible, but you can't compare it to Helmut and me. For me, it's about something completely different."

"Really?" Evelyn said sharply. "Step back and look at yourself. You're wasting years doing nothing, waiting for a dream to be fulfilled. And all you're doing is marking time. You're hoping that well-meaning fate will come to your aid. You might even nudge it in the direction you want . . . My God, do you know what that would mean?" Abruptly, she grasped Seraphine's hand and squeezed so hard that her knuckles turned white. "You're married to a good man! Why not forget your old dream of the love of your life and be satisfied with what you have? Why not simply live your life? Helmut is not all there is."

Seraphine gave a little shrug—a gesture that Evelyn had not expected and was not sure how to interpret. "And why . . . ," Evelyn began again, but then, feeling suddenly feeble, she released Seraphine's hand. She had said everything she had to say; she had done her best. *Why am I going to so much trouble?* she wondered silently. *What difference does it make to me if this stranger makes a mess of her life or not?*

"Why do you shave off your hair and walk around like a sinner? You haven't done anything wrong!"

Evelyn blinked. Her hair? Her hair . . . when she realized what Seraphine was saying, she let out a loud, shrill laugh. Then she remembered the woman sleeping on the bench and stopped again.

"Lice! Head lice, that's all. That's why I cut my hair off."

266

Seraphine's sleeplessness that night had nothing to do with the hard floorboards beneath the bed Evelyn had made for her. Nor did it have anything to do with Hannah, who groaned in her sleep with every slight movement she made. No, it came from the thoughts racing through her mind like wild bees, bumbling into her hard skull, flying on, confused and quivering.

What power of heaven had led her here, to this decrepit farm, the very sight of which had made her feel ill, and that she had approached with such trepidation? To *Evelyn?*

It had felt so good to finally speak from her heart, to tell another person everything. At first, she had not trusted herself to do it—Evelyn was a complete stranger, after all. But in the end it was Evelyn's unfamiliarity that had put her mind at ease, and before she knew it she was telling her everything. *You'll never meet her again. You don't have to care what she thinks of you,* she had told herself.

And what a clever woman Evelyn turned out to be! So much braver than she, Seraphine, had ever dared to be. Evelyn had truly snatched the reins of her own life. And the fact that she played down her courage and her drive—talking about it almost as if it were a bad thing—was evidence only of her modesty.

Evelyn could listen, too. And in the end she had found plainspoken words to talk about Seraphine's life. What was it she had said? *"You're wasting years doing nothing, waiting for a dream to be fulfilled."* Those words had nearly knocked Seraphine off her chair. Evelyn had spoken the truth. It had taken a stranger to put into words what she herself had never wanted to admit.

She had been waiting and waiting . . . and for what? For a catastrophe to come and wipe Hannah out of their lives? For Valentin to fade away into thin air? For Helmut to take her hand and spirit her away across the seven seas to a place where they could live together happily until the end of their days?

Silly little fool.

Sitting, waiting, suffering. Suffering for the sake of perfect love instead of seeing that one had to *do* something for a perfect love. She suddenly felt a strength inside her that she had not felt for a very long time, as if she were waking from long hibernation.

She frowned. Evelyn had been right: *"All you're doing is marking time."* It was true; she sat and did nothing, and waited for some higher power to intervene.

Well, perhaps she was not doing nothing, exactly, she comforted herself. But the little gibes she had directed at Hannah and nasty things that she had done seemed childish. As if a woman as tough as her sister-in-law would let things like that intimidate her!

Evelyn was a clever woman, but there was one point about which Seraphine had to contradict her. She would never be able to simply forget Helmut.

As if that might even be possible! Helmut was her life. If he did not exist, then perhaps . . .

Valentin was a good man, and life at his side was not hard. She might even be able to love him, if Helmut did not exist. But he did exist. Her love, her life, her curse. Evelyn, of course, could not know that.

Seraphine pressed her hands to her chest and felt a hot confidence burning inside her.

She would win Helmut back.

To do that, she needed to plan carefully, and put her plans into action as soon as possible. No more fear, unswerving, strong. Stronger than Evelyn, who had waited too long. She had admitted that herself, hadn't she? *"I should have snatched the reins of my own life . . ."*

Snatching the reins of her life—that was exactly what she would do!

Chapter Thirty-Six

Never in her life had Hannah felt so miserable. And lonely.

She could not walk. For the first few days, she was barely able to hobble. As soon as she put any weight on her injured leg, it folded beneath her. The slightest twist of her right foot sent spasms of pain all the way to her hip. Now her left leg had begun to hurt, too. *Self-pitying weakling,* she berated herself, but the pain was more than even her robust nature could bear, and it overwhelmed her constantly. Thanks to Evelyn's herb compresses, the open wounds had not become infected, but the herbs had done little to heal the injury.

Evelyn had gone into the woods the morning after the accident and come back with two forked branches, which she had fashioned into crutches and given to Hannah to test. Hannah's first thought was that Evelyn wanted to get rid of them as soon as possible. She had gathered her strength, snatched the crutches out of Evelyn's hands, and pushed them under her armpits; a splinter from the roughly hewn wood immediately dug into her skin. One of the crutches was a little shorter than the other, and Hannah hobbled into the room with a loud clack-clack. She managed five steps before she was racked by such pulsating pain in her leg that tears sprang to her eyes, and Evelyn's look of annoyance did not exactly stem the flow.

So walking was out of the question, with or without crutches. Evelyn and Seraphine went out, and Hannah was left alone in her little camp beside Evelyn's table. If only she had had someone to talk to . . . that would at least have helped her pass the time and drive out her gloomy thoughts. It would at least have alleviated her homesickness, and she would have missed Flora and Helmut and her home in Gönningen a little less. But there was no one there to dry her tears, no one to take her in their arms.

Seraphine might have been lazy at home, but there on Evelyn's farm she busied herself from dawn till dusk, helping with repairs around the house and out in the yard. Until then, Hannah did not think that Seraphine even knew which end of a hammer to use. But there she was, her sister-in-law, climbing bravely onto the rickety roof to replace some rotten slats. She helped clean out the chicken pens, fetched water without complaint, and marched off to the nearby stream to wash clothes. Evelyn said boo and Seraphine jumped. *All that's missing is a joyful whinny,* thought Hannah furiously, while she sat idly in Evelyn's gloomy parlor. The two women seemed to have become the best of friends and talked to each other in a way that Hannah found strange. Sometimes, she had the feeling that they talked without actually opening their mouths. That kind of understanding had never happened between her and Seraphine. Hannah caught herself actually feeling envious toward the eccentric hermit.

Because the pain did not slacken, Hannah was convinced that her ankle was broken. If only there were a doctor in the area to take a look at her injury. A doctor from Herrenberg would not deign to make the journey out to her farm, Evelyn told her in such a tone that Hannah could raise no objections. Besides, a visit from a doctor would cost money. They had money, of course, but it was to cover the expenses of their accommodations and food on their travels, that was all, and Hannah was reluctant to make use of any of it for herself.

Every evening, before she went to sleep, she convinced herself that things would be better the next day. In the morning, the swelling would be down, and they could finally get away from that terrible farm and that terrible woman, she told herself. But the next morning she always woke to the same swollen foot she had fallen asleep with.

Their days began with a particular ritual. As soon as all three were awake, Evelyn and Seraphine came to Hannah on her bench. Evelyn lifted the blanket and unwrapped the rags with the herbal paste. Then all three scrutinized Hannah's leg expectantly. And every morning, the looks of displeasure on Evelyn's and Seraphine's faces made Hannah feel like more and more of a failure. It was *her* foot, after all, that would not heal. *She* was the uninvited, troublesome guest in Evelyn's home; *she* was the one who had destroyed all their travel plans. And as if that were not enough, she was doing it *now*, when the family already had to contend with one serious setback.

All she had wanted to do was help . . .

"We have to talk." It was their fifth day on the farm. Seraphine had not gone out with Evelyn as on the day before, but instead joined Hannah.

Rays of pale sunlight streamed through the window, making Seraphine's hair shine. *How beautiful she is* . . . The thought came to Hannah unbidden. She reached up and touched her own hair nervously— it was desperately in need of a wash.

"What is it?" she asked grumpily as she stared out the window. Directly in front of her, one of the last roses was leaning toward the sun. Its leaves were already dark at the edges, withered after the long summer. Soon, everything would be gray, gray, gray. No colors, no flowers. And winter so long . . .

Just before their departure from Gönningen, Hannah had planted several dozen tulip bulbs in Wilhelmine's front garden. Hour after hour, she had dug holes in the earth with a small trowel, and little Flora, beside her, had dug into the soil with her bare hands. It was a lovely, cheerful afternoon. Wilhelmine complained about the cost of the bulbs, but Hannah was not to be dissuaded. "At least like this we have something to look forward to in spring," she had asserted.

Who knows if I'll be able to work in the garden or fields at all, come spring, she thought. *Who knows if my leg will ever be healthy again.* She bit her lip to stifle a sob. *Damn it, damn it, damn everything!*

"Hey! Are you even listening to me?" Seraphine was shaking her arm. "The way things look, you're not going to be much use for a while. Realistically, we are not going to be able to travel to Alsace together."

Hannah sighed. She had not wanted to be the one to suggest organizing a cart and driver for the homeward journey to Gönningen. But now that Seraphine herself . . .

"Our seed sacks are still full. Gottlieb's customers are waiting for their goods, and we need their money," said Seraphine.

Hannah frowned. Since when did her sister-in-law have such far-reaching thoughts? Once again, Seraphine's newfound drive took her by surprise, and she wondered if she might actually prefer the old Seraphine, with her dreamy, absent air, deep sighs, and perpetual weariness.

"What do you suggest?"

"That Evelyn and I travel to Alsace together. By the time we return, your foot hopefully will have healed, and we can think about getting home again. Of course, we would have to give Evelyn a share of our profits, that's clear, but—"

"But you can't leave me here by myself!" Hannah grabbed at Seraphine's sleeve as if her sister-in-law were going to get up and leave for Alsace that moment.

"Hannah, please, don't go getting upset. Am I supposed to travel on by myself? You know it's much more dangerous like that. Remember what happened to my father?" With cold fingers, Seraphine pried Hannah's hand from her sleeve and edged away.

"Of course you shouldn't travel alone . . . but perhaps, if we wait a few more days, then I could . . ." *Don't burst into tears now,* said a voice deep inside Hannah. *Don't give her this little victory.* But the first tears were already rolling down her cheeks. Left alone in that terrible house, no one there at night, noises all around that she did not know how to place. The very idea made her tremble. "What if you sold the seeds around here? Evelyn could take you to the farms, and you'd be back every evening—isn't that a good idea?"

"Poach on another seed dealer's territory—oh yes, a wonderful idea! Helmut would certainly approve." Seraphine sighed and stood up. "On the other hand, it is an emergency situation . . ."

Hannah nodded eagerly. "I know that in Gönningen not respecting someone else's territory would be considered dishonorable, but I'm sure the people at home would understand the difficult situation we're in." She was already feeling a little better. If Seraphine played her cards right and did a good job of selling their seeds, they could go home in just a few days and—

"Dishonorable—a flattering description. In Gönningen, what we're planning is practically a crime!" Seraphine shot back harshly, looking down on Hannah and shaking her head. "It's amazing, really. You always mean well, I know, but all you do is make everyone else's life harder. That's certainly a special talent."

"Now you listen to me," Hannah flared. "God knows, I didn't choose to step in that stupid trap. It could just as easily have been you, the way you were always charging off ahead. If there's anyone around here who's responsible for this miserable situation, then it's your dear Evelyn—she was the one who set the trap in the first place!" She inhaled deeply, exhaled. It felt good to vent her pent-up anger. From now on, she would not let anything bring her down, not her pain, not Seraphine's hostility, not Evelyn.

"Oh, Hannah, if only your mind wasn't always so . . . blinkered," said Seraphine condescendingly. "It started with your nonsensical suggestion to go on this trip at all. Didn't you ever wonder why I wasn't instantly thrilled about the idea?"

"Actually, no," Hannah said, glaring at her sister-in-law. "You're usually quite good at shirking work."

Seraphine laughed. "Lazy little Seraphine—how simpleminded. And so much the better for you, isn't it? But the truth is more complicated, dear Hannah."

Wonderful—now they had gotten into a full-blown quarrel. Hannah, a bitter taste in her mouth, lifted her throbbing leg and laid it along the bench. It was only days since Seraphine had offered her friendship. Well, now she saw what that was worth.

"No doubt you'll explain what 'complicated' means," Hannah said, and when Seraphine did not immediately reply, she prodded, "So, what is it?"

Seraphine looked suddenly uncertain. The way she glanced aside almost guiltily . . .

"I didn't . . . I didn't want to tell you at all, actually," Seraphine began, her voice faltering, but then her eyes locked onto Hannah's. There was a gleam in them that did not fit at all with her hesitant tone. "But maybe it is better for you to know the truth. Helmut and Valentin served all of us a lie about the robbery in Vienna. The truth is, they got mixed up with some women who led them on a very merry dance indeed."

"What? Women? What are you talking about?" Hannah sat up straighter and crossed her arms as if to protect herself.

A malicious smile played on Seraphine's lips.

"If you want me to spell it out: your darling husband was out whoring, and it went wrong! *That's* why I was not keen to help them out of their mess. They dug their own hole, and it was up to them to dig themselves out ag—"

Hannah threw both hands in the air, interrupting Seraphine. "How do you know that? I don't believe a word of it! It's not possible."

"Believe what you like," Seraphine snapped. "Why would Valentin lie to me? Why would he paint himself and Helmut in a worse light than necessary? Although he did stress that the whole affair had been Helmut's idea."

"But . . ." Hannah swallowed. Helmut with other women? Lying to her, his wife? Deceiving her, making a fool of her? Hannah clasped the armrest of the bench so tightly she felt she might break it off. Tears were flowing warmly over her cold skin, and she let out a whimper.

"Don't act so horrified. Helmut is still the old Helmut. He used to go whoring on his travels when he was engaged to me, and he's still doing it. Did you seriously think that *you* had changed him?" Seraphine's voice broke a little.

Is she telling the truth? Or is she just trying to torture me with her mean words? Hannah wondered, but she was in too much turmoil to think about it for long.

Seraphine, merciless, continued. "*You* with your stupid idea to send off all the seeds and bulbs by post! It was you who made it possible for Helmut to go to Russia. For him to realize his dream. Ha! What great dreams those were. And *you* absolutely *had* to help out afterward. Now look where it's got you, lying there like a cripple. You're nothing but a burden!"

Hannah shuddered.

"The truth hurts, doesn't it, dear sister-in-law? But it's about time you faced up to it. Here comes oh-so-clever Hannah with her magic wand to make everything right, but the truth is she has no idea what she's doing." Seraphine spat every word, savoring her moment. "The outsider waltzing into Gönningen, trying to tell us how the world works!"

All a lie? Helmut . . . dreams . . . cripple . . . as if peering into a fog, Hannah perceived no more than scraps of words.

"How could he do that?" Her voice was hoarse, and barely even a whisper.

"Now *I'm* supposed to tell you about your own husband? *Me*, of all people? You're in a better position than I to know that." Seraphine laughed, then stalked out of the room.

An hour later, Seraphine and Evelyn set off, laden with the two seed sacks. They had decided, finally, to try to sell the seeds as quickly as possible in the local area. Evelyn had put out something for Hannah to eat, and Seraphine had suggested sitting out on the bench in front of the house to make the most of the sun . . . as if nothing had happened between them at all.

Hannah stared off into nothingness.

Helmut had betrayed her. And once again, it was Seraphine who knew what was going on. Hannah could not say which betrayal hurt her more.

She sat on the bench inside the house for hours, rocking back and forth, her spirit and her body hurting. She felt as if she could no longer breathe; everything felt too tight, cutting off her air, her life. All she felt was pain, as red and greedy as fire.

When she could no longer stand being inside, she hobbled outside. Evelyn's dog came to her immediately, wagging its tail and straining toward her, as far as its chain would allow. Hannah lowered herself carefully onto the bench and scratched the dog's head, her fingers trembling. The dog was no longer the barking creature it had been that first night, and it gave itself over to Hannah's touch. But after a minute of her stroking, it nuzzled its head against her chest. At first, Hannah was startled—no dog had ever done that to her. But then she understood that the dog was doing its best to stroke *her* in return, as if it could sense her sadness. There was something consoling about that.

After a little while, Hannah's hands began to tremble less. Carefully, she took a breath and felt the iron cage that had clamped itself around her chest ease a little. When she exhaled, it came out as a choking gasp, and the dog looked up suddenly, its ears pricked up in surprise. Hannah had to laugh. "You think I'm utterly mad, don't you?"

She leaned back against the wall and stretched out her injured leg. She sensed herself growing calmer and calmer, and felt the tension in her face melt away. She sighed and closed her eyes, felt the warmth of the sun on her face. Maybe things weren't as bad as she thought. Perhaps, earlier, Seraphine had just been injecting her usual venom in a particularly malicious way.

How could she know exactly what had happened in Vienna? As if Valentin would confess his and Helmut's womanizing to Seraphine in detail! If he'd told her anything at all, then Seraphine had no doubt misinterpreted his words.

And if not?

With an effort, Hannah jerked open her eyes, which immediately began to tear up in the bright sunlight. What if Helmut really had betrayed her?

No, she simply could not believe he would do it. She would *feel* something like that, wouldn't she? She was sure that whatever had happened in Vienna had been completely harmless: a bit of chat, flirting with some pretty girls over a glass of wine or mug of beer—even the thought of that made Hannah angry and jealous . . . but one could not forbid a man something like that, and certainly not a seed merchant!

Hannah patted the dog's head. "Seraphine was just being spiteful. And I fell for it."

As much as she clung to that thought, the doubt that Seraphine's words had sown would not let go. She had to talk to Helmut—only then would she find peace again. But until she could do so, she would not let Seraphine's venom drive her mad any longer. She bit her bottom lip. And if Helmut really had . . .

Chapter Thirty-Seven

Two weeks later, Seraphine had sold almost all the seeds they had, and Hannah still could not walk properly. Evelyn marched off to one of the neighboring farms and talked the farmer into driving both women to Gönningen in his wagon.

"Did you really have to give Evelyn so much money? The leftover seeds would have done just as well! There's enough there for vegetables for an entire family," Hannah hissed almost as soon as they were sitting on the wagon seat. The goose Evelyn had given them as a farewell gift, perched in its basket between them, was stirred up and began to jabber and honk excitedly. Good God, a goose was the last thing they needed!

Seraphine stopped waving to Evelyn's diminishing figure and spun around to face her. "I don't know how things work in Nuremberg, but in Gönningen we say that giving charity to those in need is like sowing seeds in good soil. You may have noticed that Evelyn lives practically hand to mouth. And anyway, I think she earned the money. She even gave us one of her few geese, not to mention putting a roof over our heads, feeding us, and helping me sell the seeds."

Hannah laughed aloud. "That was the least she could do, considering that she was to blame for my accident. Besides, you more than earned your board and lodging with all the work you did around her farm."

Seraphine looked down at Hannah's still bandaged right leg.

"*I* did . . . ," she said slowly.

Hannah fell silent.

The two horses were old and slow, and they were forced to stop for the night halfway home, although Hannah would much rather have driven on. The farmer—a taciturn man with a cleft lip that caused him to mumble indistinctly—offered to drop them at a nearby inn and return to pick them up the following morning. After a quick discussion, however, Hannah and Seraphine decided to save the money and spend the night in the wagon, if the man was willing to sleep beside or beneath it.

It was a gloomy, cloudy night, but not especially cold. Hannah, her leg in pain again after all the hours of jostling on the wagon, wrapped herself in her cloak and closed her eyes. The empty seed sack served as her pillow.

She was falling asleep when Seraphine cleared her throat beside her and said, "Let me give you one bit of advice before we arrive in Gönningen tomorrow."

You can keep your advice to yourself, Hannah almost said, but she was too tired for a fight and muttered, "Do tell."

"I think it's for the best if you don't say anything to Wilhelmine or Gottlieb about what happened in Vienna."

Hannah propped herself on one elbow. "You think I'd go to them and complain about Helmut? This has nothing to do with his parents. It's just between me and him."

In the darkness, she suspected Seraphine's shrug more than saw it.

"I mean . . . if I were you, I wouldn't say a word to Helmut, either."

Hannah snorted. "That's out of the question. He has some explaining to do! Or do you think I'm going to put up with something like that? Assuming there's even a grain of truth in the story."

Seraphine sighed extravagantly. "Whether you put up with it or not . . . that's not such an easy question to answer."

The question was rhetorical! Hannah wanted to say, but Seraphine went on. "Who knows if your foot will ever work properly again. There's a good chance you'll spend the rest of your life with a limp. And as the wife of a seed merchant . . ."

"I—" Hannah broke off, at a loss for words. How could anyone be so mean?

"There's one thing you'll have to prepare yourself for: Helmut will not be happy to see you like this. He didn't want you to go on this trip at all, so he'll say it's your own fault that you . . . well. And then"—Seraphine hesitated, but only for a moment—"you know how he pokes fun at Käthe and her bad leg. He never would have married a woman with a physical malady like that. That's what the men are like. They'll come back from their travels with frozen toes—or toes that have already dropped off—or fall into bed with pneumonia, but woe betide the women if they're not fit as fiddles. Suddenly, the woman is a dead weight they have to carry. So to come back to your question: if I were you, I wouldn't be too quick to open my mouth."

Again, Hannah fell silent.

"It seems to me that primarily the ankle has been affected. Does it hurt when I press here?"

Hannah cried out.

Flora, who had just crawled onto her mother's lap, looked up wide-eyed at the doctor. Since Hannah's arrival the evening before, she had not left her side.

The doctor nodded knowingly and prodded more carefully at Hannah's swollen foot. "Some kind of fracture, I suspect. But it might also be just particularly bad bruising. Hard to say. The kind of trap that you described could cause both."

"And what does that mean for me?" Hannah asked, her mouth dry. She made an effort to smile for Flora.

The doctor packed his instruments away in his bag. "That you have to wait. And you have to be very gentle with yourself. Of course, you can walk around, do some work in the house, but don't overdo it. If it's a bruise, then the leg needs rest most of all."

"Can't you do anything, then? Isn't there a medicine to let me put some weight on my leg again?"

The doctor shrugged. "I could have put a splint on a fresh break. That would have improved the chances of the bones knitting. But so much time has passed that there's nothing more to do. The healing process began long ago. Now all we can do is hope that the bones have realigned themselves. If not . . ." He snapped his bag closed.

"If not . . . then what?" Her voice was reduced to a whisper.

"Then you will probably never be able to put all your weight on that leg again."

"Never . . ." Hannah's voice failed.

"Right, now we have to peel the potatoes and let them steam out, or the dumplings won't work at all. I learned that from your mama. Nana would rather make spätzle, but we have to cheer your mama up a little and get her healthy again as quick as we can. That's what your Auntie Seraphine says, too." Red-faced and with two pot holders in her hands, Wilhelmine lifted the lid of the roaster. The goose was bubbling away nicely inside. With a spoon, she basted the goose in the fat from the bottom of the roaster. After more than two hours of this treatment, a gold-brown crust had formed on the bird, and Wilhelmine's mouth was watering as she worked. A goose for St. Martin's Day—that was something they had never had before. Normally, half the family was away traveling in November, and it wasn't worth preparing anything so elaborate for the rest.

"Seraphine brought us a fine roast there!" Wilhelmine said, smiling down at her granddaughter.

"Goose dead! Don't eat!" Tears brimmed in Flora's eyes, and not for the first time that day. She had become quite attached to the bird over the previous two weeks, and had watched that morning as Wilhelmine laid the goose on the chopping block and, while Seraphine held the bird firmly, lopped its head off with the axe. It did not help that Wilhelmine had given the little girl a particularly pretty goose feather. Flora, who had seen an animal slaughtered for the first time in her life, was inconsolable.

"If you keep on like that, you'll turn the cow's milk with your bawling!" She looked impatiently from the red cabbage to the roaster, and from there to the potatoes. If she wanted to get the meal on the table in time for Gottlieb's return from the town hall, there was still work to be done. Aunt Finchen was having another bad day and had gone back to bed, so she was of no help. And Seraphine had chosen that morning to go off to see old Fritz Steinmehl and give him a share of the profits from selling the seeds—to make up for poaching on his territory.

Gottlieb had been furious when he heard where Seraphine had sold the seeds. Of course he knew whose *Samenstrich* was around Herrenberg. He also knew that Fritz Steinmehl had suffered a hernia and was unable to go out on the road that year—which one could almost see now as a blessing. Now old Fritz would also profit from Seraphine's work.

Dear Seraphine! How well she had dealt with a difficult situation. The two young women had returned exhausted, but Seraphine had not rested long, oh no. The very next day, she had taken over Hannah's old tasks. Not that Hannah thanked her for it—God forbid! The rancor between those two was worse than before they left. So much for her hope that the journey would bring the two young women closer together.

Wilhelmine glanced at the kitchen clock. Almost twelve. Hannah would be back from the washhouse soon.

"Best if I do the washing, too," Seraphine had said. "Or they'll start saying in the village that we're mistreating our invalid."

Wilhelmine agreed, but stubborn Hannah wanted to do the laundry as she had before.

"I may not be as quick to get around, but I'm not chained to my bed, either. You don't have to act like I'm good for nothing!" she had snapped, and then she had grabbed the wash basket and hobbled away. She promptly lost her balance on the steps; Gottlieb's shirts landed on the pavement and his underwear in the bare rosebushes. And, of course, fat Gertrude from next door chose that moment to pop her nosy head out of the window.

Wilhelmine shook her head disapprovingly.

All that hobbling around was certainly not doing Hannah's foot any good—Wilhelmine saw how Hannah twisted up her face in pain when she thought she was not being observed. But woe to anyone who tried to tell her anything. Hannah would fly into a fury.

Flora's crying, meanwhile, had escalated into a hysterical fit of wailing not to be stopped by either scolding or soothing words.

Wilhelmine looked at the child in annoyance. If the little brat didn't calm down, no one would be able to enjoy the meal.

"You know what?" she said in an exaggeratedly cheerful voice. "Nana's going to make you some semolina. My Flora likes semolina, doesn't she?" Something else that had changed with the times, she thought grumpily. No one would ever have made such a fuss about a child. Her mother would have shut her in the cellar and been done with it!

Flora's expression brightened, but she was not yet completely won over.

"So, we need milk, a bit of sugar, semolina . . ." With her wet hand, Wilhelmine lifted the porcelain semolina container down from the shelf. "Oh, not now," she muttered—they were out of semolina. Just then, the lid of the roaster began to rattle.

That was all she needed. She lifted the roaster lid but forgot to use the pot holder, and she yelped in pain when she burned her fingers on the handle.

"That's what you get when you have to do everything alone!" she grumbled to herself as her hand began to throb.

"Can I help?"

Wilhelmine jumped, then turned. Hannah stood in the kitchen doorway. Flora ran to her mother and threw her little arms around her legs.

"Oh, it's you. I thought it might be Seraphine . . . well, never mind."

"I can help you, too," Hannah repeated.

"We need semolina. Your—" Wilhelmine interrupted herself. "Oh, it isn't important. I'll send Seraphine when she gets back."

"If you need semolina, then I'll get you some. Or do you think Seraphine can do that better than I can?" Hannah's voice grew loud. She pulled herself free of Flora's grasp. "I may be a cripple, but I think I can just about manage to get to the store and back!"

And she was gone. Wilhelmine was left gaping behind her. What had she done now? "If that girl keeps on like this, then good night . . ."

No, this had nothing to do with basic temperament anymore. Hannah wasn't herself. It was time for the boys to come home. Helmut would straighten out his wife's head.

She hoped.

"A fox trap—just the thought of it! Poor Hannah, trapped like an animal . . ." Gertrude puffed out her cheeks, making her plump face look as if it were about to explode, and supported herself on Almuth Maurer's counter. "I once saw a trap with a hare caught in it. The little beast's leg was almost off, with just a few sinews holding it together."

Annchen gave Gertrude a look of disgust. "But setting out a trap where a human can step on it! That oaf ought to be brought before the law before anyone else suffers the same fate as our poor Hannah."

Elsbeth Wagner, the pharmacist's wife, turned to Seraphine. "I think I would have fainted with fright. What luck that you kept such a cool head. Without you, poor Hannah would truly have been lost."

Seraphine shrugged. "One of us had to keep a cool head." She laughed softly. "That's how it was from the very start of the trip," she added, though more to herself. The others pricked up their ears.

"When someone goes off traveling . . ." Gertrude nodded knowingly.

"They'll come back with something to tell," Annchen added. "What did you mean just now?"

Almuth Maurer sighed. One thing was certain: until the women had squeezed every last detail out of Seraphine, none of them would spare a thought for what they had come there to buy. She clapped her hands. "Oh, look at the time! I have to close in ten minutes."

Other than Annchen, who cast a rather casual glance toward the clock behind the counter, none of the women took the slightest notice of Almuth's announcement.

"Oh, nothing special." Seraphine waved her hand dismissively. "It's just . . . you know yourselves what it's like on the road. You have to be able to rely on each other."

Gertrude's cheeks puffed up again. "Oh God, yes! But tell us, Hannah—"

"She just isn't from here." Seraphine smiled apologetically at the circle of women. "She doesn't know our rules, perhaps doesn't have the right sense for things—but you can't think ill of her for it." She shook her head and closed her eyes for a moment as if struggling with some uncomfortable memory. "And I wasn't feeling very well myself. You know I had that . . . bleeding. Just a few weeks before we were meant to leave. Something like that weakens you, but she gave no thought to that at all."

Seraphine opened her eyes again and blinked a few times, as if surprised.

"It wasn't as if I was asking Hannah to look after me. I can be quite strong when I need to be. But she . . . she ran along as if we were in a race! Always dashing off ahead thoughtlessly. And I didn't want to go to that farm from the very start. We would have found the road to Herrenberg ourselves. But before I could say a word . . ." She lifted her hands in a helpless gesture. "The trap was well hidden, under a bush. Evelyn—that's the woman who lives alone at the farm—had put it out for her own protection. She'd heard someone creeping around her house at night on several occasions, she said. So, I mean, you can understand why she would put out the traps, can't you?"

The others dutifully nodded.

"To be honest, Hannah had no business tramping through where she did." Seraphine's forehead creased in annoyance. "But she always had to know better."

Elsbeth put on her most knowing look. "Oh yes, that comes when someone always has to be first. And won't listen to a word you tell them!"

"But that's how Hannah has always been," Gertrude added. "I still remember how she planted tulips in front of the house before she left. Much too deep, I could see that at a glance. But when I tried to tell her, all she did was shrug and insist that she was doing it right. Well, I ask you, which of us has spent her entire life in a village full of seed merchants?"

"It can't be easy for Helmut, can it?" whispered Annchen.

Seraphine sniffed. "Helmut doesn't see more than half of what goes on! Hannah is very good at putting herself in a good light. And me in the shadow. It's not only Helmut who's fallen for it. I think she's deceived half the village . . ." Her last words sounded pained.

Guilty looks passed among the women.

"But perhaps I'm to blame for that. Maybe I should have tried to get all the attention, like she does."

"You're not to blame for anything!" Elsbeth replied vehemently. "We had no idea that Hannah was so self-important. Who really looks beyond the facade of a house? And —" She stopped speaking when the bell over the door rang. Then all the women froze.

"Speak of the devil," murmured Gertrude.

"Hannah! We were just asking after you!" Almuth was the first to regain her composure. "How nice to see you so healthy again after your accident. How is your leg, anyway?"

"Good," Hannah replied curtly, her eyes scanning the assembled women. When no one said anything, she turned to the counter. "A pound of semolina, please."

Almuth reached mechanically to one of the upper drawers and weighed out a pound of semolina. "Anything else I can get you?"

Shaking her head silently, Hannah put down her money. When she was at the door again, she turned to Seraphine and said, "When you're done with your chat, you should come home. Lunch will be ready soon."

"You see?" said Seraphine triumphantly when she was certain Hannah could no longer hear her. "She can't even find a friendly word for me."

"And she ignored the rest of us completely." Elsbeth, annoyed, raised her eyebrows. "Too good for the likes of us, apparently!"

"Well, I've always said she thinks she's that bit better," said Gertrude.

"That's outsiders for you," said Almuth firmly, and the others nodded vigorously.

Chapter Thirty-Eight

In the next few weeks, Seraphine transformed into a night owl. After everyone had gone to bed, she unpicked old aprons in the kitchen and made new ones from what she could salvage. She darned socks and knitted a scarf. She would much rather have worked on a new dress for herself, but she could not find any good fabric cloth anywhere, and she did not want to leave the house to go to Reutlingen to buy it.

It was not that Seraphine had developed a particular love of sewing, knitting, and darning. But for what she had in mind, she would have licked the kitchen floor clean. If Helmut and Valentin returned from their travels while the others slept, she wanted to be awake. She wanted to be the first to welcome Helmut home. Before the family, but most importantly before Hannah.

It had been easy to convince the rest of the family not to write any letters to the brothers to inform them about the outcome of their ill-starred Alsace trip. It would only make them worry unnecessarily, the family agreed. Which meant that the brothers knew nothing yet of what had happened.

And now Seraphine hoped and prayed that Helmut and Valentin would not return during the day, but by night. If they came home in daylight, it would be impossible to talk to Helmut alone. But at night . . .

A week before Christmas, her wish came true.

It was after nine, and Seraphine was sitting at her mountain of mending when she heard the latch on the front door. She jumped up as if bitten and ran into the hallway.

"Shh, shh, the whole house is already asleep!" she said, greeting the brothers, and she had to fight her impulse to throw her arms around Helmut and kiss, kiss, kiss him . . .

He looked so tired! His face was gray with fatigue, his hair lank, his chin covered with a stubble that showed how long his day had been.

"Then let's wake them up!" Helmut said so loudly that Seraphine groaned inwardly. "It isn't every day that we come home after three months on the road, is it? There's a lot to tell, but first I need something to eat. I'm starving! We haven't eaten since this morning." He stomped off toward the kitchen.

"Seraphine, sweetheart! I missed you so much." Before she could stop him, Valentin pulled her close to him. His arms wrapped around her like an octopus's.

Seraphine took a deep breath and kissed him with as much affection as she could muster, but then she twisted free of his grip.

"There'll be time for that later," she hissed, listening all along for any sound on the stairs. So far, she heard nothing.

She left Valentin where he stood and trotted after Helmut into the kitchen, where he was already lifting the lid of the soup pot.

"Barley soup—not exactly what I'd call a meal to welcome home traveling men."

"There's ham and bread, too. I'll put something out for you in a minute," said Seraphine, still doing her best to keep her voice down.

She took Helmut by the arm and led him to the kitchen table. "First, we have to talk, urgently! Something has happened that you absolutely have to know about." Before he could say a word, she began to tell him her carefully planned version of what had happened on their way to Herrenberg.

"Hannah . . ." Helmut could manage no more than to croak her name. As if paralyzed, he sat and listened to the rest of her story. Valentin took a seat at the end of the table. *This must be a bad dream,* he thought. He had been looking forward to coming home so much. To the warmth, the security, Hannah and Flora . . . and he was hungry, so hungry that, for the last few miles, he had hardly been able to think of anything else but a thick bean soup with chunks of ham and—

I'm thinking about food, and Hannah is lying injured upstairs in bed.

He felt tears coming to his eyes. He was so unaccustomed to the feeling that he was momentarily overwhelmed by it. And anxious. He stood up abruptly and went to the window. For a long moment, he stared out into the darkness, which mirrored what he felt inside. Darkness, with the blackest conscience at its source. *He* was to blame for Hannah's accident. If only he had talked her out of that disastrous trip.

Seraphine's "No!" struck him like the lash of a whip and made him flinch. "She's sure to be sleeping, and she needs her rest. The whole thing has been a terrible strain for her and—" Breathlessly, Seraphine threw herself between Helmut and the door. Her face was less than a handsbreadth from his, her eyes wide, dark shadows on her cheeks making them look even thinner than before.

It must have been hard for her, too! Seraphine, so delicate and frail, and so brave.

Another wave of bad conscience swept over Helmut. All because of him . . .

Spontaneously, he pulled her to him, pressing her against his chest, and she nestled against him, trembling.

"What would I do without you?" he whispered in her ear, his voice choked with tears. Over her head, he looked at Valentin, who nodded back with tired eyes. It was no time for jealousy. Even so, Helmut gently pushed Seraphine to arm's length a moment later.

"Thank you from the bottom of my heart for everything you have done for Hannah. If you hadn't been there . . ." He paused. "I don't like to think what would have happened."

"Helmut, pull yourself together! Hannah needs you now. You and your help." Seraphine shook his arm. Her eyes were insistent, almost beseeching. "If I can just give you one piece of good advice . . ."

"Yes! Yes, of course. Tell me: What should I do?" He would do *anything* to make things better for his wife.

Seraphine's eyes darkened briefly as if she were reliving a terrible moment, but then she had herself under control again. "Hannah is naturally tough. But . . ."

Helmut nodded impatiently. "Go on."

"But I really think the whole episode has affected her very badly indeed. She tries to make as little fuss as possible, and she tries to hide her pain, but anyone can see she's doing badly. She won't take any help from us at all, stubborn mule that she is!" Seraphine laughed softly.

Helmut also managed a smile. "Oh, she can be stubborn, my Hannah."

Seraphine grew serious again. "But she doesn't see that her pig-headedness is just making more work for the rest of us." She shook her head. "Hannah has changed a lot. She doesn't want any advice from anyone about anything. Even having Flora around bothers her. She . . ." Seraphine fell silent again.

"What is it? I have to know what's going on!"

"I believe that she is thinking about going back to Nuremberg."

"What? But—"

But Seraphine cut him off. "I'm sure it will pass, but right now Hannah seems to have little interest in Gönningen and our way of life. She blames everyone and everything for her disability. But she alone is to blame for it!"

Nuremberg? Disability? No interest in Gönningen? Helmut frowned. What was Seraphine talking about?

"I don't know what I'm supposed to say," he answered uneasily. "What can I do?" His eyes moved from Seraphine to Valentin, who looked just as uncertain as Helmut himself felt.

Seraphine sighed. "Hannah has to rest a lot now, or she'll be a cripple forever, the doctor said, you understand?"

"For God's sake . . ." Yes, yes, of course he understood. Not everything, but . . . Hannah a cripple. Forever. Because of him.

Seraphine smiled angelically. "You have to get her to look after herself. We are all happy to help her. She doesn't have to act as if nothing has happened."

Helmut nodded grimly. He understood. He had to protect Hannah from herself, even if it meant tying her to her bed. He would make absolutely certain that her foot got the rest it needed and that she would be healthy again.

Chapter Thirty-Nine

"I'm just going to take two loaves of bread over to Emma." With her coat slung around her shoulders, Hannah was already standing in the kitchen doorway.

Helmut jerked his legs off the chair he'd propped them on and put aside the newspaper he'd been reading.

"You're already going out? But you haven't even had breakfast. Come and sit, keep me company for a while." He hurriedly pulled out a chair for her.

Sighing softly, Hannah hung her coat over the back of the chair and sat, her injured leg stretched out in front of her.

Normally, the entire family would be at the table; it was only on rare occasions that the two of them could sit and talk over a simple meal. They both used to treasure those times; today, however, Hannah did not seem happy at being alone with her husband.

She was looking at him with such hostility! *What is going on in there?* Helmut wondered yet again. He hadn't done anything to her, as God was his witness. No, he went to great lengths to help her whenever he could. But she did not make it easy for him.

If only she would talk to him! In the past, her constant chatter was sometimes a strain for him, but now he longed for those days to return.

"Helmut?" She spoke his name so suddenly that he jumped.

"Yes?"

"Well, now that we're alone . . ." She cleared her throat.

"Yes?" he repeated, and at the same time was ashamed of himself for sounding so insistent. Hannah hesitated, then shook her head.

"Oh, never mind."

"Never mind? I can see you've got something on your mind. Out with it!"

"It isn't so important. I . . . oh, forget I said anything." Her last words were spoken so softly that Helmut could hardly catch them.

She sat with her head down, her shoulders hunched as if she were carrying the weight of the world on them. That picture of misery was his Hannah. Helmut swallowed. He wanted no more than to take her in his arms. In the past, Hannah could not get enough of his hugs and kisses, as was normal for a man and his wife. Now, the slightest touch made her stiffen, and she would twist free of any attempted embrace. He was living as celibate a life as any monk, and that was far from normal!

Seraphine understood Hannah's behavior. "You have to be patient with her. The accident damaged her more than she would have any of us believe," she warned him constantly.

Damn it! he swore inwardly. But then he forced himself to smile and said, "Would you like a slice of bread? Or a piece of *Hefezopf?* I'll see if we have any in the pantry."

"I'm not hungry," she said before he could stand up.

"But—"

"But what? If I don't want to eat, then I don't want to eat. Why do you always try to dictate what I should or shouldn't do, like I'm a child?"

Helmut shook his head in confusion. "I didn't mean it like that. I just wanted . . ." He fell silent when Hannah stood.

"Then I'm off."

Helmut sighed. "No, wait! I can take the bread to Emma. There's some other business I have to take care of anyway, and The Sun is practically on my way." He smiled and reached out his hand for the bread.

"Thank you, but I'd prefer to go by myself. Or should I say, I'd prefer to limp by myself?" Her laugh was raw as she turned away.

"Then I'll come with you. I can support you. The roads are horribly slippery this morning. I noticed it already when I was shoveling snow . . . Hannah, wait! Hannah!"

Deeply hurt, he watched her leave. How could things go on like this?

It had snowed overnight, and early in the morning Gönningen still wore a virginal coat of white. Later, the countless footprints left by busy housewives getting in the last of their errands before Christmas Eve would mar the blanket of white. Horse dung, coal falling from passing wagons, wash water poured out the front of houses—all of it would smear and muddy the snow. For now, at least, everything was still white.

Everyone in the village was happy that the snow had held off until the seed merchants had safely returned. A white Christmas—the children would spend the days riding their sleds down the hillsides, and their laughter and squeals would be heard throughout the village. The church looked as if it had been coated in powdered sugar, and on the way home from the Christmas service that evening, the candlelight in the windows would look especially festive.

Why can't I be happy about it? Hannah asked herself, and added immediately, *Because happy Christmases are no longer granted to me. It's that simple.* The previous two Christmases had been sad affairs for her, so why should this year be any different? The thought that her downcast mood might simply have something to do with Christmas comforted her at least a little.

An icy wind pelted between the rows of houses, and the branches in the naked trees crackled like old bones. Blinking hard, Hannah stamped through the snow, away from the house, the loaves of bread wedged under her arm.

Don't get teary now just because it's a bit windy, she snarled inwardly at herself. *And don't keep looking back. It's time to start looking ahead again.* She abruptly stopped, however, and did exactly what she had just forbidden herself: she looked back, at the irregular prints her own feet had left in the snow. There the clear prints of her left shoe, completely normal. And next to them the smudged traces of her right shoe, undefined, like the traces left by an old dog no longer able to lift its leg properly.

Tears sprang to her eyes, tears that had nothing to do with the chill wind. In the past, she had been so happy to walk with Helmut though Gönningen. Or go with him up to the summit of Rossberg. Her husband was a head taller, and his legs were much longer than hers, but she could march just as fast as he could. She knew that she did not have the light-footed gait other women could claim, but her fast pace had pleased Helmut. "A man can cover a lot of ground walking with you," he had once said to her, his arm stretched lovingly across her shoulders.

Well, those days are over for now, she thought morosely. Helmut would certainly not want to be seen out and about with a cripple.

When Emma opened the door and saw Hannah standing in front of her, she was not sure if she should be happy or not. Käthe was in bed with a cold and would be no great help that day. The dishes and cutlery from the night before were still stacked in the kitchen, and Emma still wanted to get to Almuth's store before she closed at midday.

"Well, you're the last person I counted on seeing today," she blurted.

"I don't want to disturb you, but this is for the two of you." Hannah held out the wrapped loaves. "Merry Christmas."

Instead of taking the bread, Emma pulled her young friend inside.

"You're not disturbing me and you know it. I've always got time for a cup of tea. But . . . Helmut is back now, and I thought you had better things to do than visiting a lonely old woman like me."

"Lonely old woman!" Hannah laughed. "Frankly, I couldn't stand being at home a minute longer. I can't listen to Seraphine's babbling anymore. Ever since the men came home, all she knows is one game, and it's called 'Do you remember?'"

Emma looked puzzled. She had no real interest in listening to Hannah complain about her sister-in-law. In her opinion, Hannah was far too sensitive when it came to Sera. But she also knew that Hannah would not leave again until she had finished with her litany.

"'Do you remember, Helmut?'" Hannah said, mimicking Seraphine. "'When Father brought the little goat for Christmas and I wanted to have it for a playmate and not in the cooking pot? Do you remember how we used to go sledding down Rossberg at night carrying flaming torches? Do you remember this and do you remember that?'" Hannah reverted to her usual voice. "Seraphine is digging up every old memory of her and Helmut together that she can think of. He can't even remember most of them, but he makes a big effort, for her sake." Hannah shook her head in disgust. "And then they laugh. Like two people who've spent a large part of their lives together. Carefree, easy laughter. Helmut never laughs with me like that."

Maybe he has nothing to laugh about with you right now, Emma thought. The way Hannah acted around him these days, grumpy and spiteful . . . She sighed and looked Hannah in the eye. "Oh, child, what's wrong with remembering the old days? People always get a little sentimental at Christmas."

"Sentimental!" Hannah spat. "Sera is only doing it to make me feel, yet again, like all I will ever be is an outsider."

Emma put two cups of tea on the table. Hannah wrapped her hands around hers, breathing in the fragrance of chamomile. Her grim expression relaxed a little. Emma, who was well aware that the calming effect of a cup of tea would not last long, said, "What surprises me is that you have time to spare a thought for Seraphine now that your husband is back. Normally, a young couple like yourselves would have more than enough to do with each other at this time of year. Don't tell me it's any different for the two of you!" She smiled mischievously at Hannah.

"Helmut, he . . . he means so well. And I'm so rotten to him!" she cried. "He asks me how I am and wants to help me with everything. If I did everything according to him, all I'd do all day is sit around and keep Aunt Finchen company. He's so worried all the time."

"That's good, though," Emma said with some dismay, shaking her head. "Not every husband would be as considerate as he is."

"But it's not what I want! I don't want his concern. He's constantly asking me about my foot. If it hurts, if I can stand on it properly, if I might want to visit the doctor again—it's driving me up the wall. And sometimes, I admit, I blow my top. I'm starting to feel like all there is to me is one miserable foot. Helmut doesn't see me, Hannah, at all anymore. And when we're alone . . ." She turned her eyes away. "It's not like it was before, in the bedroom. He treats me like I'm fragile there, too."

Emma's forehead creased. "Could it be that you're being a little unfair, my darling? I'm sure it was horrible for Helmut to learn about your accident. It's really no surprise that he worries about you and is extra considerate." She nodded to where Käthe lay sick in bed in the back room. "My Käthe has to get by with her clubfoot all alone. She would like nothing more in the world than for someone to coddle her like that."

Hannah's hand came down on the tabletop with such force that Emma jumped. But it was Hannah's words that made her freeze.

"But I don't want to be treated like a cripple, damn it! I'm a normal person, a completely normal person!"

"Oh, and Käthe is not a 'normal' person because she's a *cripple*?" Emma shouted back. Then she closed her mouth hard before she said something in her anger that she would later regret. But there was really nothing else to say.

Emma felt a deep sadness come over her. She stood up so suddenly that her chair tipped over backward. "Maybe it's best if you go now."

Out on the street, Hannah looked at the loaves of bread that Emma had given back to her.

What had she done?

What part of what she had said had hurt Emma so much? Her own pain was too great for her to be able to see it clearly in other people. But she did know one thing: she had hurt Emma, her only friend in Gönningen. Emma, who had always been there for her.

She was not only a cripple and a burden. She had become a bad person, besides.

And now she was all alone.

Chapter Forty

The year went out the door like a guest who has overstayed his welcome and realized too late. But the start of 1852 made life hard for some of Gönningen's residents. Heavy snowfalls broke branches from trees and caused some rooftops to sag. Chimneys did not draw as they should.

Emma and Käthe departed for Hohenlohe without saying goodbye to Hannah.

When it came time to prune the fruit trees at the start of February, it was Seraphine who carted the trimmings to the fire pit and burned them.

"All you'll do is stumble over a bundle of wood," she said to Hannah. And Hannah stayed home.

She was not there when they turned over the fields in March. It was Seraphine who went out with the men to hoe and fertilize the soil.

"You wouldn't be much help," said Seraphine when Hannah was about to pull on her work shoes. "With your foot, you'll go at a snail's pace."

And Hannah stayed at home.

In mid-April, when the tulips started to bloom, Hannah took no more than a passing interest in the flowers. Of the dozens of bulbs she had planted so laboriously the previous autumn, only a fraction actually bloomed. Some put out just a few long leaves, but there were entire patches in the garden bed where nothing grew at all.

"I suspect the mice had the bulbs for their Christmas dinner," Wilhelmine said.

"It's the cold winter that's done it," said Gottlieb.

"No, it was me," said Hannah. "I probably planted them too deep."

Helmut complained bitterly that Piet, the Dutch tulip supplier, had foisted low-quality bulbs onto him. "We can look forward to some complaints from our customers! That's what you get for ordering by mail and not visiting the suppliers in person," he said angrily, but Hannah had already stopped listening. *How could I have imagined that I had any talent for gardening at all?* she wondered silently. She did not speak to Helmut, who for her sake had pushed the blame onto Piet, for an entire day.

When Aunt Finchen died unexpectedly at the end of April—she simply failed to wake up one morning—Hannah was left with no other choice but to leave the house. She shed no tears at the church service, although all around her the mourners were sniffling. But the moment they arrived at the cemetery, her dam burst. No one suspected that it was the sight of the thousands of tulips that adorned the Gönningen cemetery every spring that made her cry. The magnificence of the flowers—that there, among Gönningen's dead, bore witness to the annual rebirth of nature—made Hannah suddenly aware of her own miserable existence. How she had looked forward to the coming of spring in the past! How she had looked forward to finally seeing colors again and not just the black and white of winter. But this year the colors hurt her eyes, and she turned almost with longing to Aunt Finchen's grave.

As she had the previous year, she nurtured seedlings on the windowsills, but when Helmut asked her whether they should plant them out together as they had before, she could muster no enthusiasm at all. Seraphine took over the task. Hannah's Field was no more.

"Are you sure you don't want to come along to Reutlingen?" Valentin asked, although he had already put the same question to Seraphine several times.

Instead of answering, Seraphine merely sniffed. She was focused on tying her head scarf at the back of her neck. When she was done, the cloth covered only a small part of her head, but it kept the silvery strands of her hair out of her face.

Valentin looked at his wife admiringly. For any other woman, a head scarf was simply a practicality when working. But with Seraphine, the blue-gray fabric highlighted the shine of her hair and her dark eyes rimmed with long lashes, making her more beautiful than ever.

"It's enough for you and Hannah to laze around," Seraphine said after she finished with the scarf.

"Laze around? What's that supposed to mean? It was your idea that I take Hannah to Reutlingen." Valentin, irritated, looked toward the stairs leading to the first floor. How long was his sister-in-law going to be? Women! They took so long to do everything! Lutz and his wagon would appear around the corner any moment, and he certainly would not want to be kept waiting.

"Well, a change of scenery can only do Hannah good. Maybe it will make her a little more sociable," Seraphine said with a friendly smile.

"A stroll through the town wouldn't do you any harm, either," Valentin replied. "You used to love going up to Reutlingen. Our visit to the stamp maker won't take very long. After that, we could go for a cup of coffee or look around the shops. God knows, you don't have to slave away every day the way you do."

Valentin, of course, was proud of the way his wife rolled up her sleeves to take the burden off Hannah as much as she could. On the other hand, Seraphine's eagerness to work and concern for her sister-in-law was close to creepy. But he did not want to get caught up in such thoughts—whenever he did, a dark cloud gathered overhead and he began to brood.

"Now that Hannah isn't able to work, the rest of us have to stick together even more," Seraphine regularly pointed out. Everyone agreed with her, which made it hard for Valentin to say anything against the idea. But he secretly believed that Hannah had been pampered too much and too long already. A blind man could see that sitting around doing nothing was not good for her. And as for Seraphine's intentions in the matter . . .

"You could easily come along," he repeated sullenly.

"Strolling around town and drinking coffee!" Seraphine shook her head. "That's the best you can come up with? And your brother is supposed to collect the potatoes all by himself?"

"I can help him with that this afternoon. You really are overeager, which I don't understand at all."

Even his mother had noticed that Seraphine welcomed even the most unpleasant of tasks, as long as she could do it side by side with Helmut. "They certainly make a fine-looking couple," she had murmured to herself at the window while she watched Sera and Helmut raking leaves together. "That really could have been something," she added with a sigh. When she realized that Valentin was standing right beside her, she turned crimson. "A hardworking wife you've got there!" Her forced cheerfulness, however, could not smooth out the steep crease that had formed on Valentin's forehead. The sight of Seraphine and Helmut laughing and tossing handfuls of leaves at each other called up the old jealousy he felt toward his brother with a vengeance. At the same time, he realized, it was rare to see Helmut smile these days. Wasn't it mean of him to begrudge his brother that happy moment? But did those happy moments have to happen with Seraphine?

Valentin forced the image out of his mind again and stared morosely at Seraphine, who was just tying the laces of her heavy work shoes. She was meticulous with the loops, as if on her way to a lovers' rendezvous . . .

"Then go out to your stupid fields," he snapped at her, suddenly furious. "But I'll tell you one thing: things can't go on like this. With all your slaving away, you're always tired at night. Too tired to . . . ah, you know what! Not once since I got back have we . . ." He kicked the door angrily. Why did he find it so difficult to talk about things like this? She was his wife! He wasn't asking for anything more than a husband had a right to expect. And why was it even *necessary* to talk about such things at all? he wondered, when Seraphine's contemptuous eyes caught his.

"Oh, so that's what this is all about." She laughed harshly. "I break my back, morning to night, and that's all you can think about. And now you hold it against me that I fall into bed half-dead every night. I've picked myself a wonderful man for a husband!" Shaking her head and without another word, Seraphine left the house.

It was surprisingly hot for the end of May. When Valentin and Hannah emerged from the stamp maker's workshop, it felt as if they were walking into an oven heated by a blazing fire. The sky was a brilliant blue, but over toward the mountains, clouds were amassing.

Hannah opened the top button of her blouse and fanned a little air onto her skin.

"I hope Helmut won't mind that we've chosen the ornate script after all," she said, while she looked around for a tree that might offer some shade. "But I think it matches the seed packets very nicely."

Valentin looked up to the nearby church tower. It was not yet eleven in the morning. Lutz would meet them with his wagon at one. Time enough to put into action the plan he had worked out especially for this trip to Reutlingen.

"Well, I for one could use a cold beer right now. I know a cheap restaurant just down the road there where we can get something good to eat, too."

Hannah gazed in the direction he was pointing. Panic flared in her eyes.

"I . . . actually I'm not hungry. Or thirsty," she said, licking her dry lips with her tongue. "And besides, your mother wouldn't want you spending money on food and drink. Couldn't we just sit on that wall there and wait for Lutz?"

Valentin, who had counted on exactly that response, said, "I'm not sitting around for hours in this heat. Forget it! Let's go and get a decent meal, my treat. And a beer!" He lifted his arm for Hannah. "Come on," he said, in his cheeriest voice.

"I can walk by myself," Hannah muttered. Without another word, she limped away. Valentin followed, suppressing a grin. *Well, what do you know!*

"So, tell me, how much longer is this supposed to continue?" he said once the waitress had set two large mugs of beer in front of them. He took a long draft from his, then leaned back with his arms crossed over his chest, as if expecting to hear a lengthy story.

"What do you mean?" Hannah said, puzzled.

"I'm wondering how long you're going to sit by and watch Seraphine take over your jobs."

"Take over my . . . But she's *helping* me. I can't just tell her she can't do that, can I?" Hannah replied in an aggressive tone. It was clear to Valentin that she was not happy with his choice of topic: she had pushed her chair back a little, as if she wanted to put as much distance between them as possible. *That won't help you,* he thought. Someone had to have things out with Hannah, and if her own husband wouldn't do it because Seraphine had filled his head full of her stupid opinions, then the responsibility fell to him.

"Ah. And I suppose you like sitting around all day watching us work our tails off?" he said, just as aggressively. Oh, he might have gone too far . . . He saw the tears brim in her eyes. He felt guilty, but he did nothing to make up for his bluntness.

"What am I supposed to do?" Hannah cried, so loudly that a number of heads turned in her direction. "I'm a cripple, in case you hadn't noticed. I'm lame, and I hobble. Without me, you would have made it from there to here twice as fast. Don't think I didn't see you walk slower for my sake. All I am is a burden for everyone. And you expect me to stand up and tell Seraphine to her face that she should go to hell?" Silently, she began to cry.

Valentin shook his head. He was tempted to take her in his arms and whisper words of comfort in her ear, but pity would be out of place. As out of place as *all* the pity Hannah had gotten from the family in the past few months. The so-called pity . . .

"In good times as in bad—that was your promise to Helmut. Or have you forgotten?"

From one moment to the next, the sun, which until that moment had been casting bright sunbeams through the window, disappeared, and the restaurant grew dark.

Hannah blinked at Valentin through a haze of tears. "What does that have to do with anything? Goodness knows, you can't throw accusations at Helmut. He *is* there for me now, in the *bad* times," she said sarcastically.

Valentin laughed gently. "And you?"

"What do you mean, me?"

"Are you there for him, too? Or are you so wrapped up in your own self-pity that you don't see how *he* is suffering?"

"He is suffering because his wife is a cripple!" Hannah slung back. "And how nice of you to draw my attention to that!" The muscles of her face had stiffened.

Just then, a sharp crack sounded from outside. The thunder made the windowpanes rattle in their frames. Valentin sighed. He hoped the thunderstorm would pass before they had to leave the restaurant.

"You're mistaken, Hannah. Helmut is suffering because you won't let anyone help you. Because your marriage isn't a real marriage anymore. Because you hardly lift a finger to look after Flora. All you do is wallow in your self-pity. You're right, Helmut is there for you, but you . . . you're not there for him. At the start, when we returned from Bohemia, you should have accepted his help. And then, after a time, you should have said to him, 'Thank you, but I don't need your help anymore. I'm strong enough now. From now on we'll do our day's work together.' That how things should be between a man and a woman, shouldn't they?"

The waitress came and put down two plates of steaming, hot tripe. Valentin had finally said everything to Hannah that had been weighing on his mind, and he began to eat with gusto. Hannah poked at her food.

"So you think I hobble for the fun of it," she said so quietly that her voice almost disappeared in the next peal of thunder.

"Not for a minute," Valentin replied, his mouth full. "But I think that things aren't nearly as bad as you take them to be. Frankly, I completely forgot earlier that there was anything wrong with your foot. And if you happen to be a little slower than you used to be, it doesn't matter—you were always too fast, anyway."

"That's what you say. And maybe it's even true. But the others . . . Seraphine . . ."

Valentin pointed his fork directly at Hannah. "Now we're starting to get to the point," he said, unable to hide the triumph in his voice. "Think about it. Maybe it suits my Seraphine to see you suffering and weak. Because that way, she has her *beloved* Helmut all to herself." Despite the irony in his words, he could not suppress his pain as he spoke. Suddenly, he was so angry at Hannah that it was hard not to take her by the shoulders and give her a hard shake.

Why couldn't she see what he did? Why didn't she see Seraphine's hand "accidentally" brush Helmut's when she passed him the bread basket at the table? Or how she held his sleeve a moment too long when she wanted to draw his attention? Or the hunger in her eyes when he entered the room, or the flush on her cheeks in his presence? Valentin himself was no master in the arts of seduction—he had had to live out his desire for Seraphine in secret. And yet what he saw with his own eyes at home was abundantly clear to him: the ancient, never-changing game of temptation. One could only see it as a virtue of Helmut that, so far, the game had been one-sided. But for how much longer?

Valentin's eyes locked onto Hannah, and in a strained voice, he said, "The Hannah I used to know would never have put up with any of it."

Hannah stared down at her plate of tripe as if wisdom lay among the innards, and as she stared, her chest swelled and sank as violently as if she had just run through town.

A muscle twitched above one cheek. Valentin felt he could almost see the turmoil inside her. *Wake up, woman! Wake up, finally, please!* he cried out in silence. *And help me, too, not lose my wife forever.*

After a long time, Hannah looked up. Her eyes were clear and determined.

"You're absolutely right. I have not been a good wife for Helmut lately, not at all. Basking in self-pity . . . that's not like me." She sounded amazed. "Why am I only seeing that now?" Her mouth twisted into a lopsided smile, and she shook her head as if to shake out the cobwebs. "Has my thinking slowed down with my gait?" Abruptly, she stood up, banging awkwardly against the edge of the table, causing the plates to clatter.

"But those days are over. I want to go home, to Helmut. There's a lot we need to discuss."

Chapter Forty-One

Seraphine shivered as she had never shivered before, but neither the cold nor the rain that had soaked her dress was to blame. She was not cold at all—she felt hot, even feverish.

What was making her shiver was the anticipation of what she knew would happen. What *had* to happen, because fate had determined that it had to be.

You see, Evelyn? I knew it would work, she said silently to her friend. *I knew it! I'm getting my life back because I'm getting* him *back . . .*

And of all places, it was going to happen in the same ill-fated shed that smelled of potato sacks and earth, the same broken-down hut where she spent her "wedding night," while Helmut . . .

No, don't think about that. Life was too beautiful and too kind for her to rail about her fate any longer.

Everything would straighten out, would be as it should.

There, in that miserable hut, of course. Where else? When she saw Helmut's curious eyes, she erased the smile from her face.

"Maybe we would have been better off going straight back to the house," he said as he stared out the window. The grim thunderclouds that had appeared from over the mountains still hung low and rain-heavy over the valley. "The rain is starting to let up. If we hurry . . ."

"But going home now would be far too dangerous. You said so yourself," Seraphine contradicted him, although a child could have seen that the storm was moving away. "The way the lightning shot across the sky just now, so wild . . . and that one bolt, I was really scared we were going to be struck." Her teeth were chattering so much that she had trouble getting her words out.

Helmut turned away from the window. "You're shivering. And we don't have anything here to warm ourselves." He turned toward the door. "I'll run home and at least get you a coat or—"

"No!" Seraphine cut him off. "I don't n-need anything. There's a pile of blankets in the bottom of the cupboard." As she spoke, she began to unbutton her top, but it was difficult. Her fingers kept slipping on the small mother-of-pearl buttons.

It would not have taken much for her to tear the dress from her body.

"Sera!" Shocked, Helmut lowered the blanket that he had extracted from the stuffy cupboard. "You . . . you can't just . . ."

"Would you dry my back? I'm so cold!" She smiled at him.

"I don't know . . ." He shifted uncertainly from one leg to the other. "It wouldn't be right, I mean . . ."

Seraphine almost laughed out loud, but instead she squeezed out a sound that distantly resembled a sneeze. Then, without much effort, she started shivering again.

"All right, then," said Helmut, with an embarrassed smile. "I don't want to be to blame for you lying in bed with pneumonia next week." He began rather clumsily to rub her back dry with the scratchy blanket.

When his hand came up to her shoulder, Seraphine reached up and held it tightly. At the same time she leaned back against his chest and turned her head up to his. Her mouth was dry with desire. She ran the tip of her tongue over her lips.

"You know, I often used to imagine how you would touch me," she said, her eyes half-closed.

"Sera . . ."

"No! Stay here. Stay with me." Before he could break free of her grasp, she pulled his hand forward to her breasts. Oh, how sweet it was to feel his hard, callused hands on her! Her nipples, taut and swollen, pressed against his fingers. "We belong together," she whispered, nuzzling even closer. "I've always known it. When I was very young, before I turned thirteen, I had a dream about you. I called you my prince. At night, alone in my bed, I pictured your hands, how they would touch my naked body, and I felt each fingertip against my skin. Like now, you see? My soft skin . . . and then, when I couldn't stand it any longer, I imagined your hand going lower and lower, how you would open my legs . . ." She quickly kicked away the heavy work shoes, which she had already untied. Everything in her urged her to press her body against his, to feel him hard against her.

His hand moved of its own accord, caressing her breast. He groaned softly.

Thank you, star fairy!

The next moment, Helmut stepped back from her so suddenly that she almost fell.

"Sera!" He stared at her in horror. "We . . . we can't just . . . what's got into you?" He shook his head, but his eyes did not leave her breasts.

She smiled her angelic smile. How helpless he was, confronted with what she was offering him. And how surprised. She was destined for him. He must know that.

Her breath came irregularly, echoing her heartbeat, and she found it hard to form clear thoughts. Everything was so soft, so warm, so sweet.

Yes, they had had to wait a long time for this. For each other.

Too long? Seraphine wondered when she saw the look of doubt on Helmut's face. That's how life was sometimes. When you spent too long waiting for something, wanting it so much, in the end it was hard to feel the joy that one had imagined all that time. That must be what he was feeling.

If he would only open himself a little, take a step in her direction. What they were doing was so right. She took his hand, raised it to her cheek, kissed his palm.

"You don't need to be scared, or fight this," she murmured, as if soothing a frightened animal. "You and me, the two of us . . ."

"I don't think I've ever been so wet in my entire life. April showers might bring May flowers, but May rain will be the death of me!" said Hannah as she climbed down from Lutz's wagon. Home again, finally. "Let's hope Helmut and Seraphine made it home before the storm broke." She pulled off her boots and hurried into the house.

Smiling, Valentin watched her go ahead, then picked up the dripping cape that she had dropped on the floor and hung it on a hook.

"They're not here!" Hannah said in astonishment as she appeared from the kitchen. "Your mother says they didn't come home before the rain hit. Let's hope nothing's happened."

Valentin frowned but said nothing.

Hannah chewed on her lip. She wanted to talk to Helmut now, immediately! She wanted to tell him how sorry she was for everything. For her teariness, her meanness, her . . . cowardice. She wanted to thank him for everything, and tell him how much she loved him. And then she wanted to throw her arms around him and never let him go.

"In good times as in bad . . ." Valentin had expressed it so poetically. So poetically and, at the same time, so plainly that her face had flushed red with shame, because she had lost sight of that very promise.

With every mile of the return journey, her inner restlessness had grown with her joy. Hannah felt as if she were waking from a nightmare, still shaky and confused, but deeply relieved to discover that it had been no more than a bad dream, and that the day was once again bright and clear, all the gloom a mirage. Now it was up to her to put things right again, and get back to her daily work.

Even without Valentin's plainspoken words, she had felt for a long time that Seraphine was trying to oust her with her "helpfulness"—she had to admit that. But she had closed her eyes to that realization, and had pretended that everything was completely normal. Because doing otherwise would have meant taking action, and she had not trusted herself to do that. But it was Valentin who had made her see how much her behavior had hurt Helmut, too.

Now she had no time to lose.

She had wanted to shout, *Faster, faster!* at Lutz's horses, and several times she had felt a strong urge to snatch the whip from his hand. In fact, though, Lutz had driven the horses as fast as he could, because he, too, wanted to get home quickly. But Helmut was not there, and Seraphine was also missing. "We put the potatoes out in the horse paddock this year," said Valentin uncertainly.

"The horse paddock? Isn't that about a mile out of the village?" A mile. That was a fair distance, certainly, but not so far that one could not have made it home before the storm.

Valentin nodded. "Our old field hut is close to that. They probably took shelter there." His expression mirrored the grim clouds still visible through the window.

Hannah's and Valentin's eyes met, and each could read more in the other's than they would have liked.

Hannah's jaw tightened. *Stay calm. All will be well,* she silently told herself.

"I'll go ahead and take them some dry clothes. Can you find something for Seraphine?" She added, "Come on, hurry!" when Valentin did not instantly follow her upstairs.

Valentin stopped in front of his bedroom. "Shouldn't I come along? It's a long way . . ."

Hannah decided to ignore the concern in his voice. She forced a smile. "Didn't you just get through telling me that I've got to stop behaving the way I have?"

"I did, but—"

"I'll manage," she said, with more determination than she felt. It was not the distance that bothered her. It was what was waiting for her at the other end. The unrest that she had previously been able to keep at bay now swarmed all around her like mosquitoes.

What if she arrived too late?

Hannah set off as fast as she could.

The rain had stopped, and fog rose from the ground as if, beneath the earth, dozens of witches were stirring their cauldrons. The leaves on the trees gleamed wetly, and the sharp outlines of the houses seemed softer, almost unreal. The air was filled with all the aromas of spring, made more penetrating than ever by the rain. Hannah saw the first Gönningers reappearing after the storm: Annchen straightening forgotten laundry on her washing line, the smith trying to puff his smoldering fire back to life, and a pair of seed merchants on their way to the nearest inn, no doubt to talk business and drink beer.

A rainy May day, as normal as any other.

Hannah took it all in only from the corners of her eyes. She ran as if her life depended on it. And she had the feeling that it truly did.

From far off, she saw the low light of an oil lamp through the dirty window of the shed.

So Valentin had been right.

She stopped a few yards from the shed and tried to catch her breath. Her leg hurt, but it felt good to know that it had not let her down in her mad rush to get there. Her hair, disheveled and wet, hung in her face, and sweat gathered between her breasts, trickled from her armpits.

Suddenly, she did not know what she should do. Just barge in? She did not have the courage for that.

The muddy ground swallowed her footsteps, and she crept to the hut and peeked in through the window.

And time froze.

She blinked as if to be certain that she was not the victim of some optical illusion born of her own fear that the worst thing she could imagine awaited her, born of her hope that the worst would not come to pass.

Seraphine's bare breasts were no optical illusion. They were as real as Helmut's hand, uncertainly stroking silver-blond hair.

Hannah looked away, and her eye fell on the wool garment in her hand. The thought of bringing something dry for Helmut to put on suddenly seemed senseless, utterly ridiculous. As ridiculous as she herself.

A ridiculous, stupid person.

Her first impulse was to run away and act as if she had seen nothing. She was a cripple, no beauty, no good for anything; she had proven that thoroughly in the last few months. Was it any wonder that Helmut would be seduced by Seraphine's charms? But suddenly she heard Valentin's voice in her ear. *"The Hannah I used to know would never have put up with any of it."*

She had hidden behind her injury for too long. Fear and insecurity had made the "old" Hannah invisible. She had given Seraphine a free hand. *She* had driven Helmut into Seraphine's arms. *That* was the truth.

Seraphine . . .

Hannah eyes narrowed to slits. That woman. That wretched beast. She would claw her eyes out and—

Her hand on the doorknob, Hannah paused.

Of course, she could storm into the hut and drag Seraphine out by her blond locks. That would feel very good indeed. She could attack Helmut, too. She could pick up the first thing that came to hand and hurl it at his head, call him a swine and a scoundrel and every name under the sun. How dare he touch Sera! Hell would be too good for them! And then?

Then she could wallow in rightful indignation like a sow in mud. But what was she actually indignant about?

In Hannah's mind, an enormous invisible wall suddenly loomed, a wall built from everything that made her life what it was, everything that had been and that would be. She did not know what waited for her on the other side of the wall. She did not know if Helmut would have anything do with her again. Or if she could have anything to do with him. All she knew was that she could not stand behind that supposedly protective barrier forever. But getting beyond it would take courage.

With a final deep breath, she grasped the rusty doorknob and flung open the door.

Chapter Forty-Two

"Hannah!" Helmut and Seraphine froze in place.

It was very warm inside the hut, the air permeated with the unmistakable odor of arousal, making Hannah choke.

From a wellspring deep inside, she fashioned a smile. She turned to Helmut, who stood and gaped at her. Then her eyes moved to Seraphine, and she looked at her as she would at a dog that had defecated in the middle of the room.

"Go home." Words as passionless and dry as her mouth, yet sweeter than anything Hannah had ever tasted.

Seraphine's face shattered into a thousand shards.

"What are you doing here?" Her voice was a shriek, no longer angelic. She moved closer to Helmut possessively; already pressed against the wooden wall of the hut, he had no escape.

"Go home," Hannah repeated. "Your husband is waiting for you." Without much fuss, she picked up Seraphine's shoes and top and threw them out the door. When she tried to grab her sister-in-law by the arm, Seraphine screamed.

"Leave me alone, you witch! You have no business here! You don't understand anything. Helmut is mine! Go, leave, please . . . I . . . not now—"

"Seraphine." Helmut's voice interrupted Seraphine's hysterical clamor. She turned to him, hungry, hope on her face. "Go." He nodded to her as if trying to calm a child.

"But . . . Helmut! Tell me this isn't true. You and I . . ." Seraphine looked nervously from him to Hannah and back again. Her skin was stark white, as if every drop of blood had drained from her body.

For a moment, Hannah feared her sister-in-law would actually faint. And then?

Well, so what!

Without wasting another word, she dragged Seraphine across the hut and pushed her through the door.

From outside, Seraphine scratched on the wood like a cat demanding to be let in. Her loud cries and whining infiltrated through every crack. Inside, Hannah sank to the floor with her back to the door, exhausted. She felt as if Seraphine's outrage was sucking the very marrow from her bones, and she put her hands over her ears to block the tirade.

Time crawled forward like a snail on a leaf. At some point, silence and calm descended. Outside and inside.

Helmut sat down beside Hannah.

"Hannah. That . . . it . . . it was all different than you might think. The rain . . . we were soaked through. So—"

His strained voice broke off and his body began to shake. His hand sought hers, and their fingers hooked together.

"I didn't want anything from Seraphine. Please believe me. And I am so happy that you came when you did. That's all that matters now. You've wanted nothing to do with me for so long. Oh, Hannah, whatever I said, whatever I did, it made no difference to you. I missed you so much. And then Seraphine was there . . . I . . . if you hadn't . . . I think I—"

"Shh, don't speak." She placed her index finger over his mouth, then kissed the same spot a moment later. His lips were dry and rough. Hannah's eyelids fluttered, and she tried as hard as she could to keep her eyes closed. She did not want to see Helmut's face, his bad conscience, his shame, or his insecurity. She did not want to hear anything, either. No excuses, no explanations. There were none to give, no protestations to steal the time and space for what really mattered.

Her rediscovered confidence was still as thin as the first ice of winter, and the danger of falling through as great.

"Don't speak," she repeated, a murmur. She leaned against him. Soon, she lay her head against his chest, and he wrapped his arms around her, holding her tightly, but also softly, tenderly. It was so good to feel him again.

Gentle fingers explored cheeks, then neck and shoulders . . . cautiously, as if each first had to reassure the other that everything was all right.

"You still love me, after all."

"Forever and ever," she whispered.

And their bodies found one another in a language that needed no words.

"Hannah is nothing but a pest." Looking down, placing one foot in front of the other, Seraphine staggered home. She was not angry that Helmut had sent her away. She didn't feel any fear or concern. She was as empty as a blank sheet of paper.

"Just a pest . . ." He would not let Hannah blind him. He had seen who really loved him. Everything would sort itself out. Hannah barging in like that had been a last gasp, a final attempt at defense before finally giving up. Pathetic, really. One could almost feel sorry for her. And Helmut, good-natured Helmut, had taken pity on her.

Why did he have no pity for her, for Seraphine? How many more tests would he still set for her? Her strength was limited. Wasn't he aware of that? Seraphine blinked through a haze of tears.

"Just a pest . . ." She said the words to herself rhythmically, like a chant. "Just a pest." Her face was tense with concentration; all her senses focused on those three words so that she neither saw nor heard anyone else. Not Almuth, who waved to her through her open door. Not Käthe, who greeted her in passing. And not Gertrude, who stood and stared at her, openmouthed. Seraphine was so wrapped up in herself that she actually walked past her own house.

"Seraphine, where are you going?" Valentin came running after her from behind. She stopped and stared at him.

He frowned and plucked at her sleeve. "You're still in your wet clothes. Hannah wanted to take you something dry to put on." He looked back the way Seraphine had come.

For Seraphine, his inner agitation was almost palpable. She heard the thousand questions he did not dare to ask, and she felt the fear that he tried to hide beneath his chatter. She turned away from him in disgust.

"Come into the house. A hot cup of tea, then—"

Seraphine slapped away the arm that slid across her shoulder like a snake. "Leave me alone!"

Just . . . a . . . pest.

Don't cry. Don't cry. If she started to cry she would never be able to stop. Crying cost strength. Strength she no longer had to spare.

Just . . . a . . . pest.

Chapter Forty-Three

As spring moved toward summer, more and more of the old Hannah reappeared with her loud, lighthearted laughter and occasional crude jokes. Flora and Hannah spent a good deal of time together again. And Wilhelmine and Gottlieb were slightly taken aback to see how Helmut clung to his wife like a burr. Whether turning the hay in the fields or picking berries in the garden, whether in the washhouse or alehouse, rarely was one seen without the other.

One of Hannah's first forays following that memorable day led her back to Emma and Käthe. Carrying a basket of the biggest potatoes she could find in their cellar, she opened the door of The Sun without knocking.

Emma met her at the entrance. "Potatoes?" she said gruffly in place of a greeting. "What am I supposed to do with those?"

Hannah had expected just such a reception. "In Nuremberg, they say that the dumbest farmers have the fattest potatoes," she said. She plucked a particularly large specimen from the basket and held it up for Emma to see. "Here you can see how dumb I've been."

The smile that appeared momentarily on Emma's face was still a little forced. "You'd better come in."

Once inside, Hannah burst into tears and admitted to the stupidity with which she had hurt those who meant the most to her. She apologized over and over for what she had done, and in the end the two women embraced warmly. They had missed each other so much and were overjoyed to finally revive their friendship.

Valentin's satisfaction at the success of his plan was clouded by the fact that only *part* of it had worked. Because as far as Seraphine was concerned . . . he could only describe his wife's behavior as strange. She was moodier than ever, either withdrawing completely or dominating every conversation. She worked from dawn to dusk out in the fields, or she didn't do any physical work the entire day, bent instead over a drawing, a poem, or a fairy story and letting everyone else take care of her tasks. With Seraphine, there was no middle ground.

Toward Hannah, Seraphine was either openly hostile—if Helmut was not present—or condescending and dismissive. Hannah took it all with equanimity; in addition to regaining her old self-confidence, she seemed to have grown a protective shell as well.

Helmut avoided Seraphine as much as possible. He would not meet her eyes and answered as curtly as possible if she spoke to him directly. When Valentin asked if there was a reason for his brusqueness, his brother said no. Valentin, of course, did not believe it. He still did not know what had taken place on that stormy May day in the little hut, because no one would give him any details.

"Nothing happened," said Helmut.

"Nothing at all," said Seraphine.

"Helmut and I spoke our minds," said Hannah.

So Valentin turned his attentions to Seraphine. To his love. And to the peace of his own soul.

"I've had an idea," said Helmut to Valentin a few weeks later, when they were together in the office. "And it has to do with Hannah. I'm so happy that she's back to her old self again that I'd like to do something nice for her." He sighed and leaned back in his chair.

Valentin shrugged disinterestedly. He could not claim to feel the same about Seraphine. His wife seemed to be doing her best to anger him. Faced with his brother's enthusiasm, Valentin asked, "What do you have in mind?"

"Why don't the four of us go to Holland together and pay Piet van den Veyen a visit? I don't want to end up with tulip bulbs as bad as the ones he sent last time and would rather choose them for myself. Hannah would see that traveling really does have a good side. Maybe it would help drive out the last bad memories of her own travels."

Valentin could hardly believe it. "You've barely said a word to Seraphine for weeks. Don't think I haven't noticed. Don't you see how much she's suffering because you act like you don't want anything to do with her? I don't know what she did to make you this way, but I'm surprised that everything is suddenly supposed to be all sweetness and light. Just this morning, you completely ignored her again!"

Helmut waved his hand dismissively. "You're imagining things. If I'm talking to Hannah, I can't very well talk to your wife at the same time."

Valentin screwed up his face. He wasn't going to let Helmut put him off so easily.

But Helmut, smitten with his idea, was already talking again. "Holland isn't the other side of the world, and Piet and his daughter— what's her name again?—speak reasonable German. I want to tell Hannah my idea, but I'd better wait until I've talked it through with Father. We'll have a great time there together!"

Valentin looked at his brother's beaming face and sensed how his own dissatisfaction threatened to overwhelm him. Why couldn't things be at least bearable between him and Seraphine again?

"How do you think you'll make the cost palatable for our parents? Father will say that we should just write Piet a strongly worded letter and threaten to buy our bulbs elsewhere. We don't have to go all the way to Haarlem to rap him over the knuckles."

"Man, what's gotten into you? Fine, if you're not interested, Hannah and I will go by ourselves. I'll sort things out with Father one way or another. He'll have to see that a personal visit to a supplier is still more effective than a letter." Helmut tapped on the last letter from Valentin's old friend, Rudi, in which he confirmed his readiness to buy their dried fruit again. Then he turned back to his order for cucumber seeds.

For a while, both worked in silence.

Valentin would have liked nothing more than to stuff all thoughts of his marriage into a sack that he could hide in the farthest corner of the cellar, where no one ever went.

He tried to concentrate on comparing the offers from several different seed producers in Erfurt. But instead of the numbers, all he saw was an image of his beautiful wife standing in front of her mirror, preparing herself for the day ahead—but the day ahead was a millstone around her neck.

"Aren't you happy that Hannah is finally feeling better?" he had asked her the previous night, before they went to sleep. Seraphine had spent most of the evening giving rancorous looks to everyone at the dinner table. At his question, she rolled away from him and pounded at her pillow as if she were in a prizefight.

"It won't last forever," she had finally mumbled from beneath the blanket. "Hannah isn't the right woman for Helmut. All she will do is make him unhappy."

Valentin had not known how to respond. Should he have asked: And what about you? Don't you know that you are making *me* unhappy? He would have felt childish asking questions like that.

He let out such a long, deep sigh that Helmut looked up from his order. Valentin quickly pretended that he was struggling with the numbers in front of him.

A trip to Holland . . . how could Helmut have come up with something as crazy as that? But the real question was whether Hannah would be willing to do it at all, considering her travel experience the previous autumn.

On the other hand, they had never been traveling with their wives. He and Seraphine at the sea . . . away from home, from all the duties and work that filled their days so much that sometimes no room remained for feelings. To see something new, and see it together, to be amazed and laugh and breathe in the salty air along the Dutch coast, to sleep in an unfamiliar bed without uneasy memories . . .

Maybe Helmut's idea wasn't so bad after all. He cleared his throat. "When would you want to leave?"

Helmut grinned. "I was thinking of the end of July. By then, the women will have done the pickling and put up the preserves, and the early potatoes will already be in. We'd still be back in time for apple picking. See, I've worked it all out!" He raised both arms in the air as if he'd just won a footrace.

Valentin nodded slowly. "And the trip itself . . . I mean, Hannah is getting around well these days, but she wouldn't manage the distance we're talking about."

"God, I'm not going to make her walk all the way from here to the sea!" Helmut replied indignantly. "We go on wheels whenever we can. We'll take trains, and hire a carriage or wagon. And we'll take our time. Hannah shouldn't overdo things. I still hope that one day she'll lose her limp completely. Anything is possible, Brother, if only you want it enough."

Valentin felt a tiny seed of hope germinate inside him. Anything was possible . . . Well, why not?

"When do you think we should talk to Mother and Father?" He held out his hand to his brother as if they were sealing a deal, and Helmut returned his handshake firmly.

"As soon as Father gets back from the town hall. If we work on him together, in the end he won't have any choice but to wish us bon voyage!"

Chapter Forty-Four

A strange clack-clack-clack woke Hannah out of a long, sound sleep. At first, she pulled the blanket up over her head to shut out the noise—the long journey and their late arrival the evening before had taken its toll. Besides, as she had so often of late, she felt like she had to throw up. But the next moment, a radiant smile crossed her face.

She was in Holland!

And that clack-clack-clack was the sound of the wooden shoes worn by the farmers and residents of Haarlem on the cobblestones outside. She swung her legs vigorously over the edge of the bed. She could hardly wait to see more of this strange and exciting country. Hand in hand with Helmut . . .

After a quick breakfast of buttermilk and very dark bread, all four set off for the house of Piet van den Veyen, the tulip grower, where the brothers wanted to buy bulbs.

When the door of their guesthouse slammed shut behind them, Hannah sighed inwardly. It would have been so lovely to go off with Helmut, just the two of them, to discover whatever there was to be discovered. Without Seraphine, who constantly tried to catch Helmut's eye, like a little child. And without Valentin's forced cheerfulness.

Hannah found the equanimity with which her brother-in-law dealt with his wife's moods admirable. Whatever she said or did, he always had a friendly word for her. But there were also times when she would have liked to see him be stricter with her.

After a short walk, they reached the market square. The sight of the many pretty shops around the outside of the square immediately brought a smile to Hannah's face. Helmut practically had to drag her away from the goods on display in the windows. She would have much preferred a stroll around town to a walk in the countryside—they were from the country themselves, after all. Why couldn't they wait until the shops were open so they could look inside as well? And while they were there, couldn't they fit in a day back in Amsterdam?

Hannah thought wistfully of the magnificent squares, the tall, elegant buildings, and the many bridges they had seen on their way through Amsterdam. But the brothers had wanted to get out of the hustle and bustle of the big city again as quickly as possible.

"There must be a shop here somewhere selling these pretty wooden shoes. I *must* take a pair home with me. And I want some for Flora, too! Look, even the kids here wear them." Hannah pointed to a group of children running across the square, their clogs clacking loudly. "Oh, Helmut, the tulip bulbs aren't going to run off anywhere, are they?"

"Nor will these shops," Helmut grumbled, and he was not to be dissuaded. The next moment, however, he gave Hannah a big kiss on the cheek. "When we're finished at Piet's house, then we'll celebrate!" He laughed. "I'll buy you whatever you want. And we'll drink mugs and mugs of beer! There won't be a shop or tavern in town that's safe from us—we'll make it a real party! It's so lovely to have you along," he said, the last sentence whispered in Hannah's ear.

"We'll buy clogs, too," said Valentin happily. "I can hardly wait to see my wife's pretty feet in them." With a laugh, he grabbed Seraphine's hand. He tried to swing her arm up in time with their step, but she twisted free.

"I don't want any cheap junk," she said indignantly. "I'd much rather sit somewhere with my sketchbook. All these lovely windmills . . ."

"You'll find plenty of good subjects for your pictures." Valentin sighed with satisfaction. "It feels very, very good to be traveling as a customer for once! You feel so . . . beyond reproach, somehow." He gave Helmut a hearty clap on the shoulder.

Hannah beamed. Everything was right: the warm weather, the pretty town, the men's good mood . . . Seraphine's grumpy mien did not even matter. And a few months earlier, she would never have dared hope that she herself would ever feel this happy again.

The next moment, she nearly ran into Valentin, who had stopped abruptly in the middle of the road.

"Take a look at that house. See the stone up there, just under the gable?"

Hannah squinted and followed his pointing finger. "There's a number carved into it. One-six-three-seven. Probably a year, but what does it mean?"

"It's a memorial to the year in which everything came crashing down, here in Haarlem," Valentin said. "A time when well-to-do citizens became beggars and the beggars starved. It's been a few years since our last visit to Piet, but I still remember the story he told us about it very clearly. It was about a street with no money and tulip mania."

"Tulip mania . . . what's that supposed to mean?" Hannah said, frowning. "And why a street with no money? Look at all the beautiful houses. And unless I'm mistaken, we've passed a few small factories along the way already, so there's enough work for the people here. Haarlem doesn't look like a town of beggars." She was not as worldly as the brothers, but that did not mean she was going to swallow every yarn she was fed.

Seraphine glowered at Hannah. "Let Helmut tell the story first. I love stories. They're as lovely and sad as fairy tales, sometimes."

Helmut yawned and rubbed his eyes. "It's Valentin's story. If you want to hear it, he'll have to tell it."

Seraphine turned away, offended.

Valentin's eyes were sparkling. "It was really quite insane, what went on here more than two hundred years ago. I'll see if I can remember it all . . . This house was called the Tulip House. And that's because it was sold for a single tulip. Can you imagine that?"

"You're joking. Who would give up his house for one tulip?" asked Hannah, hooking her arm into Helmut's possessively. Seraphine was gazing adoringly at him again. Hadn't she got it through her thick skull that he wanted nothing to do with her?

"It's no joke. At that time, all of Holland was caught up in a tulip mania. Two hundred years ago, tulips were as valuable as gold. Piet told us that there were particularly rare varieties for which buyers would pay four thousand guilders plus a coach and two white horses—all for a single bulb. Wait, I'll remember the name . . . Semper Augustus, it was called. And any buyer had to consider himself lucky, because there were only two or three Semper Augustus bulbs in the entire world."

The women shook their heads in disbelief.

"It would be a dream, wouldn't it?" Helmut sighed, as all four began to move on. "I can just picture us walking into a town somewhere with our seeds, and the people begging to buy them. People offering us horses and coaches and houses for a handful of seeds . . ."

"Radish seeds." Hannah giggled. "Or turnips. I mean, a tulip bulb isn't valuable, is it?"

Valentin shrugged. "Not really. Still, the rich people then were mad about them. Everyone smelled great business, and anyone who could call a little bit of earth their own became a tulip grower. For a while, it looked as if the gamble would pay off. From one day to the next, bulbs that had been bought for a few guilders were suddenly worth several hundred or a thousand. The taverns here and in Amsterdam, Piet said, were turned into improvised trading centers, where the bulbs were bought and sold, and sometimes long before they were ever dug out of the ground!"

"Incredible!" Seraphine's eyes were shining like a child's. "The people would have gotten rich overnight! Like a fairy tale."

Hannah looked at her sister-in-law contemptuously. "What's that got to do with fairy tales? You can't eat a tulip bulb. You can't wear one. It isn't even pretty! If the people were mad about beautiful oil paintings, I could understand it. But tulip bulbs? That's . . ." She tapped her forehead with one finger. She could not find the words for that degree of folly.

"Everything always has to be so practical," Seraphine spat back. "That's so typical of you. But I can understand how those tulip lovers felt. When your desire for something is so great that it outshines every other feeling, all sense and reason, oh, the temptation to give *everything* for that is incredibly powerful! But only a person with passion could understand that," she sneered.

"Do you two want to keep on like this, or do you want to hear the rest of the story?" Valentin looked from one woman to the other.

"Yes, keep going, so Seraphine can see how fairy tales turn out." Hannah gritted her teeth. There were moments when she still felt nothing but hatred for Seraphine. There she stood, babbling something about passion and gazing at Helmut. Not Valentin, oh, no! Helmut had assured her a hundred times that he had no feelings whatsoever for Seraphine, but that could not fully erase Hannah's jealousy. She tried hard to concentrate on Valentin's words.

"A lot of money quickly found its way into the hands of families that the day before had no idea where their next loaf of bread would come from. Instead of putting some of the money aside or investing it in their business, they did stupid things. Suddenly, everyone wanted to outdo their neighbors. Many spent more than they had and didn't care about the consequences. The next tulip harvest would make them richer than ever."

"That happens in Gönningen, too," Helmut said. "Instead of investing the money they make, some of the seed dealers throw their money away with gambling or some other lunacy." When he saw Seraphine flinch at his words, he stammered, "I mean . . ."

Hannah, who had no sympathy at all for Seraphine, certainly did for her husband, and she helped him by changing the subject.

"So I guess something terrible happened. When so many people suddenly start growing tulips, then at some point they're not going to be so rare. And that means—"

"That the prices fell!" Valentin cut in, not wanting to be robbed of his punch line. "Exactly!" He looked at Hannah with respect. "Suddenly, there were tulip bulbs everywhere. And the buyers refused to pay what they had before."

"The tulip growers were left sitting on their bulbs. Finally, the entire industry collapsed. There were many who had invested everything they had in tulips, and they were left destitute," Helmut added. "If you think about it, there was not just one street with no money, but many. One might be bigger, another no more than an alley, but all of them bear witness to human unreasonableness and stupidity." He shook his head. "One thing's for certain: when we get to Piet's, we're not going to act as greedily as our ancestors!"

Chapter Forty-Five

They put the outer reaches of Haarlem behind them and walked on through a dunelike landscape, following dikes and footpaths through tall, bizarre grasses, and crossing several canals that joined Haarlem with the sea. The ground underfoot was sandy and warm, and Hannah insisted on going barefoot. The men rolled up the legs of their trousers and carried their shoes. Hannah had never seen soil this dry in her life—it was really pure sand. She found it hard to believe that tulips grew so well in it, but Helmut told her that the sandy soil was a prerequisite for success as a tulip grower.

After an hour traveling on foot past squat farmyards, windmills, and a great many neatly plowed, bare fields, they finally reached Piet's flower farm.

"And there he is!"

Laughing, Helmut waved to a small man gesticulating wildly in the midst of three horse- drawn carts.

The tulip grower looked up, and a broad grin appeared on his face. "Ah, the Swabians!" he called, waving. "Welcome once again! I'll be there in a minute."

Beside Piet stood a woman with hair redder than any Hannah had ever seen. She had not tied it up, but wore it loose. The young woman seemed to be talking excitedly with the drivers on the carts.

"What are the men doing?" Hannah whispered to Helmut. "And who's that pretty woman?"

"If I remember right, that's Piet's daughter," said Helmut. "It looks like they're loading up with bulbs. Piet ships tons of them off to England, Sweden, and as far as America."

As he spoke, he rolled down his trouser legs.

"We look like beggars," he said to Hannah. "Not like customers with money to spend."

Hannah laughed. "All the better. Like this, you can push the prices down even more. Assuming Piet still has anything left to sell . . ."

"Here they are, my precious treasures!" Piet looked out proudly over long rows of tables covered with baskets upon baskets of smooth-skinned bulbs.

Precious, maybe, but not beautiful, Hannah thought. It was amazing that anyone would pay much money for these bulbs. They did not look much different from regular onions.

She looked around for a chair or bench she might sit on, but there was nothing. After the heat outside, the barn they were in was comfortably cool. The negotiations, however, seemed set to be a boring and drawn-out affair—one look at the countless baskets confirmed that, so best to sit and be comfortable while they took place.

"Here in the front we have the Duc van Tholl in red, yellow, and pink. Next to those are the Tournesol and behind them the Keizerskroon. All you have to do is decide what you want." Piet shrugged and turned up his hands inquiringly.

"The Duc van Tholl are low-growing and bloom early, isn't that right?" Valentin said.

"Exactly. I'd add that the color of each variety is particularly vivid, which comes out best in planters and garden beds. The result of many years of breeding, I would add, which is just what the better class of customers appreciate so much, as I would also add."

Hannah yawned. Piet seemed to want to add quite a lot. If she wanted to enjoy tulips in their fullest splendor, all she had to do was visit the Gönningen cemetery in late April, where the seed merchants remembered their dead with the most magnificent tulips.

"We'll certainly take some of the Duc van Tholl, but shouldn't we also have taller, later-blooming varieties, too?" said Valentin to Helmut, who had stepped up to the table and was hefting several bulbs in his hand.

"Look at them as close as you like," Piet invited them. "The quality is top-notch. We had a good year. Just the right amount of rain, so the bulbs developed nicely. And you can't compare the sandy soil we have here with anywhere else. Perfect for tulips, I would add."

"Uh-huh. Although the bulbs you sent us last year were certainly not up to the quality of these." Helmut abruptly tossed the bulbs in his hand back in their basket.

"To be honest," Valentin added, "we were wondering if we should buy from you again."

"Gentlemen, please, I won't hear it!" Piet cried theatrically. "You can always come to an arrangement with Piet. And if you had less success with last year's bulbs, then I will make up for your loss. Just look at the lovely Yellow Prince! Or the White Swan! Or the Couleur Cardinal—magnificent blooms, just what you need. I can tell you have an eye for beauty." He turned his gaze to Seraphine, who reddened beneath his lewd smile. Piet stepped toward her and took her hand. "The tulip is the queen of flowers, as the diamond is the finest of all the gems. As the sun rules the day, so does the tulip outshine all of God's creations. A woman like yourself knows this to be true. Perhaps you would be kind enough as to advise your husband . . ." He looked her straight in the eye as he spoke.

Good Lord, he can spread it on thick, Hannah thought, puffing out her cheeks.

Seraphine beamed. "Oh, Valentin, the man is absolutely right. Buy the loveliest kinds you can. The most surprising colors, the rarest markings, the . . ." She looked to the grower for help. He was still holding her hand in his weather-beaten fingers. "I can't picture all your different tulips exactly," she admitted meekly.

"Wait a moment, I'll get my tulip book; then you can get a better idea of the beauty of my treasures." Piet trotted off. "I'll be right back," he called over his shoulder.

"What are you doing?" Valentin said, the moment they were alone. "Of course we'll buy some of his more unusual varieties, but we don't have to let him in on that. You're ruining our bargaining with your eagerness. We want to push his prices down!"

"But . . . I . . ."

"Oh, leave her be," said Helmut. "At least Seraphine finds the business interesting, unlike certain other people here who'd rather snooze." He narrowed his eyes at Hannah, who flicked one hand at him dismissively and then smiled.

"Here! Here it is, my very special treasure." Piet reappeared, balancing a large book on both hands.

Another treasure . . . the man seemed to be surrounded by them, Hannah thought. She had a sardonic remark on the tip of her tongue but swallowed it.

She looked outside longingly through the open door of the barn. The sun was shining and the sea was not far away. She would see it that afternoon with her own eyes—what stories she would have to tell her mother!

"This is amazing! Helmut, Valentin, have you seen this?" Her eyes gleaming, Seraphine held up the tulip book. "Hundreds of pages . . . the artist must have spent half his life painting tulips." She looked up at Piet in fascination. "These colors—so bright and vibrant. I've never seen anything like it."

Piet smiled. "A tulip book like that is truly a magnum opus. Especially because new varieties have to be added all the time."

Helmut cleared his throat. "Helpful for laymen, too, of course. But we know what we want. Perhaps we can get down to business?"

Finally, Hannah silently rejoiced.

"Helmut . . ." Seraphine frowned. But her brother-in-law did not react.

"What is it, sweetheart?" asked Valentin instead.

"The more I look at his book," she whispered, "the worse I find the illustrations. Look, the stems and leaves are the same—the same height, the same green. How boring is that? All the artist did was paint a new flower on top."

"Does it matter? The flowers are what it's all about. Who looks at the stems and leaves?" Valentin looked over at Helmut, who was already in the middle of the negotiations.

"These illustrations have no soul," Seraphine declared, a touch too loudly. Piet and Helmut turned toward her. "I can do better than this." The next moment, she picked up her pack. From inside, she extracted her paint box and a new sketchbook—a gift from Valentin.

"You're not going to start painting now, are you?" Hannah glared at her sister-in-law.

"I certainly am!" Seraphine retorted. "These beautiful flowers deserve a fitting tribute."

"But you can't just paint hundreds of tulips. We'll be here until Christmas!" Valentin tried to take the sketchbook gently from her hands, but Seraphine fended him off.

"I'm not planning to. How idiotic do you think I am? I'm only going to sketch the ones you decide to buy. I'll do the final artwork at home."

"And what about our trip to the seaside? Some of us want to see the sea!" said Hannah icily. "Do you think I'm going to stand around any longer than I have to?"

"Where you stand around is up to you," Seraphine snapped back. "I am going to start my own tulip book right here, right now. It will be a great help for Helmut and Valentin when it comes to selling the bulbs."

"Sera, what the devil . . . ?" said Valentin reproachfully. He grimaced apologetically toward Hannah, but she was already on her way to Helmut, who was just shaking hands with Piet. The deal was done.

Valentin sighed.

"If painting the tulips means so much to you, I'll stay with you here on the farm. We can meet Helmut and Hannah a little later." His shoulders hanging low, he waved goodbye to his brother and sister-in-law, who were smiling radiantly as they walked away.

Chapter Forty-Six

"Get away!" Hannah swung one hand at a particularly brazen gull, one of the dozens circling above them hoping to snatch a scrap of mackerel.

"Vermin," Helmut grumbled, but he still tossed them the head of his mackerel. The birds instantly descended on the tasty morsel, squabbling and pecking wildly. Helmut belched. The oily fish and the boiled mussels they had had as an appetizer sat heavily in his belly, and he reached for the bottle of schnapps. The liquid ran hot and pungent down his throat.

Hannah, also finished, wiped her fingers on the hem of her skirt. Then she unlaced her shoes, pushed up her skirt and petticoat, and lay back bare-legged in the ragged dune grass. She let out a long, moaning sigh.

"What's this?" Helmut asked with a wink. "Are you trying to tempt me, or has the fish just landed in your stomach, too?" He began to pick at her bodice, but Hannah slapped his hand away playfully.

"Neither," she said. "I'm just so happy!" She sat up again. "You know, we've never done anything like this before." Her eyes were soft and full of love.

Helmut decided to play dumb. "Belched and moaned?" he said, earning a poke in the ribs. Of course he knew what Hannah meant:

they had never had an entire afternoon to themselves. Not alone, not without work to be done.

He planted an oily kiss on her forehead. He was happy, too, and Hannah's energy was infectious. Through her, he began to see all the details of their journey with fresh senses: the unfamiliar food, the smell of new territory, the way the people dressed.

He took her right hand in his and playfully stroked her fingers one at a time. She had swept her hands through the sand at the beach like a child, and her fingernails were white and polished from rough grains of sand. Every crab, every shell, every strangely formed piece of driftwood earned a cry of delight, and she would have collected every last piece if she could have. And there were the wooden clogs that she had fallen in love with. When they passed a small farm advertising the shoes, he suggested they go and knock on the door. And now five pairs of the clogs were in a bulging sack beside them. He hated the idea of having to lug the heavy bag back to Gönningen, but the shoes were a sign that Hannah was back to her old self again. Helmut was almost embarrassed—it was rare for him to pause and reflect on such things. He quickly took a swig of schnapps, then offered the bottle to Hannah.

She shook her head, then giggled. "If you keep going like that, you'll be blind drunk by the time we see Valentin and Seraphine again."

"*If* we see them again," Helmut grumbled. "Once Sera starts painting, it could be hours. Sometimes I really have no idea what's going on in her head."

Hannah's expression darkened. "She's doing everything she can to make our lives hard. Poor Valentin," she said, although she did not sound particularly sympathetic. "Stuck there on the farm, bored out of his mind, while she indulges her artistic leanings . . . oh, let's forget about them. There's something I want to tell you . . ." She broke off then, because Helmut was pointing toward a small group of fishermen hauling their boat and the day's catch onto land. He stood up to see better whether they had had much luck.

"What a life. Exposed to nature's elements, day after day. Weather-beaten faces, hands rough and salty, backs bent," he said dreamily.

"You almost sound like you envy their hard life," said Hannah, who also stood up. Shielding her eyes from the sun, she watched the men.

"There is something enviable about them, isn't there? To have this vast expanse all around you, every day. It has to free your mind for big, bold ideas. Freedom, yes . . . that would be the main thing."

Hannah pulled him back down onto the grass. "Freedom. With a bent back and hands crusty with salt. And nothing to eat but fish, fish, fish, every day. And the work must be so very dangerous."

Helmut scratched his ear. As beautiful as this place in the dunes was, it was infested with countless sand fleas and annoying little mosquitoes.

"Maybe you're right. Maybe, from the outside, a fishing life looks far more appealing than it really is. The sea is mesmerizing, but we have our own beautiful view of the wide world from the top of Rossberg, don't we? And it's not as if a seed merchant's life is so hard. If anyone has freedom in their lives, then it's us."

"*Now* you're talking big! As for that freedom, remember how bad-tempered you were when you came home from Odessa? How you complained about the condescending way the rich people treated you? Maybe you should have told them about your freedom . . ."

Helmut groaned. "The trip to Odessa was enough experience for a lifetime," he said, trying to keep his tone light, but Hannah always managed to put her finger right on a sore point. She knew him too well altogether.

Hannah smiled with satisfaction but soon grew serious again. "In good times as in bad . . . when the minister had us repeat those words, that's all they were: words. A ritual that was as much a part of a wedding as flowers and the reception afterward. But now . . ."

Helmut took her hand and squeezed it. He understood only too well what she was trying to say. Their mutual silence wrapped around them like a warm, protective blanket.

"You know, when you first arrived in Gönningen, I can't say that I was thrilled," he admitted abruptly.

She laughed softly. "I noticed. You really took some coaxing! Which was not the most honorable behavior, I have to say. On the other hand, you were in a rather . . . special situation, so it was understandable."

Before Hannah could say anything about Seraphine, Helmut said, "What I actually wanted to say was that everything has turned out for the good. I . . . I can't imagine any other woman at my side. Last winter and in spring this year, when you were so withdrawn, well, I missed you. I missed you more than anything. And I realized that life without you was no fun at all." A little abashed at his display of feeling, he quickly stood up, then reached down his hand to Hannah. "Let's go before these mosquitoes suck out our last drops of blood."

Hannah shook her head. "Not yet. There's something I want to tell you, too."

He hesitated, then sat beside her again.

"Back then, in the hut . . ."

Helmut groaned. "Hannah, not that story again, I—"

She interrupted him by placing a finger over his mouth. Golden light danced in her eyes, and her cheeks were a little red.

"Back then, when we slept together again after so long apart . . . Well, what I want to say is . . . perhaps we need to buy another pair of those shoes. Tiny ones. We'll be able to use them in February . . ."

Chapter Forty-Seven

The seconds dragged into minutes and then into hours. Valentin had dutifully watched Seraphine paint, although she did not look up at him even once, let alone speak to him. Then without a word he had stood up from the table that Piet had cleared for her in his barn and walked outside.

He had to squint against the sun. His stomach snarled with hunger, and he was bored. Helmut and Hannah must already have reached the sea by now and surely were enjoying the beach and the breeze. And they would have stuffed themselves first.

Valentin looked back at the barn. She probably had not even noticed that he was no longer sitting beside her. She probably wouldn't notice if he did a handstand naked in front of her . . . Ungrateful woman!

So far, this trip had gone nothing like he had hoped. He was no closer to his wife at all—further away, if anything. Confronted constantly with Helmut and Hannah's attachment to one another, he felt the chill from Seraphine even more than he did at home.

What now? His belly growled again in reply, but he could not just go into Piet's kitchen and ask for something to eat. It was embarrassing enough to have to extend his visit to the tulip farmer so unnecessarily.

Perhaps he should go to Seraphine, pack up her painting gear, take her by the hand, and drag her out of there. But no . . . instead, he strolled around the yard as if it were the most normal thing in the world.

He was heading toward the apple trees to lie in the shade when a noise coming from a shed made him stop. It was a woman's voice, singing in a way he had not heard before, not especially beautifully but, for that, all the more heartfelt.

He paused for a moment, then, curious, went over to the shed.

"Can I help you, sir?" Not at all startled, the young woman looked up from her work and smiled at Valentin, who felt his face redden and wished he could disappear.

"I . . . I'm sorry if I'm disturbing you. But you sang so . . . forcefully," he stammered. Piet's daughter. He tried desperately to remember her name.

She laughed, and small folds appeared across the bridge of her nose, which seemed adrift upon a sea of freckles.

"Forcefully singing—how flattering! My father always says that when I sing, the bulbs shrivel in their baskets. But I don't care. Are you looking for him?"

Valentin shifted his weight to his other foot. "I . . ."

She gave an exaggerated sigh. "You're looking for him. I thought as much. So you're one of those who'd rather talk to the organ grinder than his monkey." She shrugged, a gesture of resignation. "My father is dealing with a load of bulbs right now. I think it might be the ones that he wants to send straight to Bohemia for you. But he'll be back here again soon. Maybe I can interest you in my *rummel* in the meantime?" She indicated the baskets of tulip bulbs on the shed floor.

"That's *rummel*? I thought *rummel* meant lower-quality product. But these bulbs look perfectly good," he babbled for the sake of something to say. And to distract himself from the woman, for his gaze was otherwise drawn to her like flies to a honeypot. He felt he was being impolite, but could not help himself. And he had recalled her name now: Margarita, almost like the flower.

Her skin was as white as milk, but not as translucent as Seraphine's—all her freckles took care of that. Her red hair shone in the sunlight falling through the shed window, and her eyes were pale brown. A droplet of sweat gleamed on her forehead, and Valentin had to resist the urge to wipe it away with the tip of his finger. She shared neither Seraphine's angelic features nor Hannah's robust femininity. And yet there, in that landscape marked by wind, salt, and sea, she was beautiful. *A bride of the wind,* he suddenly thought. At the same time, he wondered what had made him think it. A bride of the wind . . . strange . . .

She picked up a few of the bulbs and let them fall back into the basket. "The quality is really very good. It's just that they haven't been sorted. If you buy *rummel,* you never know what's hiding in your bulb. A pure white? Or maybe one of the rarest of the rare? Could it be a freak of nature never seen before? I think it's very exciting. Don't you?"

Valentin was unsure if she actually expected an answer, but while he was pondering, she stood up.

"I'm Margarita van den Veyen." Her handshake was firm and warm.

"Valentin Kerner," he said.

"I thought you had left long ago. Didn't my father arrange a coach to drive you all to the sea?" She frowned.

"He did, but only my brother and my sister-in-law used it. I—"

Margarita waved off his explanation. "I'm being impolite! You're more than welcome, of course, especially if you make my boring work *less* boring while you're here. We're very sociable in Holland, you know." She laughed and pulled him down to a crouch beside her baskets of bulbs. The next moment, he had a bundle of jute sacks in his hand.

"A hundred bulbs in each sack, tie it off, done! And I'll take them to the market in Leiden next Saturday. A sack costs five guilders. That's a fair price, isn't it? Father has given me permission to keep whatever I make from the *rummel,* so do your work well! Whether I return from the market a rich woman or a poor one depends on it." With every word, Valentin felt the warmth of her breath on his cheek.

"You're already a rich woman! Your happy heart can't be bought for any money in the world." The words came out before he could stop them, and he felt the crimson rise to his face.

What was he doing, saying things like that to a woman he hardly knew? Was it her distinctive fragrance—something herbal—that was making him dizzy? Or was it his relief that Margarita had banished his boredom?

"A philosopher from Württemberg!" She clapped her hands, and then both of them had to laugh.

Working together, they filled the jute sacks while Margarita told him about whatever came to her mind. She was happy to have a silent listener, and when she asked a question she answered it herself in the same breath. When she made a joke, she was the first to laugh at it. She seemed contented with who she was, and radiated a satisfaction that made Valentin envious.

Although the breeze coming from the far-off sea could no longer do much against the day's heat, Valentin felt better than he had for a long time. His hunger was forgotten along with the excursion to the sea. Even Seraphine was forgotten . . . almost, at least.

Margarita was so refreshingly uncomplicated.

"You're laughing at me!" she cried in horror.

"I laughed because . . . I feel so good right now!"

She raised her eyebrows inquiringly.

How was he supposed to explain to her that since their departure from Gönningen, he had barely been able even to breathe? Seraphine's coldness toward him locked around his chest like an iron ring, pressing the air out of him, robbing him of strength, courage, confidence. Not to mention her touchiness. He weighed every word he said to her with extreme care, aware that the most harmless remark could send her into sullen brooding.

When he did not go into any more detail about how good he felt, Margarita said, "Well, if I don't sell enough *rummel* to come back rich, what then? Maybe I should join the traveling fair? They're just putting up their tents in Haarlem, and it will be open by tonight in case you didn't know. What do you think they could use me as?"

He creased his brow in mock earnestness. "You could juggle tulip bulbs."

"How dull!" Margarita cried. "No, if that's all it's to be, then I'd rather hire on to one of the ships that sails off to foreign lands with my father's tulips. What do you think of America? Would that be adventurous enough? Would there be enough surprises waiting for me there? A journey by ship on the high seas is not simple. I'm sure the captain would be overjoyed to have me help him with the navigation. And if not, I can always watch over the crates," she added seriously, as if the hypothetical journey were weighing anchor the next day. She dropped a final bulb into a jute sack and then tied it off.

Valentin laughed out loud. "You can only go to America if you take me with you. Because you have to know that going to America has been *my* dream all along."

"A philosopher *and* a dreamer from Württemberg!" Margarita shook her head. "Our journey to America seems promising . . ."

They worked on, filling out their visions in more and more detail as they did. They were so engrossed in their game that neither at first noticed the shadow that suddenly fell over them. It was Valentin who finally looked up.

"Seraphine!" He had forgotten about his wife completely.

Chapter Forty-Eight

Seraphine watched the juggler through half-closed eyes. He had five balls aloft. Spurred on by the audience, he added a sixth. The glittering paint he had used to decorate his juggling balls caught the light of the setting sun, and one of the reflected rays blinded the juggler himself. The balls went tumbling to the ground, one of them rolling to a stop at Seraphine's feet. She picked it up and handed it back to the man, who thanked her with a sweeping bow.

Seraphine rubbed her eyes. The day and life had made her tired.

Wasn't she a juggler, too? With too many balls in her hands, and one after another escaping her grasp . . .

After all the hours spent sketching, she could have done without the visit to the fair. But the other three had insisted. Helmut and Hannah had returned from their seaside outing hand in hand, and laughed as they counted their dozens of mosquito bites. Valentin was also in high spirits, and it was he who had suggested the fair.

Seraphine looked at him peevishly. Nothing in his head but his own pleasure.

"Let's go on," Hannah cried beside her. "They say there's a man back there with a dancing bear. And see those geese over there?

Looks like they're going to start a race!" She laughed. "Shall we bet on one?"

"Why don't we try our luck at throwing balls first? At least I'll be relying on myself and not a goose," said Helmut, and Valentin nodded in agreement. Without waiting for her assent, he pulled Seraphine along by the hand after him. After two steps, she felt a bump against her back, and beer splashed onto her arm.

"Watch out, idiot!" she yelled at the drunk, but he was already staggering away and slurred something unintelligible as he went. Seraphine turned away in disgust.

It was a warm evening and the fair was busy. There were men standing with beers in their hands at the ring-the-bell, shouting encouragement at the one with the hammer; parents as wide-eyed as their children; young girls more interested in the young men than the entertainers, giggling and pushing each other out of their circle at every good-looking boy walking past.

While Hannah shouted encouragement to Helmut and Valentin as they flung balls at cutout figures, Seraphine turned back to where the juggler had been. The crowd that had cheered him on had moved away to other attractions. Abandoned and looking dejected, the man manipulated a single ball in one hand.

What if things go that way for me? Seraphine wondered. What if all her hard work and tactics and juggling were in vain? She blinked hard and ran her tongue over her lips. She heard a buzzing sound in her ears, and perceived the ball-throwing brothers as if through a fog.

I feel like I'm going to faint. Seraphine's hand sought something to hold on to. What if it was all for naught? *"You can't bring fate to heel,"* Evelyn had said. What if she was right?

It was the first time Seraphine had allowed herself to dwell on the thought. Which is not to say that it was the first time it had occurred to her. The idea that fate was beyond her reach had been hovering around like an annoying insect for a long time. And ever since their departure for Holland, it had been buzzing and thrumming in her head. If only she could catch it, maybe even kill it! Some days the buzzing was louder, and it took a huge effort to banish it from her mind. There were days, too, when all the effort in the world made little difference.

Today was one of those days. She knew it was a mistake to let Helmut and Hannah go off by themselves, but she could not watch anymore while Hannah made *her* Helmut dance like a marionette on indestructible strings. The tulip book had done her a world of good. But on better days, she would not have traded anything in the world for precious time with Helmut.

Since getting up that morning, dark thoughts had been brewing in her mind like storm clouds. Like an animal able to feel a storm far in advance, she was restless in a way that had made her simultaneously tired and excited and—

Something was lurking, coiling itself to leap, to sink its claws into her, her flesh, her life. So far, she had been unable to see it or smell it clearly, but she could sense it.

"You do think some silly things," she murmured to herself, hoping that a spoken word might release the negative tension in her. But nothing happened.

The men had had enough of throwing balls. With a pained smile, Seraphine accepted the three silk flowers that Valentin had won.

"I'm thirsty, and my legs are tired," Hannah announced. "Why don't we sit at one of the tables over there and get something to drink? We have some news for you . . ."

"Exactly!" Helmut agreed, with a wink at Hannah.

Now! Now it comes! Seraphine reflexively hunched her shoulders a little higher and closed her eyes like a child who believes herself invisible because she herself cannot see.

"Some news to announce? So officially?" Valentin asked, and Seraphine could have slapped him for the innocence in his voice. "What is it?"

"Oh, no you don't. I want something to drink first." Hannah laughed. The next moment, she cried, "Look, a fortune-teller."

Seraphine's eyes followed Hannah's pointing finger. Just a few yards away was a small tent, shabbier than most, lit from inside by a milky oil lamp. A tiny woman, her face and hands as wrinkled as walnuts, sat on a stool in front of the tent. She had her eyes on Seraphine, and she seemed to be calling to her. The woman had something to say to her. Something good, she was sure it was something good. Seraphine's lethargy fell away, and she tugged excitedly at Valentin's sleeve.

"Let's go to her! I want . . ." How could she explain her desire for a grain of hope from the woman?

Valentin screwed up his face doubtfully. "I think that's all a load of nonsense. If God wanted us to see our future, he would have given us the knowledge in advance. Lucky for us he didn't! On the other hand"—laughing, he jabbed his older brother playfully in the side—"it might have saved us from an adventure or two, eh?"

Hannah groaned. "Don't get started on that again, or do you want to spoil my mood? I know *I* don't need a fortune-teller." With a sly smile, she turned to Helmut. "Shall we tell them? Now or later doesn't really matter." Standing on tiptoes, she whispered something in his ear.

"I want to go to her." Seraphine took a step toward the shabby tent. She could not, would not let Hannah stop her now.

Helmut laughed. "Why not?" He slung one arm around his brother's shoulders and the other around Seraphine's, who immediately felt as if hot coals were burning her. She tried in vain to free herself from his grasp.

"Let the old woman gape at her glass ball. I can tell you myself what the future holds," Helmut said. Hannah looked as if she would explode with excitement at any minute. "The fact of the matter is . . ." Helmut took a deep, proud breath.

No, star fairy, no! I don't want . . .

"I'm going to be a father again! And this time it will be a little man who sees the light of the world."

"No," Seraphine said dully.

"Oh yes," Helmut said, beaming. "It's true! I mean, no one really knows if it will be a boy, but if you ask me—"

"Noooooo!"

The longer Valentin searched for Seraphine, the more intense the fury in his belly grew. It had come as no surprise to him, of course, that she had not jumped for joy at the news of Hannah's pregnancy.

Did she have to fly off the handle like that? *That* was what had made him so angry. Seraphine's constant dramatics and the way she always managed to spoil what should have been a wonderful moment for him. And in this case not only for him, but especially for Helmut and Hannah. Seraphine had run away as if the devil were after her, and they had only been able to stand and watch helplessly. Her shriek had made everyone around them turn and look—what a spectacle!

He should have just stayed with Hannah and Helmut and drunk a toast to their happy news, but like a fool he had taken up the chase. It was hardly possible for anything to happen to Seraphine here. She was probably off sulking in some corner, waiting for him to come and console her. He ought to tan her hide! Maybe that would make her see that her childish dramas achieved nothing. Not with him and certainly not with Helmut. With rage in his belly and a lump in his throat,

Valentin went back to the benches where his brother and sister-in-law were waiting. They were already in sight when he spotted Seraphine. She was crouched with her back against a tree trunk, huddled with her hands over her face.

His wife . . . as difficult as any child. She had not gone far after all. And he had searched the fair top to bottom for her.

He stood in front of her, arms crossed, legs apart. "So here you are! What do you think you're doing, behaving like that? You will stand up and apologize to Hannah and Helmut and—" Frowning, he broke off. "Sera, what is it?"

Great, loud sobs erupted between her fingers, and her body shuddered violently. She looked so helpless and hurt. Valentin kneeled beside her and tried to ease her hands away from her face, but she fended him off. His fury was gone. He stroked her hair.

"Don't cry. I . . ." He could not have known that she would take the whole matter like this. "I know it's not fair. They're having a second child, and we don't even have one. But that's no grounds for envy. And it doesn't have to stay this way. There's nothing I would want more than to be a father, too. You and me and a child . . . then you would have something that would be yours and only yours." He stroked her hair. "If you want, I'd be happy to give you a child . . ."

He rebuked himself immediately for the trace of lustfulness that tinged his words, and he spoke on rapidly. "But it takes two, you know? And you so rarely . . . If I think back to when we were still newlyweds . . ."

Without warning, Seraphine jerked her hands away from her face. Her eyes were huge and black.

"I don't want a child from you," she spat at him. "I could have had that long ago if I had wanted it."

"What do you mean by that?" Something drew tight in his gut.

She turned away sourly, but he grabbed her by the hair and turned her face back to his.

"Seraphine. What do you mean by that?"

Her face twisted with contempt. "You are an imbecile. You understand nothing. Nothing."

"Seraphine . . ." He could hardly speak her name. He did not want to fight with her. Oh God, how he hated doing that. No more harsh words, not today. He wanted to celebrate, to share a drink with the others. He wanted the evening to end on a bright note. A wave of dejection washed through him, and his grip on her hair relaxed.

Seraphine twisted free of his hands. She jumped at him, her fingers digging into his scalp and skin, drawing him closer until his face was just a handsbreadth from hers.

"Your child is dead. I killed it last summer. Because I did not want it." Her voice was shrill, and grew shriller with every word until it threatened to break utterly. "Remember all that blood? Remember oh-so-frail Seraphine? Ha! I was not as weak as you think. Not everyone could have done what I did, let me tell you that!"

Valentin felt himself fall apart.

She took a breath. "Now you know. And are you satisfied? Can you finally leave me in peace? You're not Helmut. Not Helmut, understand? Never, not ever. And your 'Seraphine, Seraphine'—stop saying it! I can't hear my name from you anymore!"

She jumped to her feet and ran away, a noise escaping her throat like something he'd heard once from a wounded deer.

The noise did not get past his ears.

It did not reach his conscious mind, in which all thought was dissolving.

It did not reach his gut, where pain and disbelief raged like foul spirits.

It did not reach his heart, which had been ripped out, spun on the wind, torn to shreds, a thousand little pieces . . .

His heart.

The part of him that made him who he was. His life.

He tried to hold on to that part of him, but it flew away, away from its place inside him. And all that remained was an empty hole, cold, lonely, and bleak. A deep sadness spread inside him, deeper than anything he had ever known.

"Something sweet to sweeten your night, sir? Sugarcoated roasted almonds, licorice, creamy caramels?" The young vendor held her tray temptingly in front of Valentin. When she saw the empty look on his face, she took a step back, but was not yet completely daunted.

"I've got candy canes, too," she said in a final, timid attempt. He looked at her as if she were a creature from another world.

Chapter Forty-Nine

From that day forward, it was as if Valentin had fallen silent. It was not that he stopped talking. But he stopped laughing, and his eyes were as empty as a fished-out pond. When he looked at someone, his gaze disappeared into the distance, beyond them, where there was nothing and no one to look at.

He did not say a word to Seraphine.

"Don't you think Valentin is acting strangely?" Hannah asked Helmut. But Helmut saw nothing out of the ordinary in his brother's behavior.

"He's probably just somewhere else in his mind," Helmut replied with a shrug. "He and I will be leaving Gönningen again in a few weeks."

Hannah did not believe that their autumn journey was the reason for Valentin's distance. It was far from the first time that the men had set off for Bohemia.

When Hannah objected to Helmut's suspicion, he said, "Then my guess is that he and Seraphine had another fight." He added, "Stay out of it. If there's strife between them, then it's also for them to work out."

Hannah acceded to Helmut's wish. She knew that if she asked Seraphine, all she would get was a snippy and useless answer, if Seraphine answered her at all. And Helmut was right. What went on between Valentin and Seraphine was none of her business. Hadn't she been upset at Seraphine's constant meddling in *her* own marriage?

Still, her concern for Valentin would not loosen its grip. She sensed that something far worse than a simple marital feud was weighing on her brother-in-law. Her thoughts kept returning to the conversation she had had with him in Reutlingen. Or rather, that he had had with her. He had been so understanding, so insightful. And now she would have gladly helped *him* in return, but her attempts to draw him out of his reserve came to nothing. He patted her arm as if to show that he appreciated her efforts, and at the same time twisted his mouth into something that was meant to approximate a smile, but which did not go all the way to his eyes. It made Hannah shudder.

It took them two weeks to get back to Gönningen, and their return was duly celebrated. Wilhelmine baked three trays of crumb cake for the occasion; Flora, in a pretty new dress, burst into wails of joy; and Gottlieb evaluated the sample bulbs and confirmed their quality. Emma and Käthe, Annchen and her husband, and many other neighbors came by to find out what they had seen and done in Holland. Hannah couldn't stop talking, and between her stories she laughed and kissed her daughter. In the general hubbub, no one seemed to care very much that neither Seraphine nor Valentin answered questions in more than a few words. Over the course of the day, more and more guests gathered in the Kerner house, and it became too many for Wilhelmine. So the entire group marched off to The Sun, where the party continued.

Hannah had actually been planning to keep the news about her pregnancy to herself for a little while, and Helmut had agreed to that.

But the wine that Emma so generously poured lubricated his tongue, and the agreement was quickly forgotten.

"Raise your glasses everyone. A toast to me!" he shouted to the welcome-home crowd in Emma's main room. His cheeks were red with exhilaration, he swung his glass dangerously, and little blood-red blobs of wine splattered onto the table.

Hannah tried to stop him, but it was too late. "I'm going to be a father again!" he blurted, and she was left with no choice but to join in the well-wishing and revelry. Which, admittedly, she did not find too difficult.

No one noticed Seraphine's stony face. No one noticed when Valentin suddenly fled. And no one would have done anything if they had.

Three days later, Hannah was up early and in the packing room before the others had risen. In front of her on the table stood a good dozen glass bowls. In each one, before her departure for Holland, she had sprinkled exactly one hundred seeds of radish, cucumber, beans, and some other vegetable. While she was away, Wilhelmine had kept the seeds damp, and now it was time to check and see how many of each type had germinated. It was a job Hannah hated, which was why she was up so early: she wanted to get it over with before the others were out of bed—then she would have someone constantly barging into the packing room and disturbing her counting—and before Flora demanded her attention, or Wilhelmine remembered that the chicken pen needed to be cleared out, a job that Hannah hated even more. She gagged just at the thought of the acrid smell of chicken manure. Maybe she could persuade Helmut . . . if she white-lied and told him she had morning sickness . . . but *that* thought made her lose count, and she had to start over.

She was done with the radishes and cucumbers and happy with the result. Almost every seed had come out. With product like that, the brothers could face their customers with a clear conscience.

She was in the middle of counting the germinated beans when, from the corner of her eye, she saw Helmut charge into the room. *He'll just have to wait,* she thought, frowning. Finally, she looked up from her work. He was standing in the doorway, not moving.

"What is it? Putting down roots there?" she asked in a mildly peevish tone. Only then did she notice how pale he was.

"Is there something wrong with Flora?" She was with him in a moment, tried to push past him, up the stairs—

"It's Valentin . . . He's gone."

"What do you mean, gone?" Her heart beat faster and faster as she looked uncomprehendingly at the sheet of paper in Helmut's trembling hand.

Dearest Mother and Father, dear Brother, dear Sister-in-law, Please pardon me for my cowardice, but I am unable to tell you of my decision face-to-face. By the time you read these lines, I will be on my way to America. I cannot say when I will come back, or even if I will come back. I only know that I have to go. Helmut, please don't try to come after me. No one can stop me. My mind is made up. I will write again as soon as I arrive. Don't worry about me, and please try to forgive me for my selfishness, though I know I am not worthy of your forgiveness.

Your loving son, brother, and brother-in-law

Father, I have taken a little money from the box. I will return it as soon as possible.

Helmut, Father, I have also filled my seed sack and am taking it with me. I have to live from something in my new home, after all.

"In my new home," Hannah whispered. She slumped onto the nearest chair and stared in disbelief at the letter in her hand, stared at every word until the ink blurred beneath her gaze. A thousand thoughts ran through her mind, and a feeling of unreality engulfed her.

This can't be true.

"This . . . this is a terrible joke, no more. Isn't it?" She looked up at Helmut, blinking. For the first time since she had known him, he was weeping. Openly, unashamedly.

And then she knew that it *was* true.

Valentin was gone.

Chapter Fifty

Helmut snatched the shaving brush out of his father's hand, while Hannah shooed Wilhelmine out of the kitchen in her dressing gown, then chased Seraphine out of bed. A short time later, all five were gathered in the parlor. They sat stiffly on the firmly upholstered sofas, taking turns holding and reading Valentin's letter, staring at it, looking at each other. Then, as if at some invisible command, all began to speak at once. Wilhelmine and Gottlieb also took the letter for a bad joke at first, but Helmut waved off their protestations with a tired hand.

"He's serious," he said in a flat voice, at which Wilhelmine began to cry silently.

None of them said anything. Seraphine's eyes wandered around the room, stopping on the gilded pendulum clock, on a bronze figurine of a stag, then on the buffet, where porcelain figures from the factory in Ludwigsburg were on display.

I hate this room, she thought. It was cold and reeked of despair, and all the ornamentation in it could not change that.

"I didn't know anything. I'm as speechless as you are!" Helmut shouted at his father.

"You can't tell me he prepared everything by himself. You can't just pack a seed sack like that! It takes careful planning. And you two are thick as thieves in everything else!" Although Gottlieb had a booming voice even in normal times, the volume he achieved now frightened Seraphine. The fine veins that laced across his cheeks were fire red, and he looked as if he would jump at Helmut the next moment. His entire body was shaking. Wilhelmine laid one hand helplessly on his arm.

"Helmut knew nothing, honestly," said Hannah. "There was never any talk of anything like this. They talked about the best day to leave for Bohemia, that's all." She raised her hands in astonishment. "I don't understand it at all."

"My son . . . how could he do this to us?" Wilhelmine sobbed. "All this secretiveness . . . if he was so unhappy, why didn't he say something?"

"Unhappy, bah!" Gottlieb spoke through gritted. "As if the boy had a hard life here."

Hannah put one hand on her father-in-law's shoulder. "Of course he had a good life here. We all do. Which makes it so much harder to understand."

Seraphine felt as if she were looking through a kaleidoscope. Wilhelmine's despair, the hostility of the men—all fragments, one moment there, the next blurred, nothing on which her eyes could find a hold. Or her thoughts. What did it all mean? What did it mean for her?

Valentin was gone. That was the starting point. He had not said a single word about her in his letter.

She was trying desperately to bring some order to the turmoil in her mind when Gottlieb turned and barked at her, "And you? What about you? How do *you* explain your husband's behavior?"

"Yes! We haven't heard a peep from you yet," Helmut added. Both of the men were glowering at her.

Seraphine shrugged.

Hannah sighed. "Oh, come on. This is no time for secrets. I know you had some kind of fight. At the fair in Haarlem, where you—"

"Fair?" Gottlieb interrupted her sharply. "What were you doing *there*? Does that have anything to do with this? Did Valentin fall into bad company there?"

Helmut shook his head. He looked gray and exhausted, and his bottom lip was trembling as if he might begin to weep again at any moment. Abruptly, he swept a few disheveled strands of hair clear of his forehead.

"To America! What does he want to do in America? Gottlieb, tell me!" Wilhelmine groped at her husband as if afraid she might lose him, too. In a rare moment of tenderness, he patted her hand gently.

"Probably visit Rudi Thumm, his old friend."

"Rudi? But . . ." Wilhelmine fell silent and looked around the small group. "Maybe he wants to sell him the seeds and then come home again."

Rudi Thumm—America—Gottlieb and Wilhelmine beside themselves—the kaleidoscope spun more and more wildly, the fragments became blurrier and blurrier, and somewhere in between appeared the same image, again and again: glittering balls swirling in the air. Blinking, Seraphine looked around the room. No balls. None.

"America," Seraphine said. "He always dreamed about that, I think." Valentin. Who was always there, an annoyance to her, but still, always there. The balls . . . had she dropped them herself? No, the juggler. She had screamed at Valentin. The evening had been terrible. She had left it behind in Holland just as she always left her terrible memories behind. That evening was far away and did not hurt much anymore. Like Valentin, far away . . .

Helmut let out a snort. "Dreams! And he leaves me in the lurch for a dream?" he said bitterly. "How can he do this to us?" He shook his head and looked at his father. "Can you tell me who's supposed to help me with the apple harvest now? And who's supposed to travel to Bohemia with me?"

"He can't be far away," said Hannah suddenly. "Helmut, you have to go after him. You have to bring him back!"

Helmut laughed, the sound of it raw and wounded. "Where should I start looking? We have no clue where he is. Besides, didn't you read what he wrote? He doesn't *want* me to go after him. He doesn't give a damn about Bohemia . . . or any of us, if you ask me." His voice grew louder and louder as he spoke.

"Then we don't give a damn about him!" said Gottlieb grimly. He abruptly let go of Wilhelmine's hand. His eyes were open very wide. "A boy who sneaks off like a thief, gives up on his family, leaves his brother to travel to Bohemia alone . . . he is dead to me."

Wilhelmine burst into a new bout of wailing. Bohemia? A small bell rang in Seraphine's ears, and she sat up and took notice.

"Bohemia . . ." No more than a murmur.

A region full of opportunity. Her opportunity! The place that cast everything, suddenly, in a new light. She felt heat spread inside her, and at the same time her hands grew cold. She kneaded her fingers restlessly in her lap. "Bohemia," she said again, a bit louder.

The others looked at her as if she had lost her mind. Seraphine took a breath. *Now tread carefully . . .*

"Perhaps . . . well, we did quarrel . . . a little," she said cautiously.

The faces around her hardened.

"I . . . I can't say exactly what it was. One always had to choose one's words so carefully with Valentin. But if I'm to blame for him leaving, I'll make up for it. I'll make up for everything!" She ignored Gottlieb's furrowed brow and Wilhelmine's pursed lips.

A derisive smile played on Hannah's lips, and she opened her mouth to say something. Seraphine could not let her get a word in now! But before either of them spoke, Gottlieb seized the moment: "A dispute between a man and his wife is no reason to run away." His eyes bored into Seraphine. She edged forward on her chair uncomfortably.

"Helmut, you have to take me with you to Bohemia. I'll stand by you always, every minute. Hannah is pregnant. A trip like that would be far too strenuous or even dangerous for her, but for me—"

"He should have tanned your hide," Gottlieb shouted, as if she had not said a word. "The fool was far too nice to you. All your paints and those expensive sketchbooks he always hauled around for you. Your wonderful trip to Holland—and you thank him by pushing him out of his own house with your moods! What days are these we live in? He is dead to me. Dead!"

"Gottlieb," Wilhelmine said placatingly.

Seraphine ignored both of them and concentrated on Helmut. "I can work hard. You've all seen me work hard, haven't you? And I've learned a lot in the last few years. I'm not the delicate Seraphine I used to be." So many words. They took so much of her air, but she had to— she had to—convince the others.

Star fairy, make him see how good and right it all is.

Gasping for breath, she spoke on, louder than necessary, as if her voice alone could overcome any possible doubts about her idea.

"I'm a good saleswoman, too. Hannah! Tell him! I sold all our seeds around Herrenberg, and there's no load too heavy for me. I'll carry Valentin's seed sack, everything—"

"Seraphine!"

She jumped. Helmut looked at her with an expression she could not interpret.

"Yes?" Just a word, a single question mark.

Chapter Fifty-One

A week after fleeing Gönningen, Valentin reached the van den Veyen tulip farm. When Margarita saw him coming, she shook her head as if to free herself of a vision. It was only when he waved to her that she approached him. Slowly, uncertainly.

"Is something the matter with our bulbs?" She stood in front of him wide-eyed, staring almost in fright.

The bulbs—what an odd thought. Valentin had to smile. It was not a smile that came from deep within, but it was a smile nonetheless. The first smile since, in another life, he had left Holland behind.

He shook his head. "The bulbs are fine, as far as I know. Is your father here?"

Margarita's shoulders relaxed. She sighed and said, "Ah, you want to speak to the organ grinder again, and the poor monkey gets ignored. I guess that's my lot in life." Then she grew serious again. "He's out plowing. I can take you out to see him if you like. It's time for his lunch anyway."

He could see the curiosity on her face, but he did not try to satisfy it. He nodded and thanked her with a smile.

While he freshened up at the well in the courtyard, Margarita packed a basket for her father. Then they set off in silence.

Valentin had made good time, covering the distance from Gönningen to the tulip farm in half the time it had taken him traveling with the other three. He had not been picky with rides, and had spent many hours in the back of ox carts, although he had covered long stretches on foot, too, with just the droning in his head and his heavy heart for company.

When the pain grew to be too much, he had broken into a run until all he felt were the stitches in his side. And yet all the questions had not left him, accompanying him step by step, day after day, night after night. He had fled . . . Did that make him a coward? He had abandoned his family . . . Did that make him a scoundrel? His wife had killed his child. Who was the devil now? He did not want to think, did not want to ponder about the rightness of his decision. Because reason had no easy answer for what he felt. Or for what he did not feel anymore. He knew one thing only: he could not have tolerated living at home one day longer.

At night, Valentin had simply sought out an empty barn or hayrick. He did not have enough money to spend the night at an inn. He would need the money he had taken from his father for more important things than a warm bed. He applied the same rule to his food. Whenever he passed some fruit trees in an orchard, he filled his mouth and his pockets with apples, pears, and plums. Even unripe walnuts drove away the gnawing in his belly for a time. Only once did he weaken, when the odor of freshly baked pastries streaming from a bakery made him forget his thrift.

Put as many miles as possible between himself and Gönningen, and as quickly possible. Everything else was secondary. Away, away.

Now he had reached his first destination. The tulip farm.

"Our man from Württemberg! What a surprise!" Piet cried, seeing him again. "And to what do we owe the honor so soon after your last visit?"

They had found him in a field a good two miles from the farm-house. Beside him, harnessed to the plow, stood one of the biggest horses Valentin had ever seen. And although a swarm of mosquitoes engulfed its enormous head, it stood stoically, only a slight twitch at the top of its mane betraying any reaction to the bothersome little beasts.

"Your charming wife is not with you? And your brother and sister-in-law?" Piet was as baffled to see him again as his daughter had been.

Valentin screwed up his face. He had, of course, counted on hearing just those questions, but as much as he had thought about them in recent days, he had not been able to come up with a fitting answer. The truth? Impossible.

"I'm here alone. My . . . family is at home." Would it be impolite just to blurt it out? On the other hand, he was in no mood at all for idle chat. He cleared his throat.

"I . . . have plans of my own. I want to go to America. An old friend has made a home for himself there, and I want to visit him. See what the Americans think of our seeds."

Frowning, Piet motioned to him to sit beside him on the blanket that Margarita had spread out. She sat as well, and handed him a slice of bread as if having him there for company while they ate were the most normal thing in the world. Bread in one hand, a cup of wine in the other, Valentin hurriedly outlined his plans in more detail.

"I am looking for a . . . an opportunity to make the crossing. And I thought, well . . ."

"Yes?" Piet held his cup out for Margarita to refill.

Valentin swallowed. How had he ever come up with such an ill-considered idea? There he was, barging in on a man who was practically a stranger, exploiting his and his daughter's hospitality.

"I thought I might be able to accompany one of your shipments of bulbs," he said, before he could change his mind. "As a kind of guard. So nothing goes missing. No one will try anything with me, believe me!"

Blustering, he flexed his muscles, a gesture for which he immediately felt ashamed.

With his teeth, Piet tore a chunk of ham from the rind and chewed at it calmly. Margarita said something softly to her father in Dutch. Piet answered in a louder and more vehement voice, and Margarita retreated a little.

For something to do, Valentin bit into his bread. The crumbs scratched his throat. *Say something,* he silently entreated Piet. *Say that you agree! Or say you don't have any more shipments going overseas this autumn. Or that you already have someone as a guard. Or that you don't need one.* If any of those turned out to be the case, Valentin was ready. He would simply go on to Amsterdam and hire on to a ship there. As a sailor or kitchen hand or stoker—it didn't matter what.

"I'll tell you what: I'll definitely think about it," said Piet after a long silence. Then he raised his mug of wine to Valentin.

"Of course," Valentin murmured, looking down. He felt like a beggar.

The situation struck him as absurd. There he sat with Piet and Margarita, eating a picnic on the sandy soil of the Dutch coastline, in the shade of a huge horse that was eating oats from a feedbag that Margarita had tied around its neck. Was he dreaming? A nightmare from which he would soon waken and turn to Seraphine and say, *I slept so badly last night.*

But the sharp-edged sea grasses that jabbed him through the blanket and through the legs of his trousers were as real as the pile of droppings the horse let fall just then. No nightmare. No Seraphine, just stirring or drowsy. Never again would he speak a word to her. Because there was nothing left to say.

Chapter Fifty-Two

Hannah stared at the mountain of materials piled in front of her on the packing table. Ears of wheat, oats and spelt, straw, everlastings, colorful ribbons—that Flora tried enthusiastically to tie together and that Hannah then had to untangle—and a coil of wire.

She sighed. What had she let herself in for?

In her left hand, she picked up a bundle of straw; then with her right she wrapped the wire around it. One hand just holds, the other does all the work—when Wilhelmine had explained the tying technique to her, it had sounded so easy. But now . . . her shoulders tense, holding her breath, Hannah worked her way around the bundle until the shape of a wreath began to emerge. Only when she had tied the two ends together did she allow herself to breathe properly again.

"Flora!" With her tongue in her cheek and frowning with concentration, Flora was doing her best to tie ferns, bright dried berries, and leafy stems into a bouquet. Something was constantly falling out of her hand, but Flora would simply pick it up and stuff it back in. Beaming happily, she finally presented her colorful bouquet to Hannah.

"You've done it beautifully," Hannah murmured to her daughter.

Flora instantly grabbed a boxwood twig, and Hannah watched in amazement as she went to work with it.

It was unusual for her daughter to occupy herself with one thing. Usually, she ran around as fast as her little legs could carry her, getting up to mischief, being shooed out of the kitchen by Wilhelmine, looking for something to hold her interest somewhere else but quickly growing bored with whatever it might be. Hannah had rarely seen Flora as absorbed and satisfied as she was at that moment, surrounded by all that greenery.

"If only this was as much fun for me. But I'm afraid I'm a hopeless case." She pushed aside the basket of everlastings that she still had to work into the wreath. A cup of coffee . . . that would be just the thing right now. And a piece of apple cake, too.

She would tell Helmut how Flora had been so engrossed in the flowers and greenery, and her face brightened at the thought. He would probably claim that she had inherited his love of nature. It would lighten his mood, and maybe he would even laugh and lift Flora into the air and spin her around like he always used to . . . before he became like someone who had lost his left arm.

Those had been his exact words just the evening before, in bed. "Since Valentin's been gone, I feel like someone has cut off my left arm. He's my brother, you know?"

She knew. And she would gladly have comforted him for the loss. Now, too. But Helmut was in Ulm with Gottlieb to collect a shipment of vegetable seeds that one of their Italian suppliers had unloaded for them there.

Lost in thought, Hannah shredded one of the little everlastings, orange crumbs sprinkling the table. Those left behind drew closer together, though they might sometimes be far apart.

If Wilhelmine had not still been so inconsolable at Valentin leaving home, Hannah would never have put herself forward to fashion a wreath for the harvest thanksgiving service. She was all thumbs, but she had wanted to do something nice for Wilhelmine.

When the door opened, she looked up in surprise. "Can you read minds now? I was just dreaming about a cup of coffee!" She took the cup out of her mother-in-law's hands. It was the first time she could remember Wilhelmine ever making coffee for her.

Wilhelmine smiled and stroked Flora's head, then sat down at the table. Hannah braced herself for the inevitable criticism of her handiwork. But all Wilhelmine did was stir her own cup of coffee in silence. "He's left such a hole behind. Would you have thought it?"

Hannah shook her head. Valentin had always been the quieter of the two brothers. You might hear Helmut coming from half a mile away, but it was possible to forget Valentin even when he was sitting at the table. Most of the time, his attentions were on Seraphine. He had been part of any discussions, but he was rarely as vehement as his brother. Hannah had liked Valentin from the start, and since they had talked in Reutlingen, her affection for him had grown even more. Which made it so much worse that she had not listened to her gut feeling. She had sensed that something was not right, and she had been recriminating herself because she had not convinced him to confide in her.

The coffee was hot and bitter in her mouth.

"We've managed for the last few weeks, though," she said to Wilhelmine. "When we were out in the fields working from morning to night, I had no time to miss him. Sometimes we were angry at him for leaving us with all the work, it's true. But now that there is not so much to be done . . ."

"Then you have to go looking for work, don't you?" Wilhelmine smiled and nodded toward the straw wreath. "The thanksgiving service is still two weeks away, you know. But the wreath will be lovely."

Hannah laughed. "You don't have to lie. I know it's warped and lumpy. But thank you anyway." She squeezed Wilhelmine's arm affectionately, and her mother-in-law instantly stiffened. But Hannah, instead of withdrawing her hand again, let it rest on Wilhelmine's arm.

After a moment, the older woman relaxed again, and even went so far as to pat Hannah's hand.

That was the way of things.

Those left behind drew closer together.

Hannah did not want the emotion of the moment to overcome her, so she said, "Where is Seraphine hiding?"

Wilhelmine's lips grew thin and tight. "She was hell-bent on riding to Ulm with the men. When they refused, she went off in a sulk. I haven't seen her since."

For a moment, both women were alone with their thoughts. No one could make rhyme or reason out of Seraphine's behavior. Sometimes she wandered around looking as if she might burst into tears at any moment. Which would not really have surprised anyone—everyone believed that she missed her husband, of course. But an hour later she would be talking to Helmut with exaggerated enthusiasm, making suggestions for the trip to Bohemia, sewing a fur collar onto her winter coat, or getting out her heavy shoes and polishing them as if it had long since been decided that Helmut would take her with him.

As if Valentin had never existed.

"Wilhelmine, you have to talk to Helmut!" Hannah suddenly cried. "Whenever I think of the two of them, alone—" She broke off. She could not explain her fears to Helmut's mother, or how justified those fears were. No, she did not want to think about the scene in that dismal hut ever again.

"I don't like it, either," Wilhelmine replied grimly. "He is your husband, after all. It would be indecent for him to go off traveling with Seraphine. And the people here already have enough to gossip about . . ."

Hannah nodded with relief. "Then talk to Helmut. I know he'll listen to you." Hannah was close to shaking Wilhelmine by the arm. "I don't understand how he can even begin to entertain the idea."

"Because he loves you. And because he is taking care of you and your unborn child. Bohemia isn't exactly just around the corner, you know . . ."

"But I'm not that far along at all. Look at my belly, it isn't much bigger than usual yet. I couldn't carry a full load, certainly, but I'd get through the trip otherwise. Or . . ." She frowned. "Is it because of my leg? Is that why he doesn't want me along?"

"Your leg?" Wilhelmine asked. "Oh, you mean because you still limp a little sometimes?" She shook her head. "Nobody notices that anymore. No, that would not be a problem for Helmut. Oh, Hannah." She sighed. "God is testing us very hard this year. Gottlieb's heel is even more infected now, just to add injury to injury. He smears his foot with marigold ointment every evening, but I don't know if it will be healed again in two weeks."

Hannah nodded sourly. They could not count on Gottlieb for the coming autumn. His heel looked terrible. A deep fissure had opened up through the callused heel, almost as long as a finger. Every step he took must have been painful. *Why didn't he take better care of his feet in the summer?* Hannah was tempted to ask. Gottlieb himself had told her that a seed merchant's feet were worth their weight in gold. But at the sight of Wilhelmine's tired face, more lined than ever by recent events, Hannah kept her annoyance to herself.

"We'll find a solution," she said with forced gaiety. And she would have loved dearly to believe her own words.

"You . . . ?" Ilse Schwarz looked up in surprise from the mountain of clothes waiting to be repaired.

Seraphine stopped in the doorway. She still had the door handle in her hand, and she stood and stared at her mother. Other people's clothes. Nothing had changed. And nothing else in the cottage had changed, either.

The September sun was shining outside, but inside it was gloomy and damp. Father's threadbare armchair, his pipe at its old place on the wall, the smell of cabbage and turnips. Had her mother ever eaten anything else?

I never should have come, Seraphine thought. What was she hoping to get from coming back here?

Her mother was already embracing her in her scrawny arms. "My poor child. First Russia, now America. Who would ever have thought that Valentin was so restless? I would have expected something like that of Helmut more than Valentin."

"Helmut would never leave me alone for so long," Seraphine snapped at her mother, who reacted with no more than a skeptical humph.

"Sit down, child, sit down!" Ilse pointed to a chair beneath a large pile of clothes. Reluctantly, Seraphine pushed the musty-smelling clothing to one side.

Ilse already had a large number of pins between her lips again, and, squinting, she began to pin up the torn seam of a skirt. Her hand trembled, and she did not pin the seam very evenly at all. Seraphine had to fight the urge to take the skirt out of her mother's hand and do it better. She had become so old! How tired her eyes were and how tentative her movements. Seraphine felt a mixture of melancholy and bad conscience at not having visited her mother sooner. But a moment later, she was wondering whether there were better ways to fight her inner unrest than to pay a visit to her mother's little house.

Only when the final pin was in place did Ilse look up again at her daughter.

"When will he be back? I can't believe Gottlieb gives his sons such a free hand . . . And then there's the money! I don't want to think about what a trip like that would cost. He would have to sell a lot of seeds. Elsbeth says she can't imagine that a trip to America would be worth it."

So the village was already talking . . .

Valentin had set off on a "normal" journey to America, a trip that had been in the offing for a long time—it was Wilhelmine who had proposed that as the official version of events. Seraphine could accept it; she did not want or need the pitying looks or eternal murmurings of the gossips behind her back. And someone might have thrown accusations at her, too . . . like Gottlieb did. He claimed constantly that she had driven her husband out of the house. No, it was better for now to uphold a lie.

"Child! I asked you something!" Ilse shook her arm. Seraphine jerked it back as if she had put her hand in the fire. "The same old daydreamer." Her mother sighed.

"I . . . I miss him," Seraphine heard herself say, her voice emotional. *I miss him?* She opened her eyes wide in surprise.

Had she completely taken leave of her senses? Coming here after so long, for no reason at all, and all she could think of to say was *I miss him!*

Ilse nodded. "I believe you do. He's a fine man, your Valentin. I only have to think about how he was there for you in your hour of greatest need. *Our* greatest need. Without him, we would have ended up in the poorhouse."

I don't want to hear that, screamed a voice inside Seraphine. She did not want to hear a word about Valentin. She was happy he was gone. She did not miss him one bit. That was nonsense. Let him be happy in America; for her he was nothing but a millstone.

Then why did it feel so good to hear his name? Seraphine shook violently for a second as if she had swallowed something bitter; then she abruptly stood up.

"I have to go. I just came by to say that I will be going away myself for a while. Helmut and I—" She paused momentarily to savor the sound of those words. Were they the reason she had come to visit her mother? "I will be traveling with him to Bohemia. Someone has to take Valentin's place now that he's away."

She set off for home, her mother's unvoiced questions in her head. She took her time. There was no need to hurry. The air was filled with the smell of the first potato-bake fires out in the fields around Gönningen. The happy shrieks of the children rang from the fields, filling the village with the sound of carefree, wild games. Seraphine stopped and, her senses alert, lifted her nose to the wind, picking up the aromas it carried.

How would the land smell in Bohemia?

Someone had to take Valentin's place . . . Had she really said that to her mother? Nonsense! It was not Valentin's place that she wanted to take. It was Hannah's.

Finally, everything that had been out of plumb for so long would once again be properly aligned.

Strange—why couldn't she take at least a little pleasure in that thought? Why did her heart not leap?

She was tired. The visit to her mother had exhausted her—that must be it. She was tired. Like her mother. Tired of life.

Chapter Fifty-Three

"Oh, blast!" Her hair dripping wet and her eyes stinging, Margarita searched the laundry floor for the chunk of soap that had slipped from her hand. It had fallen behind the stupid tub!

"Child! What gymnastics are you up to?" Piet, grinning, was standing in the doorway.

"And what are you still doing here?" Margarita shot back. "I thought you and Valentin had left for Amsterdam long ago." She looked with disgust at the recovered soap, now encased in a layer of dust and grime. "I think I have to have a serious word with Antje. This room hasn't been cleaned properly for ages."

"Valentin's decided not to come after all. He's out in the stable grooming the black." Piet sighed. "And Antje is the reason I'm still here. She . . . she isn't well today, and she wanted me to call the doctor for her. Then she said a little rest would get rid of her headache just as well."

"Headache! The maid has *another* headache . . ."

To avoid getting any more water on the laundry floor, Margarita wrapped a towel around her head. She glared at her father; she hated to be disturbed when washing her hair. And she hated to hear what he had just told her.

"Correct me if I'm wrong, but last week she had a sore back, and the week before that it was a cramp in her left hand. Could it be that our Antje is a little illness prone? Doesn't seem to matter what kind of illness . . ." She took some satisfaction from the way her father avoided her eye. "And could it be," she went on, "that all the maladies from which she takes sooooo long to recover started when *you* first got her into your bed?"

"Nonsense," Piet mumbled.

"It is not nonsense at all. It's the truth. Since then, the girl thinks she can get away with anything. If things go on like this, I'll throw her out myself!" Margarita dipped one hand in the water. "Lukewarm. Just wonderful." Now she would have trouble getting the soap foam out of her hair. It had already started to congeal.

"Listen to you! Do you think you can talk to me like that? Anyone would think you were my wife, the way you work yourself up."

Margarita had to laugh, the way she always did when her father tried to be strict.

"Oh, Papa, no wife would put up with you—you and your womanizing!"

"Well, if I have too many love stories, you have too few! Instead of being dressed and ready to accompany me when I go to see Max Kuyper in Amsterdam, you dawdle away here washing your hair."

"Max Kuyper!" Margarita rolled her eyes. "He's got nothing but tulips in his head. He might be the best grower around, but otherwise . . ." How could her father ever think of wan-and-weedy Max as a suitor for her?

"Ungrateful as ever, that's you! Didn't he just name his latest hybrid Margarita?"

"Which I sincerely hope you are not going to buy!" She lifted her finger threateningly. "Seldom have I seen such a pallid, boring bloom. It's such a tedious pink . . . Is *that* how he sees me? Couldn't I be something fiery and mottled? Or an exotic parrot tulip?"

Piet sighed. "Child, no one is good enough for you. It will be years before I get you married off . . ."

Margarita just laughed. "But it won't be years before I run out of patience with Antje. If she doesn't pull herself together, I'll find us a new maid. One so ugly you won't even look at her a second longer than necessary!" She laughed out loud, and watched her father scurry off toward his wagon and Amsterdam.

With her freshly washed hair, Margarita sat out on the small bench in front of the house. She spread her hair carefully over the backrest to avoid getting her blouse wet. In September, the sun was still strong enough to dry her hair, but she did not look forward to the winter months at all, when the same procedure inside the house would take hours.

She turned her face to the sun, indulging in its warmth, which felt golden and good. So good that she even forgot about her freckles, which would show more after a sunbath.

Margarita rarely had time to be idle. There was the work in the tulip fields or in one of the barns, and then there were all the customers who came to visit. Two hands and a brisk pair of feet were never enough to get through a day's work. But she had never known any other kind of life. Her mother had died before Margarita turned three, and she had lived with her father, the farmhands, and various maids ever since. Her father had introduced her very young to the work it took to run the farm, and there was nothing she did not know about tulips and how to grow them.

Her father . . . a smile slowly spread on Margarita's face. He'd stood there like a scolded schoolboy when she mentioned his little tryst with the maid. *"If I have too many love stories, you have too few"*—ha! As if he could hardly wait to walk her down the aisle. The truth was that he deliberately chose the most ill-suited candidates for her because he could not bear the thought that Margarita might one day leave him and the farm.

Is that why he was so gruff with Valentin? "I'll be a happier man when that ship leaves in two weeks," he had said to her the evening before. "He's a hard worker, and his hands are a great help around here, no argument about that. But . . ." He had left the "but" hanging in the air unexplained, though he peered keenly at her as he said it. Because he instinctively sensed that Valentin was a man that she might like? Perhaps . . . if Valentin weren't . . . if there were not a thousand "ifs."

Enough lazing around! Margarita opened her eyes and blinked. Work was calling. Though, since Valentin had done the heavy cleaning in the storeroom the day before, she could allow herself a little rest today in good conscience. She took her little toiletries case out of her pocket and began to trim her fingernails.

Margarita knew that her father had to put up with a lot of ridicule from his fellow tulip farmers because of her. Probably the most harmless description of her as a twenty-eight-year-old unmarried woman was that she was an old maid. Add to that her freckles, her flaming red hair . . .

At the same time, it was not as if no one had ever been interested in her. There had been an occasional suitor over the years. She was, after all, what was commonly known as a good catch. Margarita was picky, though, and that was one point on which her father was absolutely right!

Most recently it had been Jan, the good-looking son of a neighbor, who had courted her. After taking her for a walk three times, he appeared at their door unannounced one day, and then had become angry when she did not immediately drop everything to go for a stroll among the dunes with him. What use were his good looks if he was as possessive and demanding as that? She was not a dog to jump when its master whistled, and she had told Jan as much. He had not reappeared since.

"A man has to be friendly toward me," she had told her father. "I won't suffer being bossed around by anyone . . . except maybe you." She smiled. "And he can't be boring. God, no! And he has to have a sense of humor, too. I think that being able to laugh with him is maybe the most important thing of all."

"You'll wipe the smile off any man's face with all your demands," he had replied drily.

Oh, Papa . . . maybe you really won't ever be rid of me.

And now a man had come whom she might find pleasing—finally, after so many years! But he was married, depressed half to death, and fleeing to America. She could certainly pick them! She looked down at her short, rounded nails.

Not a sound came from the house. No clattering of pots, no shifting of chairs, no beating of mats. Well, if Antje imagined for a minute that she, Margarita, would take over her work, she was sadly mistaken.

Without wasting another thought on Antje, she stood and marched off toward the stable. *Don't do it. Leave it be. Give him his space and give your own soul its peace,* a voice inside beseeched her with every step. But the large, heavy door creaked when she opened it. *Then don't say later that I didn't warn you.*

Margarita smiled.

It was dark and cool in the stable. The black was tied up in the passage and stretched its neck while Valentin brushed it with long, sweeping movements.

"You seem to know what you're doing." Margarita nodded toward the horse, which stood with its bottom lip relaxed and hanging.

"When I was younger, I always wanted a horse of my own," Valentin said without looking up or pausing. "I tried for years to talk my father into it. For seed merchants like us, a horse would really be useful, but Father always said that we would have to make do with shank's mare."

"Shank's mare?"

Valentin looked up then. He lifted his right foot and made a little circle in the air with it. "Shank's mare."

Margarita laughed and nodded. *A man I can laugh with.* Even one as unhappy as Valentin . . .

"If *Helmut* had said he wanted a horse, he would have gotten one. Helmut always got what he wanted. He never had to try very hard." He let his hand with the brush drop. The horse gave him a bump to say, *Don't stop*, but Valentin seemed not to notice. He was staring off somewhere between the pitchforks hanging on the wall and the tack room.

Margarita waited and said nothing.

If he felt he had to tell her, then good. If not, she would not push him. She did not know whom she was trying to protect. Herself, from things she did not want to know? Or him?

In recent days, their guest had been on the verge of opening up, but each time he had thought better of it.

Now, too, she was prepared for a casual, bitter remark that would put the matter to rest.

She was not prepared for the man to burst into tears in front of her.

Later, Valentin would say that he did not know what had gotten into him. Suddenly, everything seemed too much. The warm body of the horse, the sharp fragrance of the fresh straw stored in bales beneath the stable roof, Margarita with her damp hair and patient silence. Too much closeness, too much warmth, too much danger to the thick layer of ice beneath which he eked out an existence. Furiously, he wiped away his tears.

Too late.

His pacing back and forth did nothing, nor did the hysterical laughter with which he tried to cover the tears . . . Like a snowfield in the spring sun, the composure he had worked so hard to maintain melted away.

He broke down. And as none can hold back the waters released by a melting field of snow, Valentin could not stem the flow of words that poured from him.

"I loved her so much! I would have given my life for her without a blink. But all that mattered for her was Helmut, Helmut, Helmut. I berated her for her hypocrisy. And hoped and prayed that she would come to her senses. But then . . ."

The horse, which had long since given up on being stroked anymore, turned to the hay in its hayrack. The grinding and tearing as it ate were the only sounds to be heard beyond Valentin's sobbing and his breathless words.

Seraphine . . . so close, so painfully close. Had he ever possessed her? Or was he nothing but a fool who imagined he had been in love? Was he like her? Blinded by his own wishful thinking? But then there were the nights . . . at least at the start. So filled with passion. He could still smell the sweet scent of her in his nose, the unbridled, feverish need with which she had given him everything she had to give. If it had not been for those nights . . . An idiot? A simpleton? Him?

The flood carried away his words, his reason. It was hard to think of everything in the right order. Was there a right order? Or was life a confusion of feelings that would take a stronger man than him to unravel. He was not strong, oh, no. He was tired. So tired. If the horse had not been standing there, he would have collapsed. If those arms had not been around him. Without those arms . . . he would have fallen and fallen, deeper and deeper. And it would all have been over. How merciful that would be! And how tempting!

But the arms held him, consoling, protecting him. A hand stroked his head.

He opened his eyes.

"Shh, shhhh," Margarita murmured, rocking him back and forth. Something bright gleamed in her eyes, her mouth, so infinitely sad, so soft. Valentin blinked, wanting to see clearly, to think clearly, but his eyes were burning and salty. He shook his head.

"Shhhh . . ." Her hand at his mouth, so cool. Feathery kisses on his forehead, his head resting at her chest, like a cradled child.

Gradually, very gradually, the flood subsided.

And with the last of his strength, he clutched at the line that Margarita threw him. He clutched at it like a drowning man, not wanting to let go ever again.

Chapter Fifty-Four

Helmut could not have said how long he had slept the night before. Or if he had slept at all. As he creaked down the steps that morning, his knees cracked and his back hurt as if he had been carrying his seed sack for twelve hours straight. Even after his wildest nights of drinking, he had not felt worse than he did then.

A glance at the clock in the kitchen confirmed that it was early, not even five in the morning. It was still dark outside. No bird cried, no cock crowed, and no lights were on in any of the houses around theirs. Cursing, he thought of his warm bed, his worst enemy that night. While Hannah slept contentedly beside him, all he could do was roll back and forth, pummel his pillow, rearrange his covers. He had stared at the dark ceiling until he saw tiny red stars. *Now I will fall asleep,* he had thought. Again and again. But sleep did not want to come. And with no sleep came no peace for his soul.

He was angry.

At Valentin, to whom it seemed to make no difference at all that his brother tossed and turned in his bed at night, unable to sleep. At Hannah, who slept the sleep of the blessed. At Seraphine, who pursued him with her plans for Bohemia as if it had long been decided that she would go with him. At himself. At God. At the world.

It was dark and cold in the kitchen, but Helmut was relieved to find a few glowing coals in the stove—enough to fan up a small fire, heat some water, and hope for the powers of hot coffee to work a little magic. He sat wearily at the table. It would still be an hour before the women rose; he would have to wait that long for a warm breakfast.

When the kettle began to whistle, he lifted it from the fire. For a moment, he had no idea what he was supposed to do with it. *Make coffee,* he finally recalled.

Helmut was not used to sleeplessness. When his mother complained about her own insomnia, he had always just shrugged in incomprehension. After a hard day's work, sleep came all by itself, and it was not as if he had had any lack of work lately. Since Valentin had left, he had been toiling not just for two but for three or four . . .

Mother wandered from room to room with her prayer book in her hand, let potatoes burn, mistook sugar for salt, and was really no use for much of anything.

Seraphine . . . just the thought of his sister-in-law was enough to make the gall rise again.

Father hobbled to the town hall on his infected heel; home again, he barely spoke a word. He seemed older and sometimes wore such an absent expression that Helmut felt like going and shaking some life back into him. He had never seen the wily old seed merchant so helpless.

The only thoughts that cheered him were of Hannah, who did what she could to support him.

At first, he thought it was Valentin's betrayal that had robbed him of sleep. It hurt deeply to have his brother simply walk away without a single word. It hurt not only him, but the others, too. And yet, they slept. While he . . .

No, it was the burden of being the only son. That was what was robbing him of sleep. That sudden awareness made him gasp. With an unsteady hand, he poured boiling water over the ground coffee. The smell that rose from it calmed him a little.

He had always been the elder son, of course. And his word had always carried more weight than Valentin's with their father. He had always borne more responsibility, as well. It was a role he had accepted with pride. Many times, he felt proud that he had managed to convince his father of an idea when Valentin, earlier, had failed at exactly the same task. The elder son—that was something to be!

Valentin had always been at his side. His brother, who supported him even when he might not share his opinion. Together, they overcame all obstacles in their path. And now, now he was alone. The burden of that oppressed Helmut more than he would have thought possible.

He only had to think of Bohemia. Certainly, when it came to the actual selling, Valentin was not much help, but in every other aspect he could not imagine a better traveling companion. Valentin looked ahead, and he watched their backs. He saw and heard and smelled more than most men Helmut knew. One could always rely on Valentin's instinct, too, be it finding lodgings for the night or the best way across a flooded stream. This year he would only have himself to rely on. And whom did he have to thank for this state of affairs? He did not have to think very long to know the answer.

The woman was nothing but trouble, and he had known it from the start. Or suspected it, he corrected himself. Acting so deceptively helpless all the time, playing so dreamily with her silver-blond hair.

And the way she stared with her large, luminescent eyes. In the past, he had allowed himself to be blinded by her beauty, her unapproachable elegance, the same qualities that set her apart from the other girls in the village. He had felt so . . . honored when she had gazed at him the way she did. But deep inside, he had always harbored a grain of suspicion about her. And now she wanted to travel with him to Bohemia. Ha! He could already imagine what *she* imagined she might accomplish. Not that he couldn't defend himself from her. He had proven that once already, in May in the hut, when she had done her best to seduce him.

He had stopped feeling flattered by her ongoing passion for him long ago. Her desire was another load to bear, no more. It was pathological!

Anger stirred in him again. Anger that drove out his tiredness and gave him strength. There he was, sitting in the kitchen thinking about how to defend himself from Seraphine's seductive wiles. As if he did not have enough to worry about already.

"Enough!" he muttered aloud. His voice was hoarse and his mouth dry despite the coffee.

He ran up the stairs two steps at a time. No time to waste.

He'd let her fob him off with her stories long enough. "*I don't know what got into Valentin, either*"—and he was supposed to swallow that?

She had driven his brother out of the house. He at least had a right to know why.

Halfway up the stairs, he paused. He took a deep breath and waited for his fury to dissipate. He knew that he would get nowhere with Seraphine with threats and rough handling. His father had berated her with his own accusations more than once, and she had proven more stubborn than a mule. How should she know, she could not explain it . . . stories, excuses, lies, that was all.

If he wanted to get anywhere, he would have to turn her own weapons against her.

With a grim smile on his face, Helmut climbed the last steps. Maybe he would hate himself later for what he was planning to do. But he would hate himself more if he did not do it.

The way was long and straight, no tree in sight, neither house nor steeple, nothing by which the eye could orient itself. She was walking barefoot, her feet sinking in the thick cushion of moss that grew over the path like the hide of an animal. The sky was a strange purple shade, as if just after a

thunderstorm, but the path beneath her naked feet was dry and tickled the delicate skin between her toes.

"Seraphine, wake up!"

Helmut? Where had he come from? No tree in sight, neither house nor steeple . . .

"Sera!"

"Helmut?" She sat up so abruptly that it made her dizzy. It was no dream. It was real. She awoke in an instant. "Has something happened? Have you heard from Valentin?"

He shook his head. "Nothing like that. I . . . I wanted to see you. Alone. Just the two of us, like we used to." He sat beside her on the bed as if it were the most normal thing in the world. His nearness chilled her and made her shiver. Why was he here? What . . . The dizziness returned.

"Helmut." She sank back onto her pillow, but not before spreading her hair over it like a silver cloth. She took his hand tentatively. She could not remember the last time she had touched him. His hand was cold and limp. Her sun, so cold.

"I was dreaming," she said sleepily. Strange. Where was the heated eagerness she always felt when she was close to him? Was she so calm and composed because she knew that now they had time? That no one would ever take him away from her again? He would be hers for all time now that Valentin was gone. Forever and—

"I had a dream, too, and I wanted to tell you about it," Helmut interrupted her thoughts. "You and I, we were sitting in a silver coach. Even the two horses harnessed to it were all silver." He shook his head in amazement. "We were holding hands, and everything was somehow very . . . intimate."

"I know that dream. I dreamed it myself a long time ago. Helmut!" She sat up and grabbed him by the shoulders, his face now just a handsbreadth from hers.

Could it be that he had finally awoken? That he finally *saw*? After all this time . . . or did his behavior portend something else?

She looked at him suspiciously.

"Perhaps the dream is trying to show you something. The start of a new era." She spoke softly, almost hesitantly, not wanting to turn him away with her own certitude. It was good, it was important, that he come to the understanding by himself.

"The start of a new era," he repeated slowly. The furrowed brow, the twitch of his lip, all signs of inner turmoil. Oh, Helmut. She smiled. The momentary mistrust she had felt vanished. He truly was starting to understand. "Then you've been right all these years, and we truly do belong together." He swallowed. "Then Valentin was . . . he was never the right man for you." His eyes were wide as if the recognition of that fact frightened him, and he took her hands in his, squeezed them, squeezed them so tightly to his chest that she almost cried out in pain. "You must have suffered so much . . . my Seraphine."

"Yes," she breathed.

"But . . ." He seemed to be struggling internally. "If there really is to be a future for the two of us, I need to know what you did for us. I have acted disgracefully, I know."

"That doesn't matter anymore," she said hurriedly, although everything inside her screamed: *Disgracefully? You behaved like a fool! You trampled all over my feelings like a blind cow. Did I not do everything I did for you? For us, for both of us—*

"Sera, tell me, how did you manage to free yourself of Valentin?" His eyes seemed to claw urgently at her, almost feverish, gazing into hers.

"It was not easy," she said. Her words sounded colder than she wanted them to. Where did this strange wrath come from, coiling around her heart like a snake? No recriminations, not now that his dream had finally awakened him. "I had to step back and watch you and Hannah play the happy couple. And I had to fend off Valentin's advances. He was quite insistent." She wanted to smile, to give some lightness to her words. To show him: *Look, I was glad to do it, it was not so hard after all, really.* But instead she felt a crease etch its way deeply into her forehead.

"I know he didn't give you a minute of peace," said Helmut grimly. "Why did I let things go on like that for so long?"

"You were busy with other things. Hannah—"

"Hannah!" He waved one hand dismissively. "Hannah is not important now. Dear Seraphine, tell me: How did you finally get rid of Valentin?"

Now she smiled. Hannah was not important. Neither was Valentin. Now there were only the two of them—Helmut and her—left.

"It was not easy," she repeated.

Easy? One would have been hard-pressed to find a worse description of her last few years. She took a deep breath.

"But at the same time I knew that everything I did, everything I went through, every ounce of effort was all for you." She hesitated a moment longer; then her mind was made up. He deserved to know exactly what she had done for him.

Once she began to talk, she could not stop. And with every sentence, her heart grew lighter. She rejoiced. He was there for her. He looked at her with his eyes wide open in amazement, left speechless by her love. Had he really been unaware of so much? Then her revelations must fill his heart to overflowing. She spoke on eagerly, telling him everything. Of the reason she even considered marrying Valentin in the first place. Of her thoughts when she had seen Hannah helpless in the fox trap. Of the child that could not be allowed to live.

"And now we are traveling to Bohemia. You and me. The start of a new era. Our era. Oh, Helmut . . ." She sighed blissfully. She closed her eyes for a moment, savoring the silence inside her that she had longed for all these years. She reached out blindly for his hand. When she did not find it, she opened her eyes again, blinked. Once, twice.

And her breath faltered.

Helmut was standing at the end of her bed, gasping for air like an old man. Tears ran down his face, and he made no move to wipe them away. On his face she saw revulsion and disgust.

"If you were the last human left in all of Gönningen, I would never take you to Bohemia with me. I want nothing—not a damn thing—to do with you ever again." He spat on the floor in front of her bed. "You . . . you're the devil!"

Chapter Fifty-Five

Valentin wished for nothing more than the day his ship would depart Amsterdam for America. But he feared its coming, too. He had been at the tulip farm more than two weeks. Weeks in which he had grown accustomed to the rhythms of the household.

To the work in the fields.

To Piet, who could work like an ox, possessed by the thought that the year ahead would bring even better yields and quality. And who looked at Valentin with a permanent air of suspicion, the source of which Valentin was not able to pin down, but which he also did not spend too much time thinking about.

To the salty air that smelled of seaweed and of the herring the fishermen sold on every corner and which were often part of the small family's daily menu.

To Margarita and her beguiling fragrance of fresh herbs.

He sighed and rolled onto his side, propped himself on his elbow, smiled.

Even asleep, Margarita looked as if she had a firm grip on the world. Her forehead was lightly furrowed, and her eyes were closed so tightly that her eyelids were covered with a fine mesh of lines. A touch of defiance played at the corners of her mouth.

Margarita, who let no one tell her who she ought to be or how she was supposed to behave. Not Piet, hissing warnings to her in Dutch that, no doubt, were about him, Valentin. And probably not even her own inner voice, warning her and warning her.

Margarita. Who was so generous with her spirit and her joy. Who gave so magnanimously of her smile and her lightness, as if they were the healing waters of one of the mineral spas that he and Helmut had once visited on their travels to Bohemia.

And he had nourished himself deeply at her well, like a man dying consumed by thirst in a desert. He had scooped up her waters with both hands, drunk greedily, wanting more, more, more—

Wretched thief! he scolded himself. That she asked for nothing in return did not justify his behavior at all. Soon he would embark on a ship and leave her behind. From what well would she then draw the strength she needed for herself?

His throat was scratchy. He tried to concentrate on Margarita's face, to suppress the need to cough. In vain.

She opened her eyes. "You're still coughing?" Valentin waved it off. "Just a cold, that's all." He kissed her forehead.

He had gone to Amsterdam with Piet a few days earlier. Piet had pointed out the freighter that would take his tulips, and Valentin with them, to New Orleans. Valentin stared openmouthed at the huge steamship, barely believing that such a behemoth could even move under its own power. In his stupefaction, he did not realize that a quarrel had broken out among some sailors beside him. Before he knew it, he was caught in the middle of their fight and ended up in the cesspool that was Amsterdam harbor. Dripping wet and stinking, he had set off toward home with Piet—so it was no wonder his throat felt scratchy, and no wonder he felt slightly feverish. All that was missing was the diarrhea. With all the water he had swallowed in his desperate attempts to cling to the quay wall, *not* falling ill would have been a wonder.

Covertly, he reached up and touched his forehead. Hot.

Margarita looked up at him with her pale-brown eyes. Driftwood eyes, with a low sheen, polished by sand and waves and the salt of the sea. Wood from far away, washed up after a long journey, finally and forever.

"Don't go," she said without warning.

He said nothing. She also remained silent, and placed her hand on her breast. The intimacy and warmth of the gesture moved him; he felt his throat tighten with emotion.

Oh, the temptation was great! Margarita was a woman with whom a man could be happy. There were moments when he imagined that this might apply to him, too. But the peace of such moments was destroyed by eyes like polished granite, mysteriously speckled and so cool. Destroyed by silver hair that slipped through his fingers as lightly as feathers. Destroyed by a mocking laugh.

"Your child is dead. I killed it last summer. Because I did not want it."

There was no escape from that horrible laugh. Sometimes it crept up and attacked him from behind. Sometimes it sneaked in at night, when everything was black with loneliness. Then he cried out. And Margarita was there. Holding his hand, stroking the sweat from his forehead, murmuring softly in Dutch until his eyes closed again.

Margarita was prepared to put up with his pain, he knew. She would be patient. She would listen to him as often and for as long as he cared to talk. If she would only speak ill of Seraphine, malign and vilify her as he did. But no, not a single bad word escaped her lips, although he could see very clearly that she had formed her judgments about Seraphine long ago. Valentin could only stand in awe of such generosity.

There were times when he did not feel like talking. Hours when he brooded by himself, withdrawn as a snail in its shell. And Margarita bore that with her own peculiar unshakability. "Time heals all wounds." She believed that.

Time? Was time really all it took? Or would those granite-gray eyes follow him forever?

What if they followed him to America? They had chased him to Holland, after all.

He could hear the usual morning sounds from the kitchen, two doors down from Margarita's room. The clattering of the blue-and-white porcelain plates for the bread soup. The squeak of the back door, where the milkman left the milk can every morning. The rattling noise of the maid hanging the poker back on its hook when she was done with the fire in the stove.

It wouldn't be long before the heavy thud of male feet passed Margarita's door: the farmhands on their way to a warm breakfast, and Piet himself, returning from his early morning rounds in the fields. Morning sounds that reminded Valentin of another house and another kitchen.

Valentin looked regretfully at Margarita and climbed out of bed. He did not need Piet to catch him leaving Margarita's room. As he bent down to fish his socks from under the bed, he began to cough again.

A gust of wind tore at the window, jerking it open, and Margarita's spinning wheel, standing in one corner of the room, began to turn. The air in the room chilled immediately. In his socks, Valentin padded to the window. Holding on to the handle, he looked outside. A clear wind blew from the sea, and the contours of the trees stood out starkly. Somewhere, many thousands of miles away, lay America. It calmed him to realize how little he actually knew about that land. Everything was new, and perhaps that would apply for him, too.

From where he stood at the window, Margarita suddenly looked small and vulnerable. He hated himself for what he was doing.

"You are a wonderful woman." His words sounded hollow. And yet they were the truth. God, why was it all so difficult? Why couldn't he simply stay and be happy with her? Why couldn't she be the one wandering like a ghost through his dreams? With her fiery red hair, her sprinkled freckles, her wide mouth. "You and me—" Valentin blurted.

She flinched a little at his words as if she had momentarily nodded off. She stood up abruptly, stumbling toward him. "It could work."

She pressed against his chest, and he felt her heartbeat, so strong and courageous, and his arms embraced her. They held each other tightly.

"I know that you are not ready. Not yet. I feel it every day. When you lie in my arms, when we make love, she is still there. But someday, the memory will weaken. I don't mean that the terrible thing she did to you can ever be undone. But time heals our wounds. And I will make sure that all that is left is a clean, well-healed scar. I could accept that."

Valentin smiled sadly. "But what if the scar only heals on the surface? What if it boils and bubbles underneath and the pus keeps oozing out? I can't guarantee anything. All I know is that I don't want to make you unhappy. Everything that has happened blankets my feelings like a layer of dust. I don't know what love feels like anymore, and maybe I don't *want* to know it ever again. Love hurts. That is my truth, as miserable as it is."

"There is always more than one truth," she said defiantly.

He almost weakened at the look in her eyes. He would so gladly have believed her. Instead, he said, "Maybe I have to leave to recognize that for myself. Maybe I have to leave to be able to come back."

"The only question is: To whom?" Margarita replied flatly. "I think, deep inside, you still love her."

"How can you say that?" he said, too loudly, and was immediately racked with coughing.

She clapped him on the back, her face a frown of disapproval, then threw on her robe. "If I don't make you a hot milk and honey, you won't be going anywhere," she said in an offhand manner.

Before she could disappear out the door, he held her back by her sleeve. "Thank you."

Her eyes were large and serious. "I will wait for you. I will be here when you return. If you return . . ."

Chapter Fifty-Six

Two days after Helmut had visited Seraphine in her room, he and Hannah set off for Bohemia. It was only the third week of September, and the work in the fields was far from done. In the kitchen and cellar, too, there were still preparations for winter to be made. But Helmut would not be dissuaded. The rest of the family would have to get by without them.

"Now I can understand why Valentin left the way he did," he had said to Hannah. "I can't spend another minute under the same roof as that witch, either." Then, with a meaningful glance at Hannah's belly, he added, "Besides, the earlier we leave, the earlier we'll be back home again."

She had no good argument against his new plan. Still, the sudden departure from Flora and the now-rushed preparations for their trip were hard. And that was not all that was weighing on her mind.

On that fateful morning, she had listened incredulously to Helmut's story, scarcely comprehending what he was telling her. She had questions: Could it be that he had misunderstood Seraphine? That she had spoken ambiguously? That she had seen that he was baiting her and had become agitated or confused? He dismissed them all.

Hannah had not wanted to believe that Helmut would use such a ruse to get his sister-in-law to tell the truth. For Hannah, what Helmut had done only showed how seriously Valentin's leaving had affected him.

When she finally understood the depth of Seraphine's machinations, her disbelief had turned to fury. "I'm going to give her a piece of my mind!" she cried and was almost out the door when Helmut grabbed her from behind.

"You'll do nothing of the sort! Don't you think I wanted to wring her neck myself?"

Screams or scolding or a physical attack would only rouse his parents, he had said, and he did not want that, because he was determined not to breathe a word to them about what had happened.

"Your mother has a right to know what kind of viper she's living with!" Hannah had protested, her voice rising, and thought about all the times that Wilhelmine had made sure she knew that she, Hannah, was an "outsider." But Seraphine . . .

Her outrage and anger had exhausted her quickly. And then the tears came. She had cried for the child that had not been allowed to live because it had the "wrong" father. For Valentin, who had loved with such ardor and whom Seraphine had cast aside so callously. For herself and for Helmut, for the blindness that had made both of them Seraphine's victims, too.

And finally, she had cried for Seraphine. What agony must it be to lead a life like hers? No life at all, really. More like an endless battle with something that had possessed her. Was Seraphine sick? Was she mad?

Hannah recalled an old man from the Nuremberg quarter where she had grown up. Rat-Martl, he was called. And in his mind he was convinced that he was the Pied Piper of Hamelin. Whenever he went walking through the narrow alleys, he would turn around to his imaginary swarm of rats, whistling for one that had strayed, carrying another that could no longer walk on his arm. It had been frightening for her as a girl. The people of the quarter tapped their finger at their temple whenever Rat-Martl walked by.

The comparison did not hold up, Hannah realized. Rat-Martl's delusions had hurt no one. But Seraphine . . .

Yet for all the suffering and grief her sister-in-law had caused, Hannah felt no hate toward her. Oh, she felt unbridled wrath still, deep down! And to sit and watch her play the innocent lamb before Wilhelmine and Gottlieb was almost more than Hannah could bear. But Helmut was resolved not to burden his parents with another tragedy.

In the end, Hannah had no choice but to take Wilhelmine aside and get her to swear on the Bible that she would never, ever leave Flora alone in Seraphine's care. Wilhelmine had looked at her as if she were out of her mind, but had finally acceded to her pleas. Only then was Hannah prepared to leave.

To make the journey easier for Hannah, Helmut had their neighbor Matthias take them with his wagon as far as Augsburg. From there they took the train to Nuremberg, where they spent three nights at The Golden Anchor with Hannah's parents. That was all the time they could spare before they boarded another train as far as Hof, but they secured a promise from Hannah's parents to come to Gönningen when Hannah and Helmut's second child was born. From Hof, the way was harder. There were no more railways, and opportunities to ride on a wagon were few and far between, so long stretches had to be covered on foot. Hannah held up courageously: at Helmut's side, she would have walked to the ends of the earth.

"So, to my Hilde, I said the seed man might as well stay home. A miserable beggar he is."

Hannah jumped as the man's fist slammed down on the table. She hastily picked up her cup of water before Bohumil Dolezil's next fit of rage sent it flying.

The farmer leaned across the table, and for a moment Hannah was afraid that he was going to grab Helmut by his collar. Instead, he began to count off his troubles on his fingers: "Flea beetles did in the turnips, yer carrots didn't sprout at all, and yer leeks were as skinny as scallions. Now tell me, seed man: Why should I buy another seed from you?"

Helmut leaned back on the bench in front of Dolezil's house, apparently unimpressed by the outburst. "All right, all right, you've made your point. None of our seeds are worth wasting your money on, and you're not going to buy from me again."

Bohumil Dolezil nodded as if justice had been served.

Hannah fixed her hat in place for their imminent departure.

"My God, I've got a thirst!" said Helmut suddenly. "Are you still hospitable enough to drink a little schnapps with a miserable beggar before he hits the road? Or will I have to do without our old custom this year?"

Dolezil shrugged. "Hannah," said Helmut. "The bag."

Helmut emptied his cup of water onto the ground beside the table, then began to pour generous servings of the cherry brandy they had brought with them.

Old custom? Hannah looked reproachfully at Helmut. Was that really necessary? The man wasn't going to buy a single seed from them; he had said so very clearly. In a situation like this, Helmut could confidently pass on any old custom. It was bad enough that Helmut would let Dolezil talk about their seeds the way he had.

They had already visited at least a dozen customers. Usually, Hannah stayed in the background and admired Helmut's quick thinking, his talent as a salesman, and his knowledge of everything to do with farming and gardening. The names of customers, until then no more than words in an order book, became faces. And those faces owned large estates or small market gardens, had children, ailing parents, disputes with neighbors, or a sick cow in the barn.

Helmut listened to each and every one of them as if he had all the time in the world, and he almost always had a word of advice, perhaps accepted grudgingly, perhaps welcomed. Sometimes he came up with ideas that Hannah would never have dreamed of. Several times, she had had to bite her tongue to stop herself from blurting out her admiration on the spot. Helmut got along with everyone they met, adjusting even his manner of speaking to suit each customer. At the start, Hannah had giggled inwardly whenever he abandoned his broad Swabian accent the moment he crossed a stranger's threshold.

"You have to adapt to the people," he had explained to her. Which seemed to work for him, because he was more than satisfied with the orders he'd received and had gone so far as to say that Hannah was his lucky charm!

So it was with annoyance now that she stared at the farmer, his red face made redder by the brandy, the biggest oaf they had yet had to deal with.

She kicked Helmut beneath the table, but he ignored the signal. *Why is he sitting here getting drunk with a lout like Dolezil?* she wondered in exasperation, when Helmut suddenly pulled out his order book.

"Last year it was four pounds of Prague kohlrabi. The same again?"

The farmer, who had his cup halfway to his mouth, grumbled something that Helmut obviously took to be assent, for he began to write in his order book.

"Six pounds of Erfurt cabbage, the radishes . . ." Taking no more notice of the farmer opposite, Helmut scribbled away in his order book. Finally, he clapped it closed and lifted his cup.

"Hannah, more!" he said.

She looked indignantly at him, but did as he asked.

"Well, then. To your health, you miserable beggar," said Dolezil. His face had grown much friendlier, and he clacked his cup against

Helmut's. Then he rolled the brandy around in his mouth and swallowed it before leaning across the table again. Hannah gagged when a wave of brandy-soaked breath hit her.

"Hilde, I said to her, Hilde, the seed man's stuff is still the best you'll find!"

After that, everything happened quickly. Dolezil signed the order, then went into the house to get the money, and with a great deal of hand shaking and shoulder clapping, he assured Helmut yet again about how satisfied he was with his products.

Hannah had to smile. Helmut knew his customers; she gave him that.

"Right, this is really the last bucketful! When I go downstairs again, then it will be to drink a beer." Huffing and puffing, Helmut tipped the warm water into the bath that Hannah and he had hauled into their room earlier. It was more of a laundry tub than a bathtub, in fact, but Hannah would have jumped into a horse trough if someone had offered her a hot bath in it. She leaned back, enjoying the delicious warmth and letting her arms float on the surface of the water.

"You just made a woman very happy," she sighed.

"I'm glad," Helmut murmured before he headed to the tavern below.

Hannah smiled after him. She hoped he would meet some good people down there, because she was not planning to abandon her tub quickly.

Who would have thought it possible to enjoy a bath there, in their tiny rented room in Budweis? Sheer luxury. At first, she had hardly dared to even voice her wish to Helmut. But then the longing for water, warmth, and cleanliness won out. Oh, he pulled a face, certainly, as if to say: *Is that really necessary?* But then he had persuaded the innkeeper to put water on to heat for Hannah.

A wave of love flooded through her. Helmut had gotten used to her being a little different from most women in Gönningen. Oh yes, she could certainly work hard. She had that much in common with the Gönningen women, but as recompense for that she needed a little something special now and then. A bath in the middle of the week instead of just on Saturday. A sweet pastry instead of bread and butter. A silver ring on her finger, not just the grime of work. Little things, certainly, but she took pleasure in them. Helmut understood that.

She had gotten used to Helmut's peculiarities as well, in particular the restlessness that always had him looking ahead to the next journey. It had been so painful for her at the start of their marriage. Only now that she had seen for herself how beloved he was among his customers, and how sensitively he adapted to each one, did she understand that traveling was a special part of who he really was, a validation of his place on earth.

Hannah's thoughts turned suddenly to Valentin. He would have known immediately that Dolezil's carping was just the prelude to a round of schnapps among old friends.

Her breasts bulged from the water, and Hannah laid her hands on them. *Like two huge balls,* Hannah thought. And she was only halfway through her pregnancy.

Valentin . . . she wondered how he was doing. Was he already on his way to America? America—Hannah shook her head. A journey to America was beyond her imagination.

With all her heart, she wished him happiness wherever he might be, but a grain of doubt still rankled, like a tiny stone caught between sock and sole. At first, one hardly noticed it, but the longer you carried it around, the deeper it dug into your skin. And hurt.

What is it about his story that bothers me? I am not so narrow-minded to think that he could only be happy with us in our little village.

Valentin without Sera—that was something hard to imagine. He had loved her so much!

The door creaked open.

"Girl, you're still in that water? Watch out or you'll end up looking like a prune. A fellow's just pulled out his accordion downstairs, so shake a leg if you want to join us!"

"Music! Oh, what have we done to deserve such a boon!" Hannah squealed theatrically. "First a bath and then music. If things keep on like this, you'll have to take me with you every time." She laughed and splashed water in Helmut's direction. "Who would have thought it was all so much fun!"

"Fun? Now I've heard everything. But if the hardships of our travels matter so little to you, then all the better. It means you've turned into a real seed woman." Ignoring the open door behind him, Helmut leaned down and kissed her on the lips.

"You know, today's the first day you've ever called me that."

"What of it? It's true, isn't it? Now hurry!" A last kiss and then he went thumping out and down the stairs again.

Hannah dreamily clambered out of her bath.

In Helmut's mind, at least, there was no doubt that she truly had become a seed woman. *And me? Do I think the same?* she wondered while she dried herself.

In her old life, she had been the daughter of the innkeeper at The Golden Anchor, a wild young thing whose reputation in her Nuremberg district was not the best. Today, she was Helmut's wife. A respectable, decent wife. She was Flora's mother and the daughter-in-law of Wilhelmine and Gottlieb. For the villagers of Gönningen, she was still the "outsider," though she had felt at home among them for a long time. More than that, she was also a seed woman!

Ha! When she thought back to her first night in Gönningen . . . sitting there in The Sun, with an anxious heart and an illegitimate baby in her belly. Staring over at the table of the market gardeners from Ulm, all the little bowls and jars full of seeds she didn't recognize. She had watched the goings-on at their table in utter bewilderment.

Today, she knew that you planted onions in rows, but not too close together, and that celery seeds sprouted better if you soaked them for a day in water first. And she didn't just read instructions on a seed packet; she *knew* about the seeds. There was still a lot to learn, she knew only too well, but she absorbed like a sponge everything she learned from Helmut. And every day, she learned something new.

Yes, her days as a silly city girl in Nuremberg were over!

It was loud in the inn and full of visitors. Helmut had to push to one side just to make room for her on his bench. Grinning, Hannah squeezed in beside him.

"You're right. I am a seed woman!" The pride in her voice was unmissable. "And you know what else? I can't imagine anything in the world lovelier."

Ignoring her husband's baffled look, she reached into the basket in the middle of the table and bit heartily into a slice of bread.

Chapter Fifty-Seven

"One thing we can say for certain: it is *not* straightforward pneumonia," the doctor murmured.

"Then what is it?" Margarita stood in front of him, wringing her hands.

The doctor looked back toward the room where his patient lay. Over the previous week, in the course of his daily visits to the tulip farm, his patient had turned into a shadow of himself. First the coughing, then the burning fever, and after that the cramping and diarrhea. He did not like the look of it, not at all.

One look at Margarita's anxious face and red-rimmed eyes made him keep his worst fears to himself. She had been tending him day and night, and apparently had had no help in that task, which did not surprise the doctor—no one wanted to risk infection.

"I don't want to rule out pneumonia completely," he said carefully. "Nor does he really show the symptoms of a typical case of dysentery or typhoid, but I cannot preclude either of those. He must have swallowed a lot of water when he fell into the harbor. With everything in there—human and animal feces, rubbish, dead animals—it's not what I'd call a health tonic."

"But that was ten days ago. The poison has to leave his body again sometime, doesn't it? Couldn't you at least let his blood again?" Margarita pleaded.

The doctor shrugged. "I don't believe that more bloodletting would do him any good. On the contrary. Each time, he's only grown weaker—very curious, which is why I suspect the man was already unwell before he was struck by his present illness. Didn't you say he had quite a journey behind him?"

Margarita nodded.

"Then he might well have picked up something along the way that we don't know about."

"Wonderful!" grumbled Piet, who had so far only listened in silence. "Can you at least tell us if what he has is contagious? I'm responsible for everyone in this household."

Piet's remark earned him a rancorous look from Margarita, which he vigorously ignored.

The doctor shrugged once again. "Nothing can be discounted. Of course, I can arrange for him to be taken to a hospital, but—"

"Out of the question!" Margarita cut in sharply. "Valentin stays here, where I can look after him."

The doctor looked at her and, in her sleep-deprived eyes, saw a fire he wished his patient had. This pale, freckled being had a will of iron. If the man in there had any chance at all, then it would come from her and her care. He told her that, and Margarita smiled weakly but with satisfaction.

"Keep doing what you have been doing: cold wraps against the fever, heavily salted food cut into very small bites, a sip or two of red wine for his general vigor."

He paused, then came to a decision.

"Still, it is my duty to prepare you for the worst. If the fever does not abate in the next few days . . . His body cannot take the kind of strain it is under forever. We can only hope."

Margarita choked as if she had swallowed a fish bone.

The doctor looked at her sympathetically. "Is the patient a relative of yours?" he asked, although he had known for a long time that that was not the case. The stranger, who had been at the farm for several weeks, was the talk of the district. And the fact that he was ill, seriously ill, had not escaped Piet's neighbors. As the patient's doctor, he had been approached and questioned by a number of them. The people were concerned, and who could blame them?

"His family lives in Württemberg," said Margarita so quietly that the doctor had trouble hearing her.

"Then I would advise you to send them an urgent message."

"But . . ." In consternation, Margarita looked from the doctor to her father. "A message like that will take days! Valentin will be well again by the time they could get here. And then we would have troubled them unnecessarily. Besides, he . . . he has no contact with them anymore," she added almost defiantly.

The doctor exchanged a look with Piet.

"Do as Doctor Bleyhuis says, my child."

The doctor cleared his throat. "In the face of death, family disputes are nothing—that has been my experience. And for many relatives, it is a comfort to be able to take the body home with them, for burial in their native fields."

Seraphine leaned back against a knotty apple tree. She scanned the fields closer to Gönningen. So far she had only seen birds flitting back and forth, but soon there would be many people—joking, laughing, and singing, making the apple harvest a joyful occasion. The field that belonged to Seraphine's mother lay some distance away from the village, and no one would stray out this far.

Seraphine had never had much love for the apple harvest. On that September morning, though, she could hardly wait to get out into the apple fields, because there was nothing lonelier than the bedroom of an abandoned woman. The room in which Helmut had reviled her. The bed in front of which he had spat. Getting out of that room was what mattered, and any excuse would do. Before Wilhelmine could saddle her with any domestic tasks, she had set off for her mother's fields to help with the harvest. When she arrived, her mother was not there. A strange disappointment had befallen her then, and to distract herself from it she had simply started to pick the apples alone.

With a sigh, she got up and climbed the ladder again. With every apple she picked, the linen sack that swung from a rope at her hip grew heavier. Soon she would have to climb down and empty it. The smell of the King of the Pippins apples made her nose tingle. As a child, it had always been her favorite kind of apple. Not because of the taste, but because of the name: in France, that particular cultivar was called Reine des Reinettes, her father had told her. The queen of the princesses— what a charming name! From that day on, whenever Seraphine had wandered past the field in which the trees grew, she had kept a lookout for queens and princesses.

There were no princesses. And no star fairies, either.

Besides the King of the Pippins, there were also Luiken, Geflammter Kardinal, and Red Boskoop trees in the meadow. Seraphine stared absently at the Luiken apple in her hand. The side that had been turned to the sun was a brilliant red, but the shade side was a monotonous brown. Without the sun . . .

And the earth brought forth grass and herb yielding seed, each after its kind, and the tree yielding fruit, whose seed was in itself, each after its kind. And God saw that it was good.

That's what it said in the Bible. And it said the same on the tapestry that hung behind the desk in Gottlieb's office, embroidered in cross-stitch by Wilhelmine's careful hand.

Nothing was good. Her knees trembling, Seraphine descended the ladder and sank onto the ground beside the baskets.

Since Helmut had abandoned her, she had felt like a baby bird cast out of its nest far too early. No protection anymore, and everything disappeared into nothing. Seraphine pressed her hands into her ribs until it hurt.

Why couldn't she be like one of these trees? Rooted firmly in place, resigned to the eternal rhythm of the seasons, each after its kind.

Except that there was no place for her kind. Nowhere. No one wanted her.

If she were an apple tree, she would bear fruit that, from the outside, looked flawless, but inside there would be rot, nothing but rot. A tree like that should be cut down so that it would not infect the other trees.

"You're the devil," Helmut had said, a curse. Then he abandoned her.

With an effort, she pulled herself together and got back on her feet. As she always had. Her hands grasped mechanically at the thick foliage of the lower branches.

One apple after another, into the basket.

But to what end? No one would ever again sit with her and share an apple. Never again would the sweet juice of the fruit run down her fingers. Never again would she wash the sticky sweetness from her fingers.

Never again.

She was the devil.

That was why no one wanted to be with her.

One apple after another, into the basket.

Even Valentin had run from her. Valentin, who had always wanted so much of her. Wanting and wanting and wanting!

Now no one wanted anything from her at all. She missed Valentin. That was something else she did not understand.

One day, the people in the village would realize that Valentin had left forever, that he had not merely left on an extended trip. She would be the forsaken wife, the one people would mock behind her back.

Helmut and Hannah would return. What then? The thought of living under the same roof as Helmut, of constantly feeling his contempt was more than she could bear.

Everything had been a waste of time. All of it in vain. She had made a terrible mistake . . . No, her entire life was a terrible mistake.

Oh, star fairy. Why did you leave me in another's place the way you did? What would my life have been if I had grown up somewhere else? Somewhere where there was no Helmut and where, perhaps, I might have been happy with a man like Valentin?

One day, the true reason for Valentin's disappearance would come out. Hannah would surely tell Wilhelmine all about it as soon as she returned from Bohemia. Seraphine did not like to imagine what would happen then.

Everything was finished. Nothing was left to her. Nothing that she might still have been able to hold on to.

One apple after another, into the basket.

How soft the skin of the apples was. And warm, like the skin of a small animal.

"You're out of your mind," Helmut had said to her. Or had that been Hannah?

Why did nobody come? Where was her mother? She did not want to be alone any longer, not alone with all the small animals that felt so warm and soft in her hand.

No more apples in the basket. No more apples in—

A wasp caught her eye. A moment before, it had been boring into a rotten apple with its proboscis. Now it rolled into a ball and lay motionless in the grass.

The end.

Seraphine broke down. She did not want to weep, but it was not as bad as she thought it would be. It was almost befuddling, almost comforting. The way the body exhausted itself with its trembling and sobbing, and more and more tears flowed until a stream trickled between her fingers.

Now it would be easier.

Seraphine stood up. She narrowed her eyes and fixed them on the ladder. She shifted it a little to the left, then leaned it against the trunk of the King of the Pippins tree. The tree of kings and queens and princesses.

With a steady hand, she loosened the rope that kept the picking bag in place at her hip. The rope was long enough.

She was surprised to find that she was afraid. Of what?

Stiffly, she climbed the ladder again. She formed a loop in the rope, knotted one end tightly to a high branch.

She went to put the sling around her neck. The rope was not as long as she had thought, and she had to climb a step higher on the ladder. The loop was small. The rope tugged at her hair, but finally lay around her neck. Now she only had to jump. To die for love . . .

Chapter Fifty-Eight

Looking back, Seraphine could not say whether she really would have jumped. Whether the courage she had would have sufficed.

Gottlieb's ringing shout had scared her. Her right foot had lost its grip on the rung, and for a moment the sling around her neck had pulled tight.

He had come running, had held the ladder from below, shouting, shouting at her.

They were not too late! Valentin was still alive. But how did she even know that Val . . . when Gottlieb had just received the message . . . ?

His shouts, more and more desperate. Confused words that made no sense. What was he talking about? What was he doing there? Where was her mother? Seraphine had closed her ears, oh yes, she could still do that. To not hear what she did not want to hear.

Then he climbed the ladder. She had smelled the sweat streaming from his pores. His sweat and the smell of the King of the Pippins.

She had not resisted when he took the sling from around her neck. The rope pressed painfully against her ears as he pulled it over her head, and the closeness of Gottlieb's bulky body was uncomfortable.

Somehow he managed to get her down from the ladder.

And they had sat together like lifeless puppets. He told her about Valentin, how he lay dying. In a foreign land.

Then they wept. Together.

Gottlieb arranged a carriage as quickly as he could. He wanted to get to Haarlem the fastest way possible. Wilhelmine decided to stay in Gönningen. Someone had to look after everything there, she had said. But the truth, Gottlieb confided to Seraphine, was that she could not face the thought of going to Holland only to bring home the body of their younger son.

Why Valentin had left, how he could dare walk away from the family the way he had, how he had ended up at the tulip farm when his goodbye letter had talked about America—for Gottlieb, now, none of that mattered; it was also irrelevant that he could barely walk on his own infected heel. Now that Valentin's life hung on a thread, what mattered was to be there for him. His son.

And Seraphine?

She prayed. Praying was alien to her. Her dialogue with the star fairy had been easy. She could tell her what she was thinking and ask her for anything. When it came to praying, she was not sure what tone to use—she had moved far away from God.

Please don't let it be too late.

Too late for what? she wondered in the same moment. Then she prayed over and over: *Please don't let it be too late.* The words sounded forced in her ears, and impertinent. What right did she of all people have to ask God for *anything*?

Gottlieb finding her at the last minute was a sign, she was certain of it, but she was still suspicious. She had seen so many signs where there were none. Had misinterpreted so much.

As she looked out the window of the carriage, she saw more than the landscape—she saw her whole life passing. Like the trees lining an avenue, misunderstanding followed misunderstanding. Her love. Her fate. Her purpose. She had been so blind!

This sudden awareness scared her so much that she buried her head against Gottlieb's chest and cried. He stroked her hair awkwardly.

She was on her way to Valentin. The urgent message had arrived by courier at just the moment she had tried to bring her life to an end. Not after. Not too late.

It *must* mean something.

Dear God, please don't let it be too late.

Valentin was a stranger to her, too. Like the God she prayed to. But she wanted to see him again. She wanted to ask him for forgiveness for something that was fundamentally unforgivable. Or was it?

Dear God, please don't let it be too late.

At some point, after many, many miles in carriages and trains and on foot, the words sounded less strange in her ears. The closer she came to Valentin, the calmer she was.

Maybe God had another task for her. Maybe she could yet make up for something. Maybe that was why she kept praying.

Valentin was alive.

Seraphine saw the red-haired woman who was caring for him. She saw the gleam in her eyes when she talked about the sick man. Saw how she positioned herself possessively in front of the door, as if she did not want to let anyone near him.

Seraphine recoiled, letting Gottlieb enter the room first. She feigned tiredness and slunk away to an unfamiliar room where the loneliness was as palpable as it was in her own bedroom. She mocked herself for the hope she had entertained that God might have a task for her to complete. What kind of task? To make things right again?

God had found another woman to do that.

It had been a mistake to inform Valentin's family. Margarita had quickly become convinced of that. But it was too late to change things. If it had been up to her, she would have tossed Seraphine and Valentin's father out of the house. Instead, she served each of them a plate of stew. After Piet said grace, the only sounds were slurping and the clattering of spoons.

The guests from Gönningen had arrived early in the morning, dusty, exhausted, and as out of breath as if they had run the entire distance. Since their arrival, they had taken turns at Valentin's bedside, although it was his father who had, by far, spent more time watching over him.

Eat. You have to keep your strength up, Margarita ordered herself, keeping one ear pricked for any sounds from the sickroom. Everything was quiet. Was it a good sign? She chewed mechanically at the beans and potatoes, not tasting any of it. Every mouthful seemed to scratch her throat, and she had to make an effort to swallow at all. The moment she raised her eyes from her plate and saw the other woman, she had to clench her jaw and neck to stop it all from coming up again.

In contrast to her, the guests slung down the food with more spirit. Gottlieb was already lifting his plate for more. Margarita managed to conjure up a smile over the ladle.

He was a good man. There was no doubt about that. He had not damaged his son. He had gone to the sickbed as soon as he had arrived. Everybody in the house avoided calling it a deathbed, although the doctor, with every visit, made sure they all knew that Valentin was no better than before. Hour after hour, the father had laid cool, damp cloths on his son's forehead and given water drop by drop between his cracked lips.

She had asked for a room where she might rest a little, because the journey had been long and arduous. And since Gottlieb was with Valentin . . .

Margarita's heart had pounded in her chest as she had showed the skinny, bloodless creature a room she could use. *That is* her, she had thought hotly. Over and over: *That is* her! Margarita had not spoken five sentences before fleeing as quickly as she could. From her rival. From the woman that Valentin had also fled from. The woman who was to blame for the bleeding of his heart, for his fever in his mind.

When Margarita calmed down, she had gone to Valentin and sat beside his father.

Gottlieb Kerner did not speak much with Valentin, unlike Margarita, who chatted away for hours about everything and nothing, because she believed he would hear her voice somewhere in his fever-ridden world. But just having his father close seemed to have a beneficial effect. As soon as Gottlieb was there, his son slept more soundly, his eyelids flickered less, and he perspired less.

For the doctor, it was a miracle that Valentin was still alive. "He is holding on to life as if waiting for something," he had said the evening before, shaking his head, and had then stated that the diarrhea, at least, finally seemed over and done with. As if Margarita had not noticed that herself.

Margarita sensed that Gottlieb was not in the best of health himself, but she did not know what was wrong with the older man. Was it the long trip? Or some malady of old age? Because he did not complain, she did not ask. But she saw the pain on his face when he thought himself unobserved. And during his first stint at his son's bedside, she had taken him a cup of tea and a slice of buttered bread; he gulped both down so fast that Margarita had a bad conscience for not offering their guests anything to eat as soon as they arrived. For the meal that evening, she had instructed Antje to make a particularly hearty stew.

With trembling hands, Margarita now passed the bread basket across to Gottlieb. He took another slice of bread and spread it thickly with butter, then sprinkled salt on top.

Margarita nodded, satisfied. A good man. A man who had come to stand by his son.

Valentin had recognized him. That was a good sign. His fever was still high and his sleep usually restless, plagued by God only knew what demons. But sometimes, suddenly, his eyes opened and looked around. "Margarita . . . you . . ."

Margarita lived for those moments. If he saw her sitting on the edge of his bed often enough, if he saw how she tried to will strength into him, then everything would be all right.

Even that day, just after midday, there had been one of those moments. Valentin's eyes had fluttered open, and he had seen Gottlieb. "Father?" Just a whisper, disbelieving, almost imperceptible. And then it came again, with a puff of breath: "Father." He had smiled. Margarita had seen that. He had smiled, and now he would be well again—she was convinced of it. The father would draw the son back to life; it was only a matter of time. Margarita was glad then that she had sent the message to Gönningen.

But then *she* had sat at Valentin's bed. Had taken his hand, the hand that Margarita herself had held for so many days, the hand on which she knew every scar, every line, every callus. *She*, it seemed to Margarita, took his hand clumsily, as if the gesture were somehow contrived. *Let him go!* she almost shrieked, but bit down on her lip instead so hard that she tasted blood.

After that, it started.

"Seraphine . . ."

Over and over. "Seraphine."

His shouts had come from far off, and his eyes had raced around the room in confusion, not seeing, but searching. No moment of alertness, as earlier with his father. More panicked, hounded, afraid.

He had not recognized her. And yet he must have sensed her presence. *Can he smell her? Is she sending him secret messages?* Margarita had wondered despairingly.

"He is holding on to life as if waiting for something." The doctor's words had come back to Margarita, cut into her heart, as painful as Valentin's cries. Had he been waiting for *her*? Margarita did not want to think that could be true.

Not half an hour later, his temperature had climbed so high that Margarita believed it was the end.

Valentin's body had jerked as if he were being struck by a whip. Spittle ran from his mouth. His eyes were glassy and far away. Margarita had shooed *her* away, had washed Valentin from head to foot, dried him with the softest towel she could find, dressed him in fresh bedclothes.

She had watched from the bedroom door as Valentin tossed and twisted as if fending off Margarita's ministrations. He had babbled incoherently, madly, and Margarita was certain that he had lost his mind for good. And in between, repeatedly, his cries for *her*. "Seraphine!" *She* had flinched at every cry. Just as Margarita had. *Why does he call for her when he dreads the thought of her? Why doesn't he call out for me?*

The clanking of cutlery against dishes made Margarita jump.

"Excuse me," Piet said as he got up from the table. "I have some business with the neighbor to take care of." He nodded a farewell. Before he left, though, he stopped in the doorway and signaled Margarita over to him. "After supper, Valentin's wife can sit watch. Try to get a night's sleep; you look like death." His eyes were dark with reproach and concern.

With a groan, Gottlieb also rose to his feet. "Your father's right. You need to rest. I will sit with my son."

"But I—" Margarita began, but Gottlieb shook his head and laid one hand on her arm.

"No arguing. You've done more for Valentin than anybody else"—his eyes glanced briefly at Seraphine, who sat hunched and silent at the table—"and God bless you for that."

Margarita had no choice but to agree. To give herself something to do, she began to wash the dishes. It was actually Antje's job to do, but the notion of joining Valentin's wife at the table and drinking a glass of wine with her was unbearable. Why didn't *she* go to her room to rest? No, instead *she* sat there rigidly like a pillar of salt. The temptation was great to go to her and slap her, shake her, shower her with a thousand curses. The woman was a witch! She was to blame for Valentin's state!

Margarita dunked her hands into the hot water and held them there until they burned. God help her if *she* tried to so much as look in on Valentin again that day, then—

"We tried to reach Helmut," she heard spoken softly from the table. "He's his brother, after all. If . . . if Valentin dies, Helmut will never forgive me for it."

Margarita let go of the plate she had just been wiping so abruptly that it banged against the bottom of the basin. Helmut?

"What are you talking about!" she snarled at Seraphine. "Valentin is not yet dead, and if he does die, then it is something for which *you* should never forgive *yourself!*"

Calm yourself, the woman isn't worth wasting your strength on. You are stronger, so pull yourself together!

"I did not want this," said Seraphine in a sunken voice. "I didn't want any of this to happen. Helmut abandoned me. Valentin, too. My father . . . everyone abandons me. I—"

"Me, me, me! That's the same old song you've always sung, isn't it!"

Margarita's fury was so fierce that her legs gave way beneath her, and she had to support herself with both hands on the side of the basin.

"Do you have any idea how much that man loved you?" Her vocal cords seemed on the verge of breaking, but she could do nothing about that. "He loved you more than his own life! *You* were his life! His great

421

love! And now he's lying in there sucked dry by you and your spiteful-ness, fevered and racked and haunted . . ."

Tears trickled down her face, dripped from her cheeks.

"He is suffering so because of the depth of his love. If he dies, it's your fault. Yours alone and no one else's! You broke his heart, and there is no medicine and no bloodletting on this earth that can stop that kind of suffering."

Seraphine ducked as if she had been punched in the face.

The door opened and Gottlieb appeared. "Why are you shouting in here? Has something happened?" He looked in confusion from one woman to the other.

Margarita raised her hands defensively. "Everything is all right," she said, gasping a little, and added, "It's just the nerves."

He waited a moment longer, not certain that he would not have to intervene, but then he turned and went back to Valentin's room.

If Valentin dies, then it will be of a broken heart. Suddenly, everything was too much for Margarita. Too little sleep, too much worry, too much standing up to Piet, who would have shipped Valentin off to a hospital in a heartbeat, and add to that the malign looks from Antje and the farmhands, their silent accusation that, through her, the sick man would infect the entire household—

Margarita collapsed to the floor and threw her hands over her face.

Dear God, I have done everything in my power. Now I can't help him anymore because I am not the one who broke his heart. Dear God, let him recover. Let him be healthy again. And if you need her help with that, then amen. Then I have to live with that. For Valentin.

Gradually, that awareness ate its way into her head, robbing the last of her strength.

I cannot help him. Because he does not love me. Because she is still . . . She had to give Valentin up. No! Never! Not for that woman!

An eternity passed and the sounds grew louder. Her sobs, her breathing, the beating of her heart—unbearably loud. At some point, other sounds mixed with those coming from her. Chair legs scraping over the floor, glass tinkling, the rustle of fabric, the ticking of the clock on the wall.

Somebody tugged at the washcloth she still clung to, and a moment later she felt something cold and smooth in her hand.

"Here, drink this." *Her* voice.

The sudden smell of schnapps made Margarita gag. *I'll not take anything from* her. *Nothing. Not a crumb of bread or any schnapps.*

But she raised the glass mechanically to her lips. The liquid ran down her throat, hot and caustic. For a moment, all she felt was its burn.

When she looked up, Seraphine was close beside her. Her first impulse was to stand up and put as much distance as possible between herself and *her.* When Seraphine sensed her aversion, she moved a little farther away, leaving an escape route free for Margarita. Their eyes met. Margarita stayed where she was.

"You love him."

Margarita flinched as if struck by a bolt of lightning. She said nothing.

"It's good that you do," said Seraphine flatly. "Valentin has earned a woman who loves him. I . . . I can't do it. Oh, I wish I could. But there was only ever room for Helmut in my heart. My love for him devoured me and took every ounce of my strength. I was possessed." She fell silent, then said, "I'm so sorry. I would give anything to be able to do something. Turn back time, be smarter, see things for what they are . . . but it's too late."

"It is never too late," Margarita replied, a trace of contempt in her voice. *Be silent,* an inner voice commanded her. *Say nothing that you will later regret.*

"I would never have believed that I would miss him so much. Valentin, I mean. Not Helmut," Seraphine hurriedly added. "Our bedroom at home . . . is so empty. As if I were already a widow. Sometimes

I think that he'll come to the door any minute and say something that annoys me. But he doesn't come. And now"—her eyes turned toward the door, where at the other end of the corridor Gottlieb was tending to his son—"now maybe he will die, and I can't even tell him how sorry I am for everything."

Margarita closed her eyes. *Please, dear God, give me the strength to do what I must. For Valentin, not for me.*

"Valentin's life is hanging by a thread. The doctor says it's a miracle that he's even still alive." Suddenly calm, she spoke as if repeating words she had learned by heart. "Perhaps it really is a miracle. But I call it . . . love."

The lump in her throat hardened, and speaking became difficult. What if her feeling was a deception? What if Seraphine was not Valentin's elixir of life, but instead his final blow? His fever had climbed again after *she* had approached his bed.

Maybe it would have been easier for her if she had sensed any love at all from Seraphine. Remorse, yes, and self-recrimination, but love? No.

Margarita's heart missed several beats. Maybe remorse would do? If Seraphine and Valentin parted in peace, if he were able to accept her apology, then perhaps, one day, he would be free for a new life, a new love. For her.

And if not . . .

Please, dear God, help me. I have to do it, for Valentin.

Margarita's lips trembled when she continued. "The doctor also thinks Valentin is waiting for something. That that is why he is still holding on to life."

Seraphine replied with a barely perceptible nod. In her eyes, Margarita saw something that had not been there before. A spark of hope?

She gave herself a final push. She took Seraphine's hand and squeezed it. "Go to him. He is your husband."

Chapter Fifty-Nine

It was the longest night of Seraphine's life.

Valentin slept, if one could call the wild, unconscious rearing up and subsequent collapse sleep. His face corpse pale one moment, burning red the next. Sometimes his breathing came so fast that she feared he was going to suffer a fit. Other times, he would lie so still that she pressed her ear to his chest to make sure his heart was still beating.

Suffering was second nature to her, something she could slip on like a close-fitting corset—in her old life, she had been convinced of that. She had thought she was better at suffering than most, but she had been mistaken. All her suffering was nothing compared to what she went through at Valentin's bedside.

They were finally united but closer to death than life.

She was afraid. Afraid the night would never end. Afraid of what the end of the night would bring. Seraphine could not imagine any more tomorrows.

Gottlieb had gone to bed some hours earlier, and Piet had returned home a little after that. He had exchanged a few words with Margarita in the kitchen, and then he had thumped up the stairs. After that, the house was quiet.

Seraphine did not take her eyes off Valentin for a second. She observed every movement he made, trying to interpret his condition. Her ears hurt from listening, her eyes burned from seeing. She had a headache—a thunderstorm flashed and pealed and rumbled in her head. Every clear thought cost her endless effort. At some point, she came to realize that the storm in her head was the same storm in whose clutches Valentin was trapped. She felt what he felt. She bore his suffering on her shoulders. And at the same time, she berated herself: *Don't go putting on airs.*

At times, he cried out her name, and other times merely whispered it, but he did not seem to know that she was there. *I am here!* she wanted to call to him—Margarita had said it would be important for him to hear her voice, even in his delirium—but she felt ridiculous doing it. Words slipped easily from Margarita's lips, as she had experienced for herself that same afternoon. She told Valentin about trivial things, asked questions she did not expect an answer to, even laughed in his presence. At first, Seraphine did not see how much Margarita's carefreeness took out of her, but later she saw the agony in her eyes. Margarita loved this man. Yet she had sent Seraphine to him.

Yet? No, *therefore.*

"He is your husband," she had said.

Seraphine could not understand it. If she really, truly loved him, why didn't she fight? The way she had fought for Helmut. In vain. Did Margarita know that her fight, too, would come to nothing? If yes, then how did she know it? And why was that knowledge denied to Seraphine? Helmut was happy with Hannah—why had she not wanted to see the truth of that? Why couldn't she be as bighearted as Margarita?

Helmut was happy—sooner or later, she should have granted him that happiness.

So many questions. And no answers. But there was so much love to feel here. It was almost tangible! More love than Seraphine had ever felt before. Margarita's love.

Seraphine fled. She ran into the kitchen, where Margarita was sitting, still sleepless, and asked her to take a turn at Valentin's bedside for a while. She did not have to ask twice. No sooner were the words spoken than Margarita was gone. So much love.

With a shawl around her shoulders against the chill, Seraphine stepped outside. The cold air on her forehead did her good, and she made herself breathe deeply. Soon, the pounding in her head eased. There was no light from any of the windows; there weren't any streetlamps. The darkness closed around her like an enormous maw. Seraphine blinked, then took a few tentative steps out into the yard. Gravel crunched underfoot, and occasionally she stepped on something soft, perhaps fallen leaves. When her eyes had adjusted to the night, she looked up at the sky. A few dull stars adorned the black heavens, and the moon looked like a blunted sickle. She shivered.

The sun and the moon—what nonsense!

Then she thought of something else—outside, thinking came easier: over there, in the tulip barn, she had sat and painted. Valentin had waited for her just as he had always waited for her.

"He loved you more than his own life," Margarita had said.

And Seraphine? She knew she had trampled all over his love.

How much did Margarita know about Valentin and her? What had he told her?

"He is suffering so because of the depth of his love. If he dies, it's your fault. Yours alone and no one else's!" Margarita had shouted at her.

So she knew everything.

Then why didn't this woman hate her?

"Me, me, me! That's the same old song you've always sung!" Now, out there in the darkness of the night, she had Margarita's words loud and pure in her ear. Seraphine paused in her walk around the courtyard, tilted her head to one side as if listening to a continuation of what Margarita had said to her. When nothing came, she listened deep down inside herself.

What would have happened if, just once, she had thought less about herself and more about Valentin? That kind of question was new to her, and she did not know what to think of it.

When she returned to the house, it was three in the morning.

Without a word, Margarita rose from the chair beside Valentin's bed, and just as silently Seraphine took her place. She felt the other woman's eyes on her back and turned around to her.

"We can also watch over him together," she said.

Margarita shook her head mutely and went out.

Seraphine watched her go. She had given up her place to Seraphine as if it were a matter of course.

Is my place really here, at this bed? Margarita seemed not to doubt it at all.

No, she really could not understand the woman at all.

Her place . . . if she could only sense the same conviction inside herself.

Exhausted, Seraphine slumped forward.

No more swimming against the current. To be carried along on the way that destiny had laid out for her. No longer having to struggle.

Suddenly, Seraphine felt an unaccustomed peace inside.

Was that what Evelyn had been trying to tell her, back then, in another life?

For a while, it was quiet in the room. Valentin's breathing was regular and the lines of his face smoother than before. No spasms rocked him. Seraphine sat and looked at him. Valentin. He was her husband.

Suffering for one's great love. Dying for one's great love. Seraphine suddenly felt hot.

He felt what she felt. Was that possible?

And now there she was, sitting at Valentin's bed, come to rescue him. So that they could discover new emotions together?

Oh, Valentin . . .

Tired, so tired. Her chin sank onto her chest; her eyelids fluttered and closed.

"Seraphine?" A gentle pressure on her arm.

She jumped and for a moment did not know where she was. She recoiled in fright when she realized that she was lying across Valentin's chest, with her weight on him. Trembling, she pulled away, sat on the chair again.

"Seraphine . . ." He had opened his eyes. His gaze was alert, though somewhat dazed. "You came." A smile, meager, but there.

She took his hand. "Yes, I came." Her voice was hoarse.

He closed his eyes and sighed deeply.

"Seraphine . . ."

Notes

In a historical novel, history and fiction are often interwoven. In this book, too, I have allowed myself to take certain liberties when they were in the interest of my story.

The mail-order system that Hannah comes up with around 1850 only really came into widespread use much later, around the end of the nineteenth century. Imaginative Hannah also comes up with new names for various kinds of vegetables, and although there really was a Gönninger Trotzköpfle variety of lettuce (called Gönninger rogue in the story), such inventive names were also only used much later.

The Kerner family ships their dried fruit off to America instead of selling it in the surrounding districts during the so-called Jakobi trade, which was the usual practice in Gönningen. I have not, however, found any evidence that such overseas consignments ever took place in reality.

Much has changed in Gönningen since the heyday of the seed trade. But even today, observant visitors with open eyes can still stroll in the footsteps of the seed merchants.

For anyone interested in paying a visit to Gönningen themselves—walking up to the summit of Rossberg, admiring the one-of-a-kind display of tulips in the cemetery in mid-April, or stocking up at one of the present-day seed dealers' outlets—a visit to the Samenhandelsmuseums (Seed Trade Museum) housed in the Gönningen town hall is an absolute must.

Acknowledgments

Once again, it is necessary to say a heartfelt thank-you to many people for their dedicated help in bringing this novel to the page.

First, I would like to thank my reader, Simone Schäffer, who wrote a very lovely letter to me in 2002 and gave me the idea for this book. The newspaper article about the seed trade in Gönningen that she had included got me so curious that I immediately threw myself into my research.

In Gönningen itself, I found a wellspring of support from the very genesis of the novel. A huge thank-you goes to Dr. Klaus Kemmler, who went to great efforts to read my manuscript for any errors concerning Gönningen and its inhabitants, who exhibited the greatest trust in putting his library at my disposal, and who always found the time to answer my many questions.

I was also supported from the start by Professor Doctor Paul Ackermann, the district mayor of Gönningen, whose door was always open to me and my requests.

Thanks are due, too, to the Stoll seed company in Gönningen, where I was able to get a taste of the "packing room atmosphere," and also to Ulrike Epp a "seed woman of the modern era."

If any mistakes have found their way into my book despite all this assistance, then the blame is mine alone.

My thanks also go to my family, who have always thrown out a life ring whenever I was in danger of drowning in one of my projects. Special thanks go to Bettina, who typed for me when, because of an injury, I could only dictate. Thank you also to Bertram for his "Vienna stories," to Katja for her philosophical observations on the topic of travel, and to Peter Theimer and Piet Nieyenhus.

Last but not least, my sincere thanks go to all the wonderful people at Ullstein Buchverlage who were instrumental in the original publication of this book in 2005.

About the Author

Photo © Privat

Petra Durst-Benning is one of Germany's most successful and prominent authors. For more than twenty years, her books have invited readers along on adventures with courageous female characters, through rich and engaging detail. Petra has written more than a dozen historical novels, many of which have gone on to be bestsellers and be adapted for television. She's enjoyed immense international success and has developed a loyal following of fans. She lives with her husband in Stuttgart, Germany.

About the Translator

Photo © Dagmar Jordan

Edwin Miles has been translating in the film, television, and literary fields since 2002.

From his hometown of Perth, Western Australia, he went on to complete an MFA in fiction writing at the University of Oregon in 1995. While there, he spent a year working as a fiction editor on the literary magazine *Northwest Review*. In 1996, he was short-listed for the prestigious Australian/Vogel's Literary Award for young writers for a collection of short stories.

After many years living and working in Australia, Japan, and the United States, he currently resides in Cologne, Germany, with his wife, Dagmar, and two very clever children.